BUFFALO MAN

Calvin C. Clawson

Copyright © 2012 Calvin C. Clawson

All rights reserved.

ISBN: 147913564X

ISBN 13: 9781479135646

*Dedicated to my parents,
Anne and Calvin Clawson*

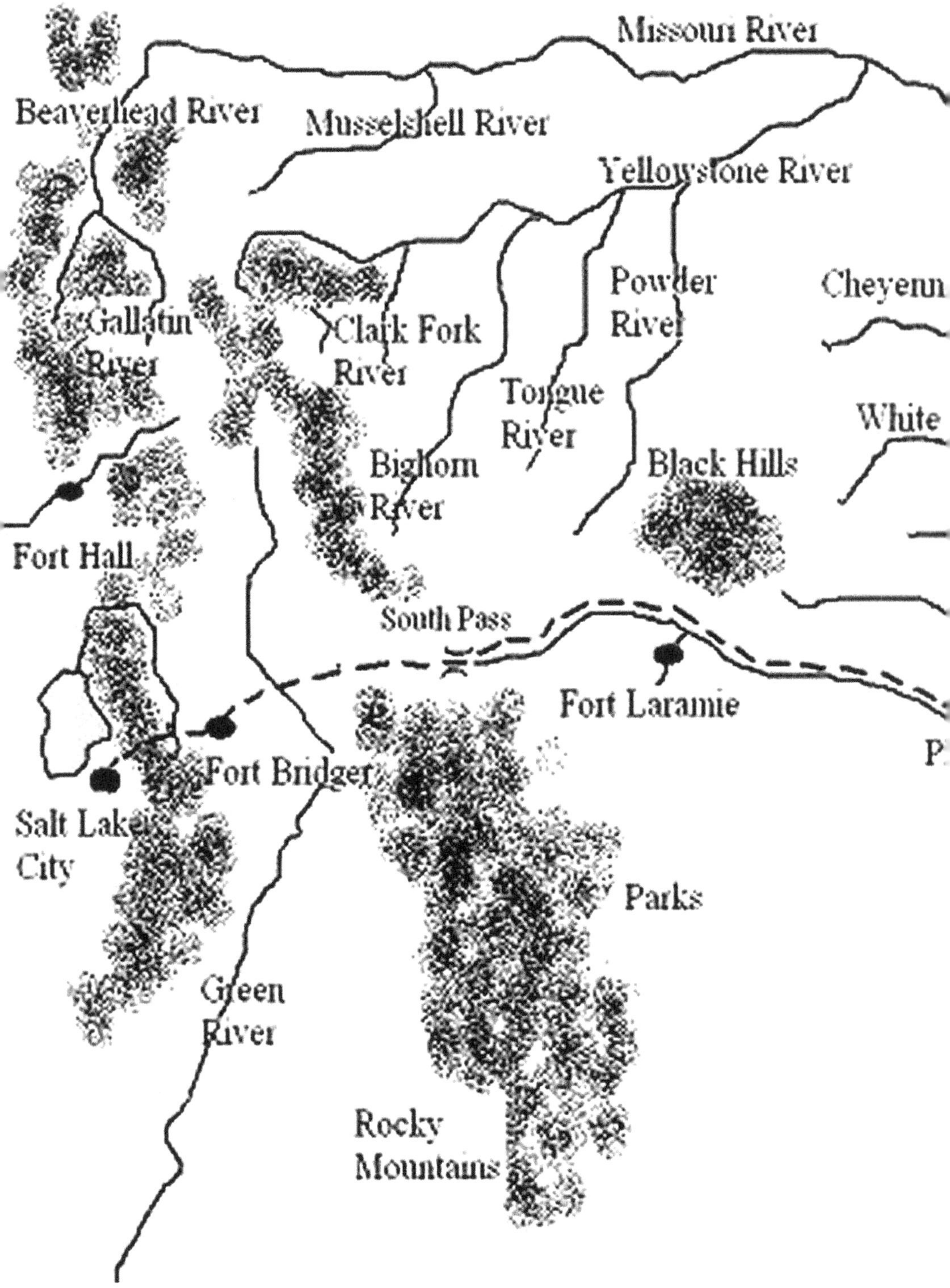
Missouri River
Beaverhead River
Musselshell River
Yellowstone River
Gallatin River
Clark Fork River
Powder River
Cheyenn
Tongue River
White
Bighorn River
Black Hills
Fort Hall
South Pass
Fort Laramie
Fort Bridger
Salt Lake City
Parks
Green River
Rocky Mountains

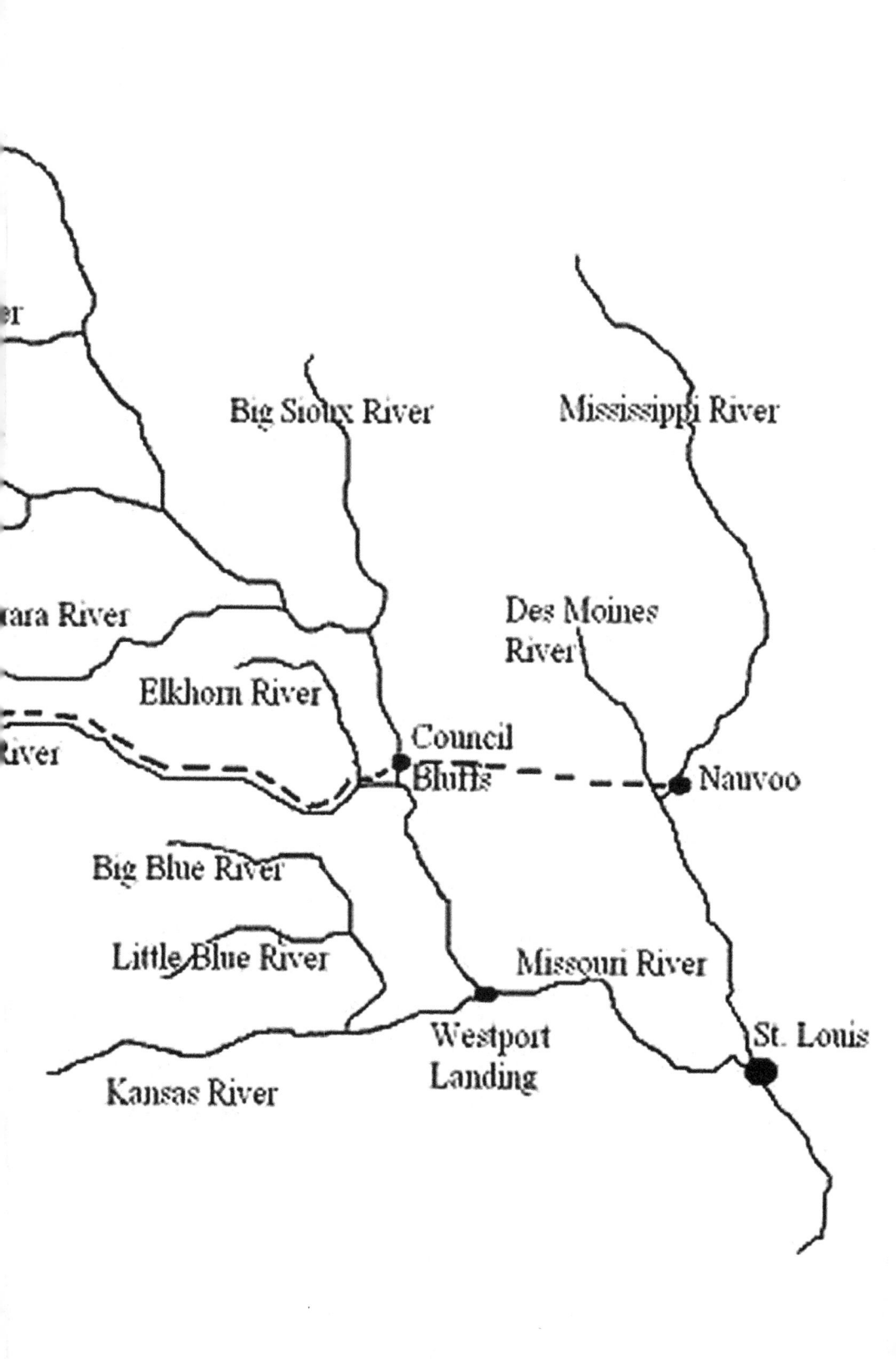

- Big Sioux River
- Mississippi River
- ara River
- Des Moines River
- Elkhorn River
- iver
- Council Bluffs
- Nauvoo
- Big Blue River
- Little Blue River
- Missouri River
- St. Louis
- Westport Landing
- Kansas River

CHAPTER 1

February, 1846

The Burning

Anna softly sang as she held her five-year-old sister, Lisa, on her lap and rocked in Ma's big rocking chair. Even though the song was one of Anna's favorites from church, she couldn't remember all the words so when she ran out she just hummed the tune. The heat radiating from the cooking stove warmed both the kitchen and small front room against the winter cold. As Anna gently rocked back and forth, occasionally glancing out the frost covered window, she caressed Lisa's long black hair. Lisa sat quietly, secure in the comfort of her sister's lap.

Envisioning the upcoming trip to the City of Nauvoo, Anna thought of the wagon rides she and her family had made to Nauvoo each Sunday to attend church and listen to The Prophet, Joseph Smith. She enjoyed church; it gave her a chance to fix up in her best dress, the one Ma had made special for her, and she enjoyed the booming sermons of the church leaders, especially The Prophet. And then there was the opportunity to meet boys. At fourteen, boys had suddenly appeared in her world as a compelling force to be dealt with. Boys were always available to talk to after the General Session, but the grown-ups kept close watch on Anna and her girlfriends. It was so exasperating! Didn't they trust her? But now things had changed so! The Prophet had been murdered, and Anna and her family were going to Nauvoo, not to attend church, but to prepare their large new wagons for the great trek West.

She stopped rocking momentarily to see if Lisa had had enough, but her little sister wiggled on her lap. "More, Anna, do some more!" Anna gave Lisa a hug and resumed rocking as she picked up the tune again.

Singing to Lisa, Anna absentmindedly glanced out the window. She could see past the barn and the fields to the edge of the oak forest, the bare trees still in the grasp of winter. Suddenly, what she saw, or thought she saw, made her stop rocking and lean forward to get a better look, the prickly feet of fear dancing inside her. Through a small clear spot on the frosty glass she caught the suggestion of smoke curling up into the cloudy sky miles toward the south. A wolf hunt! She quickly put Lisa on the floor and rushed to the front door.

"What's wrong?" asked the little girl. "Where ya going? I want to rock some more."

Ignoring her little sister, Anna opened the door's peephole and spied out. She saw a half dozen chimneys of smoke twisting up into the cold February sky. Realizing it must be the mob again, her heart jumped into her throat. "Ma!" she called over her shoulder. "Ma, come quick!" Anna pulled the door's latch and swung it open, letting in a blast of cold air. As she watched the southern horizon, she heard her mother's footsteps hurrying from the kitchen.

"Anna!" exclaimed her mother. "You'll freeze us out. What's wrong with you, child?"

As her mother reached her side, Anna pointed toward the smoke.

Her mother put a hand to her mouth. "Oh Lord, it's the mob! Anna, run and get your pa. Hurry!" She gently, but firmly, pushed Anna onto the front porch.

The icy porch planks stung her bare feet, but Anna hardly noticed. She paused just long enough to check the woods to the left and the right of the barn which stood sixty yards from the house and, satisfied no

The Burning

mobbers were hiding, she dashed off the porch and toward the barn to find her father. Halfway across the frozen yard she saw her father and brother, Michael, exit the barn and begin walking toward her, leading one of the new oxen purchased for the trip West.

"Pa!" she yelled, still on the run, "Look, Pa! Look at the smoke!"

Her father quickly turned and scanned the horizon, stopping at the sign of smoke in the southern sky. As Anna reached his side, her brother also stopped to stare at the black-grey columns twisting into the cloud covered sky. "Pa, they don't usually come during the day," exclaimed the boy as he nervously stared at the southern woods.

Pa looked at both Michael and Anna and tried to smile but the worry and fear were written in the wrinkles on his brow. "I don't know," he said as he looked back toward the southern horizon. "Can't tell whose farm it is."

"Are they comin' here?" asked Anna.

Pa quickly slipped an arm around her shoulders. "If they do, we'll be waiting. Michael," he ordered, "take this animal back and then come to the house." He firmly took Anna's arm. "Come on, Peaches, let's run!" While holding her, as if she would somehow be snatched away, they ran back to the house and up on the porch. Her Ma was already there, holding two old flintlock rifles and a hunting pouch.

"Quick!" said her pa. "Everyone inside!"

"Where's Michael?" asked Ma.

"Putting the ox away, he'll be here." Inside they shut and latched the door and then closed the heavy wooden window shutters on each side of the door. Lisa, left alone while everyone else hurried about, began whimpering.

"Anna!" pleaded Ma. "Pick up your sister and give her a rock. That's something you can do. Help with Lisa, all right?"

Her father had finished with the shutters and was loading his rifle in the now dim light of the house. Ma retrieved a lantern and, removing the glass chimney, lit the wick with one of the new sulfur matches. "They burned out Berner and Eveeda Thornley just last week," she said as she put the lantern on the table. "Burned the barn, the house, and all their belongings." She looked at her husband, the fear reflected in her voice. "What about Jack Jr.? What if they stop him on the road?"

Pa stopped tinkering with his gun. "Jack will be all right, he knows what to do." Looking at his wife and then nodding toward Anna and Lisa in the rocker, he spoke in a low but firm voice. "We got two young 'ens right here, Mary."

Ma looked at Anna and her sister in the rocker and, tears coming to her eyes, walked to the rocker where she knelt down, wrapping her arms around her two daughters. "It'll be just fine; they won't come here, you'll see."

Now the pain and tears swelled up inside Anna as she felt her mother's trembling. "What if they do come, Ma? Will they kill us?"

"No, child, they just burn barns and houses; they don't kill anybody."

Anna was about to ask why Ivan Scrouther, a Mormon neighbor, had been shot and killed by the mob when, suddenly, she heard footsteps on the porch and men's laughter. Anna knew it wasn't the mob for she recognized the laughter of her brother Michael and her Uncle Stan.

Her father hurried to the door and, sliding back the latch, pulled it open. Her uncle and brother quickly stepped inside the house. Pa allowed Michael in and then forcefully swung the door closed behind them.

"My!" said Uncle Stan. "Ain't we all prepared for them mobbers! Well, Jack, you can put yer gun away. It ain't the mob; it's just a brush burning."

"Thank goodness, ya came, Stan! We were about to go to war!" Laughing, her pa quickly walked to his brother, and the two men embraced, giving each other a powerful hug.

As Stan pulled away he smiled at Pa. "I came to see how you was getting on. Brother Allison told me about the smoke. I expect it's got plenty of Saints in a sweat."

Michael laughed while he opened the shutters. "That's right, Pa! It's a burning on one of the Gentile farms to the south. That's all. They's just clearing brush and trees!"

"Well I'll be hog tied!" exclaimed her pa as he put his rifle away. "We thought the mob was out for sure. Lord, what a scare!"

Suddenly the world was bright and friendly again, and Anna brushed away the tears on her cheeks. The smoke was from brush clearing, not the mob! Her ma mumbled something about hot tea and hurried to the kitchen as Michael put away his gun. Without warning, Lisa jumped off Anna's lap and ran to her uncle. "Stan! Stan, pick me up!" she yelled as she danced about in her bare feet and held up her arms for him to take her.

The Burning

He swiftly reached down and scooped up the five year old. "How's my Little Lisa? How's my little rabbit? Have you been good?"

Anna stood and walked toward her uncle. "Hi, Uncle Stan."

Uncle Stan looked at her and smiled. "Is that Anna? Why you've growed a foot since I seen you Sunday and yer prettier, too. Sure yer my Anna? But let's not stand about, ain't we gonna sit?"

She felt herself blush as she looked at her feet and shyly tried to dig a toe into the plank of the floor. Her Uncle Stan was tall and thin with silver hair, his lips turned up at the ends in a perpetual smile. He was clean-shaven, unlike her pa who had a full beard. Anna believed her uncle to be one of the most handsome men alive and his infectious laugh and dancing eyes only added to her conviction.

"Come on," replied her pa, "we'll have something to warm our innards." The two brothers, Stan carrying Lisa, hurried into the kitchen while Anna and Michael followed.

Everyone found seats around the large kitchen table. Ma placed tin cups before the men and filled them with tea from a large tea pot. "Are ya hungry, Stan? I got Johnnycakes left over from breakfast."

Uncle Stan shook his head. "Thanks Mary, but I'm fine." He turned to his brother. "Brother Lissman wants us to be ready to move out with the others around the first of the month. That's only five days away. We got to get a move on. The Lord waits for no man. Jack, we've got to go now; we can't wait any longer. We've got to get to Nauvoo. There's still much to do!"

Her father picked up a cup of hot tea and warmed his hands. "I don't know, Stan. We're not ready—things aren't all packed un' Terral Jackson ain't paid me for the farm, yet."

"Never mind Terral Jackson. He can send you the money, or you can send one o' yer boys to fetch it. He ain't paying ten cents on the dollar, anyway! It's robbery the way them Gentiles are taking our farms for almost nothing. Jack, I tell ya we got to go. I've got most things to Nauvoo already, with only 'bout one load left and I can do that tomorrow."

"But Stan," said her father, "I've got too much to take in one load."

Uncle Stan shook his head. "Lissman said the big wagons will be ready in a day or two. The company ain't going to wait on us, Jack. We got to be in Nauvoo with everything loaded by the twenty-eighth or the first at the latest." There was silence as her pa shuffled his chair,

Buffalo Man

and then her uncle spoke again, his voice lower. "Ya got to remember the mob. They can strike anywhere. Tomorrow it might not be a brush burning. Too many farms have already been destroyed, especially farms away from Nauvoo like yo'r and mine. Brother Allison heard word that some of them at Appanoose were forming up for another wolf hunt."

At the sound of the words, Anna felt her heart skip a beat. She knew only too well what a 'wolf hunt' was. Adults talked of such things in low voices or made the children leave the room, but a wolf hunt was when the mob came and burned your house and maybe killed ya, too! She couldn't understand why the Gentiles hated the Mormons so. They were just plain farmers with a love of God and a desire to be left alone. But since The Prophet had been murdered by the mob, all the Saints had been told they had to leave, to go west into Indian Territory. It was so unfair. Pa said he was getting only a pittance for the farm. She didn't know how much a pittance was, but she knew it wasn't much. They had such a nice log house to have to leave it behind. They were even abandoning the two glass windows her father had shipped by wagon all the way from Springfield; there would be no room for them in the wagon. Her ears picked up again as Uncle Stan continued.

"The mob can strike anytime, Jack. Even Nauvoo isn't going to be safe soon. Better to leave now than be burnt out. Please, Jack, listen to me, pack the rest of yer things and leave, leave tomorrow."

"I would, but I've got too much to do in one day."

"No, listen, load your Dearborn with everything it will carry and send it in with your boys. I'll send Jason with the boat, and he'll dock at your pier. You can load the rest of yer things in the boat and just float 'em down to Nauvoo. You can do 'er all in a day. That'll give us time to get the teams together and the wagons ready."

Another silence hung in the air before Anna's mother spoke in a solemn voice. "We could do it, Jack. The boys have most things ready, and we can do the rest today. The mobbers might strike here next. We've got Anna and Lisa to think of." Again the little house was filled with a heavy silence as if it were holding its breath to catch the next words.

"It must be the will of the Lord," said her father as he shook his head. "I know we've got to go, but it's hard giving up what we've worked for. Don't worry, Stan, we'll be ready. Send Jason with the boat and we'll be

The Burning

waiting at the pier." Pa's eyes became watery. "It's just so hard leaving a good home again."

Stan smiled. "Good, it's settled then. We'll meet in Nauvoo and get our wagons ready with the others. I got to go now, Alice is expectin' me."

Her mother, father and Uncle Stan stood and walked into the front room, followed by Anna, Lisa and Michael. Uncle Stan gave Anna's mother a hug. "Alice has some pickles and dried peaches for you, Mary. I would have brought it, but I plumb forgot! I'll give it to you in Nauvoo." Uncle Stan buttoned up his heavy brown wool coat as Pa opened the door, and everyone walked out onto the porch to see Stan off.

Suddenly they were aware of a horseman patiently watching them from his mount before the hitching rail. They all stared without speaking as the man slowly leaned over and spit a large chaw of tobacco onto the ground. He then leaned back in the saddle and proceeded to run his tongue over his teeth before speaking. "Hello, Mister Sinclair," he said in a deep voice as he looked straight at Anna's pa.

"Afternoon, Sheriff Hawes."

The Sheriff looked at Uncle Stan and then back to her pa. "That smoke is a burning at Tillman's. Don't want ya to worry."

Her pa nodded. "I thank ya, Sheriff, but I already heard of the burning."

The Sheriff gazed at the Mormons on the porch for a moment before continuing. "I understand yer brother, here, is packing and getting ready to go. I came to see if maybe I couldn't encourage you to do likewise."

Her pa's eyes narrowed. "You come to throw me off my land? Can't ya wait for the mob to do it?"

Hawes' forehead knotted up. "These outlying farms ain't safe no more, Sinclair. If you left with the other Mormons, there wouldn't be no raid. Ain't that so? If there's a wolf hunt, someone might get hurt."

"You don't have to fret, Sheriff. I'll be leaving tomorrow. But I'm warning you, this farm has been legally sold to Terral Jackson. If you let the mob burn this place then they'll be burning the property of one of their own."

The Sheriff smiled and gave a slight nod of his head. "I'm glad to hear you've made the right decision. I'll be leaving now." He reined his horse to the left, but then, with a slight hesitation, turned once more toward the Mormons. "For what it's worth, good luck, wherever it is you're going." He gave a gentle spur to his horse and rode out of the yard.

Everyone watched as the Sheriff trotted down the road toward the woods. Finally, Stan turned to his brother and sister-in-law. "I guess that was our farewell!" Both her pa and uncle laughed. Anna didn't understand why, it was some sort of private adult joke between them.

"Ma, are we leaving now? Is it time?"

Her mother reached over and stroked Anna's curly, black hair. "Yes, child, we'll leave tomorrow."

Anna felt a trembling deep inside. "Is there a wolf hunt, Ma? Will they come here?"

Her mother smiled and gave Anna a quick hug. "No, sweetheart, they're not coming here. We're leaving to join Brother Lissman and the Company in Nauvoo; we're going to a Promised Land. But you've got to help–you're my right arm. No more talk of wolf hunts. We have lots to do. I want you to gather up your things and Lisa's, too. Have her help, you know, make a game of it. And tomorrow we'll take your uncle's boat down the Mississippi. You've never been in your Uncle Stan's boat. It'll be a great adventure, you'll see."

* * *

The clouds in the west broke, yielding a red sunset, as the smoke from the burning brush and trees gave the land a look of desolation. The men had finished their work in the fields and were now heading toward the log house for their supper. This was Ned Tillman's burning, and his neighbors had helped clear new fields which he would plant in the spring with wheat or corn.

Wes Hamlin rubbed his cold hands together and then began trudging toward the house, carrying the spade and ax he had used to dig out stumps and bushes. The work had been hard since the ground was almost frozen, but worth it because now he could join the others in the sumptuous supper prepared by his mother and the other women and, afterward,

The Burning

he could stand around the fire and listen to the older men discuss religion or politics.

When he reached the house he saw men already standing before the long rough-hewn table, eagerly stacking mountains of food on their tin plates. Wes hurried to the end of the table to fetch a plate. As he reached for a piece of cornbread, a voice came from behind him, and a strong hand grabbed his wrist.

"Wes!" said his mother in a stern, sharp voice. "Look at those hands! You march right over to the wash basin and clean 'em good. You hear me? Now get!"

He felt everyone's eyes on him, and a blush came to his cheeks. He was sixteen! Why did his mother treat him this way? "Yes, Ma, I'm going." He turned and, dancing around her, retreated to the wash stand where he spotted his cousin, Jimmy Dixon, intently scrubbing his fingers and knuckles over a basin of soapy water.

Jimmy turned and grinned. "Where ya been, Wes? I ain't seen ya since noon."

Wes found an empty wash basin and filled it with spring water from the bucket next to the table. "I was working on a powerful stump 't the edge of the field. It were so big that the horses couldn't pull 'er free. They gave me the job, special, to get her out."

Jimmy showed little interest in the story of the stump. "Where was your brother, Gunner? I ain't seen him."

"I think he must o' had a job to do cause he wouldn't miss a burning. Maybe he'll come later." Wes was now drying his hands as Jimmy impatiently waited for his cousin so they could get to their meal.

"Did Gunner really fight Injuns in the Territories? I heard he's been to St. Louie and to Santa Fe. What kind of gun does he carry?"

Wes smiled, for Gunner was one of his favorite subjects. His half brother was the only child from Wes's father's first marriage and, at twenty-four, had developed a reputation as a rogue. Wild stories circulated about his fighting, whoring and traveling, and Wes believed them all, not afraid to accidentally embellish the stories, himself. He knew that some day he would be just like Gunner and go West where he could fight Indians and shoot buffalo and make a name for himself. Bert was his full brother and, at four years Wes' senior, had already taken over the farm since their father's death. Wes couldn't see himself in Bert's place: a farmer, tied to one spot. He knew he was meant to roam, to be famous, like Gunner.

"He carries a Walker-Colt revolving cylinder. You've heard of that one, ain't ya? Now, come on! Let's get our share of the grub."

They hurried back to the dinner table and stood in line as several other boys, all neighbors, joined them. Carrying plates heaped with smoked ham, beef jerky, cornbread, beans and preserved pears and peaches, Wes and his friends moved away from the house and found a large fallen tree to sit on. They had to have some distance from the women and young girls so they could talk of "men things."

"I tell ya, our boys will go down there and kick them Mormonites across the Mississippi. You wait and see." It was Melvin Ingertal speaking, a tall blond boy who was barely seventeen. "I'm going to go, too! Soon as I get a chance I'll join up with the Carthage Grays. Those Mormonites started this war and we'll finish it."

Jimmy swallowed hard to down a piece of ham. "You can't go, Mel–your pa won't let ya. How you goin' if'n he don't let you join up?"

Melvin looked at Wes and back to Jimmy, and the other boys leaned closer in anticipation of some secret. "I tell ya, I'm going. If ya go and just do it, then it's done. I'll be in Carthage before my pa finishes milking the cows. I'll just be gone some night." He turned to Wes and placed a hand on Wes' shoulder. "You should come too, you're old enough. Sixteen is almost seventeen and you look as big as anyone. You and me could just sneak away and be in Carthage, ready to sign up, before the cock crowed."

Jimmy would have none of it. "Your dad would skin ya alive, Mel."

Melvin slowly turned to the fifteen-year-old. "I weren't talking to you, Jimbo, so go suck an egg. I was talking to my friend, Wes." He turned back toward Wes. "Now how about it, do we go?"

Wes felt the excitement rush through his blood. It was perfect; he and Mel would sneak off, join the militia and be fighting the Mormons in a single day. He fixed his eyes on Mel's and grabbed his friend by the arm. "I'll do it! We'll join up and be soldiers. I hear they issue a pair of boots and a new gun to each recruit. Them Mormons don't stand a chance, we'll chase them all across the Mississippi."

Greg Oldmyer couldn't take it any longer. "I'll go too! I can fight."

The Burning

Several others also affirmed their intent to join the brave new warriors. Jimmy was the only one to keep a cool head. "Greg, you're only eleven. How you going to get in? Them army men will take one look at you and laugh. How yer folks going to do with no one to help with the planting this spring?"

Wes's new dream was too full to let go. "But there's always planting or harvest or feeding or something and besides, them Mormons will be long gone before spring. Some of them is already across the River and in Iowa Territory. We got to do it now or it'll be all over. We just got to go. When ya get to be a man, ya just got to decide one day that ya can't stay tied to yer ma and you've got to do a man's job. Now, I'm fer going. Who else is with me?"

A number of boys, of all ages, raised their hands. Wes was about to caution his cousin to be quiet about the secret operation when laughter from a group of men standing around a large bonfire attracted the boys' attention. With mutual understanding the group broke up and the boys slowly sauntered over to stand around the fire, too. Wes found his brother Bert and slipped up next to him.

"I tell ya, men, those Mormonites must be wiped from the face of the earth." It was preacher Tammerman speaking on his favorite subject. "They are an abomination in God's sight! They take multiple wives and they perform vile and lascivious rites in their temple, and God will smite them for their wickedness."

Wallace Tucker grunted and then smiled at the preacher. "Now I don't know as it's such a bad idea to have a second wife. When the winter gets cold it's nice to have both yer sides warmed at once." The men around Wallace began laughing but caught themselves before they overstepped good taste in front of the preacher.

As the glow of the fire danced over Tammerman's scowling face his eyes locked on Tucker. "You're mocking the Lord's commandments, Wallace Tucker. If you hold to such vile and unsavory beliefs, then God will lock you from heaven. Do you want that, Wallace? Do you want to be locked out of Heaven?"

"Preacher, I was just funnin'. God likes a joke too, don't he? You will forgive an old sinner, won't ya, preacher?"

The preacher seemed mollified for the moment, but he had a powerful memory and a man was well advised to soothe an insult with him.

"Now, men," began Samual Davidson, one of the workers at the Newtown Mill, "it ain't them extra wives we got to ponder on. It's them Mormons kissing up to the Redskins. Them Mormons have been preaching to the Injuns and telling them they is God's own children. There's thousands 'a Injuns west of the Missouri and if they get stirred up they can cut this country in half. What of the folks that's already gone to Oregon? What about them that's going to California? Them Injuns could cross Iowa and the River and raid our farms and burn our homes, and it would be them Mormonites doing the devil's own work. Remember the Blackhawk War." There were numerous nods and grunts of agreement around the fire.

Wallace Tucker leaned on his rifle, his buckskin clothes adding an aura of legitimacy to his words. He had been a trapper and a scout for the army, and his opinions regarding Indians were taken with great weight by the local farmers. "Don't worry none about them Injuns; we can take care of their likes. It's them Mormons. President Polk is going to get us in a war, you mark my words. It's going to be Mexico or the British, Oregon or the Rio Grande. When it happens the State of Illinois will be calling men to join up. What will those Mormons be doing? If they leave the United States, are they going to join the British in Oregon or maybe the Mexicans? What if we go to fight the Bean-Eaters. Why, them Mormons can come right back to their holy city, Nauvoo. It took us enough years to get them pig suckers to leave our State, now they have a chance to come back and, if we was at war, the Governor would be helpless to do anything."

A heavy silence fell as the men pondered his words. Preacher Tammerman cleared his throat to say something when a man on horseback rode up and, with a grace showing both strength and youth, slid from his mount and stepped before the fire. Wes' heart took a jump–it was Gunner! The tall, young man slowly scanned the faces around the fire. "By yer soberness, I take it yer speaking of the Mormons." There were grunts of affirmation.

Wes spoke before he realized it. "Mr. Tucker says that the Mormons are coming back to Nauvoo as soon as the men all march off to fight Mexico."

Gunner peered through the smoke. "We at war? Who is that? That you, young Wes? Well, I don't know about them returning to Nauvoo

The Burning

'cause I got me some plans of my own. As long as we make sure them Mormons is crossing the River from this side to the other then we got the problem licked. I say we have ourselves a little wolf hunt. There's still them two families over by the bend in the River; they haven't joined the retreat. I say tonight would be a perfect night to give 'em a little shove. What da ya say men, ya with me?"

"I am God's own servant and as such I can't take up the sword," said the preacher, "but I say Gunner Hamlin has hit the mark. I say that to speed up the exile of them swine from our fair state is to do God's work." The men began talking to one another in excited tones and someone passed a jug of corn whiskey.

Wes felt his own excitement surge to match that of the others standing about the fire. He had never been on a wolf hunt, but he had heard plenty about them. When the moon was gone and the night was black, men would slip out of their homes and join up. By morning another Mormon farm house or barn would be burned to the ground. It was a tactic that the people of Western Illinois had used for years, and it was a tactic that the Mormons had used themselves. Now Wes might get to go on one with Gunner!

The men were getting worked into a fighting pitch when a figure abruptly appeared before the fire. He was on the short side but with broad shoulders and a neck as thick as a man's leg. At first he was silent; and, as the farmers came to notice his presence, they fell silent, too. Soon there was no movement or talking, the only noise was the crackling of the bonfire. Everyone watched and waited on the newcomer. Finally, Wallace Tucker found his voice. "Evening, Sheriff. Will ya take a pull on the jug?"

Sheriff Hawes nodded and someone handed him the whiskey. He locked his finger in the handle and expertly tipped the jug off his shoulder and took a long drink. "Awh, now that's drinking whiskey. Just the thing to take the chill out of the bones. My compliments to the maker. Ya know, when I first walked up to this here fire I heard something that I know must have been a mistake 'a hearing. I could of swored I heard someone talk of a wolf hunt. You boys all know we don't have wolf hunts around here, now don't ya? The Mormons have been a thorn in the side of Illinois for years, but now they're on the run. Joe Smith, their prophet, is dead. Their leaders have already crossed the River and the others will be going. It would pain me greatly to bury one of my friends or neighbors for some damn foolishness that was leading nowhere. Do each of you get my meaning?" He paused and looked about as everyone stared at the ground in embarrassment. "Good, now you boys have had a hard day helping Ned clear his fields. Your women and kids is back at the house waiting to go home; they're tired, too. I think it's time we called it a day's work done and each of us go home."

As the Sheriff watched, the men slipped away to fetch their families and leave. There would be no wolf hunt on this night.

Later, Sheriff Hawes rode his large chestnut down the Old River Road. Even in the dark, he knew the way. Reaching his destination, he reined to a stop and quietly dismounted. He tied the rein to a willow branch and walked down a narrow path toward the black shape of a shed. Standing very still by the side of the shed, he peered through the trees toward the cabin and caught the flicker of a lantern at the cabin's window. Leaning against the shed he watched the cabin and impatiently waited.

After several minutes a woman's voice whispered his name. "Taylor? Is that you?"

He turned to see her coming toward him. "Yes," he whispered back. She glided into his arms, and he held her tightly. "Oh, Sarah, I didn't think you would come. I was afraid you were gone."

She firmly pushed against him and broke his embrace. "I wasn't going see you again, but I had to tell you."

"Don't say it, Sarah, don't say anything." He began pulling her into the dark shed.

"No, Taylor, I can't. Not this time. I came to tell you I'm going. We're leaving tomorrow for Nauvoo."

The fear he had carried for so many months now burst out. "No, you can't. You don't love him anymore. You told me that yourself. You love me! How can you go? How can you leave everything for some wilderness with a man you don't care about?"

"You don't understand, Taylor. I'm a Mormon and I have to do what God commands me to do. The Apostles have ordered everyone to prepare, and there's nothing I can do about it. My loving you has been wrong, it's been a sin. I'm here just to tell you it's over, done with. I'll be gone tomorrow and we'll never see each other again. You have a wife, Taylor, you belong with her."

The Burning

He pulled at her dress and kissed her neck. "You can't go. We'll go off together, just you and me. We'll go back East and start over." He felt her body tremble.

"No, Taylor, it's too late." As she spoke, she didn't pull away or try to stop him. "This must be the last time, my sweetheart, the last time." She helped him with her dress as they backed into the dark shed and sank to their knees on the cold hay.

CHAPTER 2

The Raid

Wes dreamed of riding Jeff, Bert's prize stallion, while chased by Mexican soldiers across a sagebrush covered plateau. He was frightened, knowing the Mexicans were out to get him, but excited too; he knew Jeff was too fast for them and he would escape. Suddenly Bert was calling and the Mexicans were gone.

When Wes opened his eyes, Bert stood beside his bed, shaking Wes' shoulders. "I said wake up, Wes. I want ya to get dressed." Bert turned and headed for the loft's ladder which led to the main floor.

Wes sat up, rubbed his eyes, and looked about, shivering in the cold morning air. The attic was dark, the only light coming from a lantern his brother held. "What time is it? Why did ya wake me?"

Bert paused on the ladder. "It's almost daylight and I need ya to go to Newtown's Mill in Appanoose and see Sam Davidson. You're to fetch a mule he's loaning us. Hurry up and don't take all day. I want ya back by noon so you can help Ma."

"Can I take Jeff?"

"No, you can't. You'll run that horse 'til he's lame. You take old Blackie." Then Bert was gone.

Wes slipped on his cold pants and boots, grumbling to himself. "You never let me ride Jeff. You ride him all the time and I never get to. It ain't fair." The complaining wouldn't help: Bert was the head of the family now, and Wes would do what his brother said. But he didn't have to like it.

By the time he'd eaten two cold biscuits and saddled Blackie, the eastern sky had brightened, warning of a cloudy day. Wes mounted Blackie and pointed the old horse north, toward the Mill. He then eased back in the saddle to daydream. Blackie sensed what was expected and plodded along as well as his tired old bones allowed. The morning air was bitter cold, and heavy clouds moved quickly overhead, threatening to add rain or even snow to the sharp briskness. Wes pulled his brown wool coat tight around himself to keep out the chill while he slipped into his dream world to fight "Injuns" and "Bean Eaters" and find fabulous treasure.

Suddenly Wes was aware that Blackie wasn't moving, but had stopped at a fork in the narrow rutted road. The right branch led north to Appanoose and the Mill while the left road went toward the River. Before leaning right and touching his heels to Blackie's sides, a thought sprang up. The left road went down to the River and passed two Mormon farms, but then it doubled back and joined the other road. The left road was a bit longer, but Wes was in no hurry and hadn't been that way for a long time. Bert and his ma discouraged Wes from going near the Mormons. Yet, today was different for the Mormons would be gone soon. If he hurried to the Mill and then back home, more work awaited him. No sense in that! He might as well take his time and have a view of the world's greatest river, the Mighty Mississippi.

* * *

The Raid

Anna was frightened even though she had been told there was no reason to be. Ma had explained that the mob wouldn't come, but Anna couldn't help looking around anxiously whenever she heard an unexpected noise. All morning the family prepared to leave the farm for the last time. Dark clouds overhead warned of rain or snow, and the way her ma and pa hurried, it was as if they were trying to beat the bad weather. Only little Lisa was unperturbed by all the hustle and hurry.

Finally they had stacked those belongings going by boat on their little pier and had loaded the Dearborn wagon for Jack Jr. and Michael to drive to Nauvoo. Much would stay behind; they hadn't had time to dispose of unnecessary items and, since all the Mormons were trying to sell their extra belongings, too few buyers could be found.

The instructions from the Apostles for each family were explicit: one thousand pounds of flour, twenty pounds of sugar, one rifle, one tent, one wagon, three yoke of oxen, two cows, three beef cattle, building tools, and all the prepared foods possible including corned beef, pickled pork, parched corn and dried potatoes. Anna and her mother worked all winter to be ready. The flour gave them the most trouble because everyone needed such a large supply. Her pa and brothers went far in search of it, selling off several cherished pieces of furniture for the money.

As her brothers hitched up the two draft horses, Anna's mother put a comforting arm around her shoulders. "I want you to watch Lisa while we load the boat. Don't let her go near the edge of the pier and keep her coat buttoned up. We don't want her to catch cold. Remember, you're responsible for your sister." Her mother smiled. "Now get ready. Your brothers are leaving and then we'll be going down to the pier to meet Jason."

Anna was pleased with the responsibility. "I'll watch her, Ma."

Soon her two brothers sat ready on the seat of the wagon. Pa gave them their last instructions, and then everyone waved goodbye. Jack Jr. slapped the reins against the horse's rump and started down the road.

Anna, Lisa and her ma and pa made the short walk west from the cabin down the tree covered lane and over the hill which sloped down to the little pier on the River. When they arrived, Jason was already there, sitting in a large flat-bottomed boat with a set of oars and a tiller. Two weeks before, the Mississippi had frozen over, allowing those Saints leaving Nauvoo to drive their wagons across to the Iowa shore. Recently the weather had warmed and the ice broke up. Anna saw large blocks of ice float down the River, yet none came close to their pier or boat.

Jason and her folks went to work, transferring the household goods from the pier to the water craft while she played with Lisa. When the boat was loaded, Pa and Cousin Jason rearranged the belongings so it would ride even.

Suddenly Pa stood up straight and stared at the wooded hill sloping down to the River. Following his stare, everyone else stopped what they were doing and turned to look. On the crest of the hill, through the trees, three horsemen rode back and forth. One of the horsemen stopped and, for a moment, was motionless. A blue cloud of smoke obscured the man and a second later something smashed into the planking of the pier, sending splinters flying. The loud discharge of a gun rang in Anna's ears.

"Oh God!" yelled Pa. "They're shooting at us!"

Anna's mother screamed at her. "Anna, get the baby! Get into the boat!"

Anna grabbed Lisa's hand and ran to the end of the pier. Another shot rang out. Everyone looked about to see where the ball struck, but nothing appeared damaged.

"Jason!" yelled Pa, "untie the stern. I'll get the girls."

Ma quickly swept Lisa up in her arms and handed her to Anna's father. As Jason untied the stern rope, Pa put Lisa down in the boat and moved to the bow of the craft. Just as he reached for the bow rope, a rifle ball smashed the stanchion holding the rope to the pier, and the report of another gun shot filled the air. The stanchion shattered and the bow of the boat pulled away from the pier as the rope, now loose, untangled and slipped into the water.

Anna, standing on the pier beside her mother, watched in amazement as the front of the boat moved farther away. She could see Jason in the stern, clinging to one of the pier's posts in an attempt to hold the boat in place. Lisa stood in the boat and danced about wildly. "Mama, Mama!" she cried, holding her little arms out toward her mother who stood helpless on the pier.

"Hold on, Jason," yelled Pa.

"I can't, it's slipping!"

The River was too much, and Jason's hold was wrenched free by the force of the current. At once the boat slipped out and was firmly caught

The Raid

by the cold dense flow. Jason, losing his balance, fell overboard into the muddy water. Pa stood with outstretched arms and called to his wife and daughter, left on the pier. "Stay there, Mary, stay there. I'll bring the boat back." He moved quickly to the center of the craft and, sitting on a box, took hold of the oars to begin rowing toward shore.

Anna turned to see her mother standing at the side of the pier, yelling down into the cold river water. "Jason! Can you get out? Do you need help."

"I'm all right, Aunt Mary. God, it's cold!"

Anna heard her cousin splashing about under the pier as he struggled to get out of the River. She looked up at the ridge of the hill and saw one of the men aiming his rifle at the boat. "Look, Ma." She pointed toward the gunman.

Her mother glanced first toward the hill and then cupped her hands around her mouth and called to her husband in the boat. "Jack! Look out!" Anna and her mother watched her father row toward shore as the current continued pushing the boat down river, while Lisa stood in the bow and cried. Another shot rang out, and her pa dropped the oars and clutched his head. Then, very slowly, he pitched forward and fell over the side of the boat.

Doubling up her fists, Anna's Mother screamed at the top of her lungs. "JACK! JACK!" His head appeared above the water and his arms reached out, struggling to propel him toward the river bank. Both her father and the boat were carried away toward a bend in the River. Her mother grabbed Anna's hand and ran to the shore end of the pier just as Jason walked out of the water. "Jason," her Ma yelled. "They shot Jack! He's in the water!"

"Stay here!" commanded the boy. "I'll get him."

"Jason, Lisa's in the boat! Get her. I'll get Jack."

Jason looked out over the River and saw the boat disappearing around the bend. "Oh, God!" he groaned as he scrambled up the hill to cut off the boat. Anna's ma called for Anna to follow. They started plowing through the brush that clogged the river bank, her mother leading, Anna following. More shots rang out.

Anna and her mother struggled to get through the willows and tree branches that blocked their path. Ma charged ahead without concern for the whipping branches or thorns. Anna, in her attempt to follow, was lashed and pricked until her arms and legs hurt from the scratches and welts. She hadn't had time to grasp everything that was happening and, in her fear and pain, began to cry. Anna heard the deep sound of a man's voice ahead. It wasn't her father. Ma stopped and held up her hand. Again the man's voice drifted to them from somewhere ahead. Ma renewed her effort to get down river to Pa, and Anna struggled to keep up.

After endless minutes, mother and daughter reached a small opening in the brush where a stream emptied into the Mississippi. Laying on the dead brown grass beside the River was Pa; blood covering his head and upper body. Ma screamed and ran to him. Falling on the ground beside him, she began wiping the blood from his face with her dress. Anna ran after her and, reaching them, knelt down next to her father. "Jack! Jack!" cried her mother, but the body was lifeless. Ma stopped her wiping and intently stared into Pa's face. As realization filled her eyes, she screamed again, pulled his head to her bosom and rocked back and forth, a low, sickening wail escaping her lips.

Anna knew this really hadn't happened; her father was only teasing. He would soon open his eyes and laugh at them, calling Anna "Peaches" and giving Ma a big hug. Yet, as she stared down at her father, he lay perfectly still, as if in deep sleep. A painful knot formed in her throat and she cried again, but the crying didn't relieve the pain. Soon she was rocking in rhythm with her mother.

For many minutes Ma held Pa as she and Anna rocked back and forth. Suddenly Anna was aware of someone standing behind her. She turned to see Sheriff Taylor Hawes frowning and shaking his head. "I seen who did this, I know the boy. Don't worry, I'll get him."

CHAPTER 3

False Accusation

Wes rode down the winding, tree-lined lane, drawing closer and closer to the River. Holding an imaginary rifle in his hands, he pointed it toward a tree, which was really an Indian, and squeezed off a round. The terrible Indian was shot through the heart and fell in a heap to the ground. Wes smiled and stroked his gun. "A Hawken, I think," he said to himself. "Yep, I'll have me a Hawken buffalo gun or maybe a Henry. The Hawken is good, but maybe the Henry is better. And a Colt, a new Navy Colt for a side arm." He quick-drew an imaginary pistol from his belt and shot a few desperadoes from the trees.

As Wes rounded a small bend in the road, movement far in front and to his right caught his eye. He reined in Blackie and studied the forest stretched before him. At first he saw nothing, then spotted three riders two hundred yards through the trees and on the other side of a steep

Buffalo Man

gully. Even at this distance Wes recognized all three horsemen. One wore a dirty green felt coat and a red bandanna. He was Roland Palmer, a farmhand from east of the Newtown Mill. The second man wore an old top hat and a long black coat; Cyrus Maggio, a drifter from Missouri. But it was the third man who drew Wes' attention. The distinctive mount and white rawhide shirt were unmistakable. It was his half-brother, Gunner!

Wes yelled to attract their notice, but none of the three men turned to see who was calling. Instead, they were looking at something at the bottom of the hill they were on; something by the River. Suddenly, a thought flashed through Wes. Gunner had talked of a wolf hunt just the night before and there he was with two friends, close to the Mormon place. Excitement surging through him, Wes realized it must be a raid. He had to join Gunner and be part of it.

Wes quickly scanned the gully separating him from the three riders before glancing again in the direction of his half-brother. Gunner sat in his saddle as he aimed his rifle down the hill. Wes knew he'd have to hurry to reach them as he urged Blackie through the brush and between tall thin trees toward the northeast where he hoped the gully broadened to become passable. After several minutes he found a washout and was able to urge Blackie down into the canyon bottom. As he struggled to find a way up the other side, he heard the first report of a gun. The hunt was on! It took Wes several more minutes to wind his way to the top of the gully and into the forest in Gunner's direction. During that time he heard several more shots. He had to hurry. He might be too late and miss everything! Even in the cold air, sweat formed on Blackie, and Wes felt the heat rise up around him. In anticipation of combat, he drew his hunting knife, the only weapon he possessed. It would have to do. In his mind's eye he could see Gunner and the other two men charging into a whole flock of Godless Mormonites, blazing away with their guns and dropping the heathens in all directions.

Wes tried maintaining a course to the north, but the terrain was broken and uneven, forcing Blackie to correct his path to the west and closer to the River. Wes crossed several small ridges and then, without warning, he and Blackie found themselves sliding and slipping down a steep embankment. It was impossible to stop their descent and Wes let Blackie take the lead and steer a course to the hill's bottom. Once on flat land Wes reined in and quickly looked about. He was in the clearing of

False Accusation

a narrow ravine containing a small stream. He felt he should be close to the fighting as more shots rang out somewhere to the north, up the hill, confirming his suspicion. In the River, not fifty paces away, something thrashed about in the water. Wes was confused, the excitement of the impending battle completely replaced by curiosity. He dismounted and walked to the water's edge to get a better view. In shallow water, ten yards from the River's bank, the thrashing stopped and a man stood up out of the River with the muddy water whirling about his waist. The man held his head with both hands as blood ran down his face.

Wes stared in disbelief as the man took a shaky step toward the shore, toward the very spot where Wes stood. The man's eyes were fixed, as if in a trance, looking up toward the top of the ridge behind Wes. The man took several more steps. Wes, realizing the distance between them was closing quickly, was unable to move or turn and run. Instead, his fear locked him in place as the wounded man closed the final few feet and, with a lunge, flung a hand out and grabbed Wes' coat, falling to the ground and tearing the buttons from Wes' garment.

The body contact broke the spell, and Wes quickly bent down and, grabbing the man under the shoulders, pulled him up on level ground. The man's eyes remained open, but the body was limp, settling onto the earth with all muscle tension gone. Wes quickly tore a strip of cloth from the tail of his shirt and knelt down, pressing the fabric of the shirt against the gaping wound in the man's head. Suddenly he recognized that the body was lifeless—the man was dead!

It had all happened too fast: an adventure on a chilly, cloudy morning shattered by horsemen and then someone in the River. First, a wounded man and now this thing on the ground; this thing with open eyes that had only moments before been a living, breathing person! Wes slowly stood and, becoming aware of the sticky blood on his hands, tried to wipe them on his trousers. He continued staring at the corpse for several moments as if that alone would change what he saw. Bit by bit, a new thought wormed its way into his brain. He shouldn't be here, he should be someplace else, anyplace else. He reached for his bloodied, torn shirt and, as he backed away, his eye caught the glimmer of metal next to the body—a single shot pistol lay on the ground. Wes knew instinctively that it had slipped from the dead man's belt. He bent over and picked up the gun as water ran out of the barrel.

"You there! Stop!" The sound jolted Wes out of his stupor as he recognized the voice, a chill running up his spine. Looking up, he saw Sheriff Hawes standing on the River's bank only thirty yards away. The Sheriff held a revolver pointed toward Wes' chest. "Now don't you move a muscle or I'll put a hole in you big enough to plant a tree."

Wes shook his head. "You don't understand! I came to help!"

The Sheriff continued watching Wes as he slowly moved toward him through the willows and cottontails. "Drop that gun!" he commanded in a loud, forceful voice.

Wes looked at the pistol in his hand and quickly dropped it as if it were a snake about to bite. The Sheriff was getting closer so Wes instinctively backed up several steps. "You don't understand, Sheriff. I came to help, I pulled him from the water."

"I said 'don't move!' and I meant it. Don't make me shoot."

Wes stretched out his hands in a pleading manner. "Please, Sheriff, I didn't!"

Sheriff Hawes stopped and took aim. "I warned you Wes Hamlin to stop! Don't make me shoot, boy."

In Wes' imagination, he could see the lead slug leave the muzzle of the Sheriff's gun and, crossing the short space separating them, enter his chest. His feet worked independently of his mind and continued moving him backward. "I didn't do it, I..." Wes' foot caught on something and, losing his balance, he toppled over backward. As he hit the soft ground, he was aware of a loud explosion. At first he was too frightened to move, but then quickly recovered and felt about his chest for the wound. Nothing! The bullet had missed! There was no confusion now! He scampered to his feet and, remaining in a crouched position, ran for the safety of the trees. As he ran he heard the thrashing of the willows behind him and knew that Sheriff Hawes was in pursuit. When Wes reached the trees he stood straight so he could sprint to safety. Dashing through the woods, he heard a second shot somewhere behind him and Sheriff Hawes yelling. "You stop, Wes Hamlin! I know who you are! Stop!"

Wes refused to stop, but ran with every fiber and muscle of his body striving for more speed. He knew he must get away and find safety from the Sheriff and from the Sheriff's gun! He ran until he thought his lungs would burst and when he could run no more he fell behind a tall walnut tree and gasped for breath. After a few moments, he held his breath,

False Accusation

ignoring the pain in his chest, and listened. He heard nothing other than soft forest sounds: a distant crow mocking him with its caw and the wind rustling the bare branches of a tree. He saw no sign of Sheriff Hawes.

Wes waited several minutes, making sure he had lost his pursuer and, when satisfied, began walking southeast through the woods in the direction of home. He was afraid to go back and look for Blackie and would have to walk all the way. He spent two hours returning to the farm house and, as he drew close, he moved forward with great caution and care. Would the Sheriff be waiting? Should he even attempt to return home? When he finally caught sight of the family's log house located across a cleared field, he stopped behind an old rotting tree. Careful not to expose himself, he scrutinized the house and barnyard. Four horses were tied to the hitching post in front of the porch. The horses did not belong to the Hamlins—it had to be the Sheriff and his deputies!

Wes drew his legs up and, putting his forehead on his knees, softly groaned. An empty pit occupied his stomach and a knot of pain found his throat. It wasn't fair—he hadn't done anything! He tried to help the man, and the Sheriff thought he had done the killing! If he returned home now, the Sheriff would arrest him. Who was that man at the River? Had it been a Mormon? Wes thought it looked like that Sinclair fellow who owned the Mormon farm on top the hill. Why did the Sheriff care about an old Mormon, anyway? Everyone was shooting Mormons. What was one more dead one? He had to find out what had happened and why the Sheriff was at his house. He would hide and, when the Sheriff was gone, would return and find Bert. Bert would know what to do. Bert could explain to Sheriff Hawes what had really happened and everything would be all right.

Wes slowly stood and, glancing once more in the direction of the house, slipped into the woods. He knew where to go: a secret place no one could find except he and his brother. Traveling cautiously through the forest for the better part of an hour he came to a small hill completely covered in hemlock. On one side stood a large rock outcropping. He moved the bushes from one side of the rock to reveal a small clearing just five yards across completely hidden by the rock and the hill. Here he would be safe. Once settled in, he wrapped his coat tightly about himself to fend off the cold. A light rain began falling. Without warning, a heavy sleepiness came over him. He couldn't keep his eyes open and soon was sound asleep.

Buffalo Man

Wes felt himself in water, heavy and cold, almost like syrup, pulling him down. The night was dark, yet he sensed the water was bloody. He tried swimming to shore when, suddenly, the river water was all blood and getting thicker, pulling him under. He tried screaming, but the blood flowed into his mouth. Wes struggled in the blood when, abruptly, the River disappeared and he was back at the hiding place with someone shaking him! He opened his eyes and tried to sit up, but his brother Bert, sitting next to him, held him down. "Shhhh, talk low," his brother warned.

Wes threw his arms around Bert's shoulders and hugged him. "I didn't do it, I didn't! It was someone else. Gunner was there. He knows."

"I know, Wes, I believe ya, but the Sheriff said he saw ya. He said he's gonna arrest ya."

Wes pulled away to better see his brother's face. "That's not what happened. I was going along the river road and I seen Gunner and two other men, that Roland Palmer and Cyrus Maggio. I figured they was on a Wolf Hunt and I wanted to join 'em. Somehow I found myself on the river bend, and this man came out of the water—he was shot in the head. I tried to stop the bleeding, but he died. Honest, Bert, that's what happened. I didn't kill nobody, I didn't!"

Bert wore a perplexed look on his face. "But Sheriff Hawes said he saw ya. Why would he say that?"

"I know, Bert. Ya see, I was holding a gun."

"Ya don't have a gun, Wes!"

"I know, I know, but I found this gun on the ground. It was on the ground next to the dead man and I picked it up. Sheriff Hawes saw me with the gun and now thinks I done it! But I didn't, ya see, I didn't."

"Sheriff Hawes says ya done it and that he's got to arrest ya for killing a Mormon. That man was Jack Sinclair. Hawes says he seen it and he's got to arrest ya. Ya can't come home now, Wes. The Sheriff isn't there now, but he could be back anytime and if he catches ya, you'll go to jail. You might even hang!"

Wes looked down at his hands and felt the tears well up inside again. "I don't want to hang! I'm innocent. Why would they hang a man fer killing a Mormon? I've done nothing. Help me, Bert!" The tears again flowed from his eyes and ran down his cheeks.

"Now listen Wes—this is what we'll do. I've already talked to Ma. You're to go to St. Louie. Ma's cousin, Lawrence Butterworth, is there;

he's some sort of merchant. Tell him who you are and what's happened. Ma says he'll help you until this thing blows over. The Sheriff will never follow ya to St. Louie and when he catches the real killer, you can come home."

"But Bert, what if the real killer ain't caught? How will I ever come back?"

"Don't worry 'bout that. He'll be caught and if he ain't, the Sheriff will forget he's after ya. Hell, lots of Mormons been killed in fights and they's killed lots of us. No one's going to count this against us. When the Mormons are gone and everything's settled down, then you can come back. What's important now is to get you to St. Louie. Here's seven dollars." Bert handed the silver coins to Wes. "It's all Ma an' me had in the house so be careful with it." Bert stood up. "You better leave now. Get as much distance between yerself and here as you can before tonight." Wes stood and brushed the dirt from his trousers. "And another thing, Wes, when ya get to St. Louie have Ma's cousin write Ma a letter so's we know ya got there. I've put some grub and extra clothes in a sack and I tied a tarpaulin to the back of the saddle. You can use it for a tent."

"Thanks, Bert."

Bert pushed something hard into Wes' hand. Wes looked down to discover their pa's single shot pistol. "Take this," said Bert. "You might need it."

His brother had tied two horses to a tree, Jeff and a brood mare, Sandy. The sight of the horses reminded Wes. "What about Blackie? Did he come home?"

"Naw, he's still out, but I'll go for him tomorrow. He'll be around." Bert handed the reins of the large black stallion to his brother.

Wes took the reins and stared back. "Jeff is your horse, Bert. I can't take him—he's yours."

Bert shrugged. "You'll need a good horse. Take Jeff and when you return he'll be mine again. Just take good care of him."

Wes, his eyes watering, stood before his older brother as a great surge of love swelled up inside of him. The two brothers hesitated for a moment before giving each other a powerful bear hug. Bert held Wes at arms length. "Don't worry, Wes, I'll see that the real killer is caught. I'll make it right. You'll be home in a couple of weeks."

"I know, Bert. I'll be all right and I'll send word when I get to St. Louie." Wes quickly mounted the stallion and, forcing a smile for his brother, touched the horse in the flank with his heels and moved off through the woods toward the south. St. Louis; it was over a hundred and fifty miles, but it was safety.

CHAPTER 4

Lost on the Mississippi

The Mississippi River slowly turned the boat around as the current pushed it along. At first Lisa cried for her mother, but soon she realized that Papa would come for her if she just sat still. She didn't know why Papa had jumped into the River, but she knew he would be back. Trying not to fidget, she looked out over the water as the boat continued its slow spiraling. Other boats were on the River, but they were far off, and she wondered if any little girls were in them.

Until it was very close, Lisa didn't see the yawl approaching from up river. The on-coming boat had oar locks and a small mast with a dirty brown canvas sail. Three people were in the craft: a boy at the tiller, a middle-aged woman in a dirty black coat and a big man with an untrimmed beard who struggled to control the sail under a constant verbal assault from the woman.

"Damn it, Toby, watch what yer doing! Forget the goddamned sail and row!" The man looked at Lisa in the flat-bottom, then at the woman, finally sitting down and picking up two oars.

The boy at the tiller pointed toward Lisa. "Look, Ma, we're going to hit it–we're going too fast."

"Well, Christ," yelled the mother. "Slow down!"

"I can't. I'm just steering. Have Toby lower the sail."

"Toby, goddamn it! Lower that fucking sail before I kick ya in the balls!"

As the yawl drew closer, Lisa was astounded. She had never heard such words, but somehow knew they were naughty and that if she ever said them her mother would spank her good. The big ugly man called Toby dropped the oars, stood and quickly brought down the sail. The yawl was too close and rammed the flat-bottom causing both boats to rock violently. Lisa yelled and grabbed the sides of the box she sat on. Toby managed to reach over and take hold of the side of the flat-bottom, holding the two boats together. "Look, Ma. Look at all that stuff," he said.

"Shut up Toby!" said the woman. She then turned to Lisa. "Hi, honey. What's your name?"

"Lisa."

"Lisa what, dear?"

"Lisa Sinclair."

"Where do you live, Lisa?"

Lisa pointed up river.

"You live up there somewhere? Is this your folk's boat?"

Lisa knew the boat belonged to Uncle Stan and she shook her head.

"Is this your stuff, honey?"

"Yes."

The woman chuckled and winked at Toby. "Well, Lisa, we'll help ya get back to shore. All right? You just sit right there and my boy, Toby, will tie a rope to your boat and we'll give you a tow to shore. Is that all right with you, Lisa?"

Lisa didn't like the woman or Toby either, but if they were taking her to shore where her mother was, then it was fine. She nodded her head.

"Good," said the woman. "Toby, tie 'er up and let's get the hell out of here. Put the sail back up and we'll head down river."

Lost on the Mississippi

* * *

Anna wasn't sure how long she and her mother sat next to her pa, but after awhile, a soft, cold rain began falling. Anna became aware that someone had draped a man's rough wool coat over her shoulders to keep out the rain, but it failed to keep away the chill. Her dress was damp and she shivered. Ma continued holding Pa to her breast as she softly moaned.

Early in the afternoon, a dozen horsemen rode into the small clearing. Anna looked up to see her Uncle Stan quickly dismount. She jumped up, discarding the coat, and ran to her uncle. "Oh, Stan," she cried. "It's Pa. They shot Pa!" She couldn't say he was dead, even though she knew it was so.

Her uncle's eyes flashed with anger as he embraced her. After holding her for a moment, he let go and walked to her ma. Bending down, he gently took her shoulders. "Come on, Mary, we'll get him up to the road."

Without a word, Ma turned and buried her face on Uncle Stan's shoulder. He carefully drew her to a standing position and then led her to a horse. Several men dismounted and wrapped Pa's body in a white sheet. A horse nudged up against Anna and a hand gently touched her shoulder. She looked up into the face of a handsome man in his forties with a neatly trimmed black shiny beard. "I'm Brother Martin, Anna," he said. "Jump up behind me and I'll take you up the hill."

She reached out her arm to his strong hand and, placing her foot on his boot, pulled herself up behind him. As she slipped her arms around his warm waist, he started through the forest. "Where's Lisa?" she asked. There was no answer. She tapped Brother Martin's shoulder. "Where's my sister, Lisa?" she asked again.

He turned his head so she could see his face. "We're still looking for her. The boat disappeared."

She couldn't believe her ears. "What?" she blurted out. He repeated what he had said, yet her mind couldn't comprehend what he was telling her. Jason had gone for Lisa! The boat had been right there, floating down the River–it couldn't have gone far.

"Where's my sister?" she repeated.

This time Brother Martin reined to a stop and turned in the saddle. "Listen to me, Anna. Your cousin couldn't get to the boat. It floated away down the River and we haven't found it yet, but don't worry, we will, you'll see. Anytime now, we'll find your little sister."

First her pa and now Lisa. She looked at Brother Martin and suddenly hated him for telling her. "NO!" she screamed and began beating her fists against his shoulder. "You're lying, you're lying to me! Where's my sister?" Brother Martin turned and urged his horse on, allowing her to hit his back.

On the road leading to the farm more riders were waiting, accompanied by the now empty Dearborn wagon with Jack Jr. holding the reins. Pa was taken from the back of a horse and placed on the wagon, and Ma climbed up to sit beside him. Anna was lifted to the wagon's seat to sit beside her brother, his own eyes red from crying. He took her in his arms and gave her a long hard hug. "It'll be all right, Anna. We're going to Nauvoo. There's nothing at the farmhouse, no beds or bedding left. Can you make it?"

She wiped tears from her eyes and nodded her head. "Have they found Lisa?" she asked.

"No."

A great knot of pain grabbed her throat. "I was supposed to watch her," she forced out as the tears began again.

He gave her another hug. "We'll find her. She may be safe in Nauvoo already." He released the brake and snapped the reins, starting the wagon down the road.

Anna woke the next morning to the sound of hammers pounding, saws sawing, men yelling and children crying. She opened her eyes to find herself in a tent of heavy canvas; it was the tent made by her father for their journey West. The memory of her father and the preceding day brought tears to her eyes, but she decided she had to quit crying and she wiped the tears from her face. The tent flap opened and Aunt Alice looked in. "You're awake!" She stooped and entered the tent, putting comforting arms around her niece. "How are you feeling, Anna? I've got some breakfast out here when you're ready. Your brothers are both here and your ma's outside now." Alice's blond hair was tied up in a bun, but a few strands had escaped, catching the morning sun.

Anna pulled away. "I want to see Ma," was all she could think to say. Getting dressed, she exited the tent and looked around. She was standing in the middle of a large field in Nauvoo. On the hill to the East the

Lost on the Mississippi

Temple shone in the cold February sunlight as workmen continued putting on the finishing touches, even while the City's residents prepared to leave. Now that the Temple was almost completed, it would soon be abandoned to the mobs. It didn't seem fair.

The field was crowded with large prairie wagons, tents, cooking fires and stacks of supplies as hundreds of families prepared for the great exodus from the largest city in Illinois. Anna spotted her mother sitting next to a fire, holding a cup in her hands. Hurrying to her, Anna sat down and put an arm around her mother. Ma looked at Anna through red watery eyes. "How you doing, honey?" she asked.

"I'm fine, Mama," replied Anna as her ma leaned her head against Anna's shoulder. "Have they found Lisa?" asked Anna.

"Not yet, but Jason and your Uncle Stan are still out looking. Don't worry. I'm sure they'll find her. The boat just drifted too fast. They'll find it soon."

"What can I get you, Mama?"

"Nothing, honey. Do you want some tea?"

"No, I don't want anything just now."

They sat together next to the warm coals of the breakfast fire, not speaking, just looking into the cinders, trying to imagine what life was going to be like without Pa.

The activity continued around them at a feverish pitch. Michael and Jack Jr. were busy loading goods into the two Sinclair prairie schooners and preparing the harnesses for the oxen. Before noon, Ma announced she would try to sleep and slipped off into their tent, leaving Anna by the fire. Anna decided she had better help and, finding her brother Jack, asked what she could do. Jack Jr. handed her a pencil and a list of goods written on a piece of paper. "You check the wagons and mark which items are in which wagon and then what's still on the ground. Can you do that?"

"Of course," she said. She had been a good student and was proud of her penmanship. She went to work at once and before long she had temporarily forgotten about Pa and Lisa and the River.

Late in the afternoon, as Anna helped her Aunt Alice and cousin Lucy prepare the fire for supper, Uncle Stan, Jason and half a dozen other men rode up to the camp. Stan and Jason slipped from their mounts and Stan entered the tent where Ma was still sleeping. Anna could hear Uncle Stan talking to her mother in a low voice. After a few moments, she heard her mother begin to softly cry, and Anna knew that her little sister had not been found. Jason walked to Anna's side and shook his head. "We looked everywhere."

Anna felt the pain in her throat again and began crying. For the first time that day, Anna spotted Gwen, her Aunt's oldest daughter, and at sixteen, Anna's senior, walking toward her. Gwen put an arm around Anna. "Come on, come back to our tent." Gwen's eleven-year-old sister, Lucy, took Anna's hand and the three girls walked to Uncle Stan's camp.

The next morning, Anna sat next to the cook fire, mending a hole in one of Michael's shirts when a middle-aged man approached and stood towering over her. She looked up at the strong brown eyes and short black beard. He smiled at her. "You don't remember me? I'm Brother Martin, Brother Carl Martin. I gave you a ride up from the River."

Now Anna did recognize him, but she only nodded her head and spoke in a low voice. "Yes, I remember."

Gwen walked by and stopped next to Brother Martin. "My Goodness, Brother Martin, it's so nice to see you today." Gwen reached down and, taking Anna under the arm, pulled her to a standing position as she whispered in her ear. "Don't you know who this is? This is Carl Martin, he's our captain of ten." She turned back to Martin and spoke in a loud voice. "You'll have to forgive Anna. You know about her father and sister."

"Yes, of course," replied the older man. "I gave Anna a ride back from the River. I just wanted to tell her that we're not going to give up on Lisa. We have men out right now. We'll keep searching every day until she's found. There's no evidence she's drowned, because if she had, we'd have found the boat. Both you young ladies should pray to our Heavenly Father. That's what you can do, because your prayers will be answered."

Anna finally found her tongue. "Thank you, Brother Martin."

He smiled again as he looked down at her. "We know who killed your father. Sheriff Hawes saw the man, one Weston Hamlin. His family has a farm south of yours. This Hamlin fellow has run off, but Hawes has sent out word that he's wanted for murder. It's only a matter of time."

Anna felt very ill at ease listening to Brother Martin talk so casually about her father and sister. "Yes, but will it bring back my father?"

"Anna!" implored her cousin. "That's no way to talk to Brother Martin. He's just trying to help."

At once Anna felt sorry for what she had said. "Excuse me, Brother Martin, I didn't mean it."

"Of course, Anna," he said as he put a hand gently on her shoulder. "You rest and get strong. The Company is leaving in a few days and you'll want to be ready."

"Of course," she replied, but she slowly pulled her shoulder free of his hand. Martin nodded and walked off.

Gwen was furious. "How could you, Anna? Brother Martin is our captain; he's responsible for ten families. He was just being helpful. You were very rude!"

Anna sat back down. "I don't like him. There's something strange about him—something strange about the way he looks at me."

"Well," said Gwen. "I just wish he would look at me the way he looks at you," and she brushed at her hair with her hand.

Anna looked at her cousin in astonishment. "You don't mean that! He's over twice your age, forty at least. And he's married!"

"Yes, but haven't you heard of Celestial Marriage? Many of the leaders have several wives. Cory Tobbs said she was asked by Brother Wheeler if she would marry him. That proves it!"

Anna shook her head. "That proves nothing. Cory Tobbs would say anything. The Apostles have denounced polygamy. It's only lies by the mob to turn everyone against us. Besides, even if it were true, which it isn't, you wouldn't want to marry Brother Martin."

Gwen frowned and sat down next to Anna. "I suppose not, but there aren't any decent men my own age. I'm sixteen, and Ma was married by the time she was sixteen. Your ma was married at seventeen. I'm going to be an old maid, all shriveled up like a dried plum, just you see. The boys around here aren't interested in marriage. All they want to do is ride horses and talk about guns."

Anna smiled and leaned closer to her cousin. "Yes, but just think when we get on the trail to Zion. Think of all the boys who will come riding by, and think of the camp at night—one hundred wagons all together. There'll be plenty of boys—boys you've never even met!"

"Hum, you're right. Say, this might be fun. We could both be married by the time we reach Zion." For just a moment, Anna forgot her sorrow, and both girls giggled at the idea of being married on the trail.

Buffalo Man

✸ ✸ ✸

A cold rain began to fall as Wes rode down a trail that led away from the Hamlin farm and his hiding place. He didn't dare ride southwest toward Nauvoo for that's where everyone would be searching for him. Suddenly, a new thought sprang up that caused him to rein Jeff to a stop. The Mormons had the secret posse known as the Danites. These were armed men ready to avenge any wrong committed against their people. Once the Mormons learned that Sheriff Hawes was after him, would the Danites join in the search? The idea made him shiver for he realized the Danites would hang him at once if he was captured. He had to get as many miles away from his home and Nauvoo as fast as he could, before the way south was blocked. He would abandon the main road heading toward Nauvoo and go southeast toward the road to Carthage. He didn't dare enter Carthage since Hawes was the Hancock County Sheriff and his office was in Carthage. Before reaching Carthage, he left the road and cut through the woods to the Warsaw road. Warsaw was on the Mississippi and approximately fifteen miles south of Nauvoo. He had to get south of Warsaw as quickly as possible. He pulled his hat down further over his eyes to fend off the rain and urged Jeff into a slow gallop. Now late in the afternoon, it was close to getting dark. He stopped by the side of the road long enough to examine his grub bag to see what Bert had included. To his surprise he discovered four biscuits, which had been cut and spread with his mother's preserves, a large slice of smoked ham wrapped in an oil cloth, his fire-making kit, a small bag of power and shot for the pistol, and a change of clothes. In addition he had a new tarp, Bert's large canteen, his knife and a small bag of oats for Jeff. He hungrily ate the four biscuits. He would save the ham until later.

Wes galloped Jeff for a while and then changed to a trot. He kept repeating this until it became too dark to gallop off road. Finally he reached the road to Warsaw. With the poor weather and the lateness, he met no one. Approaching Warsaw he saw the lights in the windows of homes and businesses on main street. Was someone waiting for him? Was someone watching? He couldn't risk finding out and guided Jeff around the main part of the town. By now he was cold and hungry, yet he still didn't dare stop. Still relatively dry, he knew the dangers of getting wet while outside during the winter. Just last December little Nancy Wanefield got lost in woods not far from her home. The next day she was found dead. The thought made Wes shiver. If he were to get wet, he would have to build a fire and dry his clothes.

South of Warsaw he kept Jeff at a slow trot and hoped no holes were hidden on the black road. After what seemed like an endless ride, he decided he must stop. Guiding the stallion off the road, he unsaddled and picketed Jeff, and then wearily rolled himself up in his tarp. He was still cold and hungry, and the rain danced against the tarp, making it impossible to sleep. In the dark, with only Jeff as company, the emotions stirred up again. How had this happened? He ached to be back home with his mother and brother, in his own bed, warm with a stomach full of his mother's good cooking. Tears came to his eyes, but he fought them off, he was going on a great adventure and he wouldn't think of home anymore.

With a start, Wes realized that he had drifted off to sleep. It was already morning, and the sun was shining although the air was still cold, and he shivered as he stood and stomped his feet to get his circulation back. Searching the stores his brother had provided, he found the sack of oats. He gave Jeff half the oats and watched as the horse eagerly consumed them. Back in the saddle he ate the ham as he headed south; within an hour he discovered the outskirts of Quincy. He was amazed for Quincy was at least thirty miles south of Warsaw. Now maybe he could relax a little. Would the Sheriff or the Danites really search for him so far south? Not taking any chances, he avoided the main streets of Quincy and headed south for Pleasant Hill. He rode slower now, but was still careful to avoid anyone he saw on the road ahead, always moving Jeff off the road while the travelers moved past. Toward dusk he passed through Pleasant Hill. He knew with his seven silver dollars he could stop at any of the settlements along the road and buy a meal and lodging, but he couldn't stand the thought of being awakened in the middle of the night by a sheriff or a gang of Danites. Yet, he didn't want to spend another cold night so he would try making a camp with a fire. Away from the road, searching for a suitable campsite, he discovered a light coming through the trees. For a long time he stood in the dark and cold and wondered who was there, and did he dare approach? Finally, he decided that it wouldn't hurt to spy out the fire. Dismounting, he slowing led Jeff toward the light.

Buffalo Man

Approaching an opening in the trees, he discovered two boys about his own age sitting before a fire and talking. They didn't look like sheriff deputies or Danites either. "Hello the camp," he called out. The boys stopped talking and turned to face in Wes' direction. "Hello the camp," he called again.

"Who's out there?" yelled one of the boys.

"I'm Wes...Tucker, and I'm alone."

He saw one of the boys draw a handgun and place it in his lap. "Come in," came the reply.

Gratefully Wes walked into their camp, leading his horse. "Hi, I'm Wes. Can I join your fire? It's a mite cold tonight."

Both boys stood and held out their hands. "Hi," offered the older one. "I'm Tom Lynch and this here is my brother, Darrell."

Wes shook their hands. "Thank ya, thank ya much."

"Sit down Wes," said Darrell. "Ya look like a drowned rat. Where ya headed?"

Wes quickly sat before the fire and held his hands toward the flames. The warmth was delicious. "I'm headed fer St. Louie. How about you?"

The boy, Tom, slapped his hand on his knee. "Crackers! So are we. Where ya from?"

"Up by La Harpe," lied Wes. "Heading for St. Louie to find work."

"So are we," replied Tom. "We're looking to join the army. They need men good with a gun, and we want to fight Injuns."

Tom's brother, Darrell joined in. "We hear you get a new gun and a uniform, too. I could sure use one of them blue uniforms."

Wes was amazed. He'd never considered the army. "Hey, I might just join up, too. I can shoot good as the next man."

"What ya carry?" asked Tom. "Ya got a rifle?"

Wes pulled out his single shot. "I only got this old single shot bean shooter. It's a thirty-six caliber."

Tom picked up a handgun from his lap. "Mine's just a single too—an old dueling fifty. Can't do much hunting with a pistol. If we had a rifle we could bag a deer. Darrell and me seen enough the last few days, but all we been able to bag is a lousy sage hen. Sorry Wes, we ate her all up."

Darrell handed Wes a cup of steaming coffee. "This might help your innards."

Gratefully, Wes sipped the coffee and felt the hot liquid fill his stomach and warm him from the inside. It was the first real comfort he'd experienced in two days.

"Well, Wes," began Tom. "See 'an how we're all headed for St. Louie, why don't we join up. Two guns is better protection from Injuns and road bandits than one. What ya say?"

Wes was very happy for the invitation and eagerly nodded his head. "Sure sounds go to me. To St. Louie and the army life fer us." They all three laughed.

CHAPTER 5

The Trapper

In addition to the belongings from Uncle Stan's boat, the dirty little cabin was full of rubbish and junk. Holes in the roof let in the rain, and Lisa's dress was now wet. She had found a hiding place between two wooden boxes and she sat and shivered as she watched the man named Toby sip from a large gray jug. Somehow she knew it was whiskey he was drinking.

"I don't give a damn," said Toby to no one in particular. "She can't order me around. I'm not her servant. I can come and go as I want." He looked about the cabin. "Little girl, where are you? Come on out, Toby wants to talk to ya. I won't hurt ya, come on out."

Lisa snuggled back farther into her secret place.

"Come on little girl. It's old Toby, I want to play. Where are ya?" He got up from the table and began searching the cabin in earnest. Lisa shut her eyes as tightly as possible, but she could still hear him bang about the small room. Suddenly she heard a scraping noise and felt his vile breath on her face. Opening her eyes she saw him on his knees, staring right in her face. "Come on, little Lisa. I ain't goin' to hurt ya. It's Ma ya got to watch out for. Come on out."

"You said you would take me to my mother."

"No, I didn't. That was Ma. She lied to ya."

"I'm not coming out until I see my mother."

"Your fucking mother is dead! She drowned in the Mississippi River and her body was ate by crows. Now come out of there."

Her ears rang from his words, but she wouldn't believe him. "No!" she yelled as she covered her ears with her hands.

Toby reached in with a fat, hairy hand and, grabbing her by the front of her dress, pulled her out. Lisa wiggled to get free. "Now don't fight old Toby. We're just gonna play a game. You like games, don't ya?" He hugged her close to his chest, and she could smell the revolting whiskey on him. He felt her dress. "You're wet, you're all wet and cold! Let's take off this here dress and Toby will get ya warm." He pulled at the buttons on the back, and she again struggled to get free.

"Don't! I don't want it off!" She knew he wanted to put his hands on her; she knew he was going to hurt her.

Without warning the door burst open and Toby's mother and brother, Jake, walked in. Immediately his mother walked to Toby and slapped him across the face with her hand. "What the hell ya doing? Ya want to ruin that child!" and she slapped him again.

Toby scurried across the floor in an attempt to escape her deadly hand. "I wasn't doing nothing. I was changing her dress, her dress was wet."

"God damn you, Toby, I know what you were doing! Ya think I'm stupid? You was getting all worked up and going to rape her and maybe kill her. What good is she then? I got plans for this child. From now on Jake will take care of her. Do you hear me, Toby, you stay away."

Hearing his name, the fourteen-year-old boy picked Lisa up and held her protectively in his arms. Lisa knew Jake was safe and she snuggled close to him. Their ma continued yelling at Toby as Jake re-buttoned Lisa's dress. "Come on, little one," he said. "Let's go outside. The sun's come up and your dress will dry."

"Jake," said Lisa, "Toby said my ma drowned."

"Naw, she didn't drown. She went on a trip and told us to take care of you."

"When is she coming back?"

"I don't know, someday."

Lisa couldn't believe her mother would leave her, especially with such awful people. Again the tears welled up and she began softly crying.

* * *

Anna sat in the back of their prairie wagon with her mother as Brother Martin and Uncle Stan stood outside, leaning against the wagon tail. "Are you sure you want this, Mary?" asked Brother Martin.

"I know what I'm doing," she replied in a low voice.

"How much flour ya got? How much beef jerky?"

"We'll do," she said.

Uncle Stan looked at Martin. "Most of the flour was in the boat, the beef jerky too. She has three hundred pounds, but we'll share; I got my full load."

"Besides," interrupted Mary. "There are some with less than us. We got a wagon and three yoke of oxen. Some don't have that much. It just won't work if both families tried to go in one wagon, and I'm not staying in Nauvoo while everyone goes to Zion."

"How do you feel, Brother Sinclair?" Martin asked of Stan.

Stan shrugged. "Jack was my brother. We're all family and can do it together. I don't want Mary and her kids to stay while I go. Don't worry, Carl, we'll keep up."

"All right, it must be God's will." He turned to go, but Mary touched his arm.

"You promised someone would keep looking for Lisa."

He nodded. "We have brethren out searching right now. Don't worry, she'll be found." Brother Martin and Uncle Stan left to get ready.

"Mama?" asked Anna, "Can I ride with Gwen and Lucy? Is that all right?"

Her mother smiled, but Anna saw that her face was still pale, dark rings circling her eyes. "Sure, sweetheart. You go ahead, I'll be fine."

Anna hurriedly climbed down the tail of the wagon and ran to the back of the next wagon in line. "Gwen," she called.

The flap opened and Gwen looked down. "Anna, are you coming up?"

"Yes," and Anna climbed up and wiggled into the back of Uncle Stan's wagon. Each Sinclair wagon was ten by four feet with sides two feet high, with six hickory bows that held the canvas tops high, making the insides roomy. Even with all their supplies, there was enough room in the back of each for passengers. Gwen and Lucy sat on a patchwork quilted blanket, which had been folded and laid down to form a small bed. Anna saw the straight figure of her Aunt Alice sitting on the wagon's seat, waiting for Uncle Stan.

"Did I tell you what Cory told me?" asked Gwen. "She said Sister Wheeler puts things in her corset so her front sticks out farther!"

"I don't believe it," said Anna as she fought to keep from laughing. "She already sticks out enough!" Both Gwen and Anna laughed.

Lucy shook her head. "Why would she do that?"

"Because," responded Anna. "It makes men look at you."

"Who wants men to look?" asked the eleven-year-old.

Gwen gave her sister a patronizing pat on the knee. "You just wait a few years, then you'll understand."

All heads turned to see Uncle Stan climb up into the seat and pick up the big whip. "You girls all ready?" he asked. He waited for the Wheeler's wagon, which was in front, to begin moving and then snapped the whip over the rumps of the oxen. The six animals grudgingly pulled, and the wagon lurched forward. They moved out of the field and onto the road leading down to Nauvoo's piers and the ferries which would take them across the Mississippi. The sky was cloudy, but only a gentle cool breeze brushed against their faces. A long line of wagons, white tops fluttering in the wind, snaked through the City to end at the docks.

As Anna watched, pride welled up in her breast. This great wagon train was going to join others in the Iowa Territory and then on to a strong new kingdom, a new Zion. She was proud to be a Latter-Day-Saint, yet she also felt a sadness. She would never see Nauvoo again, but more importantly, she would never see her father again. And what about Lisa?

The Trapper

Would they find her? It had been whispered around the campfire at night that river bandits had taken her away to sell to Mexicans and that the Sons of Dan were in hot pursuit. Everyone knew that Brother Martin was a Danite. Would God's Avengers find and punish the man, Hamlin, who had killed her father?

Anna looked again at the long line of wagons and knew this was going to be a great adventure. If only it weren't so cold and rainy all the time.

* * *

The boys rode south along the Mississippi River toward St. Louis. From their camp just south of Pleasant Hill, they had just over one-hundred miles to go. They reached the ferry at Kampsville where they crossed the Illinois River, Wes paying the dollar-fifty ferry fee as Tom and Darrell had no money. Finally, after four cold days and nights with little to eat, they crossed the Mississippi to sit, sore in the saddle, cold and tired to the bone, in a muddy St. Louis street.

St. Louis was the fur capitol of the West and portal to the vast Indian lands west of the Missouri. At the piers behind them rested paddle wheelers, lined up along the St. Louis waterfront. Before them stood the stores and shops that hosted a wealth of goods from all over the world: rum from the West Indies, fine guns from Germany and England, wool from Scotland and buffalo robes from the Indian Territories. Wes knew that here was the place where a young man could make a fortune for himself if he had the brains and guts.

People hurried about in all directions, and Wes felt out of place in all the motion and movement. Near the waterfront the majority of buildings were two story wood frame warehouses and shops fronted by wooden sidewalks and hitching posts. The streets were crowded with wagons of all types from the large prairie schooners with white tops, blue boxes and red tongues to little push carts. Men in tall beaver top-hats walked with beautiful women dressed in fine Eastern fashions followed by buckskinned mountain men or Indians. Excitement hung in the air, and the boys breathed it in.

Buffalo Man

Feeling generous and thankful for their company, Wes paid for a full meal for the three of them at an old hotel and kitchen. It consumed another dollar, but they all agreed it was worth it. "Hell," announced Tom. "What we got to worry about? We're joining the army. They'll feed us just fine."

Darrell was finishing the last of his pie. "We got to find out where they is recruiting. We got to get a move on. Without no money, we got to be in them army barracks tonight."

They left the kitchen and, walking their horses, asked directions from a boy pulling a pig down the street on a rope. He pointed west. "Ya just go down this here street and keep going until ya come to a big church that's red. Turn left and then go to a grey brick building where the army is." He smiled and held out his hand, palm up. Wes took his hand and shook it. "Much obliged, I'm sure." But the boy frowned and abruptly walked away. Wes, Tom and Darrell walked their mounts to the grey brick building where they could see blue uniformed men through the open double doors. They quickly tied their horses to the hitching rail.

"Well, this is it, boys," announced Tom. "We're gonna do it."

Darrell was staring at the open door with worry dancing on his brow. "We really going to do this? We really going to join up right now?"

Wes was not to be delayed. "No time like the present, Darrell. We just walk in and volunteer."

An old man in a black top hat was sitting on the porch, smoking a corncob pipe. "You boys joining up?" he asked.

"That's right, old man," proclaimed Tom. "We're here to be soldiers and fight Injuns and bean-eaters."

The old man smiled and puffed on his pipe. "That's good. Army needs recruits. Bunch of them army boys just been scalped by the Pawnee. They is in need of replacements."

Wes would have none of the old man's nonsense. "You're funin us, old man. The U.S. Cavalry carries rifles and pistols and hunts down warring Injuns."

"Used to," said the old man. "But they plumb run out of horses. Soldiers now have to walk into battle. Them Pawnee just swoop down and scalp them on the run."

"Don't listen, Darrell," commanded Tom. "He's just an old man whose jealous 'cause he's too old."

The Trapper

"Ya, guess so," and he puffed more on his pipe. "Lots of bandits and murderers join up with the army. Guess that won't bother boys like yerselves. 'Course the sheriff tries to weed them out."

Suddenly, Wes' ears burned with the news. He turned toward the old man. "What did you say about the Sheriff?"

"I said he checks recruits against wanted posters. Any you boys been robbing the river boats? Sheriff will get ya sure."

Wes turned to Tom. "I been thinking, Tom. I want to join up, I really do, but I just remembered—I got to find my ma's cousin. I promised her. I got so excited, I just forgot."

A discouraged look came to Tom's face. "Hell, Wes, I thought we would all go. I though you wanted to fight with us."

"Oh, I do, Tom. I just need to find my ma's relative. Soon as I do that, I'll come right back here and join up. Hell, I'll probably be back by supper time."

Tom held out his hand. "Well then, Darrell and I will be off. We'll be seeing you soon, Wes. And don't forget we still owe you for the ferry crossing and the food."

Darrell stepped forward. "We'll be seeing ya soon, Wes." With that, the Lynch brothers left Wes and walked to the recruiting station. As Wes watched them leave he knew he'd never be back. It was time he found Butterworth.

He untied Jeff and walked back the way they had come. On the next block Wes spotted a bearded man holding a broom and standing in the doorway of a harness shop. Deciding there was no better time than the present to begin his search for his mother's cousin, Wes tied Jeff to the hitching post and stepped up on the sidewalk before the man. The gentleman with the broom looked at Wes' muddy boots and the trail left on the sidewalk and tilted his head, showing Wes a sour face. Wes looked at the mess he had made and immediately became embarrassed. "Excuse me," he said. "I didn't mean to track."

"What do ya want?" asked the man with the broom.

"Can you tell me where Mr. Lawrence Butterworth has his shop? He carries dry goods, I believe."

"Butterworth? Sure! He used to have a place down on King Street. Burned down some time ago. Don't know what happened to Butterworth."

Wes was stunned. "Ya sure?"

"Of course I'm sure. Go down to King Street and check for yourself. Now get out of here, I've work to do."

Wes was upset over the news of his mother's cousin. How was he going to find Lawrence Butterworth now? What if he had been killed in the fire? Wes walked Jeff down the streets of St. Louis, occasionally looking about for a King Street. Several times he spotted drunks lying in alleys or next to the sidewalk, dirty and sick. He realized he'd end up in an alley if he didn't find a place to stay. For now, he would walk about looking for King Street. Maybe someone would remember Butterworth and tell Wes where the man had gone. Wes meant to ask directions from those encountered on the streets, but nervousness kept putting it off until later.

Without warning the sky grew dark and many businesses closed while the taverns and whorehouses kept their doors open. Wes was completely lost and tired from all the walking. He looked in several taverns to see men and women drinking, eating and having fun, but he was afraid to enter. He had never been in such an establishment, his mother schooling him well on the evils of such places. Yet he had to do something; he couldn't walk the streets of St. Louis all night. Finally, he passed a stable as the proprietor was closing the front door. Wes stopped and asked the fee for leaving Jeff. "Ten cents without oats, just hay."

Wes reached in his pocket and pulled out one of his remaining dollars. The man gave him change and then led Jeff into the stable and closed the door. Wes had meant to sleep in the stable with his horse, but now he was too embarrassed to go and knock on the stable door. Slipping his tarp and canteen over his shoulder, he again began walking the streets. A light rain fell as he cussed under his breath. He would have to find some place to spend the night soon or put down his tarpaulin in an alley.

After passing an especially noisy tavern he stepped in front of an alley and heard a low groan come from somewhere in the dark. Walking into the alley he squinted into the blackness. A man was bent over something on the ground. "You need some help?" asked Wes.

The man looked up but continued doing something with his hands. Another moan came, but it issued from the lump on the wet ground. Suddenly it was clear to Wes. Some poor soul, some beggar or drunk, was being robbed by this person standing over them. Wes pulled his pistol from his belt and took three steps forward. "Stop! Thief!" he shouted, but it came out with only half the force and strength he had intended.

The Trapper

"Get out of here!" growled the man before him.

"What are you doing there?" shouted Wes, trying to sound brave.

"Get out sonny or I'll put ya under."

Wes pointed his pistol at the man and slowly pulled back the cock, which gave off the distinctive click of a firearm being armed.

The man stared at Wes and the gun for a moment more and then, with one word—"Shit!"– stole off toward the other end of the alley.

Wes put his gun away and hurried to the victim on the ground. Kneeling down, he turned over a skinny man dressed in buckskin from head to foot and smelling of rancid grease and whiskey. "God!" exclaimed Wes as the full odor hit his nose. Evidently, this man was a drunk or bum. What had the robber hoped to steal? Rain fell on the man's face and slowly one eye opened and then the other.

"Oh, shit!" said the downed man. "What hit me?" He slowly reached behind his head and began to rub.

"Can ya stand?" asked Wes. "Come on, I'll help ya. Somebody tried to rob you; did ya know that? I chased him off." Wes got a hand under the man and helped him to his feet.

The man swayed and held on to Wes' arm to steady himself. "Stomped by a bufler, kicked by a mule. Who done this? Were it that half-breed?" He looked straight at Wes. "Say, I don't reckon I've seen ya," he said.

Wes couldn't tell how much of the man's unsteadiness was the result of being hit on the head and how much was from whiskey. "Did ya hear me?" asked Wes. "I said someone tried to rob ya, but I chased them off. Look and see if anything is missing! Do ya want me to take you someplace?"

The man felt his person and belt. "God Awful!" he yelled. "That sneakin', thievin' half-breed stole my Green River! I'll scalp that suckin' lizard!" He stopped his harangue to look at his rescuer. "Say, you're just a calf. You saved me? Well, Hot Jesus and the Holy Ghost, ain't that somethin'!" The man took hold of Wes' arm with substantial force and began to lead Wes toward a door that faced the alley. "Come along, little calf. Old Crock will do ya right."

Wes put up little resistance as the man pulled him along to the door. With a kick of his moccasined foot, the door burst open revealing the noisy, smoky tavern that Wes had passed on the street. They entered the tavern and the man pulled Wes to a long bar that ran the length of a large rectangular room. The place was full of men drinking and yelling and pawing at the few women who sat at round tables and sipped light brown liquid from shot glasses. Tobacco and sweat were the predominate odors, but whiskey and sour clothes fought to be acknowledged.

Leaning on the bar with one arm, the man pulled Wes up to the bar with his free hand and yelled at the bartender. "Hey! Barkeeper! Come over here!" He then laughed and Wes realized the man was very drunk.

The barkeeper appeared, a big man with gray hair and wearing a dirty apron. "What will it be, Crock?"

Pointing to Wes, the man slurred his speech. "Get me and my friend here a whiskey and put it on my bill." The bartender disappeared as the man called Crock leaned back to take a better look at Wes. "You're a farm boy! What's yer name, farm boy?"

"My name's Wes Ham....Wes Tucker."

The bartender put down two drinking glasses, half filled with whiskey. Crock picked his up and, bringing it to his mouth, he downed half the liquid, shuddering and gasping. "Holy Christ! That's real drinkin' whiskey–real Taos Lightnin'. What ya say yer name was? Wes..."

"Wes Tucker."

"Wes! What's that short fer? Weston?"

"Yes, Weston Tucker."

"Well, Weston Tucker," he said, holding his glass up to toast with. "This old griz is Crocker Sloan, the meanest, dirtiest, most awful son-of-a-bitch that ever spit in the devil's eye. Ya got that, farm boy? I've kilt men for looking cross-eyed. I've fucked bear and bufler and half them herds is my own offspring. Ya got that, farm boy? You can call me 'Crock' cause you saved my life and this coon never went back on an Injun who saved his life. Drink up!" and he downed the rest of his whiskey.

Wes stood, holding the glass of whiskey, not knowing if he really wanted to be here, next to this drunk, crazy man. He held up the glass and then, taking a mouthful, swallowed. The vile sourness puckered his mouth and he gasped for breath. Crock's eyes rolled in his head. "God Almighty! Is that how ya buggers drink good whiskey back on the farm? Give me that!" and he grabbed the glass and swallowed the remaining whiskey. "Now! That's how ya do 'er!" He turned and began pounding on the bar. "Barkeep! Barkeep!" he yelled at the top of his lungs. "More whiskey here!" and he pounded again.

The Trapper

Wes looked around, but no one seemed upset that this Crocker was making so much noise. Wes realized that the man couldn't be just a penniless, ordinary drunk or the barkeeper wouldn't serve him. The man must have some source of money. Then Wes noticed that most of the other patrons were dressed in frontier garb: rawhide, moccasins and black felt hats. And everyone wore a wide belt with a knife and pouch. Several Indians were mixed up with the other patrons, drinking and yelling. Wes felt a hard poke in his ribs and turned back to face Crock.

"Say!" yelled Crock. "What'd ya say yer name was?"

"Wes Tucker."

"Oh yeh, Wes! Well Wes, what ya after in St. Louie? Ya here to make yer fortune? What?"

A second glass of whiskey had been placed in front of him and as he took another sip of liquor, he felt the warmth come to his stomach. "I'm just here to...see a relative."

Crocker's eyes narrowed. "Ya don't seem too sure. You're not lying to old Crock now are ya?"

Wes looked at Crocker and felt his heart pounding. Crocker was older, maybe in his fifties, and stood several inches shorter than Wes. His coal-black hair hung down on his shoulders and black stubble covered his chin. Heavy eyebrows, with just a hint of white, crowded over piercing eyes. Even though the man was skinny, old and shorter than Wes, he saw under the dirt and rawhide a rock-like power and knew it would be a mistake to test this drunken degenerate.

"No, I'm not lying. It's just that I'm supposed to find this relative of my Ma's and I can't."

"Relative? What's the name?"

"Lawrence Butterworth."

Crocker turned his back on Wes to face a large, broad shouldered man on his other side. With little formality, Crock pushed the big man away from the bar. "Get over, ya big bufler turd."

The big man stumbled backward, caught himself and turned as if to strike at Crocker, but seeing who it was only stepped back and smiled. The next man at the bar was tall, dressed all in black, and wore a beaver top-hat which made him appear even taller.

"Hey Professor!" yelled Crock. "Come here! This coon needs yer help."

The Professor stepped closer and put a hand to his mouth, coughing from deep inside his chest. His watery eyes slowly cleared as he held on to the bar. "What can I do for you, Crock?" he said in a low voice.

Crocker pointed a thumb at Wes. "My friend, here, is looking fer a coon. Name's Butterworth, Lawrence Butterworth. Ya ever heard of him?"

The Professor extended his hand toward Wes. "Good evening young man. My name's Sterling Harkless, Professor of Natural History. What might your name be?"

"Fer God's sake, Professor! His name's Wes," interrupted Crocker.

Wes took the Professor's weak, toneless hand and shook it. "I'm Weston Tucker. I'm looking for Lawrence Butterworth."

"Aw yes, Lawrence Butterworth. Did he run a shop, a mercantile establishment?"

"Yes, he did!" exclaimed Wes.

"Down on King Street?"

"That's the one!"

"I'm afraid he's no longer there. His shop burned down, poor fellow. Left him destitute and suffering, I'm afraid, from the same malady that affects me–consumption. Not long ago, I believe, I saw his name in the obituaries, fallen to this damnable disease. I am sorry. Were you close?"

Wes shook his head. "I didn't know him, myself. He was my grand-cousin, my mother's cousin. She asked me to get in touch with him." Looking at the Professor, Wes could imagine his mother's cousin, thin and frail from consumption, eyes sunken and dark, breath sour and weak. He felt a twinge of sorrow and wondered how his mother would react when she received the news.

"Well," said the Professor, "we all have to face the Great Reaper and we can't always choose our demise. For myself, I always believed I would die in a soft bed, surrounded by my wife and beautiful children, all crying of course. Now look at me! Here, alone at the edge of the Great American Frontier, dying of an ignoble ailment. How do you wish to die, young Wes? I don't mean to cast a black spirit over our festivities, but in my condition I seem to be obsessed with death and how men wish to greet Her."

Wes glanced about and noticed that Crocker had disappeared, but two glasses of whiskey were on the bar before him and the Professor. He

The Trapper

reached for his glass and took a sip. "You know, Professor, I haven't really thought about it too much."

"Aw, but you're so young. The young never think of the inevitable. But try."

"Well, I suppose I see myself being chased by Injuns and being shot full of arrows. Or maybe in a gunfight with some bandit."

The Professor took a deep drink and his eyes sparkled as the liquid moved down his throat. "Just so," he said. "The young see death as the end of an unsuccessful battle. Very good, Wes. Keep that in mind. Don't go to Her without a fight. Too many of us old birds just give up. Don't let it happen to you. Now, tell me, what do you hope to accomplish in the immediate future? Do you have a grand plan to offer?"

Wes took another drink and suddenly felt warm and secure. "I'm not sure. I've always wanted to be an Injun fighter. Maybe I'll go out to the Injun Country and fight the Redman."

The Professor put a finger to his lips and gently shook his head. "Oh, watch your tongue in here. Do not be so free to debase the American native. This is the Rocky-Mountain House. Most of these men are, or have been, trappers and traders with the Indians; some of them have squaws for wives. To speak so boldly of killing Indians may precipitate a violent quarrel."

Wes was shocked as he looked about the room. "These are trappers?" he asked. They looked so dirty and common, not rich and glorious at all.

The Professor laughed. "Yes indeed! But you are seeing them at their worst—letting go, as it were. But they are really a fine bunch. Your friend, Crock, has been a mountain man for years. Surely, you knew!"

"I just met him."

"Oh, I see."

"Well, maybe I won't go after the Injuns after all. Maybe I'll do some trapping, myself. They still buy beaver, don't they?"

"Oh, yes," said the Professor. "But I'm afraid that the price is terribly depressed on the European market. But other skins are worthwhile: otter, mink, and buffalo hide."

Just then, Crocker stumbled in between Wes and the Professor carrying three glasses of whiskey. Slamming the glasses down on the bar he addressed the two men. "Great fat cow! I got here just in time—time to drink, that is!" and he roared at his own joke, pushing a glass along the bar at both Wes and the Professor. Wes picked up his glass and swallowed a mouthful as the other two men did likewise.

The Professor belched and, at first looking embarrassed, put a hand to his mouth and smiled. "Crock," he said. "Wes here, tells me he might go out after the noble beaver."

Crocker looked at Wes with watery, whiskey eyes. "Goin' fer the beav?" he slurred.

Wes felt very confident and accepted. "Yes, think I will. I've done some trapping up by Hamilton. Might as well go out after beaver."

"Hamilton!" yelled Crocker as he tilted back and forth. "Hell, this coon has been everywhere in Illinois: Kaskaskia, Shawneetown, Vandalia, Springfield, Rock Spring, Albion, Fox River. You name it, I've been there. Been every place in the West: the Parks, Colter's Hell, South Pass, Fort Hall. You name it, I've been there." He reached out a hand to steady himself against the bar. "You goin' fer beav? I'll go too. Beav ain't dead. I know where's there's hundred pounders—bigger than bufler. Meaner too! Hell, we'll be partners, me and you, Farm Boy!" and Crocker turned, spotted someone else, and stumbled away.

"Ya hear that!" said Wes, addressing the Professor. Wes felt warm and a little light-headed, but most of all he felt good. "Crocker Sloan and I are going to be partners! We're going trapping fer beaver. We'll be rich men! You should come, too, Professor."

The Professor shook his head. "I wouldn't take Crock too serious. He's very drunk!"

Wes waved the remark aside with his hand. "Hell, Professor, I saved his life! Did I tell you that? Some thief was robbing him in the alley and I chased him off with my gun—saved his life! We're partners, now. Say, did I tell you I fought the Mormons? Up by Nauvoo, that's their city. They put up one hell of a battle, but we finally beat them back. They've give up now, leaving for Injun Territory. Some say they're going to Oregon and some say they're going to Mexico."

"Aw, yes—the Mormons! A very interesting people. I've heard that their leaders take multiple wives. Think of it, young Wes! Every man's secret desire—two wives. Be honest! Haven't you at least once thought of climbing into bed with two women? Two loving creatures to fulfill your every desire. I went to bed with two women once, but was so intoxicated I don't remember what happened. Probably nothing. They say the

The Trapper

Mormons' late leader, Joe Smith, talked to God. If you could talk to God, Wes, what would you ask?"

Wes had been finding that he was following the Professor's comments with ever more difficulty. But now he understood the question perfectly. Draining the last of the whiskey from his glass he held it up. "I would ask God fer another drink!"

The Professor burst out laughing. "Another drink! Perfect! And so it shall be, and on me this time. Barkeep! More drink!"

Wes wasn't sure just when it happened. He was having the best time of his life; Crocker kept drifting in and out of the conversation and the Professor was a secure constant, introducing Wes to several more patrons of the Rocky-Mountain House who were as famous, Wes was sure, as his own half-brother, Gunner. Then, all at once, Wes didn't feel good any more. In fact, he felt awful. The room began spinning and his stomach and everything attached to it wanted to come out his mouth. He ran for the side door through which he had entered, for he certainly didn't want to embarrass himself in front of his new friends and especially his new partner, Crocker.

He made it to the door without incident, but outside the cold rain of early March didn't relieve his discomfort. He staggered and stumbled to the side of a building and then everything came up. When his stomach was empty, he continued to retch, sinking down on his knees in the mud and the goo. When it was over he was wet and very cold, but he knew he couldn't make it back into the tavern. He would just have to die in the cold. Falling forward, he lay in the muck, afraid to open his eyes. He was unconscious when strong hands pulled him from the mud and dragged him into the storage room behind the Rocky-Mountain House.

CHAPTER 6

Leaving Nauvoo

All morning the line of wagons moved down the road toward the piers. Finally, just after noon, the two Sinclair wagons and the Wheeler wagon were driven onto a large ferry and secured with heavy hemp ropes. The trip across the Mississippi had begun. Ice still floated in the River, and the men manning the ferry took their time. On the western bank the three wagons were driven off the ferry and started down a muddy road.

The Wheeler wagon led the two Sinclair wagons. Brother John Wheeler was the captain of their company of one hundred wagons. Although he was generally away managing the affairs of the company, he might appear at anytime to help his son, Paul, and his wife, Sarah. He was a strict and forceful man, tall and broad shouldered; not one of the Apostles, but it was rumored he was one of the Fifty, the secret group of

Saints that managed the Church's affairs after the Twelve Apostles. Sarah Wheeler, a tall beautiful woman with auburn hair and a clear, strong face, ruled the Wheeler household with an iron hand during John's absences, yet she could be gentle and her rebellious sense of humor often brought a rebuke from her straitlaced husband. Anna liked Sarah, but sometimes felt uncomfortable when she made unkind remarks about the Church or its leaders.

The wagons moved slowly, and soon the day's light faded, making it apparent to Anna they would not reach Sugar Creek, their immediate destination, this first day. Brother Martin rode back along the line and announced that his company of ten would make camp just ahead in a small clearing off the road. Soon Uncle Stan turned the six oxen to the left and, joining other wagons, reined to a stop. Saying goodbye to her cousins, Anna jumped from the wagon, wrapped her coat and scarf tightly around herself, and trudged to where her mother stood beside their wagon. Although she covered only thirty paces, Anna struggled to pull her booted feet from the gray-black mud. "Come on, Anna!" commanded her mother. "We've lots to do. You look for wood while your brothers put up the tents."

"But Ma, everything is wet! How am I to find wood when everything is soaked?"

A streak of anger crossed her mother's face to be replaced with compassion. "Now Anna, that's easy. Just look under things. Look under logs and leaves and places where it's still dry. Bring back anything that will burn."

Anna nodded and trudged off toward a clump of willows. This close to the Mississippi, trees and thick brush grew in all the hollows and gullies. At first, Anna found nothing as she kicked over branches and last fall's leaves. Soon, however, she spotted small sticks which had somehow stayed dry. Cupping the front of her dress, she collected her treasure of wood.

By the time Anna returned to the wagons it was dark. Under her dress and slips she wore wool knee-high stockings, but these were soaked through. Her coat was wet up to the elbows and she was shivering. Gwen and Lucy had been more successful in their wood-gathering, and Jason had found several dry logs. The fire burned brightly as her mother checked a cooking pot hanging over the fire-pit.

Leaving Nauvoo

They ate beans, beef and barley stew, pickled onions and cornbread by the light of the fire, but exchanged little conversation; the rain and the cold depressed everyone. At eight-thirty the Sinclairs gathered about the fire for evening prayers and then trudged off to their tents. Uncle Stan announced that the women, Alice, Mary, Gwen, Lucy and Anna, would take one tent while the men; Uncle Stan, Jack, Jason, and Michael occupied the second. Gwen laughed and put an arm around Anna. "Just like a visit, huh, Anna? It will be fun."

Aunt Alice cautioned the girls. "We have much to do in the morning, so it's to bed now. No talking! Everyone is to go to sleep."

They hurried into the tent, removed their outer clothes and found a place to snuggle under the cold blankets. Anna left on her long underwear and flannel shirt and replaced her wet socks. In the small tent, she could feel Gwen on her left and her mother on her right. Gwen wiggled a little closer. "Isn't this exciting! This is going to be the best camp-out we're ever had."

"No talking!" came Aunt Alice's voice in the dark.

The next morning the Sinclairs ate oatmeal with hot bread, baked on the fire's coals under a tin reflector, and fresh milk from one of the cows. Aunt Alice made butter and opened a jar of her special apple jelly. They said morning prayers after which the women cleaned up from breakfast and put the tents and bedding away while the men hitched up the teams to the wagons. Finally, just after nine in the morning, the line of wagons moved out onto the road.

The now frozen ground allowed the wagons to proceed with little difficulty, and shortly after noon the Sinclair outfits rounded a bend and moved down a gentle slope to stop at Sugar Creek. Through Anna's eyes, Sugar Creek was the same bedlam as the ferry landing but on a grandiose scale. Wagons occupied every free space among the willow trees and ground brush, and next to each wagon a tent or lean-to had been constructed. Camp fires warmed dinners as people of every description sat by their fires, worked on their chores or wandered aimlessly through the camp. Everywhere Anna turned, a new activity met her eyes: here a blacksmith repaired the rim of a wagon wheel, there two women hung out wash, at another spot four men had a cow on her side, doctoring her by forcing medicine down her throat.

Standing next to the wagon, Gwen spotted Cory Tobbs. "Hi, Cory," she yelled. "Wait for me." Turning to Anna she took her cousin's arm. "Come on, Anna, let's go see Cory. I've got to talk to her."

Anna shrugged her shoulders and gave out a simple "All right," The two girls ran over the hard ground to catch their friend. At fifteen, Cory Tobbs could pass for eighteen; she had prematurely developed into one of Nauvoo's true beauties with bright curly red hair that fell in locks over her shoulders and a nose full of freckles, which highlighted her penetrating green eyes. She had more suitors than she could count, much to the distress of her retiring and pious parents.

Cory kept walking and allowed the other girls to catch up and join her. "Hi, Cory," said Gwen. "Lucy says you've been sparking with Joey Taylor."

"Joey Taylor!" exclaimed Cory. "That smelly little kid is just a nuisance. If there was any sparking, it was on his part. I think he's silly."

Gwen's face glowed with pleasure. "Oh no, I think he's kind of cute. Don't you, Anna?"

Cory would not be persuaded. "Cute! Really, Gwen! I'm going to have to introduce you to some real men, not these boys."

"Well, who are ya sparking with, then?" asked Gwen.

Cory stopped and, turning to Gwen, lowered her voice. "Please, Gwen, ladies don't call it sparking. It's simply a show of affection."

Anna laughed. "When I give my brother a hug, that's affection. When Gwen's with her fella, she's sparking!"

"Please, Anna," implored Gwen. "We're trying to have a serious conversation here." She turned back to Cory. "Tell me again about Brother Wheeler asking you to marry him."

"Gwen," cautioned Cory. "Isn't your cousin a little young to hear about such things?"

"Anna's fourteen, just a year younger than you, and I'm older than you are, Cory, so tell us what happened."

"I can't, I've been swore to secrecy. I couldn't tell you if I wanted to."

Gwen wouldn't give up and Anna, in spite of her usual dislike for Cory's comments, was dying to hear about this new doctrine being whispered around the wagon train. Gwen leaned closer to Cory. "Don't tell me, Cory. Just tell me if what ya told me before was true. That's not giving away secrets."

Cory seemed satisfied. "All right, but not a word to anyone. You both have to swear."

"We swear." proclaimed Gwen.

"I swear." said Anna.

"All right. What I said before is absolutely true!"

Gwen was beaming. "Then it's true! Men can have more than one wife!"

Cory stopped again. "Gwen! It is so common to talk about it right out here in the middle of the camp. It's a secret doctrine and very sacred. We shouldn't be talking about it at all."

"Very well," said Gwen as she nudged Anna. "Let's talk about something else: let's talk about boys. What new boys have you met here in Sugar Creek?" The three girls continued walking about the camp, lost in that special world full of young men, all interested in just them.

* * *

Wes woke with a pounding head and a nasty tasting tongue. He opened his eyes to discover he was laying on his tarp and under an old blanket in a storeroom. Sitting up, he rubbed his eyes and stretched his aching muscles. The room was dimly lit, but he could tell from the whiskey and beer kegs that he was in the storeroom of the Rocky-Mountain House. He stood and brushed the dirt from his soiled pants and shirt and rolled up his tarp, placing his canteen by his side. He tried remembering how the night's celebrating had ended, but all he could recall was that he had wandered outside to relieve himself; then everything went fuzzy. He certainly didn't remember coming into the storeroom.

With tarp in hand, he walked through the door and entered the barroom. The place was empty except for two men sitting at a large round table: one of the previous night's bartenders and Professor Sterling Harkless. The two men were sharing a freshly baked apple pie and drinking beer from tall mugs.

"My goodness!" exclaimed the bartender. "Look who we have here: the young Mormon fighter!"

Buffalo Man

The Professor pointed toward an empty seat. "Put your body down here and join us in some pie, Wes." He reached behind him and took an empty mug from the bar and filled it from a wooden bucket of foamy beer. "Have yourself a cool beer. It will relieve your congested head."

Wes sat down at the table but gently pushed the mug of beer away from him. "I think I'll pass on the beer this morning, Professor. Say, what time is it?"

The barkeep wiped several pie crumbs from his mustache. "It's almost ten o'clock. You've slept half the morning."

"How'd I get in the storeroom?"

"I don't know," replied the bartender. "But if'n you'd wandered outside, you'd 'a froze."

"Have some pie," offered Harkless. "It will put something on your stomach. You imbibed a considerable amount last night and need your nourishment."

"Oh, no," replied Wes. "I think I'll wait a little while. I don't feel too well. Where's Crocker Sloan?"

"Can't say, exactly," said the Professor. "But I would guess he is several miles on his way to Westport."

"Westport! That's toward the west, along the Missouri!"

"That's right," offered the barkeeper. "Westport's more than two hundred and fifty miles up the Big Muddy. Best place for jumping off into the Injun Lands. That's where Crock will be headed if I know him. He ain't one to stay in civilization longer than it takes to get drunk."

Wes felt confused as he looked from the barkeeper to the Professor. "But we were going to be partners; we were going out trapping beaver."

The Professor laughed and stroked the stubble on his chin. "I wouldn't be too sure of that, young man. Crocker was pretty drunk last night. You can't hold him to a statement he won't even remember today. Besides, he's a strange fellow; prefers to be alone."

"But I was planning on it. I was counting on it!"

"You had best get a job here in St. Louie," advised the barkeeper. "The prairie is no place for a farm boy. To be frank, the prairie is no place for any civilized man."

"James is right," interjected Harkless. "Get a job here and don't bother about Crocker and trapping beaver. It will just cause you trouble."

But Wes stood up and took his belongings in his hands. "I've got to catch him. I'm sure Crocker meant it. He said to my face we'd be partners. He just forgot."

The Professor gently took Wes by the elbow. "Don't deceive yourself. Crocker Sloan doesn't take partners. He's a mean, surly mountain man who would rather warm up to a rattlesnake than a human being. Some men are like that: meant to live out their lives in solitude. They don't appreciate human company. It was the whiskey talking for Sloan last night–nothing more."

Wes pulled away. "You don't understand. I have to go. Thank you, Professor, but I can't stay here."

The bartender glanced at the tarp and canteen. "That all ya got. You going out in the badlands with no bedroll?"

Wes shook his head. "I got some things at the stable."

"A bedroll?"

Wes just stood, not knowing what to say.

The bartender jabbed his thumb in the direction of the storeroom. "If ya got a quarter, I'll sell you that blanket you was on. It's wool and has few holes."

Wes pulled a quarter from his pocket and placed it on the table next to the barkeep. "Thanks much." He quickly retrieved the blanket and walked from the tavern as the two men at the table watched in silence.

Wes stopped on the sidewalk in front of the tavern to let his eyes adjust to the bright sun and get his bearings. He would get Jeff and head down the road toward Independence and Westport. Surely, he would find Crocker on the road and the man would honor his commitment from the night before. After all, wasn't it Wes who had saved his life? Without warning, Wes' stomach rolled over and he regretted not partaking of the apple pie; he was famished. He reached into his pants and found the remains of his money–two dollars and one nickel. Where had the rest gone? Had he really spent almost two dollars on spirits the night before? His stomach rumbled again and he decided a short delay wouldn't hurt. He hurried along the sidewalk in search of a cafe for a good meal before starting out.

After breakfast, Wes retrieved Jeff from the stable and, from strangers on the street, found the right road leading to Westport. The day was warm for early March, even though it had frozen the night before. Large white clouds hurried across the sky, changing the complexion of the weather every few minutes. The road was damp and showed the tracks of many horses and vehicles. Wes moved Jeff along at a good pace and was soon overtaking carriages, wagons and travelers on foot, some headed back toward St. Louis and others headed west. Starting his quest just before noon, he was convinced that he could overtake Crocker quickly, but by four in the afternoon, he decided that he might not catch Sloan until the next day.

That night he made his camp by the side of the road, not far from the Missouri River. In the distance, he could see other fires–travelers making supper and preparing beds. Was one of them Sloan? There was no way of knowing and it would be impossible to go out and check each one in the dark. Wes began reconsidering what he was doing. In the half day of travel, he didn't think he had covered more than thirty miles which left more than two hundred to Westport. He had no food left and little money. He would have to find food tomorrow and he refused to consider the possibility of stealing in order to eat. Maybe he should have stayed in St. Louis! True, Butterworth was dead, as reported by the Professor, but he could find a job and if no one inquired, there was no reason for the Sheriff to come for him. The thought of slipping out onto the prairie and trapping beaver with a real mountain man had temporarily dimmed his judgment. Yet, he felt committed now, and on the morrow would try again to overtake his partner-to-be.

* * *

Gunner Hamlin sat at a table fashioned from packing crates and boxes at a river bottom tavern known as Sally's. Roland Palmer, Cyrus Maggio and Ned Tillman sat at the table with him. Their conversation stopped while Mary McNaughton delivered a wooden canteen of whiskey to the men. Once she turned and walked back behind her bar, the conversation resumed.

"Yes sir." said Ned Tillman. "I remember the day. It was when I had my burning."

"No," said Gunner. "It was the day after. I came to your burning, don't ya remember? I was at the campfire."

"Oh yes, you're right," said the farmer. "It was the next day, ya say?"

"Yes," said Gunner. "I had just paid Jack Sinclair off for his farm. I was delivering the money for Terral Jackson—he's my cousin. Anyway, I was just leaving, having given Sinclair the money, when the shooting started. Well, I didn't know what the shooting was about; after all Sinclair was a Mormonite. I just decided to keep my head low until I figured out who was what. That's when I seen my own half-brother, Wes, shoot this Jack Sinclair."

Ned sipped at his whiskey and made a sour face. "They say there was three men up on the hill shooting at the Mormons."

"That's right, that's right," proclaimed Gunner. "I seen them myself, up on the hill, shooting down on them. But Wes was down at the River. Wes must of robbed Sinclair after shooting him. That's where Terral's money went."

Ned shook his head. "It just don't add up right, just don't figure."

Gunner gave a quick glance at Palmer and then Maggio before looking back to Ned. "What's odd? What don't add up?" he asked in a soft, low voice.

Ned shook his head again. "We've all been fighting them Mormons. They've killed some of us and we've killed some of them. Why all this trouble about one killing?"

Gunner smiled and leaned back in his chair. "Well, Ned, here's the difference. Wes did it fer robbery, he did it fer money. We been fighting for our State, but he done it just fer greed. See the difference? Ya can't let people go about killing anyone they want just because a war been going on. Ya see that, Ned?"

Ned shook his head a third time. "I see what yer saying and ya got a point. But, still, something's amiss. This Sheriff Hawes—why's he carrying on so? He's always been partial to them Mormons, and now he's gone crazy over this Sinclair thing. No one would say he's wrong to just forget it. The kid run off. If and when he comes back we can have a trial and hang him. But Sheriff Hawes won't let 'er go and he's gone off after the kid. Said he'd bring the boy back. And then I talked to your brother, Bert..."

"Half-brother," corrected Gunner.

"Well, yes, half-brother. Anyway, Bert says he talked to Wes before the boy run off. Swears the boy is innocent. Say's others did the killing and he just stumbled on Sinclair. Even says the boy saw you there, Gunner."

"Well, of course he saw me–I said I was there. Now, I saw Wes do it! Ya doubting the word of an eye witness?"

"Naw, of course not. I'm just saying something seems odd, that's all. Let's have another drink."

"Good idea, Ned," replied Palmer as he picked up the canteen and refilled everyone's glass.

"My guess is," continued Ned, "that we won't know the truth until Hawes brings back Wes and we have a trial."

"I don't know," said Gunner. "Sheriff Hawes might find it harder to find that kid than he bargains fer. I think the kid went south, toward St. Louie, but Hawes was fer trying across the Mississippi. Thinks the boy might be passing as a Mormon and traveling with them. I say that's crazy. And remember, Hawes is looking fer a Hamlin. We Hamlins don't give up that easy."

"That Hawes is a strange one, that's fer sure," responded Ned.

Lisa could hear the men talking in the tavern from her place in the back room. She would have thought nothing of it, except she heard the name Sinclair. She was a Sinclair! Maybe these men knew her mother and father. She glanced at Jake who sat at a table and poured whiskey from a bucket into bottles. He'd never let her go into the tavern and talk to the men. She snuggled closer to the wall between her bunk and the next room to see if she could hear what they were saying, but after a while they didn't mention her name again and she fell asleep.

CHAPTER 7

Sugar Creek

Wes, walking Jeff, stumbled down the dusty road leading to Westport, Missouri. On the trail from St. Louis for eight days, he'd eaten nothing but two rabbits and beans purchased from a freighter on the road. Nearly broke and low on lead shot and powder for his pistol, he was ravenously hungry. To make matters worse, it had rained at least once each day, and he was covered in streaks of mud and dirt, and chilled to the bone. As he led Jeff down the hill toward the ramshackle frontier outpost on the Missouri River, he wondered if prison wouldn't be an improvement over his present condition. He had hoped to overtake Crocker Sloan somewhere on the road to Independence. Failing that, he tried locating Sloan within Independence, but a blacksmith informed Wes that Sloan had already passed through on his way to Westport.

Buffalo Man

Beyond Westport lay Indian Territory, and Wes felt his chances of finding Sloan there were slim; Westport might be his last hope.

Wes stopped long enough to brush the dirt and dust from his shirt and pants and then mounted Jeff. If he were to enter Westport broke and dirty, at least he could enter mounted, his head held high. Reaching Westport, Wes found the main street a sea of mud and muck separated by shallow pools of water. Frontiersmen, Indians, pioneers and teamsters crowded both the street and wooden sidewalks, hurrying from one little shop or building to the next as if some great event were in the making and paid no attention to the Illinois youth on the large black stallion.

The first places to check, of course, were the taverns, for Wes knew Sloan's taste for whiskey. Locating the first drinking establishment Wes tied Jeff to the hitching rail and, scraping his boots, entered through a narrow, open door. Inside several candles fashioned from buffalo horns filled with tallow gave off poor light but great streams of black smoke. At noon Wes was the second customer; the first, an Indian, dressed in dirty rawhide, snored softly as he slept with his head on a poker table. As Wes stepped to the bar, a tall, thin man in his fifties looked up from behind the counter. "Whiskey?" he asked.

Wes shook his head. "Sorry, I just need information."

"Whiskey ya pay for, information is free," said the bartender as he smiled.

"I'm looking for Crocker Sloan. I understand he's here in Westport." As Wes waited for the man's reply, he held out little hope his question would produce anything but a blank stare.

The smile vanished from the barkeeper's face. "Sloan? Why ya after Sloan?"

"No, I'm not after Sloan. I want to join up with him, I want to be his partner."

The man leaned back and laughed, showing tobacco stained teeth. "Partner to Sloan? You're crazy! Sloan don't have partners, he's a loner. Besides, ya don't want to hitch up with the likes of him–he has a nasty disposition. Kind of like a grizzly in heat."

Wes sighed and shook his head. "Could ya just tell me if he's in town?"

"Sure. He was, but ya just missed him. Left this morning for the prairie. Ya can catch him on the road to Fort Leavenworth, but you'll have to hurry. Sloan don't travel on roads much."

Wes leaned on the counter and sighed again. Once more he had missed his mark. "Well, I'll just have to go fer him out there."

The bartender's eyes narrowed. "You ever been to Injun Country? You look like a farm child."

Wes was tired of being called a "farm boy" and "farm child" by everyone. "Farm child! Hell, I'm a personal friend of Crock. He wants me to be his partner. We're gonna hunt beaver."

A smile crept across the barkeeper's face. "Hunt beaver? You mean trap them!"

"Sure, trap them. Of course that's what I meant." Wes, to cover his nervousness, dusted off his shirt. "Well, thanks fer the news. I best be going. Ya say Sloan headed out on the road to Fort Leavenworth?"

"Ya."

"Well, thanks again."

Wes hurried from the tavern and, just as he stepped from the door to the sidewalk, heard the barkeeper call out, "Hey, Chief, wake up. Guess what I just saw!" Wes quickly mounted Jeff. He would ride like the wind and overtake Crocker before noon. If, perchance, he met Indians on the way, he still had some shot left; he could drop them without any trouble.

Fast moving clouds came from the west, signaling another storm on the way as he urged Jeff down the street and out of town. Leaving Westport, the road was dry, and Jeff made good time. For several hours Wes travelled northwest along the road and parallel to the Missouri River, or Big Muddy as the locals called it. Finally, the clouds thickened and a soft rain fell. Wes slowed Jeff's gait realizing he would have to save his horse's strength. He passed other travelers and loaded freight wagons headed for Fort Leavenworth plus a small train of pioneers in their large Conestoga wagons going for Oregon. Numerous Indians moved along the road in both directions, but Wes, much to his great relief, found them completely pacified.

At mid-afternoon the road moved down a ravine and closer to the River. As Wes reached the bottom of the ravine, he heard yelling and laughter through the trees toward the Missouri. Deciding to check on the disturbance, he reined Jeff to the right and off the road. Cautiously moving through the brush, he came to the bank of the River and found a bullboat resting on a sand bar. A dozen men were about the boat, pulling on ropes, trying to free the keel from the sand. On the near shore, three men stood on the River's bank, jeering and laughing at the predicament of the men in the River. One of the men on shore was Crocker Sloan.

"Get yerself a good bufler!" called the mountain man. "Hook 'er up and she'll pull ya out!" All three men on shore laughed.

Wes spurred Jeff on to where three horses and a mule were picketed. There he hitched Jeff and set out on foot to reach Sloan and his friends. As Wes approached, Sloan and the other two men nodded, acknowledging his presence, but then returned to the fun in the River, Crocker seeming not to recognize Wes. One of the men pulling on the boat slipped and fell in the muddy water. All three men on shore laughed again.

"Hello, Mr. Sloan," said Wes.

Crocker turned and carefully looked Wes over but still didn't appear to recognize him. "Do I know ya, young fella'?"

"Yes, I met you at the Rocky-Mountain House in St. Louie. Remember, ya invited me to go beaver trapping with ya."

Now the other two men turned from the River and looked at Wes as Crocker's eyebrows arched up and his mouth dropped open. "Why, it's the farm boy! Yes sir–it's Wes. Now I recognize ya."

Wes felt a sense of relief. "Yes, it's me. You left St. Louie without telling me, and I've been looking for ya for more than a week. I didn't ever think I was going to find ya."

Crocker's face wrinkled up in a frown. "Why would you want to find me? What did I do?"

"Don't ya remember? You said we would go beaver trapping!"

The other two men laughed at Wes' remark.

"BEAV?" yelled Crocker. "We were going after beav– TOGETHER!"

"Yes," whined Wes in a half whisper.

"Lord, God-Almighty! I don't go fer beav with no one! I was drunk. Ya can't hold a coon to what he says when he's drunk. Ain't that right, men?" and Crocker turned to his two companions.

They both chuckled and one with a gray beard and a fox tail hanging from his black felt hat shook his head. "A man's word is his word. Don't matter if'n he's cock-eyed or not. Look's like ya got yourself a partner, Crock!"

The men hooted again, but Crocker Sloan was not to be undone. He pointed a finger at Wes' nose. "Now ya listen to me, ya little mutton-head. Yer not ready fer out there," and Crocker pointed out toward the

West. "You got some growing still to do. Them Redmen will skin ya alive and the bufler will have ya fer supper." Crocker stepped back from Wes for a better look. "You ain't even prepared. Where's your possibles? You got traps? You got a gun? Galena? How much money ya got? You're just a kid and if'n I see your ugly face again, I'll take my Green River and peel the skin from your whangdangle and hang it from my hat." He stepped close to Wes and spoke in a low voice. "Now get out 'a here!"

Wes' impulse was to turn and run for his horse to escape this bully, but he had to say one last thing. "Mr. Sloan," he squeaked. "Don't ya remember? I saved yer life! I saved yer life from that robber!"

With this, Crocker was rocked back on his heels and his two friends opened up with another round of laughing. "He saved yer life, Crocker!" yelled the graybeard. "He saved yer life and yer in his debt!" They couldn't control their merriment and, slapping their legs and grabbing their stomachs in their hilarity.

Crocker's face was red and his brows moved down close over his eyes. Stepping up so his nose almost touched Wes' nose he spit out the words in a whisper. "You get the hell out of my sight!"

Wes felt something sharp in his stomach and looked down to see a vicious knife in Crocker's hand with the point pressing against his shirt. Wes jumped back. Crocker stood still, holding the knife and staring back at him. Wes decided it was time to leave and, taking several steps backward, turned and hurried to Jeff. As he mounted, he heard the laughter of the two men and Crocker's cussing.

While Wes rode back down the road toward Westport, the shock slowly wore off and he realized what had happened. As he recovered his senses, anger welled up inside. He had saved Sloan's life and Sloan had asked him to go trapping; he hadn't made up any of it! This man, Sloan, obviously wasn't a man of honor. Like his friend had said—"A man's word is his word!" Sloan couldn't go around making promises to everyone and then breaking them. In addition he had pulled a knife on Wes without provocation. That wasn't manly or fair! Someone should teach this Sloan fellow a lesson. As Wes slowly walked Jeff down the road, his thoughts continued to churn about in his head and his anger continued to grow. Finally, he reined Jeff to a stop. "God damn it!" he said, addressing his horse. "This Sloan isn't going to get off the hook so easy. I'll show him a Hamlin ain't bullied about. Killing Injuns and shootin' buffalo is one thing, but insulting a Hamlin is to tease Death Herself!" Wes reined Jeff around and headed back up the road toward the ravine.

Returning to the site of the river boat he found Sloan and the two companions gone, but their trail was obvious and he followed it through the trees and back to the road. Apparently, they were still headed for Fort Leavenworth, and Wes hurried Jeff down the road until he saw three riders far ahead. It was them! Wes slowed so as not to overtake the three for he still didn't know what he meant to do or if he really meant to do anything. He followed them until late afternoon when they turned off the road to make camp. Wes tracked them into the woods and then waited until he could see their camp fire. Satisfied he knew their location, he picketed Jeff and prepared his own bedroll. Rain began falling in great, heavy drops, and he quickly snuggled down under his tarpaulin and blanket, still undecided as to how he was going to redress Sloan's insult.

The next morning Wes woke to find the sun shining in his eyes. The clouds from the previous day had cleared, and the sun's rays were drying the ground and surrounding vegetation. He looked in the direction of Sloan's camp but saw nothing. Curious, he packed up his bedroll and then stealthily crept through the trees, leaving Jeff picketed at his camp. After several hundred paces he saw a thin column of black smoke curling up through tree branches. Only one horse, one mule and a single man remained at the camp, but Wes could tell it was Crocker Sloan. Crocker sat next to the fire, working on a strip of leather he held in his hands. Wes quietly backtracked and settled behind a large tree so as not to be seen.

Sloan worked until just before noon when he packed his belongings on the mule and, saddling his horse, rode off toward the northwest, away from the Leavenworth road. Wes didn't dare stay close enough to watch Crocker, but he had tracked animals many times through the woods and so was content to follow Crocker from a distance. For an hour Wes continued through a maple and hickory forest until he broke out upon a great open plain. He saw Crocker's tracks still leading toward the northwest, but the mountain man was out of sight. Looking out over the great expanse, Wes suddenly felt very small and very alone. At least on the Leavenworth road he had passed other travelers and had the Missouri for company, but here, it was nothing but grassland. Wes took a deep breath, patted Jeff on the neck, and started out, following Sloan's trail.

Sugar Creek

All afternoon Wes rode northwest but not once did he see Sloan. By sundown he still hadn't overtaken the mountain man and had to dismount to continue his tracking, the failing light making the task progressively harder. Finally, he spotted a stand of trees in a small hollow and saw a flicker of light–it must be Sloan's camp fire! Relief washed over him as he slumped to the ground. He still didn't know what to do: he didn't want to barge into Crocker's camp and demand hospitality. However, it was now cold and windy and the thought of a night on the open prairie was discomforting. Besides, his empty stomach grumbled for food. He decided to enter the trees but stay away from the fire and Sloan. Maybe in the morning he would confront the man.

Wes waited until he imagined that Sloan had finished his meal and gone to sleep. Then, as quietly as possible, Wes walked Jeff into the trees and, once in the grove, saw Sloan's fire and the man sitting at its side. Wes yearned to join the mountain man, warm his back at the fire and fill his stomach with food. He hadn't eaten all day and his stomach constantly reminded him of the fact. For long minutes he just sat and watched, too hungry and cold to sleep, but unable to face the older man.

After some time, Sloan added wood to the fire causing sparks to spring up into the night air. The mountain man looked in Wes' direction. "Well!" Sloan yelled. "This old hoss ain't fooled by you're sneaking around. I know you're there, Farm-boy. Might as well come on in!"

Wes couldn't quite believe he had been spotted and simply stared back at Sloan.

"Well?" called the mountain man. "Are ya deaf as well as stupid? I said come on in!"

With heart pounding, Wes untied Jeff's reins and led his horse into Crocker Sloan's camp. Crock looked the boy up and down. "My God, but you're a sight! Sorriest looking coon this side of the Big Muddy. Injuns look better 'en you. Sit down while I decide what to do with ya."

Wes tied Jeff up and, returning to the warmth of the fire, sat down cross-legged. "Are you going to knife me?" he asked.

Crocker looked at him and his eyes narrowed. "Might. Might skin ya or maybe hang ya or bury ya up to your head. Don't rightly know. Maybe, I'll sell ya to the Pawnee fer a beav skin or bufler robe, although I doubt you're worth as much." He then reached down and carefully rolled several grayish bird eggs over the sand and closer to the fire. "I thought I told you to skee-dattle home?"

"Can't go home. Got no home."

Crocker laughed. "No home? Likely story! Your ma is probably crying her eyes out right now. What did ya say your name was? Wes something?" He turned and rolled the eggs a little closer to the fire.

"Wes. Wes Tucker. I'm from Illinois."

"How old are you, Wes?"

"Eighteen."

"Eighteen? Bufler balls! You're seventeen or sixteen. Now don't lie, for I'm not likin' to repeat my questions. Why ya tagging after me?"

Wes shifted his weight to get more comfortable and felt his stomach turn over again. "I went to St. Louie to find a relative and work for him, but learned he was dead. When I met you in the Rocky-Mountain House you said we could go trapping together. I got no place else to go."

Crocker picked up one of the eggs and tossed it from hand to hand several times before throwing it to Wes. Wes caught it and found it was freshly cooked. Disregarding the heat, he quickly peeled off the shell, blew on the egg and popped it in his mouth. It was delicious.

Crocker laughed. "When you eat last?"

"Yesterday."

Opening a bag, Crocker withdrew several pieces of buffalo jerky and two stale biscuits and threw them to Wes. Next, he bent down and poured Wes a cup of hot coffee in a tin cup. "Might as well eat before I put ya under. No use meetin' yer Maker with an empty stomach."

As Wes bit into the tough, cured meat, his mouth exploded with flavor.

Crocker took a stick from the fire and lit a corncob pipe. "Where's yer gun?"

Wes pointed to his pistol. "It's my pa's. A Parker, 36 caliber dueling single shot."

Crocker nodded. "A pea-shooter? God-Almighty, I can see ya don't have no real possibles. Ya got traps? A pack mule? Food?"

Wes shook his head.

"Well, coon, let me tell ya how it is. I don't take no partner. Can't get along with other men–always end up puttin' 'em under. If I told ya I would take ya trapping then I'm going back on my word. I was drunk and

Sugar Creek

ya should be old enough to know the difference between drunk-talk and real-talk. And ya can't make it out here alone; you're just a kid fresh off the farm. A party of Pawnee or Kiowa will find ya and slowly roast ya over a fire, and your ma will hear your screams back in Illinois. We're less than a day out of Fort Leavenworth, so tomorrow I'll take ya there and turn ya over to the soldiers. They'll know what to do with ya. Maybe make ya into one of them Dragoons. Now, have ya got anything to say for yourself?"

Wes swallowed to clear his mouth. "I can't go to the Fort."

"What do ya mean, ya can't go to the Fort?"

"I can't go. I just can't go."

"Now listen here! I should 'a just slit yer throat and left ya back at the River. But, because I said what I said in St. Louie and ya claim to have chased away a thief, I'm taking ya to the Fort where you'll be safe. But I don't want to hear another word from that mouth of yours or I'll kick it closed. Now finish your eats so we can go to sleep. Any trouble from ya and I'll hog-tie ya to a tree." With that Crocker began putting out the fire and cleaning up the camp.

Wes hurried to finish the meat and biscuits, afraid to protest further about the Fort. His confusion increased as he watched Crocker pack his mule and saddle his horse. "Where we going?" he finally asked.

Crocker looked at Wes who sat cross-legged before the now dead fire. "Lunkheaded. Just plain old stupid! How'd you make it this far? We're going away from the fire so's we can sleep, less ya want some fucking Pawnee to sneak up on us in the night?"

Wes quickly jumped to his feet and fetched Jeff. They rode out of the stand of trees, Crocker leading the pack mule. On the open prairie, thousands of stars shone down on the two travelers, the moon still hidden behind the eastern horizon. They rode side-by-side as Crocker led them toward the east. In the darkness, Wes heard Crocker's saddle squeak as the man turned toward him. "Now boy, what do ya smell?"

Wes took in a deep breath, but found nothing unusual. "Nothing," he replied.

Instantly, he felt the back of Crock's hand across his face. "God Almighty!" whispered the older man. "It's the smoke from our fire! That's what ya smell and that's what every living critter fer a hundred miles smells. Never sleep where ya eat! Not if ya want to wake up in the morning. God Almighty, Farm-boy, you're wolf meat!"

Buffalo Man

Wes rubbed his aching cheek, not daring to reply for he didn't want to risk another blow from the mountain man. He decided that Crock was mean and vicious, and it was just as well he wasn't going trapping with him. Prison was his only future since the soldiers would surely find out he was wanted back in Illinois for murder. Nothing turned out like it was meant. If only Bert were here, or maybe Gunner.

* * *

The first time Anna became aware of trouble at their camp was when she returned with an armload of firewood. They had been camped in Sugar Creek a week now, and it was necessary for her to forage farther and farther from the wagons for her quota of wood. Tired from walking the long distance back, she only wanted a place to drop her heavy load, but as she walked to the side of their wagon, she heard Brother Martin speaking. "Don't fret, Sister, it will make your wagon lighter."

Anna dropped her wood and hurried around the tail end of the wagon to find Brother Martin, Brother Lissman, Uncle Stan, Aunt Alice and her mother. A Dearborn wagon was loaded with sacks of flour, and Anna realized the flour had just been unloaded from their wagons. She saw her mother give a scornful look at Uncle Stan. "Do what ya will, Stan. You men don't listen anyway," and her ma turned and walked away.

Aunt Alice put her hands on her hips as she looked at her husband. "She's right, ya know! Better to have some fully prepared than everyone only half prepared."

Brother Lissman stepped forward from the Dearborn. "You don't understand, Sister Sinclair. There are those who have nothing. They can't stay in Nauvoo; no one will be able to stay there soon. It's not like you're giving it away. We're just consigning it to the Company Wagon for now. Remember, I'm responsible for fifty families and Brother Martin is responsible for ten families, including yours."

"We understand," responded Uncle Stan. "But we do want it recorded, that's all we ask. We just want it put down that four hundred pounds of flour was transferred from our stock to the Company Wagon."

"Huh!" said Aunt Alice. "Ya can't eat a record!" And she walked away to join her sister-in-law.

The men looked at each other, frowns on their faces, and Stan shook his head. "It's hard on the women. Don't worry, they'll come around." Suddenly, Uncle Stan was aware of Anna watching from the wagon. "Anna, say hello to Brother Martin and Brother Lissman."

Anna gave a slight curtsy. "Hello," she said in a low voice and then decided it was better to retreat back with her mother and Aunt. Hurrying to the campfire, she found them both standing before the fire with arms folded.

"I tell ya, Alice," said her mother, "they just don't think ahead! Where we gettin' flour out on the prairie? They say they can always kill a buffalo, but I haven't seen any buffalo meat since we've been in Sugar Creek! Trying to live off beans and bread is bad enough, but now we don't have the flour we need for bread."

Aunt Alice nodded. "What can I say? You know how Stan is. Jack was the same way. If the Apostles say to do something, they don't even ask questions, they just do it. To tell the truth, I'll be glad when we leave this place and we're on the trail."

"We're leaving?" asked Anna.

"You haven't heard, yet," replied her mother, "but Brother Lissman has decided to take the company west, toward the Missouri. Some companies have already left and ours will be leaving tomorrow."

The next morning, the entire Sinclair family was up before sunrise. Again the clouds had come up during the night and now the sky delivered a generous rain storm which soaked everyone and everything. The women fixed a big breakfast of potato cakes and oatmeal while the men prepared the teams. After eating and saying morning prayers, they had to wait at their wagons while other families made last minute adjustments. Finally, the horn sounded, signaling the lead wagons to start up. Within minutes, one hundred wagons were heading west, through Iowa, following the trail laid out by the preceeding companies.

From the passage of so many wagons, the trail soon became a sea of mud. Stan reined in his wagon, forcing the wagons behind him to stop. Walking to the back of his wagon, he poked his head in under the canvas. "Gwen, you girls will have to walk; we have just too much of a load in this muck."

"All right, Pa." said Gwen as she pulled on her boots. Anna and Lucy followed and soon all three were standing in the rain and mud beside Uncle Stan's wagon. Anna looked down the line and saw others getting out of their wagons. The train started up again with the girls plodding alongside the slow moving schooners. Anna slowed a little until her mother caught up to her. "We aren't going to have to walk all the way to Zion, are we Ma?"

The rain got under her mother's bonnet and ran down her face. "I hope not, sweetheart. If we do, it's going to be a long trip."

"Ma?" asked Anna, "is it true what they say about the Apostles? That they have more than one wife?"

Her mother laughed. "That's just talk started by apostates. They want to discredit the Church and the only way they know how is to make up stories."

"But Cory says she was asked by Brother Wheeler to be his wife? What about that?"

"Anna, sometimes people say things to get attention. They don't mean to lie, but they get carried away."

"You mean Cory lied?"

"Well, maybe she just misunderstood what Brother Wheeler meant. That could happen, don't ya think? Maybe he said something to her in fun, but she thought he was proposing. That's probably what happened."

"But Ma, Cory said she was swore to secrecy; that it was a secret doctrine only a few knew."

Her mother frowned. "I think Cory has gotten carried away a little. I'd pay her no mind. Brigham Young has told us these lies are false. It's just our enemies trying to get at us. Now put it out of your head. A good Christian man can have only one wife."

A lump came to Anna's throat. "Ma? Now that Pa's gone, are you going to marry another man?"

Her mother was silent a moment before slipping an arm around Anna's waist and giving her a squeeze. "Don't worry about such things now. Our first job is to get everyone to Zion. Then the Lord will provide, you'll see."

The next day began without the rain, but by early morning a slow drizzle came down. At mid-day everyone was again ordered out of the wagons to lessen their load. The first day Brother Lissman's train made almost seven miles, but on the second day they covered only four and a half. The flat territory of Iowa lay before them and the rain gathered in every creek and tributary to become a flood. Small streams required agonizing detours and the mud and filth were everywhere. By the end of the second day, little Lucy Sinclair was coughing, but everyone was too tired to really notice.

CHAPTER 8

On to Pappan Ferry

Wes was secure in his mother's kitchen, warmed by the stove and smelling steaming biscuits covered with melted butter and fresh honey. Without warning, the kitchen was gone, replaced by darkness and something very cold flowing over his head. "GET UP!" came a voice.

Wes recognized it at once as the mountain man, Crocker Sloan, and realized he was back on the prairie! He quickly sat up and tried shaking the water from his face. "What the hell! Why did ya do that?" he complained.

The moon shone through tree branches and stars still covered the sky. The black form of Crocker gave a grunt. "Had to wake ya, didn't I? Why do ya sleep so long? You're a rawheel, that's sure. Out here we get up 'for sunrise or someday we don't get up at all. Now you get wood and start a fire. I'm takin' a look-see around the camp." The dark form slipped away, leaving Wes alone.

Wes removed his wet shirt, replacing it with his spare, and then pulled on his boots. Wood was plentiful and using his tinker box he soon had a warm fire brightly burning in a shallow fire pit. Without a sound, Crocker slipped up next to the campfire. "Well, at least ya can do somethin' right! Here," Crock dropped a cloth-covered bundle in Wes' lap, "you put some bufler on a stick so we can eat breakfast. You bake?"

Wes nodded. "Sure."

"All right, get some flour and soda from my possibles bag and whip up a batch of biscuits, and start the coffee. I'm grazing the horses." Again Crocker quietly slipped from camp.

Wes unwrapped the bundle to discover large smoked strips of buffalo meat. He gingerly brought a piece to his nose and sniffed. It was turning rancid, but might still stay down, so he quickly cut two branches and placed two cuts of meat over the fire. He opened Sloan's supply bag, extracted the coffee pot and rummaged about for the flour.

They ate their breakfast as the eastern horizon brightened to a pale blue and a cold breeze gently stirred the tree leaves. Crocker broke open a biscuit which was nearly black on the outside but only partially done in the center. "Augh! What'd ya do? Throw the tin in the fire?"

Wes winced. "I didn't let the fire die down enough–it was too hot!"

"Damn it, Farm-boy! Next time rake out the coals and let 'er bake. This is poor bull!" Suddenly, Crocker laughed. "Almost forgot; ain't going to be no next time. I'm handing ya to the Dragoons today!"

Wes tried to ignore his remark. "Where'd the buffalo meat come from?"

"Them two coons at the River. Traded it fer a twist of 'bacca."

Wes realized he had only today to talk Crocker Sloan out of going to Fort Leavenworth and turning him in, but he wasn't sure how to proceed. "Good tasting meat," he lied.

Crocker looked at him and his eyes narrowed. "Good? Don't lie, Farm-boy. This meat's poor bull. Don't go bamboozling me fer I'm not taking ya with me."

"What I mean," said Wes, embarrassed to be caught in his fib, "was that meat is good. Didn't always have it at home–greens mostly and beans when we could." Maybe his second lie would cover the first.

On to Pappan Ferry

Crocker looked him over again and smiled. "You ain't no Jim Crow from a river bottom rat hole. And what about that fine horse of yours? Ya steal him?"

Wes felt defeated. "No, he was my brother's. Bert gave him to me for the trip to St. Louie."

"That's more like it," said Crocker. "Now, you clean up this mess and put out the fire. I'll have me a smoke and we'll be off."

Wes shrugged his shoulders and, struggling to his feet, began his assigned chores. When Wes was finished cleaning up and had loaded the mule, they mounted their horses and left the grove of trees, moving northeast at a leisurely pace. For once the sky was clear and blue, and no rain threatened. The sun dried the earth, and every living green thing struggled to free itself from the mud and cold of winter. Wes wasn't sure how much time he had, but he was desperate to turn Crocker's mind, short of telling the truth, for he was afraid Sloan might turn him in if he thought Wes was a wanted man. Yet, he knew that getting through to this old mountain rat was going to be difficult.

They rode over grass covered hills and through tree lined gullies, passing several Indian farms. "Now that's an Ottawa farm," announced Crocker, "ya can tell by looking at the ponies. Ottawa ain't natural to these parts. 'Course ya knew that. Government moved them here and the Shawnee and Wyandot and some Fox. North of Leavenworth is the Kickapoo Village. The real Injuns of these parts don't farm yet. Still run wild and free."

Maybe Wes had a chance. "Who are the real Injuns?"

"Oh my, let's see: Arapaho, Kiowa, Comanche to the south, Cheyenne and Pawnee. We got Kansa and Osage. Now that first farm we passed was Kiowa."

"I thought you said the old Injuns didn't farm."

"Well, not most. Some are changing."

"How did ya learn about all these Injuns?"

"God, Farm-boy, I been out here for a donkey's years. I've been everywhere. I was with Henry in twenty-two when we went way up the Big Muddy and built Fort Union on the Yellowstone. We was going to build a string of forts all along the upper rivers and take in the beav but the Arikara burnt us out. I could 'a been with Jed Smith when he found South Pass but I weren't. I've worked for Bridger in the Rocky Mountain

Buffalo Man

Fur Company and fer the American Fur Company. But mostly, I just go my own way. I been to Santa Fe and Oregon, I've seen the Great Salt Lake in the Great Basin. It's been a life, it has–a real shining." Crocker turned and looked at Wes. "And ya know why I'm still here, still here to live and breathe?"

"Why?"

Crocker quickly leaned over and reaching began slapping Wes about the back of the head. "Cause I don't sleep late! Ya got that, Farm-boy? I don't sleep late!"

"Damn!" thought Wes as he tried to duck Crocker's blows. "I almost had him softened up!"

Before mid-morning they again reached the road to Fort Leavenworth and Crocker was pleased. "We're almost there, Farm-boy, just a few more miles. You'll take a shine to the army. They'll teach ya to be a real ripsnorter, you'll see. You'll be fightin' Injuns and Spaniards before ya know it."

But Wes wasn't pleased. A knot formed in his stomach and sweat ran down his sides even though it wasn't yet a hot day. Prison awaited him and he didn't know how to avoid it. If he just dashed off, Crocker would probably chase him down, but he wasn't absolutely sure that's what the mountain man would do, and now bolting off was beginning to sound like a good idea. He would try one more strategy. "Crocker?"

"Ya?"

"We're close to the Fort. Why don't I just mosey on down the road and you can be on your way now?"

Crocker reined to a stop and leaned forward on his horse's withers. "You don't really want to go to Leavenworth, do ya?"

"Oh, it's all right. Being a soldier will be just fine."

Crocker spurred his mount. "We're so close, I'll just mosey along with ya. Don't want nothing to happen to my Farm-boy."

They continued along the road and the knot of pain grew in Wes' gut. He had to do something! They were getting near and the closeness was sucking the breath right out of his lungs. He had to act. Without planning, or thinking ahead, he leaned forward, spurred Jeff in the ribs, and give out a yell. Jeff bolted forward and they dashed down the road.

Suddenly, Wes was free and the exhilaration poured through him. He couldn't be stopped; Jeff was too fast and Crocker would never catch

On to Pappan Ferry

him. He looked over his shoulder and saw Crocker still walking his horse. He hadn't even tried to catch Wes! There would be no Fort Leavenworth or army now. As soon as he was out of Crocker's sight, he reined Jeff to the left. He would have to go West. North was the Fort and east was the Missouri. Only the west offered the open expanse to get lost in. What if Crocker went to the Fort and found out he was a wanted man, a murderer? By then it would be too late because Wes would be gone!

He galloped Jeff over a hill, down into a tree filled ravine, back up the opposite side of the ravine, twisting from left to right and back to left again. Breaking out of the ravine, Wes looked at the sun to get his bearings. It was almost straight overhead, but he knew which way west must be. Spurring Jeff on, he galloped out onto the prairie, continuing his flight until Jeff was covered with streaks of white sweat. The horse was young and strong and Wes knew his limits. He could continue his escape for a ways before stopping.

He rode down into a creek, flooding from the recent rains, and carefully picked his path, maneuvering Jeff through the creek and willows and up the opposite bank. Reining in, he looked about, momentarily confused. Which way should he go? It must be to the left again. He urged Jeff on and galloped down the creek as the creek bottom widened and became clogged with trees and brush. Had the stream turned south? No, that couldn't be–that would mean it was flowing west where he crossed it, away from the Missouri! He turned Jeff around and crossed the creek again, going to the right and up a hill.

After many minutes, Wes decided he had to be far from both Sloan and the Fort. He determined to gallop to the near tree line and rest his horse while he made his plans. Approaching the trees his heart took a leap. A road! But there was only one road out here–the road to Fort Leavenworth. Reining Jeff to a halt, he looked about. It was the road he and Crocker had just been on and, worse, he couldn't tell if he was above or below where he had started. Exhausted, he bent forward and leaned on Jeff's neck.

From behind he heard the slow, methodical plodding of a horse. "Ya through, Farm-boy? Ya had yer fun?"

The pain returned to his stomach and sweat beaded on his forehead. "Did ya see that, Sloan? Jeff, here, just bolted out from under me. Never seen the likes of it. He gave me quite a ride!"

"Yep, I got eyes. Now let's get on to Fort Leavenworth."

They continued along the road and Wes resigned himself to going to prison where he would surely die from over-work and torture. His life was finished. They rode up a slight hill and around a bend to find the fort laid out before them. It had no stockade or bulwarks, consisting of several blockhouses around an open parade ground. The Fort was alive with activity, soldiers moving about everywhere.

The two travelers rode to the parade ground where they stopped a soldier and Crocker asked for an officer. The soldier pointed out a lieutenant and then ran to fetch him. Crocker took Wes by the arm and gave a pull. "Come on, Farm-boy. Let's get you hitched up. Army life fer you!"

Wes resisted. "What if, Crocker, what if I had reason to not be here?"

Crocker stopped and looked at Wes, confusion written on his face. "What do ya mean?"

"I mean, what if a fellow had a good reason but didn't want to share it?"

"What in the world are you talking about?" Abruptly, Crocker's face cleared and a smile replaced the frown. "You're wanted!" he whispered. It wasn't a question, but a statement.

"Well, it could be, but then maybe not."

Just then a tall young officer approached. "I'm Lieutenant Rosenberg. Can I help you?"

Crocker looked at the officer and then back at Wes. Wes just held his breath.

"Well?" repeated the soldier, "can I help you?"

"Yes," responded Crocker. "Can you...was there a party of trappers came through the Fort lately?"

Wes expelled the air from his lungs with such force that both Crocker and the Lieutenant looked at him. Immediately, he put a hand to his mouth and gave a little cough. "Cold been clinging to me for days!"

The lieutenant returned his attention to Crocker. "A bullboat came up three days again. That yer group?"

Crock nodded. "Yep, must be them. Much thanks and give my regards to yer commander." Without further comment, he wheeled his horse and started toward the road. Wes quickly followed.

They traveled in silence, Crocker content to just take in the countryside and Wes too nervous to start conversation. By evening they were

On to Pappan Ferry

again out on the prairie. Crocker located a small thicket of hickory where they could cook their meal and Wes was quick to build a fire. As the western horizon grew dark, they sat by their fire and ate buffalo meat. Finally Wes couldn't stand it. "Ya changed yer mind about the Dragoons?"

Crocker smiled. "This don't change nothin'. Ya still can't come with me, but I could see giving ya to the army was making yer eyes bug out."

Wes cleared his throat and spoke in a soft voice. "I'm wanted in Illinois."

Crocker only nodded and continued chewing on his supper.

"I'm wanted fer murder, but I didn't do it! It was someone else, but the Sheriff thinks I'm the one."

"If ya say you're innocent, that's good enough fer me."

"You're not going to turn me in?"

"Illinois don't pay me to bring in fugitives."

"There might be a price on my head."

Crocker laughed. "Whatever it is, it's too high!" They both laughed and the tension in Wes was gone. He felt like crying, but held back the tears as he took another strip of meat from the skewer.

When Crocker finished his meal, he lay back against a log and lit his pipe. "Ya know, Farm-boy, we got to figure out what to do with you. I reckon we'll head southwest to Pappan's Ferry; that's where the Oregon Trail crosses the Kansas River. Lots of rawheels are heading fer Oregon this summer; I've seen their wagons everywhere. Maybe you can hire on one of their trains. How'd ya like Oregon? No lawman will go fer ya there!"

"How far is Pappan's Ferry?"

"Not far. Two, three days."

Wes nervously bit his lower lip. "Crocker, I could be a great help. If you're going after beaver, I could set the traps and cook your meals and you wouldn't have to do a thing. I'd do everything."

"Now what did I just say? Didn't I just say ya couldn't come? God, you're a lunkhead!"

"But Crocker, I can take care of myself. I got my pistol and I fought the Mormons in Illinois. I can ride a horse. I can..."

Crocker had reached down and, picking up a rock the size of his fist, threw it at Wes' chest, striking the boy in the breast bone. Wes let out a hurting grunt and grabbed his chest.

"Now shut up!" yelled the mountain man. "I told ya it wouldn't work, didn't I tell ya that? You're a kid, you're a rawhorn and don't belong out here. Ya got that pea-shooter that ain't no good in a real fight. I'll bet ya got no Galena or powder. I don't know where I'm going so I can't take no kid."

Wes rubbed his chest. "I ain't a kid and ya got no call to hit me with a rock!"

Crocker puffed on his pipe and was silent as he watched Wes. Finally he took the pipe from his mouth. "Yer right! I'm sorry I throwed at ya, but ya don't listen! I'm trying to tell ya something. This here is a rough land. People die, people a lot stronger and smarter than you. Some day all this wildness will be gone, the Injuns dead and the land full of farms, just like back East. Then it will be safe, and the rawhorns will think of us trappers and dream of what a fun, exciting life we had, just like you're thinking now. But it ain't fun and the kind of excitement ain't the kind ya want. It's hard and it's boring and ya can't make no money out here."

"Then why are you here?" asked Wes.

"Cause I can't live with town-folk. I get in trouble. That's how it is with most trappers: we mix in with civilized folks and soon we're killing or they're trying to kill us or something. That's why most of us stick out here where we can't bother no one but the bufler and the Injuns." Crocker refilled his pipe and lit it from the fire. "Now you, you're young. You got a whole world to play in. You fool around out here and you'll go under. If ya can't go back to Illinois, ya can go to St. Louie or down the River to New Orleans, or ya can go to Oregon or California."

"I just don't want to join with a strange wagon train and work for someone else."

"Well, yer going to have to get used to it," said the mountain man. "Now let's move camp and get some sleep." Crocker stood and began packing his possibles bag.

"Crocker?" asked Wes. "How do ya do it? How do ya get up before sunrise?"

Crocker laughed. "Ya take a big drink before going to bed. When ya get up to pee, don't go back down, stay up. That's how the Injuns do it and it works fer me."

Wes woke in the half-light of dawn and rolled over to see Crocker already sitting before a small fire. Quickly scurrying from under his tarpaulin, he dashed for a large tree. His over-full bladder was killing him. As he stood behind the tree and relieved himself, he heard Crocker laughing. "You still can't beat me up, can ya, Farm-boy. Better drink another gallon before laying down."

Wes joined Crocker at the fire where the older man was cooking buffalo meat. Handing Wes a long, steaming strip, Crocker cautioned him. "Ya better fill yer crammer 'cause this is the last of the bufler."

"You mean we ate the whole thing?"

"Whole-hog. This here is the last."

"But shouldn't we save some, shouldn't we ration it out?"

"No, can't do that. Meat don't keep anyway, and it's best to fill yer gut full when ya can."

"But what about tonight? What about tomorrow?"

Crocker chuckled. "You won't go under skipping a day or two and by then maybe we'll make meat."

Wes looked at Crocker, his eyes narrowed, and his chin stuck out as he considered his suspicions. Was this mean old man going to starve him just to prove how rough it was? Well, Wes was no saphead to fall for Crocker's hornswoggle. He would just tighten his belt and outlast the old crow.

They moved southwest, toward the Kansas River. Early March, the wind still carried a chill, and the wet season continued drenching them with rain whenever they believed the sun was about to bring relief. That night they dined on biscuits and a few strips of jerky. Afterward, Wes was surprised he still felt hungry and his thoughts kept drifting back to fresh buffalo meat. Before bedding down he walked to the creek and drank cold, clear water for he wasn't going to let Crocker beat him awake again.

In Wes' dream, Bert was chasing him with a branding iron, trying to brand his feet. Running, Wes felt the ground grow hotter and hotter until the dream vanished and he opened his eyes to see smoke curling up from the foot of his bedroll. He was on fire!

He jumped up and began stomping out his smoldering socks. Deciding this action was ill advised, he sat down and quickly pulled them off. Crocker roared with laughter. Wes looked down at the bottom of his bedroll and found that Crocker had built a small fire just close enough to get cloth smoking, making it uncomfortable for anyone still asleep. Wes beat out the remaining hot spots in his blanket. "Damn it,

Crocker!" he yelled. "Ya ruined my bedding! Look at this! What the hell ya doing?"

Crocker, standing in the half light of dawn, swallowed part of the biscuit he was holding. "Ya ain't getting up early enough so I'm helping ya. I'm just doing ya a favor." And he stuffed the second half of the biscuit into his mouth.

Wes clenched his jaw shut as the anger boiled about inside him. Was this just more meanness so Wes would want to join a wagon train? Well, he would smarten up and be ready for Crocker next time. But now, he'd have to hurry because his gut was bursting and he had to relieve himself.

Biscuits and coffee were breakfast, after which the two travelers packed up and moved west again. At mid-day they sat on their mounts on top of a bluff and watched a family of Indians move through the valley below them. "What are they, Crocker?" asked Wes. "They Pawnee?"

"Hell, no! Pawnee would be up here by now to cheat us out of something or put us under. No, they's Osage. Just moving east, although I can't say why. Most Injuns is making tracks west to hunt bufler this time of year. Maybe they's joining with family." The Indians waved and Wes and Crocker waved back. "Ain't you the one who's fer killing Injuns?" teased Crocker.

"Hell," replied Wes, "they's just a family. I'm fer fighting real Injuns, you know–braves. I'm planning on taking scalps. I seen a scalp on a man's belt in St. Louie." The thin smile on Crocker's face made the hair stand up on Wes' neck and he decided to save his boasting for later. That night supper was beans and coffee. Before retiring, Wes swore he would awake before Crocker. He didn't.

In the waking instant that he knew something was wrong, he felt a warm, wet and sticky liquid dripping on his face. Crocker was at him again! He opened his eyes and found a sage-hen hanging over his head, blood falling on him in gooey drops. Again he had overslept until almost dawn, and again he had to hurry to relieve himself. Crocker giggled as Wes jumped up and wiped the blood from his face. "Lookie! I got our breakfast, Farm-boy!" Wes ran behind a tree, refusing to give Crocker the pleasure of a response.

After a breakfast of roast sage-hen, which barely quieted Wes' grumbling stomach, they headed southwest again and by early afternoon found the Kansas River and the Pappan Ferry. The trail was empty of wagon

On to Pappan Ferry

trains or travelers, and Wes gave a sigh of relief for he wanted one more try at beating Crocker. They moved west along the north bank of the Kansas River before making their cooking camp.

That night, as Wes lay beneath the star-filled sky, he decided tomorrow was the morning he would best Crocker Sloan. At first he planned to stay awake all night, but soon reversed his decision, hoping that early sleep would allow him to awake early. His plan began to unravel as sleep sidestepped his will and he lay on the hard ground, eyes open. The more he wanted sleep, the farther it slipped from his grasp.

His eyes snapped opened and he knew with a certainty that something was very wrong—wrong in a way beyond a simple joke. Something was in his bedroll with him, something very dangerous, slithering along his side. Giving out a horrendous yell, he jumped from his bed and discovered a large black snake on his blanket. Anger flooded over him like a great wall of water. "God damn you, Crocker Sloan!" he screamed and twisted about to find his target.

Crocker sat on a log, razor in hand and a smile on his face, as he prepared to shave in the early morning light. "You say something, Farm-boy?"

Wes ran at the bigger man, doubling up his fists and letting out a grunt of anger. Crocker stood, still holding his razor and soap still on his face. Wes stopped in front of Crocker and, without hesitating, threw a sidewinder, striking Crocker on the side of the chin.

Crocker dropped his razor. "Why are you so cantankerous?" Without warning, a fist shot forward striking Wes in the mouth, causing him to fly backward and land on his bottom. In stunned silence, Wes looked up at Crocker and felt the warm blood begin to flow from his split lip and down his chin. Crocker pointed to his own chin. "Your turn!"

In frustration, Wes doubled up his fists and pounded the earth, cussing between his teeth.

They continued along the trail until noon but encountered no wagon trains, Crocker remarking that it must be too early for them to be on the trail. Sloan didn't want to make camp too close to the trail so, after supper, they moved several miles north of the River and made night camp in a small grove of trees. Wes felt moody, convinced Crocker was using his superior strength and experience to torment him. That night Wes took his now customary drink of water and slipped under his blanket.

He didn't even consider what the mountain man would surprise him with in the morning.

A slight noise reached Wes' ears, a small animal in the brush or one of the horses shifting his weight, and Wes' eyes popped open and he was awake. The night was black, not a sliver of light showing on the horizon. He glanced about but discovered nothing unusual. Could he be so lucky? He slowly turned and looked toward Crocker, tucked under his great buffalo hide, but saw nothing except a black mound. Hearing only soft snoring coming from the mountain man, he wanted to shout out in relief and scream insults at Crocker, yet he controlled himself. Silently getting up, he crept behind a tree and relieved his aching bladder.

Now, what to do? He could just build a fire and wait for the man to wake up, but that didn't quite seem adequate revenge. Slowly, a plan began forming in his mind. The delight of his scheme felt too good and he fought the temptation to giggle and, instead, quickly dressed. Picking up his bedroll and Crocker's possibles bag, he loaded the animals and led them from the trees. Of course he had to leave Crocker's Hawken, since Crocker always went to sleep with his rifle and six-shooter safely tucked under his buffalo robe.

In the dark, Wes rode Jeff and led Crocker's horse and mule south toward the Oregon Trail. Old Crock would have to walk a few miles before breakfast–payment for oversleeping! Wes laughed each time he thought of it. He reached the Trail and, picketing the animals, started a small breakfast fire. Rummaging through the possibles bag he found enough flour and baking soda to whip up a batch of biscuits–no use making Crock starve after his morning walk.

The eastern sky brightened and soon the sun came up. Wes tried calculating how long it would take Crocker to reach the trail, but he couldn't be sure. Hungry, Wes ate half of the biscuits–still no Crocker. Deciding he could always make a second batch, he ate Crocker's biscuits. Still no Crocker, and Wes began to wonder what had happened. The morning wore on and he found himself walking around the fire, turning toward the north every few minutes to scan the horizon. Nothing moved. The sun crept higher and Wes' worry increased. Finally, at mid-day Wes had to admit that his plan was failing. Crocker was out-waiting him back at the grove of trees. Oh well, it had still been a fine joke and he had stranded the mountain man on the prairie.

On to Pappan Ferry

He loaded up the pack horse and, mounting Jeff, started north again. Soon he was back at the previous night's camp. Riding directly into the grove of trees he looked around, but Crock was nowhere to be seen. He dismounted and, cupping his hands around his mouth, he called out. "Oh, Crock! Where are ya, Crock?" Suddenly, it came to him that Sloan was at this minute walking south, and they had somehow passed each other. A stupid thing to happen, but, of course, that was it. Then Wes spotted something red on the ground. He bent down and touched it–blood! Standing, he looked around and saw lots of blood splattered on the ground around the fire pit. Goose bumps ran up his back and a cold chill made him shake.

He withdrew his pistol, primed the pan, and began a close search of the ground. Moccasin tracks were everywhere, yet Wes remembered that Crocker wore moccasins. He looked again and his heart dropped as he saw hundreds of tracks–too many for just one man. By a bush he picked up a lone eagle feather! The truth was overwhelming: Indians had come and overpowered Crock, killing him or wounding him and carrying him off. Wes' gut became a great hollow; he wanted to scream out for his joke to be taken back. He didn't mean this! He would have to go after Crocker–this was Wes' fault and even if the Indians killed him, he had to try to get Crock or Crocker's body back.

Wes searched the rest of the trees but found nothing, however; making a slow circle of the grove, he discovered a trail of moccasin tracks heading directly west. Two parallel marks showed in the soft earth–heels dragging along the ground. Mounting Jeff, he took the lead line to the other animals and started west. If only he could catch up before they tortured Crocker to death; that is if Crocker were even alive!

Wes followed the tracks all afternoon. Periodically, he broke out in tears from a combination of fear and sorrow. When it grew late he realized he would have to make camp for the night; it was getting too dark to follow the tracks. He didn't eat and didn't dare make a fire. Picketing the animals, he lay down in his bedroll and soon was sound asleep.

All night he dreamed of Indians chasing him and scalping Crocker. When he finally awoke he found it was light–he'd forgotten to drink a bellyful of water the night before. He was on his back and, as he turned to get up, discovered he was pinned to the ground. Looking at his arms, he found them held by rawhide tied to stakes. Looking down, his waist and groin were covered with twigs.

A great screech reached his ears and he looked up into the brown face of a Redman, standing naked and holding a blazing torch. My God! They had captured him and were going to burn him to death! The savage danced about and waved the torch toward the kindling piled on Wes. "Oh, please! Don't kill me! Please!" screamed Wes. He could see in his mind the wood bursting into flame and almost feel the scorching heat of the fire as it worked to consume him. He began to cry. "Oh God! Please save me!"

The Indian stopped his dancing and kicked the twigs off of Wes' groin. "Don't ya ever learn, Farm-boy?" The Indian knelt down and looked into Wes' face. It was Crocker, naked and covered in dried mud to darken his skin. "You sleep too late!" and he pulled up his Green River and cut the rawhide.

As Wes sat up and rubbed his wrists, Crocker danced over to a fire, whooping and hollering like some crazy man. Wes' relief was overwhelming. Crying, he fell back on the earth and rubbed his face.

"Oh, I'm an Injun and I'm eating that boy," sang Crocker as he danced about. "Come on, Farm-boy, get up. I'm hungry. Let's eat."

After breakfast they rode along the Oregon Trail as it led northwest away from the Kansas River toward the Big Blue, and Crocker laughed again. "You done all right, Farm-boy. Yes sir, you done all right, indeed. Ya beat this coon in gettin' up, but what's more, ya figured out a plan and carried it out. Old Crock was bug-eyed when he got up." Crocker laughed again and slapped his leg. "But ya should a-seen yer face when ya thought I was a Pawnee! Oh, that was a ripsnorter, it was!" Crocker continued giggling and complimenting himself on his wonderful joke.

Wes smiled. He had to admit Crocker had turned the tables on him, scaring him out of his wits, but now it didn't seem so awful. Suddenly, Wes saw movement ahead, off the trail. Looking more carefully, he spotted a small herd of cattle grazing on new grass just coming up from the mud of winter. Just beyond, several Conestoga wagons slowly moved along the trail. "Look, Crock. It's a train."

Crock squinted his eyes. "Yep, you're right. Ya got good eyes, Farm-boy. If all works out, this is where we'll say our goodbyes."

They passed the cattle and approached the wagon train, which had stopped for dinner. The pioneers quit what they were doing to watch the two strangers ride up. Crocker asked the first man he came to where the captain was, and was directed to the head of the column. At the lead wagon Crocker and Wes found a tall man about Crock's age, mid-fifties, with a long black beard and a black top-hat. He wore a great, black overcoat and a wide, brown belt which held two single shot pistols.

"Morning," said Crocker. "You captain of this here wagon train?"

The captain's eyes narrowed. "I am Randall Earnst, Captain of the Earnst Pioneer Company. Who might you be?"

"I'm Crocker Sloan, and this is Wes Tucker. Where ya headed?"

"Oregon, Mr. Sloan. I see by your dress that you are a trapper."

"Yes, a trapper." Crocker dismounted and Wes followed. Another man approached. He was of medium height with long brown hair, which fell over his shoulders and a short salt-and-pepper beard. Dressed in white buckskin from head to moccasined foot, he held a shiny-new percussion rifle. Captain Earnst gestured toward the new man. "Let me introduce our guide, Mr. Jacob William Hunt. Mr. Hunt is a famous trapper and Injun fighter. You, Mr. Sloan, and Hunt may know of each other."

Hunt extended his hand and Crocker took it, a smile on his face. "Don't believe I've heard of ya, son. You a relative of old Wilson Hunt? I think he's still in St. Louie, selling possibles. Was a hell of a trapper in his day."

A slight hint of embarrassment danced across Hunt's face as he continued to shake Crock's hand. "No, no relation. But, I've heard of you, Mr. Sloan."

Crocker quickly dropped Hunt's hand and stepped back. "Well, none of it is true. Ya got that, Hunt?"

Wes put a hand to his mouth to cover his urge to smile. Did Crocker really think evil rumors had been spoken against him or was he just pulling Hunt's leg? Wes couldn't tell–Crock was too good of an actor.

Captain Earnst looked confused. "You say you haven't heard of Hunt, here. But, it is my understanding that he is known throughout the West."

Crocker leaned forward and squinted as he carefully looked again into Hunt's face. "Ain't never seen this coon in my life, so help me God! But, I'll say this, he's got the prettiest duds I've ever seen on a famous trapper, yes sir. That's bleached rawhide, ain't it?"

Hunt's face was blushing red, but Captain Earnst was still looking at Sloan. "Hunt says he's not too familiar with the trail in this part because he did his trapping farther north. Perhaps you can inform us of the land from here to the Platte Valley."

Crocker lost his smile as he considered the question. "Well, it's flat! This trail is new, the old one went up past Fort Leavenworth and stayed against the Big Muddy. This one will save ya some time. It crosses the Big Blue and then follows the Little Blue River, going northwest until you're 'bout twenty or thirty miles south of the Platte River. Ya leave the Little Blue just before its headwaters and go north. Ain't no way of getting lost. 'Course the Pawnee or Sioux can pinch yer tit."

Captain Earnst looked worried. "Injuns? Are the Injuns on the warpath?"

Crocker smiled. "Before we get into that, I would just like to ask a little favor."

"Of course," responded the Captain. "Anything you want. We have lots of women and children and we can't take any trouble from the Injuns."

Crocker pointed toward Wes. "This boy, here, is a strong and honest working youth. Now, where I'm a goin', I can't take this boy 'cause the Sioux only allow old Crocker onto their sacred hunting grounds, 'cause I saved the son of one of their chiefs, see. Now if you could see yer way clear to hire Wes, here, onto your wagon train and let his work be payment for passage, he would help drive yer livestock and guard yer camp. What do ya say?"

Captain Earnst carefully looked Wes over and then turned to Hunt. "Can ya use the youth?"

Suddenly Hunt regained his composure. "He looks strong enough. Ya got your own horse? Ya got a gun?"

Crock nodded. "Oh, sure, he's got a beauty of a black stallion there. Just look him; sixteen and a half hands at least and only four years old. And he's got a gun, too. Show Hunt your gun, Wes."

Wes pulled his pistol from his belt so the men could see it.

"I suppose I could use the lad, if he don't eat too much," announced the guide.

"Then it's a deal!" said Earnst as he held out his hand. First Crocker shook the Captain's hand and then Wes shook it. "Well," said the Captain, "what about them Injuns?"

Crock's eyebrows came together as a worried look made his eyes shine. "It's them Pawnee. Ain't that right, Hunt?"

On to Pappan Ferry

Abruptly, Hunt was confounded again. "Well, yes, but I'm used to the northern tribes, you see."

Crocker chuckled. "Yes, I'm sure you are. Well, anyway, them Pawnee are sore as hell at the Whiteman just now. Don't know why, but they's been milling around looking fer trouble. You let any of your folks wander from camp and get caught by the Pawnee, they'll go under, sure. But the Pawnee are cowards, see, and if ya stick together and show yer bullthrowers they'll stay a distance. You'll meet Pawnee on the Little Blue clear up to the Platte. On the Platte you'll find Oglala, Minniconjou, Cheyennes, Brule and Sioux. But around Fort Laramie, you'll run into mainly Sioux. Them Sioux are different. They's a proud people and will make peace if ya treat 'em well. They ain't mad at us just now."

As Crocker talked, all three men listened with rapt attention, for Crocker gave a detailed description of the tribes Captain Earnst would encounter all the way to Oregon City and he outlined just how the pioneers should act toward each tribe. When he was done, Earnst extended his hand to Crocker again. "I want to thank you, Mr. Sloan. That was a most helpful recitation regarding the Redman and will help us profoundly. Is there anything I can do for you? Would you like to travel with us to the Platte?"

"Oh, no," responded Crocker. "I can't go that slow. Just take Wes, here, and see he gets to Oregon."

Earnst patted Wes on the shoulder. "You can be assured we'll take good care of him, Mr. Sloan. If you change your mind, we would be pleased to have you join our company for as long as you find convenient."

Crocker shook his head. "No, I'm a goin'." He turned and took Wes' hand. "This is it, coon. It's been a shinin'. Don't forget your nightly drink," and Crock winked.

Suddenly Wes realized that Crocker was really departing while he was staying with the wagon train. "Goodbye, Crocker," was all he could manage through a cracking voice.

Crocker waved to the other two men and quickly mounted his horse. Leading the pack mule, he wandered up the trail and disappeared.

Captain Earnst looked at Wes. "Well, boy, you're bound for Oregon. Better come over here and get a mouthful of grub before we get started. You can ride pick-up on the cattle today. How does that sound, Hunt?"

The guide was still watching the trail ahead where Crocker had disappeared. "What? Did you say something?"

"I said," repeated the Captain. "Wes, here, can ride pick-up on the cattle. Is that all right with you?"

"Sure," replied the guide as he looked Wes over and then turned his eye on Jeff. "Fine horse. What's his name?"

"Jeff."

"Yes, sir. Fine horse!"

* * *

Anna was bored walking beside the wagon, trudging along in the sameness of the flat Iowa landscape. At least the sun had come out and warmed the air, but the ground was still covered with mud. Usually, she found something interesting to do as she walked along: naming off the Twelve Apostles or repeating a Sunday school lesson, but she had spent the morning doing such things and now she yearned for something more exciting.

The trail was wide and smooth, so the company's wagons pulled four abreast. In Anna's group were the Wheelers' wagon on the right, the two Sinclair wagons in the middle and the Taylors' wagon on the left. Since the second day, everyone who could manage was required to walk because Uncle Stan and the other men were afraid the teams would tire if the loads weren't reduced. Anna didn't understand why more teams couldn't be added so everyone could ride. Sometimes, it seemed to her, men just invented rules to make things harder for everybody. She smiled at the thought. It reminded her of something Sarah Wheeler might say.

Suddenly Anna heard coughing from their wagon. Lucy, sick with the fever, was being cared for by Gwen in the back of Anna's wagon where a bed had been prepared. When Gwen grew tired, Anna would take over, holding Lucy and wiping the sweat from her head. Yet, after two days, Lucy hadn't improved, and Uncle Stan sent Jason back down the trail looking for a doctor. Brother Lissman told Aunt Alice that not a single doctor could be found on the trail and not to expect Jason to return with one. Anna was appalled. Thousands of people out on the prairie and not one doctor! How could that be? Brother Martin said doctors weren't

On to Pappan Ferry

needed; that all the Saints were safe in the hands of the Lord. Yet, Anna wished the Lord would send a doctor to make Lucy better.

Lucy coughed again and Anna walked to the back of the wagon and looked in. "You want me to take over?" she asked her cousin. Gwen looked at her and smiled. "No, I'm fine."

"How's Lucy?"

Gwen looked at the eleven-year-old laying under the old woolen blanket and shook her head. "She's not good. I wish we'd stop."

Anna looked at the sun, low on the horizon. "It won't be long. We'll be stopping for supper soon." To make better time, the pioneers had ceased stopping for dinner, the midday meal, and simply ate leftovers from breakfast while on the move. That made supper, the evening meal, the main meal of the day. As if hearing Anna's words, a trumpet sounded and the two girls heard Michael calling a halt to the oxen. The wagon slowly came to a stop. Gwen smiled. "You're magic, Anna!" Soon, Brother Wheeler and the Captains of Ten maneuvered the fifty wagons into a large circle for night camp.

As evening fires were lit, concerned brethren from other wagons congregated to check on Lucy. Alice Sinclair climbed up and told Gwen to help with supper while she watched the child. Uncle Stan shook his head. "She looks pale, Alice! Is she getting enough water? You giving her water, Gwen?"

Gwen looked at her father with a hurt expression. "Of course, Pa, but she can't take much. She's too sick."

Uncle Stan shook his head again. "I wish Jason would come back," he said, and he turned and trudged off with the other men to water the teams.

Sarah Wheeler clapped her hands. "Come on, ladies, let's get some supper for our men; they've been working hard. Gwen, you start a fire while Mary and I get the bread kettle ready. Anna, you set up the table." They turned away from the wagon and went to their chores. During night camp it was convenient for the four wagons belonging to the Taylors, Wheelers and Sinclairs to share one fire. The supper bread had been rising in the wagons and was now ready to bake. Anna set up the little table and began arranging other food: dried catfish, raisins, rice, fresh butter and peach preserves. Dorothy Taylor, Joey Taylor's seven-year-old sister, tried helping Anna, but for some reason, the little girl just annoyed her.

Dorothy tried lifting a bucket of water to the table, but it proved to be too heavy. Anna rushed to her side and lifted it into place. "Dorothy!" Anna snapped. "You shouldn't get the bucket so full. It's too heavy. You'll spill it all over the table!"

The little girl looked up, a tear forming in her eye. Suddenly Anna felt awful. What if someone were yelling at Lisa at this very moment? She knelt down and scooped Dorothy into her arms. "Oh, honey, Anna's sorry! You did just fine. Do you forgive Anna?" She leaned back to look at the seven-year-old.

Dorothy shrugged her shoulders. "Ya, sure," she said. Instantly recovered, she wiggled to the ground and dashed off.

Without warning Joey Taylor was standing by Anna's side. "Hi, Anna, need some help?" He looked over the table and moved some of the dishes about. "What can I do?"

Anna's heart was pounding. He wasn't here just to help out. He was here to flirt with her and she knew it. "Nothing, I think everything is ready." Of course everything wasn't ready because the women from the other wagons hadn't brought their dishes and the bread wasn't baked, but Anna wasn't paying attention to what she was saying. She was watching Joey Taylor watching her. Somehow, this was wrong, for it was Gwen who was sweet on Joey, not her. Her heart pounded harder.

Joey picked up a piece of catfish and popped it in his mouth. "That's good! What is it?"

"Catfish."

"Catfish? Well, it's very good. Do you fix it?"

"No, my ma did."

"You're a good cook, if you fixed it. Did you know that Jason is back? I seen him down at the creek with some man."

"Jason's back? Was it the doctor? Was the man a doctor?"

"Naw, it was some Gentile sheriff from Hancock County. Jason said he got almost to Sugar Creek before turning back. He said he couldn't find a doctor."

Before Anna could respond, Gwen was at her side. "Hi, Joey," she said.

Joey turned toward Gwen and his eyes sparkled. "Hi, Gwen. Jason's back."

Gwen reached over and gently took Joey's arm. "He's back! Where is he?"

On to Pappan Ferry

Watching them, Anna felt a sadness: Joey may have flirted for a moment with her, but it was obvious now that it was Gwen he really liked, and Gwen wasted no time in returning his interest.

All at once, people crowded around; women placed dishes of food on the table, and men dusted off their pants and shirts. Three horsemen rode up to the wagons: Jason, Brother Martin and a man who looked vaguely familiar to Anna. All three quickly dismounted and joined them at the table. The stranger was introduced as Sheriff Taylor Hawes, and Anna's memory was jolted back to the River on the day her father died. It was the same man, the man who was there!

Soon everyone had their dish piled high with food and had found a place to sit around a small fire. Anna and her mother sat close together on the hard ground. Mary wasn't eating so Anna sat with her plate on her lap, the smell of fresh bread reaching her nose, but not eating either. With Sheriff Hawes' presence a tension had entered the camp and conversation was nervous and short. The Sheriff sat on a log, holding his plate on his lap and casually taking a bite from his supper, more from politeness than hunger. Occasionally, he glanced at Sarah Wheeler. Anna could understand why. Sarah was a beautiful woman.

Finally, Sheriff Hawes put down his fork and cleared his throat. "You all know," he began, "that I was at the River and saw Weston Hamlin shoot Jack Sinclair."

A lance of pain plunged into Anna's heart. To hear this near stranger, this Gentile, speak so directly about her father renewed Anna's suffering. Tears filled her eyes and she felt her mother's arm slip around her shoulders.

Hawes removed his dark, wide-brimmed hat and placed it on his knee. "I wish I had better news for you. I haven't found Hamlin, although I've found another witness, Hamlin's half-brother, Gunner Hamlin."

"Sheriff," interrupted Uncle Stan. "Did you actually see this Weston Hamlin shoot my brother?"

"No, but I caught him holding the gun and Gunner Hamlin saw the shooting, so there's no doubt. There's also the fact he fled. An innocent man wouldn't do that. I had hoped he'd come out into Iowa Territory, but I might be wrong. No one's seen or heard of him."

Again Stan stopped the Sheriff. "What about our Lisa?"

103

Hawes shook his head. "I've searched the entire River's east bank from above Nauvoo to Parker's Dock. I couldn't find a sign of her. Of course, your people sent out search parties, too and they failed to find anything. There is one point of hope. The boat never turned up. In all likelihood, it didn't swamp, which means Lisa is alive somewhere. The River bottoms from Nauvoo south are dotted with rum holes whose occupants represent the worst of humanity: robbers, Greasers and Jim Crows of every description."

"What are you suggesting?" asked Brother Martin.

Sheriff Hawes fidgeted with the rim of his hat and shot a quick, but short, glance at Sarah Wheeler. Anna looked at Sarah and realized that she was blushing! Why would Sarah blush?

Hawes looked back at Martin. "I'm saying there's a good chance your Lisa was found by these river rats and taken in. That means she's still alive, but it also means her life will not be as pleasant as it would be home with you folks."

A silence overtook the group as they considered Sheriff Hawes' words. Mary turned to Anna and, with tears streaming down her cheeks, squeezed her shoulders. "He thinks she's still alive, Anna. Did ya hear? He thinks she's still alive!" She smiled and the hope danced in her face. Anna began crying, too.

Uncle Stan's face was stern and hard. "What do we do now, Sheriff?"

"Nothing ya can do. I've put out word of your little girl. Hopefully, someone will see something or hear something and I'll check it out. But I wouldn't hold out too much hope she'll be returned home in the near future. I think the best you can wish is that she's in the hands of kind people, like yourselves."

Uncle Stan nodded his head. "We understand." He then turned toward the others sitting about the fire. "We owe a great deal to the Sheriff, here. Not many Gentiles would have been so helpful and taken such great effort."

Everyone nodded and a few whispered quiet thanks to Hawes.

Stan turned back to the Sheriff. "If there is anything we can do, please let us know. Feel free to stay with us as long as you want. You can see our homes are only these wagons, but you're welcome as long as you like. I know that God will provide and that, through prayer, our little girl will be returned to us some day. In fact, I think this would be a good time to offer up a prayer to our Lord. Would you do the honors, Brother Martin?"

Carl Martin stood and clasped his hands together. "Our Almighty Lord..." he began.

Anna opened one eye just enough to look at Sheriff Hawes and Sarah Wheeler. While everyone else had their eyes tightly closed, Sheriff Hawes had his head lowered but it was turned and he was looking directly at Sarah. At first Sarah remained still with her head bowed, listening to Brother Martin. Then, very slowly, she turned her head slightly and gently opened her eyes, staring back at the Sheriff. Even from this distance, Anna could see that Sarah was blushing again. Anna felt her heart skip a beat as a sensuous excitement filled her, watching the two adults in their secret flirt.

That night Anna couldn't sleep even though she was very tired because Lucy's coughing kept her from drifting off. Yet, when a time passed and Lucy didn't cough, Anna grew worried and began listening for the next cough. The hour was late, past midnight, and in the little tent, lit by a smoky lantern, Aunt Alice held and rocked Lucy while Gwen, Mary and Anna looked on. Lucy hadn't been conscious for hours. As Alice rocked her, she wiped Lucy's forehead with a damp cloth and hummed a little tune. For many minutes Lucy didn't cough, but then when she did, it was weak and feeble. The little girl still didn't open her eyes.

Alice slowly reached over and gently touched Mary's arm. "I think it's time. You'd better get Stan."

Anna knew what Aunt Alice meant and tears came rushing to her eyes as she placed a hand over her mouth to stop from crying out. Her mother wrapped her coat closer about her, pulled on her boots, and slipped out into the blankness and rain. Aunt Alice looked at both Gwen and Anna, tears filling her eyes. "You two be strong for me, now, won't you."

A soft moan came from Gwen as she threw her arms around Anna and began to sob.

Minutes passed. Lucy's coughing grew weaker and less frequent. Finally, the tent flap opened and Uncle Stan poked his head in. "Anna, you take Gwen outside. We're going to bless Lucy and need the room."

Anna helped Gwen on with her boots and then pulled on her own boots. Because of the cold night air they were wearing their coats, even in the tent. Taking Gwen by the hand, Anna left the tent and stood up in the blackness and rain. Uncle Stan held a lantern, and beside him were Brother Martin, Brother Taylor and, to Anna's surprise, Apostle Willard Richards. Suddenly, she felt very proud of her uncle, for in the middle of the night he had gone to an Apostle's tent, awakened him and asked him to bless Lucy. Anna was proud of Uncle Stan and she was also proud of Apostle Richards for coming. She and Gwen stepped away from the tent so the men could enter.

Once the men were inside, Anna, Gwen and Mary could easily see from the shadows cast on the tent by the lantern that the men shifted around to make a circle, placing Lucy in the center as Aunt Alice sat at the back of the tent and watched. Anna felt a presence in the dark and turned to see Jason, Michael and Jack Jr. standing beside her.

"Is that right?" It was Uncle Stan's voice.

"Yes," responded Apostle Richards. "Now place you hands on mine."

Even though the shadows from inside the tent were indistinct, Anna could picture what was happening. Brother Richards had placed both hands on Lucy's head and the other men placed their hands on his. Anna knew because she had been blessed when she was confirmed a member of the Church and had seen hundreds of other blessings. All the men of the Church held the sacred Priesthood, so all four of the men inside the tent held the power to heal her cousin.

Apostle Richards started the blessing. "Our Heavenly Father, we are gathered here to bless this child…"

Anna listened to the words and felt the power of the Priesthood flow from inside the tent to the outside and over those standing in the dark. If any power on earth could save Lucy, this was it. But Anna knew it didn't always work, because sometimes God wanted a person to die and join Him in heaven. Would God let Lucy be saved or would He take her?

For many minutes Brother Richards continued his blessing, and no other sound came from the tent. When it was over the men began moving around and, one by one, they whispered to Aunt Alice. The first out of the tent was Uncle Stan, crying quietly. Taking Gwen in his arms he hugged her. "Lucy's gone, Gwen. She's with God in heaven."

Brother Martin stood next to Anna, his strength and warmth drawing her as she slipped into his arms. He held her tight. "Your cousin has gone to meet God and Jesus Christ."

"Yes, I know," whispered Anna through her tears.

On to Pappan Ferry

"Your hurt will go, Anna, and it will turn into joy for you know God's Spirit is here with us on earth. We have the Priesthood and that is God's power." In that last instant, Anna felt that Brother Martin was holding her just a little too tightly. She gently pushed away. At first, he resisted, then let go. In the dark, she found the comforting arms of Michael and was safe again.

Lucy was wrapped in a clean, white sheet and, in the early morning light, Jason and Michael dug a grave on a hillside, overlooking the trail. Another grave digger had already been busy, and a second hole, next to Lucy's, waited for its occupant.

The rain stopped as gray clouds raced across the bleak sky, and the families of Brother Lissman's Company gathered on the hillside to say goodbye to the two fallen Saints. The services were subdued, and when they were over the families returned to their wagons to prepare for another day on the trail. Anna was dog-tired, but she was resigned to walking all day beside the wagon. As she made her way down the hill with Gwen, she caught sight of her mother helping Aunt Alice back to camp. Anna was startled by her Aunt's deep furrows and sunken, dark eyes. She seemed to have aged many years during the last twenty-four hours. Then Anna remembered how her mother had aged when her father had died and Lisa was lost. Was that what age was? Was it watching loved ones die? Could she postpone aging by hiding from death? Anna felt older, too, and it was a sadness she carried inside that gave her that feeling of age.

She began thinking of Brother Martin and his holding her tightly the night before. Was it her imagination that it had been something more than simple comfort? Brother Martin was at least forty and married. Had she only imagined that his comforting was covering something else? It had seemed so then, but now, she wasn't sure. Maybe she was seeing things that weren't there; like Cory thinking Brother Wheeler had proposed. Yet, she felt her instinct was right about Brother Martin. Should she tell Gwen her suspicions? No, not yet. Gwen would surely tell Cory and soon it would be all over camp that Brother Martin had flirted with Anna. Better to keep it to herself for now.

CHAPTER 9

Brigham's Sermon

Anna shielded her eyes as she glanced at the bright March morning sun. Spring had officially come and, for once, the sun was shining and no clouds threatened in the western sky. Maybe they could dry their clothes and wash up before the mud and rain came back. She bent down and picked up another small branch and placed it in the fold of her dress. Today was Sunday so The Company would stay in camp and hold a church service. Everyone was supposed to rest today, but Anna knew her mother planned on doing a big wash as long as the sun was shining; that's why Anna had been sent out for more wood after breakfast.

Brother Lissman's Company had left Nauvoo three weeks before, yet, to Anna, it seemed they had been on the trail between the Mississippi and Missouri Rivers for years. Her Uncle Stan complained that they had covered only ninety-five miles in all that time and at this rate would never get to Zion. Yet their Company wasn't alone, for everywhere they went along the trail other companies or parts of companies were camped or even preparing temporary towns. She had seen Mormons planting spring wheat, building barns, and fencing pastures for those parties that would come later. One such town was Garden Grove, halfway between Nauvoo and the Missouri River. Anna hoped that when they reached Garden Grove they would be allowed to rest a few weeks. Living out of a tent was hard and, after the first excitement wore off, it became boring.

She bent over to pick up another stick, but stopped when she heard a rattling noise. Slowly straightening up, she looked about. She knew the sound—a rattlesnake! Carefully, she stepped backward and the rattling stopped. Anna quickly turned and hurried back toward the camp. That had been the first rattlesnake she had encountered, or at least heard, and it was frightening. Joey Taylor told her that an old man, an Iowa man, had told him that each spring the rattlesnakes come out by the hundreds! Anna thought Joey might be making it up, but now she wasn't sure. Was this warm weather going to bring many more snakes out?

When Anna reached camp she dumped her load of twigs and sticks on a large pile of kindling next to the fire pit. Gwen was waiting for her. "Anna! We've got to get ready for meetin'. You don't know who's here!"

"Who?"

"Brother Brigham! Brigham Young rode into camp! He's going to be at meetin'."

Anna suddenly became infected with the same excitement as her cousin. "You mean he's here from Garden Grove?"

"Yes!" said Gwen. "He's moving down the trail on the way back to Sugar Creek and he's only going to be here today."

Anna followed her cousin to their tent. "We'd better hurry and dress. You're not ready either!"

"Yes, but I know what I'm wearing. I'll be ready in a jiffy." Gwen started removing her coat and then her dress. "Everyone is going to be there. He even has some of the other Apostles with him. I hope Brother Lissman doesn't take up all the time with one of his boring sermons."

"Me too," replied Anna. Brigham Young was the head of the Quorum of Twelve Apostles and everyone believed he would soon be made President of the Church and take the place of Joseph Smith, their martyred leader. Anna had felt the special strength and power of the Priesthood radiating

Brigham's Sermon

from Church Apostles before, and she knew the feeling would be even more splendid with Brother Brigham. She had seen him speak on several occasions in Nauvoo, but that was before the death of Joseph Smith.

Anna's mother put her head in the tent. "What is taking you girls so long? Don't ya know Apostle Brigham Young is here? When you're ready, I'll come in and we'll do some last minute fix-up. But hurry, now, the meeting is just about to start and you don't want to be late."

The church meeting was held on a grassy hill overlooking the Chariton River. Brigham Young and the other Apostles and company captains sat on the crest of the hill while Mormon families from three different companies gathered on the side of the hill. With hundreds of people present, Anna decided it was the largest gathering she had seen since Sugar Creek. A gentle wind blew as the noon sun beat down and gave a festive mood to the services. The Sinclairs all sat together on the soft grass and waited for the meeting to begin.

Anna studied Brother Brigham's face. He was stocky and powerfully built with a full head of golden hair and piercing blue-gray eyes. His face was full and friendly, yet not as handsome as Joseph Smith's chiseled face and stunningly handsome profile. Brother Lissman sat at Brigham's left, and next to Lissman were Apostles Parley P. Pratt, Willard Richards, George Q. Cannon, Brother Martin, Brother Wheeler and several other company captains or sub-captains.

Brother Wheeler gave the opening prayer and then sat down after introducing the Apostles. A hush fell over the crowd as Brigham Young stood to address the gathering. "My brothers and sisters," he began, his voice full and pungent. "We are embarked on a great mission in the Lord's name. Like Moses and the children of Israel, we are cast into the wilderness to find a new Zion and to establish the Lord's true Church here on earth. I want you all to take a moment to think about this. Think what this means! We, the Latter-Day-Saints, hold the sacred Keys to the Lord's Priesthood. No one, and I tell you again, no one else carries the authority of God's power here on earth. We are God's chosen people. We are the people God has picked to hold His Priesthood and administer in His name."

"What does that mean for you as an individual in His family? That's right! Each and every one of you, as Latter-Day-Saints, are members in Jesus Christ's own family! It means that the Priesthood and God's authority are in your hands. For God's Church to survive here on this earth, you must carry it forward to the new Zion. If we fail, the Keys will be lost for another thousand years! As we depend on God, He depends on us. Each of you men personally hold the Priesthood. In you, in your hearts and hands, is the power to do works in God's name. This power resides with no one else! It is yours and it is what it means to be chosen by God. For you wives and daughters, your salvation is locked up in your men, your husbands and your fathers. As you are bound to them, they will open the doors to heaven and you will enter, through them."

Anna felt the breath being sucked from her breast. His words electrified her as they seemed to fly from his mouth straight to her bosom. Not a soul in the congregation stirred, but all sat and gathered in each word he spoke.

"Now we have enemies!" Brigham Young continued. "Satan has gathered his forces to stop us and to deny God's Church from being established on the American Continent. If Satan has his way he will unleash wickedness and evil which will cover the land and tie the hands of God's people. We cannot let this happen. Yet our enemies are everywhere. They are the mobbers of Illinois who killed Joseph and other Saints and robbed and forced us from our holy city of Nauvoo. They are the Missourians who attacked us in that state. They are the apostates who now would leave the Church and turn against God and fight on Satan's side. Besides all these enemies, there are more, for Satan has unleashed devils from his underworld to attack our spirits. We must cast these spirits out of our hearts as we cast the physical enemies out of our camps."

"The trail ahead will be hard. God will call on us to make many sacrifices and if we are to be deserving of the Priesthood, if we are to be deserving of working in God's name, with God's power, we must make these sacrifices. I am ready! God has filled my heart with love. Our beloved prophet, Joseph, turned my eyes from wickedness and toward God and now my heart is full of God's love. I will never turn back! All that go forward with me will go to God's glory here on earth, to the new Zion which will be a place of peace and holiness. I give you my testimony. I know in my heart the Church is true. I know in my heart that Joseph was the true prophet and that he walked and talked with our Lord Jesus Christ and with God. I know the Priesthood that I hold in my hands is from God and I will use it in God's name." Brother Brigham stopped and looked over the crowd. Holding out his hands he asked the Saints, "Let me hear what is in your hearts, let me hear your testimony." And he sat down.

Anna felt her body filled to overflowing with Christ's love and she knew that Jesus had come to them while Brigham talked and touched each of their hearts until the very air was saturated with God's holiness. She began crying. She knew with a rock certainty of the truth of Brother Brigham's words. Someone stood near her and Anna turned to see that Uncle Stan was on his feet, tears flowing from his eyes.

"I have the Priesthood," he sobbed. "My heart is full of God's love and I know the truth of the Church. I am not an educated man, I've not read many books or gone to great universities. Yet, I can see with my eyes and my heart and I know Joseph was my prophet and that the Lord wants me to go to the wilderness and build his Church in Zion."

Stan sat down and Anna was filled with joy and pride in her uncle. Now, as she looked about her, it seemed that everyone was crying. Another man stood and gave his testimony and then another and then a woman stood. The offering of testimony continued all afternoon and their hearts were made strong again in that special knowledge that they were God's personal servants, that they walked the earth in His name and that they held His power in their grasp. The world was theirs to save and a thousand times a thousand armies of Satan's demons could not sway them from their true course.

Early the next morning, the sun was not yet up when Anna went to gather her wood. Off to her left Cory and Gwen collected their supply of kindling. She preferred working beside them, but if all three girls gathered wood together, they couldn't find it fast enough, so Anna usually wandered off alone to collect hers. Even though the morning was chilly, Anna could tell from the pre-dawn sky that the day was going to be hot. The heat would bring out the flies, and the dust would swirl up to cover everything, but she didn't care. Anything was better than the rain and the wet and the mud. She was so tired of mud!

Suddenly the air was filled with a terrible scream, and Anna recognized at once that it came from Cory Tobbs. Anna dropped her wood and began running toward her two friends. Cory screamed again, that high-pitched scream that signals great hurt or fear or both. When Anna arrived, Cory was sitting down, screaming, while Gwen was standing and screaming, holding both hands against her cheeks. They were both staring at a large rattlesnake coiled a few feet from Cory. Cory held her leg, and Anna saw small rivulets of blood coming out from between her fingers.

Neither Cory nor Gwen appeared ready to do anything but stare at the snake and continue their screaming. The rattlesnake was shaking and rattling and preparing to strike again. Anna quickly looked about and, finding a large round boulder, picked it up and without hesitating threw it on top of the snake. At once Gwen found her tongue. "Anna! Anna! Kill it! Kill it!"

Anna selected a long stick from the wood that Gwen had dropped on the ground and, carefully walking to where the snake was withering under the boulder, she began beating that part of the snake that still showed. She continued beating until the snake stopped moving.

"You got it!" yelled Gwen.

Cory stopped screaming long enough to move her right hand and look at her wound. "It got me! It bit me!"

Already people from the camp were running up to see what had happened. Gwen pointed first to Cory. "Cory was bit by a rattlesnake." Then she turned to Anna, "and Anna killed it. Look! See the snake under the rock!"

Cory began crying. "I'm going to die. Rattlesnakes are poisonous! I'm going to die!"

Two men gently picked up Cory and carried her back to her wagon where she was carefully laid down on a bed made of blankets. Brother Tobbs appeared and rolled down Cory's white stocking to get a better look at the bite while Cory's mother held her daughter in her arms. Dozens of people stood around and tried to get a glimpse into the back of the wagon. Gwen told each newcomer what had happened. "Cory and I was gathering wood and this big rattlesnake just jumped up and bit Cory on the leg. Anna killed it with a rock."

Cory's pa squeezed the two puncture holes, forcing blood out, but seemed unsure what to do next. Suddenly, Brother Martin was standing at his side. "Here, John, let me see," he said. For a moment he looked at the wound and then, without speaking a word, he withdrew a hunting knife, made cuts across each puncture, bent down and began sucking out a mixture of poison and blood. After spitting out the blood, he instructed Cory's mother on how to properly bandage the wound.

"Will she be all right?" asked Cory's pa.

Brigham's Sermon

Brother Martin stroked Cory's bright red hair and smiled down on her tear-stained face. "I think so. Rattlesnakes ain't always fatal and I think I got most of the poison out. But just to be on the safe side, send for Apostle Richards. He's up ahead in the Cliffard Company. We'll give Cory a blessing."

"God bless you," exclaimed Cory's ma. "You saved my girl!"

Brother Martin turned and spotted Anna and, moving through the crowd, he stood before her. "Is that right? Did you kill that snake?"

Anna felt uncomfortable with everyone looking at her. "Yes."

"Well, I'll be! That was very brave. You're no longer a little girl, are you; you're a young woman." He put his hand on her shoulder. "God has need of young women like you, Anna."

She was too embarrassed to speak so she just nodded. Sister Taylor put an arm around Anna. "You are a brave girl, Anna. We're all very proud of you."

Brother Martin turned and walked away and the crowd turned back toward the wagon to see how Cory was doing.

Anna hurried back to her wagon to tell the news to her mother, but when she got there, she completely forgot the news because her Aunt Alice and Uncle Stan were having an argument. He had loaded a one-hundred pound sack of flour on his horse and tied it down. Her Aunt held a second flour sack that contained only a few pounds of flour. "Look at this, Stan! Just look at it!" she said, holding the sack up for him to see. "Now you tell me we can spare more flour!"

Uncle Stan rocked the first sack back and forth to make sure it was going to stay on the saddle. "I tell ya, honey, we do what we have to. Now we're getting credit for this."

"Credit! How we going to feed these growing kids with credit? You already gave half our flour away and now you're giving away another hundred pounds."

"We only gave four hundred pounds—not half!"

"But you're giving another hundred now. When will it end? Will they want another hundred tomorrow?"

The softness left Uncle Stan's face and his eyes narrowed. "I've listened to your objections and now it's done. Saints are out here on the trail with nothing and we can't let them starve. We'll help out now and if we get in a bind, someone will help us."

Alice placed her fists on her hips. "Sure, we give now because we have it to give. What happens when we run out and no one has any to share with us? What then, Stan? Do we eat sagebrush?"

"God will provide."

Alice tightly clenched her fists and turned her back on her husband to faced Anna. "Damn him!" she cussed in a half whisper to Anna. "He'll give everything away before we get there, if we do get there." Confusion suddenly showed in Alice's eyes. "Anna! Where's the kindling? Where's Gwen?"

"Oh, Aunt Alice, you won't believe it! Cory got bit by a rattlesnake!"

Rattlesnakes and arguments aside, at nine that morning, the trumpet sounded and the wagons moved out onto the trail. Cory continued riding in the back of her wagon, much too sick to walk. Gwen told everyone who would listen how Anna killed the snake until, finally, Anna was embarrassed about it. "But, Anna," said Gwen, "you should be proud. I was too scared and Cory was dying on the ground. You saved her life. You saved me!"

"But that snake wasn't going to bite you."

"It was, it was going to bite Cory again and then me. I could see it in its eyes. Brother Martin said you are a hero." Gwen blushed and smiled. "Brother Martin is sweet on ya. Can't you tell?"

"He's as old as your pa!"

Gwen's lips pouted. "Just cause you're old don't mean ya can't be sweet on someone. And I say Brother Martin is sweet on you."

Anna knew Gwen was right, but she didn't want to say it out loud because she didn't want it to become a topic of conversation around the camp. Brother Martin still made her nervous, yet she admired the way he had handled the snake bite. No wonder he was the captain of their ten families.

Late in the afternoon the company pulled into their night camp and drove their wagons into a circle. Anna looked up at the sky to see fast moving clouds rushing in from the west. A breeze blew, occasionally gusting and causing the wagon tops to flap. They were still miles from Garden Grove.

Later that night, as Anna, Gwen and their mothers lay in their tent, they listened to the wind whistling past the wagons and angrily flapping the wagon tops against ropes and wagon sides. Abruptly, the wind stopped, and they held their breaths waiting for what would happen.

Then, without warning, the rain began falling, beating against the tent. The wind picked up again and the rain beat harder against the tent's canvas.

"Anna?" asked her mother. "Did you and Gwen tie the tent down good, like I said?"

"Yes, ma."

"I hope so," replied Aunt Alice.

Anna snuggled closer to her cousin and whispered. "Did you tie your side good?"

Gwen giggled. "Of course I did. It's holding, isn't it?"

The storm was too intense for anyone to sleep and too noisy for them to comfortably talk, so they lay awake and listened to nature's wrath. Just when they believed the wind might be lessening, a new gust whipped the tent and let them know the storm was still building. Very late, the tent flap opened and Uncle Stan poked his head in. "Alice?"

"Yes, Stan?"

"Some of the cattle and oxen broke loose. The boys and me are going after 'em."

"All right, Stan. You want us to do anything?"

"No, go back to sleep," and his head disappeared.

Anna and Gwen giggled. "Back to sleep!" exclaimed Gwen. "They must think we're in a luxury hotel!"

Another gust rocked the tent. "Alice," said Anna's mother, "do ya hear that wagon top flapping. Ya think it's going to tear?"

"No," said Alice. "I think it's..." without warning, a gust of wind hit the tent and tore the canvas cover away, leaving the women lying in the open, rain falling on their bedding and faces.

"Oh, sweet Jesus!" cussed Aunt Alice. "This is all we need!" Mary began laughing. "What's so funny?" demanded Alice.

Anna's mother laughed harder and soon Alice and the two girls joined in. Finally, Alice sat up. "Well, we can't sit here and have all this fun all night. We have to get the tent back up."

Mary nudged Anna and Gwen. "Come on, we've got to fix the wagons or the wind's going to tear the tops off. We'll take them down." Everyone hurried to get boots and coats on. Outside, they discovered that the tent used by the Sinclair men had blown down, the canvas twisted around a wagon wheel.

Even though the wagons were only a few feet from where their tents had been, the blackness forced them to feel their way. Anna's hands grew cold while the wind and rain stung her face whenever she turned it toward the west. She struggled with the others to untie the ropes restraining the wagon top, but her fingers soon became numb. Finally, after the torrents of rain had thoroughly soaked her, the wagon top was down and out of danger. Finished with one Sinclair wagon they had to feel their way to the second wagon and remove its top.

Anna's mother found her and put an arm around her. "We're going to pull the tent canvas over the supplies in the wagons to keep out the rain." Mary had to yell so Anna could hear; the wind was blowing even harder.

The wagon top had been easy compared to using the tent as a cover. The women pulled the wet canvas over the boxes and sacks of supplies only to have the wind whip it off again. Whenever Anna got the chance, she put her fingers under her armpits or blew on them to get the feeling back so they would obey her commands. After much struggle, they achieved their goal and had the tents snugly tied down over their belongings in both wagons.

Retreating to the leeward side of Uncle Stan's wagon, they huddled together and tried to take shelter from the storm. Alice yelled to be heard. "We can't stand here! Let's drape a wagon top around the bottom of this wagon and get underneath." Once again they went out into the rain and struggled with the heavy canvas to construct a temporary shelter.

Using both tops they managed to enclose three sides of Uncle Stan's wagon. Hurrying for cover, the four of them crawled under the wagon and Mary lit a lantern, which flickered with every gust. Each of them looked at the others. Wet hair hung down over dripping faces; clothes clung to shivering bodies.

Mary smiled. Alice looked at her sister-in-law and laughed. Soon all four of them were laughing and pointing at each other. Anna couldn't remember when she had felt so miserable and had had such a good time. Uncle Stan poked his head under the wagon. "My God in Heaven, what is going on here?" He made no effort to hide his anger. "We've been out in this God-awful storm all night, chasing animals to hell and back and here you sit, warm and cozy and laughing!"

The four women sat absolutely still, stunned at Stan's harsh words. Finally, Aunt Alice reached down, picked up a wet dirt-clod and threw it at her husband. The clod hit Stan in one eye and exploded into a gooey black mess which slithered down his already wet face. Stan's one open eye told them his anger had been rudely replaced with astonishment.

Alice put both hands before her open mouth and tried to control herself, but for the others it was hopeless. Anna wrapped her arms around her stomach and fell over, convulsing in laughter. Peals of laughter gushed forth from under the wagon as all four of them screamed in hilarity. Anna laughed until tears streamed down her cheeks and her sides throbbed in pain. Then, as they tried to stop and see where Stan had gone, they looked at each other and laughed again.

* * *

Captain Randall Earnst's train was composed of fourteen wagons and one hundred and fifty-five cattle and oxen. The wagons carried the possessions of eleven eastern Missouri families, all hoping to make a new start in Oregon Territory. Captain Earnst's family occupied the lead wagon, driven by his oldest son, Theodore. The guide, Jacob Hunt, generally rode ahead of the wagons, scouting the trail; however, he had little true scouting to do since the trail was well marked in this part of the prairie. For several years, pioneer wagons had traveled the Oregon Trail, and in many places pairs of wagon tracks could be clearly seen on the soft ground.

Behind the wagons came the cattle herd where Wes was assigned pick-up requiring that he ride at the very end of the herd and catch any cow or oxen which tried to wander off. Since he was the last along the trail, he was held responsible for missing cattle in addition to the unpleasantness of eating the worst of the dust kicked up by the wagons and livestock. Four wranglers, including Wes, drove the cattle: Wes at pick-up, a wrangler on each wing, and the head wrangler, Jerry Flint. Flint, a tall blond youth of nineteen, was Captain Earnst's second cousin. Flint's job was to scout out water and feed, indicate just where to move the herd and supervise the other three wranglers. Both wing riders, young men Wes' age, were sons of families in the train. To add to Wes' discomfort, Captain

Earnst required him to stand frequent night watches while the other men of the wagon train stood watch only once every four or five days.

Jacob Hunt, Jerry Flint and Wes shared a common campfire since they didn't belong to one of the pioneer families. Wes, being the youngest of the three, was frequently sent to perform their chores and errands. To be bossed about on the farm by his brother, Bert, was one thing, but to be ordered about by these strangers was galling to Wes. Yet he made no complaint since he was new to the wagon train and wanted to be accepted.

After five days on the trail the wagon train crossed the Big Blue, moved west to the Little Blue and then trudged along its east bank toward the Platte River. Inquiries to Jacob Hunt regarding the distance remaining to the Platte Valley resulted in a grunt and a simple "not far" from the guide.

The night air was mild and the stars shone as Wes, Hunt and Flint sat about their fire. Flint kept looking at the western horizon since he still had to check on the herd's guards. He stirred the fire, causing sparks to shoot into the air. "I say we started too early." said Flint. "Ya don't see any other trains on the trail, do ya?"

Hunt gave a thin smile, but his brows came down over his eyes as he stared at Flint. "I advised the Captain to start early cause we don't want other trains to take all the grass. We're depending on these oxen and keeping them fit is important."

Flint stirred the fire again, but didn't look up at the guide as he spoke. "Grass! Ain't no real grass–just little outcroppings of new growth. Be another month before the real grass comes up. Besides, the fucking mud is so thick half the cattle bog down. You're out front, riding your little pony while Wes and me are at the back, trying to pull dumb beasts from the muck. Ain't that right, Wes?"

Wes glanced through half closed eyes at the head wrangler but said nothing. He didn't want to side with Flint and he wasn't going to say anything to help Hunt. Better to just keep his mouth shut.

The guide became agitated. "Now listen here, sonny! You ain't never been out on the prairie before and ya don't know what you're talking about. You're just a wild kid. Them wagon trains still in St. Louie will find the trail a bare and empty place by June or July when hundreds of wagons have passed and thousands of cattle have eaten everything in sight. We're in good shape and things are just going to get better for us."

Brigham's Sermon

Flint seemed bored with their argument so he turned again to Wes. "Where ya get that stallion? Ya must 'a stole him."

"I told you, Jerry, I get him from my brother."

"Ha! If I had a horse like him I wouldn't give him to no egg-sucking kid brother. Why don't ya trade with me for my roan? My horse is broke in and trained, your Jeff is still half wild. Needs the hands of a man to teach him who's boss."

"No thanks," said Wes.

"Leave the kid alone," butted in Hunt. "If anyone needs a fresh horse, it's me." Something about the tone of Hunt's remark made Wes' ears perk up.

Flint leaned up on one elbow. "You? Why you? You don't never go nowhere. I thought you was a scout; why don't ya do some scouting? You're always riding up in front of the Captain's wagon where the trail's already well marked. I swear, I don't know why we need a guide anyway."

Hunt laughed. "You wait, sonny-boy! Wait till them Sioux savages come riding down on ya. You'll want old Jacob Hunt then."

Wes couldn't resist taking a jab at the guide. "I thought Sloan said the Sioux weren't on the warpath just now."

Flint began laughing. "Hey, that's right. Ya get your Injuns mixed up, Hunt?"

The anger in Hunt's eyes flashed as he stared at Wes. "Don't you have early duty tonight?"

Wes shook his head. "Nope, second watch."

Flint jumped up and brushed off his pants. "Got to check on them Jim Crows. They'll lose half the herd if I don't get on 'em. Sam Walker fell asleep again last night, fell asleep right in his saddle and was snoring like a storm. Ya got to tell the Captain, Hunt. Tell him to get on Walker and Walker's son, too. The kid's no better than his pa. When they fall asleep, they's supposed to walk the next day, but them two never do."

"Why don't ya tell him yourself?"

"Cause he don't listen to me. You tell him or we'll have the whole herd wander off some night." Hunt only grunted. As Flint was leaving the campfire, he turned once more toward Wes. "Hey, let me ride your Jeff just for tonight. Then I'll let you ride my Red tomorrow."

"Nope," said Wes as lay back on his bedroll and closed his eyes.

"Ya leave that horse alone," yelled Hunt while Flint walked from the camp.

Wes tried to go to sleep, but the remark from Hunt stuck to him. What had Hunt really meant by saying he needed a fresh mount? The guide had eyed Jeff ever since Wes joined the wagon train. Wes didn't like the guide and didn't trust him, but Flint was no ally, either.

During the next day's dinner stop, Wes headed Jeff toward the Captain's wagon where he was to join the Captain's family for noon meal. As he drew close to the front of the column he spotted Hunt and Captain Earnst talking next to Hunt's small chestnut mare. Hunt was holding the horse's rear left hoof off the ground and pointing to it. As Wes drew closer he caught the drift of the conversation.

"Ya can see it's in poor shape. Look at the crack and swelling," said Hunt.

Captain Earnst glanced at the hoof and straightened up. "Yes, I can see it. You'll have to use that mare of Lloyd Hanson's. He's driving now and your horse needs to mend."

As Wes approached and dismounted, Hunt glanced at him and dropped his horse's hoof. Turning back to the Captain he began to whine. "But Captain, that mare has ringbone; she's wore out. I need a strong horse in case I get in a fix and have to get back to the train in a hurry. You can see that, can't ya?"

"Ringbone? I didn't know she had ringbone."

"On top of that she's fallen hipped."

"But not bad." replied the Captain. "Well, if ya can't use Hanson's horse, which one do ya want?"

Wes just stood before the two men and made no pretense he wasn't listening. Hunt glanced nervously at Wes and then back to the Captain. "Well, I'm not sure–let me think on it. It will probably be one of the wranglers' horses; they got extra."

"They need their horses, Hunt. Those boys are on horseback all day and they need fresh mounts."

"Well, let me think on it." The guide took his horse's reins and led the animal away.

Wes was alarmed for he knew Hunt was up to some plan to go for Jeff. He decided he'd better make plans, himself, in case Hunt tried some trick. He tied Jeff up and approached the Captain. "Sir," he began. "I need some provisions. I got this pistol, but it ain't no good without shot and powder."

The Captain looked at Wes and then at the pistol in Wes' belt. "You don't have any shot?"

"I got two balls left and powder for maybe two more, but what good will that be if the Injuns attack and I'm cornered back by the herd? I'll have two shots and then I'm done."

The Captain thought for a moment. "Yes, I see your point. What caliber?"

"Thirty-six."

"I'll make some shot tonight. Now you better get your dinner 'cause we'll be pulling out soon."

All afternoon, as Wes moved back and forth across the rear of the herd, pushing the reluctant cattle forward, he considered what Hunt's plan might be. The guide could ask Captain Earnst for permission to ride Jeff while his mare was on the mend, but Jeff didn't belong to the Captain, and Wes could simply refuse. Wes didn't warm up to Captain Randall Earnst, yet the wagon train's leader seemed to be a fair man.

That night Wes ate alone while both Hunt and Flint made excuses and disappeared. When he was finished, Theodore Earnst came for him. "My pa wants to see ya, Wes; he's at our campfire."

"Of course," thought Wes. "He's got my shot."

At the Earnst campfire the Captain, Theodore, Flint and Hunt sat about the fire with several other pioneers. As Wes walked up they silently watched him, and Wes' heart began to pound–something was wrong. Captain Earnst pointed to a log. "Sit down, Wes. We've got some talking to do."

Wes overcame the urge to touch his pistol for reassurance before sitting down. As the Captain continued the other men watched. "Now, Wes, we seem to have a problem here. The men of the Company have been complaining. I know I agreed to take you on to Oregon in exchange for your wrangling, but the plain truth is that most men have to pay for passage with a wagon train in addition to working. The others feel I've been unfair to allow you to come on without any payment."

Wes could see it now. "What about Flint? You're paying him."

The Captain shook his head. "Not really. What he gets is just for expenses and he's contributed three horses and a supply wagon."

Buffalo Man

This was the first Wes heard of Flint's extra horses and wagon. He glanced at the wrangler and saw Flint smile and nod his head. Wes cleared his throat. "But it wasn't my idea to join with ya, it was Sloan's."

"That's beside the point," responded Earnst. "We've still got the problem of the unfairness of you not paying and everyone else paying or contributing goods."

"What do ya want me to do?" asked Wes. "Ya want me to just leave the train?"

"No, of course not. We're smack-dab in the middle of the Great American Desert: nothing for miles in every direction but Indians and rattlesnakes. Now I've got a solution, if you'll just pay attention. You can sell your horse."

"I ain't selling Jeff," protested Wes.

"Now wait just a minute. The real thing is to get to Oregon. We get to Oregon and we'll all do well. You can have a herd of horses if that's what pleases you. But face it, Wes, you've got a good horse and we need a good horse for our guide, Mr. Hunt. His chestnut has gone lame."

"What if I just loaned Jeff until the chestnut were better?"

"That won't do. There's no telling when the chestnut will heal and, besides, there is still the problem of your contribution. Now, I say you sell your horse to Hunt for a small amount; say ten dollars. The horse is worth more, but the difference is your contribution to the wagon train. That way, everyone will know it's fair and you'll end up with ten dollars."

"What horse will I have?"

"Well, you can use one of the extra wrangling horses until we get to Oregon."

"What if I say no?"

Captain Earnst shook his head. "I don't see any other way, now—do you? If you see another way then tell me. We can't just let you wander off alone out here; that would be criminal. After all, you're still just a boy and we're responsible for you. You have nothing else besides your horse to give."

"How about a marker?"

For just a moment, Earnst glanced at Hunt, but then quickly turned back to Wes. "You know no one takes markers on the trail, and besides, you're too young to sign a marker."

Brigham's Sermon

That was the last straw, for Wes was convinced he was being bamboozled. All this talk about not taking markers and him being too young to sign was just bull. But, as he slowly looked around the campfire, he knew he had to think of something fast. Each man was sitting and watching him, and Wes realized he wasn't meant to leave the Earnst's campfire in possession of Jeff. "All right!" he said. "I'll do it, but Hunt has got to promise that I can buy Jeff back in Oregon for...for fifty dollars."

Hunt nodded and smiled. "Ya got a deal. Fifty dollars when we reach Oregon."

Captain Earnst let out a sigh and leaned back as the tension of the previous minutes dissipated. "I'm glad that's all settled. Hunt, you take the stallion and Wes, you choose the horse you want to use out of the wrangling stock. Welcome aboard, Wes, you're a full-fledged member of Captain Randall Earnst's Pioneer Company." The older man held out his hand. Wes took it and looked the Captain in the eyes.

"What about the shot and powder and what about the ten dollars?"

Earnst stood up. "I almost forgot. Hunt, give the boy the ten. Theo, get Wes that shot and powder out of our wagon." The guide approached Wes cautiously and handed him a ten dollar gold coin. Wes looked at it in the dim campfire light and then put it in his pocket, thinking he must find a good hiding place for it later. Theodore returned and handed Wes a small cloth bag of shot and a buffalo horn filled with powder. Wes smiled and nodded. "Thank you, Hunt and thank you, Theodore. Well, guess I'll get some sleep, I got second watch." Turning, he slowly walked back to his own fire.

As Wes prepared his bed, the ball of anger inside just churned around. He hadn't dared to show his true feelings at the Captain's camp and he didn't dare show them now. Yet, he had an almost uncontrollable urge to seek Hunt out and smash him in the face. Instead, he went to the nearby creek and took a long, long drink.

* * *

Gunner sat in McNaughton's rum hole and stared across the table at Cyrus Maggio, contemplating how his friend was getting uglier each day and how he was tiring of Maggio's company. Besides, Maggio never seemed to have any money, so what use was he as a friend?

Mary's boy, Jake, came to the table with another bottle. He put it down and, searching through the coins laying on the table, selected the correct change and left. Gunner didn't bother to count what Jake took because he knew Jake was just about the only honest one in the tavern. Jake was honest or dumb, but to Gunner it was the same thing. If the boy wasn't clever enough to pocket an extra coin when he could, then he was just plain stupid.

Gunner laid his head on his arm and stared at the money left. When it was gone, he would be broke. There wasn't much there, certainly not enough to get through tomorrow. Better to use it to get drunk today. He looked again at Maggio who gently snored, his forehead resting on his arm. Maggio hadn't shaved for a week and then Gunner felt his own beard, realizing he couldn't look any better than his friend. Gunner smelled the heavy odor of decaying animals and plants—a permanent fixture to those who drank and gambled in taverns along the river bottoms. It was land no one wanted so you just put up a shack or tied up a houseboat and opened business. No one asked for a title; no one cared. Just have whiskey available and a girl or two and maybe some gambling, and everyone would bring money. Gunner wished he owned a rumhole. He could sit and drink all day and when the mood came to him he could have a woman. That would be the life!

A scraping sound told Gunner someone had just entered the tavern, and he lifted his head, squinting through the half darkness of twilight. The newcomer was a man he didn't recognize dressed in clean clothes and wearing an expensive revolver on his side—certainly not the usual patron for here. The man stepped to the bar and ordered a whiskey. Young Jake poured half a glass from a bottle and took the coin offered. The newcomer tipped the glass to his mouth and took a drink, his nose wrinkling up as he swallowed. "God, that's awful!"

Gunner smiled to himself. Of course it was awful; the McNaughtons watered down most of their whiskey.

"What's in that?" demanded the stranger.

Jake barely turned enough to face the man. "Whiskey."

"Well, it don't taste like whiskey. A man stops to refresh himself with a drink and this is what's forced on him?"

Brigham's Sermon

Gunner stood and walked to the bar. "Jake," he ordered, "get that crock up here, that brown one from under the bar." As the boy bent to fetch the crock, Gunner turned to the man beside him. "Good day, sir. My name is Gunner Hamlin. Let me get you a decent drink."

The stranger held out his hand. "I'm Edwin Bottiggi, in from Springfield with a load of dry goods."

Jake put the jug on the bar. Gunner emptied Bottiggi's glass on the floor and filled it again from the jug, the liquid carrying a considerably darker color. "Now you try this, Edwin. It's all the way from St. Louie and I know for a fact that no one has messed with it. You just try it."

Bottiggi took a healthy drink. "Say," he said, a smile on his face, "that's fine liquor. Smooth!"

"Jake, put that on my bill. Edwin, what brings you to these parts?"

"As I was saying, I've got goods from Springfield. I might move across the River and sell to those Mormons or maybe move down river and catch some of those leaving for Oregon. Got linen, wool, pots and pans, leather goods. You know, Mr. Hamlin, there is a great deal of money to be made with the Oregon Territory opening up. But I'm rude! You're not drinking. Let me buy you one."

Gunner held up his hand. "No thanks, Edwin. I only have one drink a day and I've already had mine."

"Oh, but I insist. You can't make me stand here and drink alone. Barkeeper, pour one for my friend, Mr. Hamlin, here."

"Just one, then. But, please, call me Gunner. That's what my friends call me. Now you say you're going to sell to them Mormonites across the River? That's a sharp idea, Edwin. It's a thought I've often had. You know we run them out of Nauvoo, don't ya."

"Yes, I'd heard they're giving up the city–that thousands have left already."

"That's correct. They was going to take over the government of Illinois with a secret plan, and we discovered it just in time. We been battling them Mormonites for years. Those blood suckers would sneak out at night and burn our farms. They would kill innocent women and children by driving a stake through their hearts. I seen it myself."

Bottiggi took another drink. "Yes, I've heard some terrible stories. But now they're going we must get back to business. Right?"

"Oh, yes. I, myself, am considering taking a herd of a hundred horses across the River to sell to the Mormons. But it don't look good. I got the horses, but can't raise the ferry fee. Shame to let all that profit go!"

"Oh, don't talk that way. You have to keep trying. Get those horses over and get them sold. Why don't ya just go to Nauvoo and sell them there?"

"Oh, no! Little profit in that. The real profit is having them horses across in Iowa. You're a businessman, you understand profit. But that damn ferry fee has me stumped."

"Surely, someone here-abouts will stake you to the ferry fee."

"Yes, in normal times a dozen men would gladly step forward to loan Old Gunner the money. But not now for no one here has money. We lost it all fighting them Mormons. Most of us are out of work or burned out–money gone on uniforms and powder. Now, you, Edwin, you're a businessman. You know the kind of profit to be made. For a small loan of...say, fifty dollars, I could get some of them horses across the River and sold. I could pay you back in a single day with a handsome profit."

Bottiggi took a half-step back. "You mean you want me to loan you the money?"

"It would be a business deal. You're a businessman."

"Oh, but I can't. I'm new here, I don't even know you. I'm sure you're a fine person but one does not loan money to a complete stranger."

"Complete stranger? Ya come in here and complain about our whiskey and I buy ya a drink. I didn't have to, ya know. But, I buy ya a drink and tell ya all about myself and ya call me a complete stranger. That's not nice." Gunner wanted to put his hand on his revolver but didn't dare; Bottiggi carried a gun of his own.

"I'm sorry, I can't loan you money. I'll buy you another drink, but a loan is out of the question."

Gunner slammed down his glass, spilling some of the contents. "You've insulted me, mister. You've insulted me and I ain't drinking with ya no more. I'm going where I got real friends." Gunner walked from the tavern without glancing at Jake or his friend, Maggio, who was now awake, watching the scene at the bar.

Outside, Gunner could see it was almost dark. Good, it would be just perfect for what he planned. Bottiggi must have come down from the high road, so he would have come on the left trail. Gunner hurried along the trail until he came to a large tree. He climbed the tree and wiggled out on a limb that put him directly over the path. Nothing to do now but wait. He drew out his gun and cocked it. But that wouldn't do, he couldn't shoot Bottiggi. When the businessman didn't show up, the sheriff would be nosing around and would learn that Gunner had left before Bottiggi and then there was a gun shot. He holstered his gun and drew out his knife. Bottiggi wasn't very big: one hundred and fifty-five or sixty. Gunner was one-hundred and ninety pounds. He wouldn't have any trouble. He didn't have long to wait. Soon the sound of a horse plodding along reached his ears. He tensed up as the form of a horse and rider came up the trail. When the rider was directly under Gunner, Gunner slipped off the limb and fell on the horseman, dragging him to the ground.

Bottiggi struggled, but Gunner had the knife in him several times before the man could get away. Gunner dragged the merchant into the bushes to die while he went through his pockets. Finding Bottiggi's purse, Gunner emptied it in his own pocket. Then Gunner dragged the body down to the River and pushed it in. The horse was another problem, but Gunner tied a branch to its tail and gave it a slap. The horse would run for some distance. Gunner knew he couldn't count the money in the dark, but he realized, from the wad of paper and the weight of coins, that he must have several hundred dollars and maybe more.

What a fool Bottiggi had been! To come into a place like McNaughton's and brag about being a merchant! Oh, well, there were plenty of fools around to keep a man with real guts in whiskey. Gunner decided not to return to the tavern. Better to spend some time somewhere else, somewhere farther down the River. Besides, he was getting tired of Maggio's face.

CHAPTER 10

Fight at a Rumhole

Wes opened his eyes and the blackness of the camp told him it was still several hours before sunup. He twisted and looked across the cold fire pit where Hunt was rolled up in his blankets, snoring lightly. Wes quietly pulled on his boots and coat, rolled up his blanket and tarpaulin, and slipped from camp. A cold wind blew from the west, and black clouds obscured the moon and stars. He was grateful for the darkness.

Wes found his horse picketed next to Hunt's chestnut mare. Jeff recognized his master and only nodded his head, but the mare whinnied. Wes quickly put a hand on the mare's nose and gently stroked her breast and throat. "Shhh, girl," he whispered. She shivered and, shifting her weight, calmed down. Wes gave her one more pat before turning back to saddle Jeff. Finished, Wes walked Jeff from the camp and away from the wagon train. Making a large half-circle, he avoided the herd and their night wranglers to arrive on the trail far south of the pioneer company. There, he mounted Jeff and began galloping down the trail. He wasn't sure where he was going, but he knew he had to get far away from Captain Earnst's Pioneer Company as fast as possible.

Wes urged Jeff on, giving the horse his head, knowing Jeff would pick out his own path in the darkness. For over an hour they moved down the road before the eastern horizon began turning a dirty gray. Wes pulled off the trail and stopped in a stand of young oak. Jeff needed a short rest and Wes had to decide what he was going to do now.

He couldn't go back to Earnst's wagon train. Not certain what they would do if they caught him, he was sure they would send someone looking for him, probably Flint or Hunt; they would come after him for Jeff if for no other reason. Yet, neither man could be spared from the wagon train too long, so all Wes had to do was to keep going–keep out of their reach. He still felt anger from their attempt to cheat him out of his horse. No one was taking Jeff from him.

He considered different places to go. South on the Oregon Trail would take him back to civilization, but Earnst might send word down the line to watch for a run-away. If he continued north, up the trail, the company would always be behind him, pressing him; north was no good. West was out of the question, too; it was all wilderness and Indians. It would have to be east, toward the Missouri. Once on the Big Muddy, he could decide what to do, and the River would reconnect him to a road and put him closer to civilization.

He patted Jeff on the neck. "Come on, boy, we got to make tracks." He gave his horse a gentle nudge with his heels and pointed him toward the light in the sky. Away from the trail, they entered an open, brush-covered prairie. In the dim light, Wes didn't dare hurry Jeff for fear of groundhog and badger holes and their progress slowed.

The eastern sky grew light enough for Wes to see the details of the terrain. The plain he was on was broken by occasional shallow gullies, some containing small stands of trees. The deeper ravines hid streams, a result of the previous weeks of rain. Wes occasionally touched his gun to reassure himself it was still there. He and Crocker had seen Indians on the prairie and he could well run into more on the way to the Missouri.

Fight at a Rumhole

Carrying only his pa's old single-shot dueling pistol and a limited supply of ball and powder, he would have to be careful.

He travelled all day, seeing nothing and too nervous to stop or eat. At each creek he walked Jeff up stream or downstream to throw off anyone who might be pursuing him. Toward evening he ran across a village of prairie dogs, but he passed on—he wasn't that hungry! After dark he found a small grove of trees and, picketing Jeff, took a long drink from a brook. His stomach growled in complaint, but there was nothing he could do— he had no food and didn't dare build a fire. Laying out his bedroll, he snuggled down under his blanket and tarpaulin.

His sleep was fitful and disturbed with dreams of being chased by Jacob Hunt. Finally, waking to a star filled sky and an aching bladder, he decided to get up. He saddled Jeff and started off toward the East again; no use sitting around and waiting for something bad to happen.

The sun came up and the day promised to be considerably warmer than the day before. Scanning the horizon in all directions, Wes saw nothing: no one chasing him, no trees, no mountains, nothing—just prairie! Luckily, sufficient new grass pushed its way through the drying mud to keep Jeff's belly full. At least his horse wouldn't starve. He took a fix on the eastern skyline and started out. Today he would try shooting something, his stomach telling him it was time to stop the fast. He wasn't going to be particular now, he would hunt anything: prairie dogs, sagehens, skunks, badgers, anything. Withdrawing his pistol, he re-primed the pan. No harm in being prepared.

Just before noon Wes spotted a jack-rabbit sitting at the base of a bush. He carefully drew his pistol, pulled back the cock and, aiming, squeezed the trigger. In a second's time, the hammer struck the pan and caused the pistol to go off. When the smoke cleared, Wes discovered he had killed the rabbit. "Oh, boy!" he said out loud. "Oh, boy, it's roast rabbit today."

He skinned and cleaned the rabbit, started a small fire, and soon was holding his dinner over the flame on a long stick. Hobbled, Jeff browsed the thin grass on the flat prairie. Before the meat was completely cooked, Wes cut off strips with his hunting knife, blew on them, and popped them in his mouth. It was delicious! Yet, after barely starting, he discovered he was finished and the rabbit was consumed! But he was still hungry! He sat back and tried to find any hidden morsels of meat on the cleaned rabbit bones.

Buffalo Man

Cracking a leg bone between his teeth, he glanced up at the eastern horizon and his heart froze. Something or someone was coming toward him.

He threw the bones away, jumped up, and kicked dirt over the remains of the fire. Checking the horizon again he saw that the something had now become a man, or woman, on a horse. Was it an Indian? Was it a Whiteman? Was it Hunt or Flint? Wes saw no place to hide and he didn't have time to fetch Jeff. Withdrawing his pistol, he found a small depression in the ground and laid down, his pistol held ready in his right hand, the barrel resting on his left arm.

As the rider drew closer Wes saw it was a man leading two pack mules. Wes wasn't ready to expose himself; he would wait.

The rider approached the extinguished fire and looked around. Spotting Wes laying on the ground a few paces away, the man, dressed in the rawhide of a trapper, stood in his stirrups and tipped his broad-brimmed felt hat "How do you do?"

Wes uncocked his pistol and stood up, brushing the dirt from his clothes. "Hello."

"I saw your fire from a distance and came here to investigate."

The man's accent was heavy, forcing Wes to listen carefully. "I was just eatin' dinner. Thought ya might be an Injun."

"Auch! An Indian! Nein! I am a trader from St. Louis. You know of St. Louis?"

Wes replaced the pistol in his belt and walked to his smothered fire. "Of course I know St. Louie. Came that way myself. You ain't American! You're a foreigner, ain't ya."

"Awh, ya. I am German! But I came here to trade. You are all alone? Ver is your horse?"

Wes pointed toward the bushes in the west. "He's eating dinner, too."

"Good," said the German as he dismounted. "My name is Peter Hoffman. I have much supplies. Vould you like to trade? Do you have buffalo hides or beaver skins?"

Wes looked Hoffman over carefully. "What kind 'a things ya got? Ya got any guns?"

Hoffman pointed toward Wes' pistol. "You already have a gun."

"Ya, but it's just a pea-shooter. I need a rifle. You got any rifles?"

Hoffman smiled and showed a large space between his two front teeth. "Ya, I have guns. You vant to see them?"

Fight at a Rumhole

"Sure."

Hoffman hurried to one of his pack mules and untied a long canvas bundle. Carrying it back to the firepit, he laid it on the ground and carefully unfolded it. Inside were a half dozen rifles. "I have pistols, too. Of course these are just for trappers and pioneers. I do not trade them vith the Redman. They told me in St. Louis that it vas against the law to sale guns to der Indians."

"Oh, hell," said Wes. "Don't pay no attention to that. Everyone sales guns to the Injuns. Government says it's illegal but everyone's been doing it so long that no one cares. Ya got a percussion rifle?"

Hoffman held up a shiny, new gun. "Ya, this is der Henry–a good gun: fifty-four caliber."

"How much?" asked Wes.

Hoffman turned the gun over in his hands. "I think you can have dis gun for forty American dollars."

"Forty dollars!" screamed Wes. "No gun costs forty dollars!"

"But we are far from a city. We are far from St. Louis. It is less dere, yah?"

"You bet it's less there. I'll bet this gun ain't more than fifteen or maybe twenty dollars in St. Louie."

"Yes," said the German as he continued to examine the rifle. "Twenty is what they were in Vestport. But we are not in Vestport."

"But forty dollars is just too much. It ain't fair!"

Finally Hoffman looked at Wes through piercing eyes. "How much money do you have?"

"Well, I ain't got forty dollars!"

"Well, then, I will let you have dis gun for only dirty-eight dollars. That is two dollars less!"

Wes leaned back and sat down on the hard ground. "I ain't got that much."

The German shook his head and clicked his tongue. "Well, then, you don't want dis gun. I have more guns. How about dis Hawken? It is a flintlock, but shoots straight."

"Don't ya have any more percussion rifles that are cheaper?"

"Yes, yes. I have a Tryon. It was made for your army. I can let you have it for twenty-four dollars. It is almost new."

"Well," responded a dejected Wes. "I ain't got that much."

"How much do you have?"

"I got ten dollars, gold."

Again Hoffman shook his head and clicked his tongue, and Wes felt that he had done something wrong but wasn't sure just what it was. The German picked up an old flintlock with rawhide holding the barrel to the hand grip. "I have dis gun. I could let you have it for ten dollars."

Wes took the gun from Hoffman's hands and looked it over. "But this ain't nothing but junk! Hell, it ain't nothing but a musket and the handgrip is broken. Injun gun is better than this."

Hoffman laughed. "An Indian sold me dis gun. I paid him nine dollars for it, so you see, I must get ten to make a profit."

"Ha! If ya paid that much ya got cheated." Wes put the musket down and looked at the rest of the rifles on the blanket. Finding an old Kentucky flintlock rifle in reasonably good condition, he picked it up. "How much is this?"

"Oh, no!" exclaimed Hoffman. "I can't let you have dat rifle for just ten dollars. It is a very valuable gun. It was used at die battle of die Alamo. It was used by a famous man by der name of Daniel Boone. It is very rare."

Wes began laughing. "If ya think this was old Daniel's gun than you're dumber than your horse."

"I am just repeating what I was told."

"Well, someone told ya a whopper."

"I do not know of such things as voppers. But you must have something else to trade. If you could add something to your ten dollars: your pistol and some skins. Then I could let you have der gun."

Wes looked the Kentucky rifle over again. "I'll tell you what. I'll give you the ten dollars in gold and you give me the rifle, a dollar back and some lead and powder. Oh, ya, and a shot mold, too."

Hoffman sat back on his behind, his mouth opened and his eyes wide. "What? Are you crazy? That would be cheating me! I can't do dat!"

"It's just an old Kentuck' rifle. Ain't even worth nine dollars."

"It is a good gun. Kentucky rifles are famous all over die world for how straight they shoot. Look, it was made right here in America; it vas made in Philadelphia."

"Now, besides the rifle, I'll need two pounds of lead and at least three pounds of powder. What's the caliber? I'll need a mold for that caliber."

Fight at a Rumhole

The bartering continued with the German complaining that he was being cheated and Wes ignoring him and pressing his demands. The sun was in the afternoon sky when they were finished. Wes ended up with the Kentucky flintlock, one dollar change, one-half pound of lead, one-half pint of powder and a single shot mold carved from soapstone. "Say," said Wes before they broke company. "Where am I?"

"Where? You are west of the Missouri River. I would say maybe twenty or twenty-five miles west. How far is die Oregon Trail?"

Wes looked toward the west as he tried to figure. He had been riding east for a full day and a half. "I'm not sure, but I'd say maybe fifty or sixty miles."

"Good! That's where I am going. I will sell to die pioneers going to Oregon."

"Well, good luck, Hoffman. I'm heading toward the Big Muddy."

As Wes rode away toward the East and Hoffman continued on his way west, the young man felt himself to be very clever. Sure, the German had made a profit; the gun wasn't worth nine dollars, but Wes had received the lead and powder. Now, he had a decent gun, a gun that could protect him. Wes had learned to shoot with his grandpa's old flintlock so he knew they could be both reliable and accurate if properly cared for. Let Hunt or that Flint come for him now. He would show them!

With rabbit under his belt and a rifle resting across his saddle, the world appeared a better place, and, for the first time, he didn't feel someone coming for him from his backside. He would make it yet and he would stay out of prison. He rode up a slight hill and, suddenly, was looking down into a gently sloping valley where two dozen Indians slowly moved west. He reined Jeff to a stop to watch. Four horses pulled travoises loaded with small children and the Indians' belongings as older children walked or herded dogs which pulled their own small travoises. The squaws rode horses or walked as a half-dozen braves led the party.

Wes sat very still, hoping his immobility would make him invisible, but several children pointed toward him and then waved. Wes waved back. Would the braves turn and see him? Would they ride after him? Slowly, the Indians wound up the valley and disappeared. Wes let out a sigh of relief. He just wasn't quite ready to deal with Indians. He gave Jeff a touch of his heels and trotted down the slope toward the Missouri.

By dusk, Wes realized he wouldn't reach the River before nightfall, so he looked for a place to make camp. The rabbit had been only a snack, and now his stomach rumbled for food, and, with annoyance, Wes was aware he would have to go to sleep hungry again. Picketing Jeff between two large cottonwood trees, he laid down his bedroll and pulled off his boots. He had seen Crocker take his rifle to bed with him at night and decided it wasn't a bad idea. Checking the prime in the pan, he pulled the gun under the tarpaulin where it would stay dry in case of rain. Without a fire or a meal, he drifted off to sleep.

The next morning Wes broke camp early and by noon had reached the road to Council Bluffs. Just beyond the road he found the Missouri River. He still wasn't sure just where he was going but decided to go north toward the trading post at Council Bluffs, which was just beyond the juncture of the Platte and the Missouri rivers. Sloan had mentioned that the post was run by Mr. Sarpy for the American Fur Company and was located in the Pottawatamie Village of Point aux Poules. Maybe Wes could find work there, hauling freight or hunting.

After fighting the brush and trees along the River's bank, Wes decided the road would be easier going and reined Jeff away from the Big Muddy. Moving north, he watched for travelers, but saw no one. Finally, late in the afternoon, he spotted a board pegged to a tree by the side of the road. "River Tavern" was scrawled in charcoal and an arrow pointed down a slightly used path toward the Big Muddy.

Wes had little money to pay for food or drink, but decided the diversion would be restful. He started down the path, but, noticing the River wasn't far, picketed Jeff where the horse could chomp on fresh grass. He decided to take both his pistol and rifle since they were the only things he owned of value besides Jeff.

Drawing closer to the floating tavern, he noticed several horses and a mule tied to a hitching post on the River's edge. A plank ran from the bank to a large barge and on the barge's deck a tent was erected to serve as the tavern. Wes started for the plank when he heard a woman's high pitched squeal and then several men yelling and cussing inside the tent. "Judas!" thought Wes, "this is a tough place." Suddenly a shot rang out. Wes stopped, one foot on the plank and the other on the River's bank. Another shot sounded.

Fight at a Rumhole

He could leave now; he could just turn and walk away and no one would know the difference and he wouldn't get into any trouble. He turned as the yelling started again and took only one step before stopping. Staring at the mule, he suddenly realized who was inside.

The yelling continued as Wes ran over the plank, onto the barge and entered the tent, rifle held high. The room was eighteen feet across and twenty-five feet long; a wooden bar stood at the far end and three small round tables plus half a dozen wooden chairs were scattered on the floor. As Wes looked about, everyone inside froze to stare back at the newcomer.

"Oh shit!" slipped from Wes' lips. A man sat on the floor next to an overturned table and held his leg as blood oozed from a nasty wound in his thigh. Another man, wearing a dirty white smock, sat on the floor with his back to the bar. He held a hand against his head trying to stop the flow of blood from his wound. Crocker Sloan stood with his back to the tent wall, holding a man with one arm around the neck and a knife at the man's throat. Crocker's teeth were firmly clamped to the man's ear as blood trickled down the victim's neck. Two more men stood facing Crocker, one held a pistol and the other worked to reload his rifle. Behind the bar stood the largest, fattest woman Wes had ever seen.

Crocker let go of the man's ear and smiled through bloody teeth. "Farm-boy! Join the fun!"

The man holding the pistol looked at Wes, his eyes dark and brows pulled together. "You best be gone, boy. This ain't you're doing!"

Wes knew there was no way to retreat from the tent because Crocker, as mean a man as he was, was still Wes' friend. Wes slowly reached down with his thumb and pulled back the cock of his rifle. The woman let out another scream as Crock laughed. "I knew ya couldn't pass up a shinin', Farm-boy. Now blow the guts out of that there coon with that bullthrower."

The man with the pistol began hissing between his teeth as he swung the pistol up at Wes. Wes followed by swinging his rifle toward the man. As the woman screamed again, a blue cloud of smoke blasted out of the pistol's barrel and the thunder of the explosion reached Wes' ears. Wes squeezed the trigger of his flintlock and the rifle bucked as another cloud of blue smoke filled the tent.

When the smoke began clearing, the man with the pistol dropped the weapon and stared with wide eyes at a hole in his left shoulder. Giving out a terrible grunt, he fell to his knees. "That fucker shot me!" he cried.

"Ya got him, Farm-boy!" yelled Crocker.

Wes turned toward the second attacker and saw that the man was ramming the charge and ball home with his ramrod as he stared at Wes.

"Wes," said Crocker, "if ya still got that dueling pistol, I recommend ya shoot that scum-ball what's loading his rifle!"

Wes moved his rifle to his left hand and withdrew his pistol from his belt. The man shouldered his rifle with the ramrod still sticking out the barrel. Moving in unison with his attacker, Wes pointed his pistol at the man's head and squeezed the trigger just as the muzzle to the man's rifle swung toward Wes' head. A third and forth cloud of smoke filled the tent while the explosions rang in Wes' ears.

Something was moving by his head, and Wes glanced to his right and saw the hickory ramrod quivering, sticking out of a post that held up the tent. It had missed him by almost a foot. He turned toward the attacker and saw that the man still stood– unhurt. Wes looked at Crocker who was shaking his head. "You two coons are the worst shots this side of the Big Muddy. Hell! Ya both missed!" For a moment, no one knew what to do. Finally, Wes dropped his pistol and withdrew his hunting knife. The attacker with the rifle grunted and, dropping his rifle, withdrew his own hunting knife. It was still a stand-off.

The man Crocker was holding let out a scream as the mountain man again clamped his teeth down on his ear. With a flick of Crocker's wrist, his knife sliced off the man's bloody ear and left it dangling in Crocker's mouth. Crocker let go of the man who stumbled forward and grabbed the side of his head. "Oh, God!" he moaned. "Oh, God! Oh, God!" he said over and over as he slumped onto a chair.

Crocker now faced the attacker holding the knife and, wiggling his head, flipped the severed ear back and forth as he let out a terrible laugh between his teeth to taunt the man. That was enough; the man with the knife grunted, turned and ran from the tent.

Wes took another look at the ramrod sticking out of the pole and felt his legs start to shake. He reached toward an overturned table to steady himself, but missed and, instead, just slumped to the floor. Crocker did a little jig and laughed as he continued flipping the ear clamped between his teeth. Wes' stomach turned over and he knew he was about to be sick. As the smell of blood reached his nose, he lay down on the floor and began retching. With an empty stomach, he had little to bring up and

Fight at a Rumhole

soon the retching stopped. Slowly sitting up, he wiped the spittle from his mouth and then noticed a burning on his neck and a wetness on his shoulder. Cautiously, he touched his finger tips to his neck and felt the warm stickiness of his own blood. He looked at the blood on his shaking fingers. "I'm shot!" he yelled.

Crocker knelt down and looked at Wes' neck. "Not bad, Farm-boy. Ball just took some skin away. You're fine. Now, up on your feet, coon. We needs a drink."

Helping Wes up, Crocker righted two chairs and eased Wes into one of them. "Rinda!" he yelled to the fat lady. "Get us whiskey!" But the fat woman was ignoring Crocker while she bent down to administer to the man leaning against the bar. "Oh, Henry!" she cried. "Are ya hurt, sweetie? Are ya hurt bad?"

"Aw, crap!" said Crocker. "He ain't hurt at all. Just banged up aside the head. Now, when do we get some of that blue ruin ya call whiskey."

"I'm all right," said Henry, as he held on to her and slowly stood. Upright, he held onto the bar. "You fetch the whiskey. I'm fine."

She poked at his bloody ear and neck. "You're bleeding all over. Hold something against yer head." Leaving her man, she walked behind the bar and retrieved a bottle of whiskey.

Crocker pushed his chair back so he could see the two wounded men on the floor and the man sitting in the chair. All three attackers held hands over their wounds and stared at Crocker with red sullen, pain-filled eyes. "Now, ain't they a sorry sight," said Crocker. "Guess they won't soon try to cheat this hoss again."

Rinda placed two glasses before Wes and Crocker and filled them with whiskey from the bottle she carried.

Crocker picked up his glass. "We deserve this, coon. That was a ring-tailed snorter of a fight! You're not such a rawheel after all. I figured we was going under, sure."

Wes picked up the glass with a shaky hand and took a sip of whiskey, grateful when its sourness cleaned out his mouth. Suddenly, a powerful sense of euphoria swept through his body. He had been in a fight for his life and here he was, sipping whiskey with Crocker Sloan. He grinned and looked at Sloan.

Crocker chuckled. "Ya look like ya just raided the hen coop."

"What happened here?" asked Wes.

"Well," said Crocker, "this hoss came on board fer a drink and," pointing to the man who was holding his leg, "that low-down skunk wanted to play Euker. When I won, them three Voyageurs joined him and tried to rob me! Henry, there, was going to help me out when they bashed him in the head. Ain't that right, Henry?"

Henry, now holding his own drink, turned and looked at Wes. "I just stepped out from behind the bar and he hit me with that pistol!"

"That Jim Crow on the floor pulled a knife on me so I gave him a taste of my bullthrower."

Wes was only half listening to Crocker and Henry. The other half of his attention was on the three wounded men. "I shot that one in the shoulder. Is he going to die?"

Crocker stood up and walked to the wounded man. Moving the man's hand, he looked at the wound and grunted. "It ain't bad, he might live."

"My God!" moaned the man in the chair. "Ya cut off my ear; ya cut my ear right off!"

Crocker began looking for something on the floor. Finding it, he picked it up and placed the severed ear on the table and then stabbed it with his knife, pinning it to the table top. "Ya? Well, there it is! Now you just get up and come over here and take it back, slime-face! If ya can't do that then I'm keeping it."

"I shot that one, but I missed that one," said Wes, still amazed he was only slightly wounded after being shot at twice.

The man with the shoulder wound began to moan. "I'm dying, I'm a dead man. Ya shot me and ya had no cause. You're a murderer and ya killed me."

Suddenly, Crocker was angry. "You she-wolves have out lived yer welcome. Now get, go on, get!" From a holster hanging on the back of the chair, Crocker pulled his six-shooter and fired a shot in the air. The explosion filled the tent and everyone jumped. "Now, I said get, vamoose or I'll plug ya good so's ya go under. Do ya hear?"

The one-eared man and the man with the shoulder wound scurried to pick up the third man under his arms and drag him toward the door. "You ain't heard or seen the last of us, trapper. We'll be back and you're dead meat!" yelled the one-eared man and they left the barge.

Crocker laughed and replaced his six-shooter.

Fight at a Rumhole

"Crocker, we got to go!" warned Wes. "The one what got away might be back with friends."

"So? They come here and we'll put 'em under. They're nothing but cowards, rumhole yellow-bellies. Hell, a real man wouldn't stop just cause he's got a little wound or is missing an ear. Had they been real trappers, or maybe Blackfeet, we'd all be dead. Now, I say we enjoy our whiskey." Crocker took another drink and coughed after swallowing the smelly liquid. "God, that's choke-dog, sure! Farm-boy, you're not bending the elbow?"

"I need something to eat!" said Wes, afraid another drink of whiskey might bring his stomach up again.

"You're plumb-right! We need a meal." Crocker looked toward the woman. "Rinda, get us something to eat."

Rinda had her hands on her broad hips. "You look at the mess in here. Who's paying for all this? You paying? My God, you men drink whiskey and ya think ya can go about busting everything in sight. Now what ya want? Buffalo steaks?"

"Ya, get us some bufler steaks," yelled Crocker. Rinda shrugged her shoulders and began rummaging around behind the bar. Crocker turned to Wes. "Now, let's take a look at you. Ya got a nick, but it's a bleedin' like a stuck calf." Crocker untied a dirty bandanna from around his neck and tied it around Wes' neck to cover the wound. "There, that'll do 'er. How's that feel?"

"Feels just fine!" said Wes. "Ya see me shoot that fellow? I got him right in the shoulder with my Kentuck. Nice shot, huh?"

"Nice shot? Hell, ya almost got us both kilted. Ya only wounded the first coon and missed the second altogether. If any of 'em had got to my revolver hanging on the chair, we'd both be fish food right now!"

Wes didn't care about Crocker's criticism. He felt wonderful. "Hey, I just thought of something: I saved your life again. I saved it back at the Rocky-Mountain House and I saved it just now."

Crocker's eyes narrowed as he stared at Wes. "Say, where'd ya come from? Didn't I send you off with that wagon train? What ya doing here?"

"Well," said Wes, sitting up very straight in the chair and holding his whiskey glass. "They tried to cheat me out of Jeff. That low-down Hunt fellow tried to take Jeff. I worked for nothing but passage, just like you fixed up with Captain Earnst, but that Jacob Hunt wanted Jeff, and they said I had to contribute something for my way to Oregon and the only thing I had was Jeff. So they made me sell Jeff for ten dollars."

"Ten dollars!" scoffed Crocker. "They was cheating ya, sure. What'd ya do then?"

"I got up early, like ya showed me, and I snuck Jeff out of camp and headed here."

Crocker slowly nodded as he continued to consider what Wes had said. "Did ya leave the ten dollars with 'em?"

"No, I took it because they tried to cheat me."

Crocker smiled. "Ya did, did ya? Well ain't you the slick one. Only one thing, Farm-boy, now they'll say ya stole the horse from them. Ya done good to keep your horse, but ya should of left the money. You're wanted in Illinois and now the word will go out on the Oregon Trail that ya stole a horse."

"But it ain't fair–Jeff is mine! I didn't want to sell him."

"Hell, I know that. Things like that happen, nothing to do about 'em. It's just that you're getting to be a wanted man everywhere." Crock took a long drink. "Christ, ya just now got in a fight! Don't know if it's safe being around ya. Christ Almighty, looks like God had decreed that I keep stumbling over ya."

Soon Rinda placed two tin plates before them, each containing a steaming buffalo steak. "Now, you boys enjoy these. Henry says they're on the house cause them Jim Crows tried to rob ya." Crocker pulled his knife out of the table and ear and, wiping it on his shirt, began to carve his meat. Wes looked around for his knife as Rinda sat down next to him and put a dirty, sweaty arm around his neck. "Say, you're a scrapper. How old are you?"

"Now, Rinda," warned Crocker. "Don't go getting any thoughts about bedding the Farm-boy. He's broke and he has the pox."

"Oh, Crock!" she said, slapping his arm. "You talk so! He's so cute, I might just do him for free."

With a mouth full of meat, Crocker pointed at Rinda with his knife. "How 'bout that, Wes? Ya want to jump on her bones? Ya could disappear in her fer a week!"

Rinda laughed and clapped her hands together. "Oh, that's good, a week–that's good."

Fight at a Rumhole

Wes smiled as he cut up his steak. "No thanks, I'll just eat this buffalo."

As the sun sank below the western horizon, Crocker and Wes rode their horses north along the road to Council Bluffs, Crocker leading his pack mule. "We got to find a place to bed down, Farm-boy. It's getting late."

"God, Crocker, did ya see me shoot them fellows? I shot 'em good. Say, ain't ya afraid they'll come after us?"

"Na, they won't come after us. They's just cowards. They'll go pick on someone else, someone they think they can lick."

"Are we really partners, Crocker? We're partners now, ain't we?"

"Now, this old dog didn't say we was partners. I only said you could hitch up with me and I'd take ya north. We're traveling together for safety. That's all! Ya got that, Farm-boy?"

"Crocker, back there in the tent ya called me 'Wes'."

Crock looked at Wes and shook his head. "Didn't. I always call you 'Farm-boy' cause that's what ya are."

"No, ya called me 'Wes' when ya spoke to that Rinda."

"No I didn't. I called ya Farm-boy."

"No, I remember. Ya said 'Wes' plain as day. I heard ya."

"Now, Farm-boy, you listen to me! I know what I called ya."

CHAPTER 11

April, 1846

Dance at Garden Grove

The sound of Captain Pitt's brass band playing a lively march reached their ears as Brother Lissman's company of fifty wagons approached Garden Grove, the midway station on the trail to Council Bluffs. Anna was so excited she could hardly contain herself. "Oh, Gwen!" she yelled. "This is it! If only we get to stay awhile."

Gwen's eyes sparkled. "Oh, we will, I'm sure of it. We've been on the trail since the first of March and we've got to rest sometime. Do ya hear the music, Anna? That's Captain Pitt's band greeting us."

The wagon train moved down the slope toward the temporary settlement, which overlooked the Weldon River. Anna saw several cabins under construction and teams of mules already turning over the soft brown earth in preparation for planting. Lissman's company made its circle just north of the cabins and across from where the road west forded the Weldon. As Michael reined the oxen to a stop, Anna looked down at the ford and saw wagons from another company crossing on their way west. Every company wasn't staying; some had to continue. She prayed their company would not have to follow too soon.

When the wagons and draft animals were secured, Uncle Stan left for a council of family heads at Captain Lissman's wagon. Anna, Gwen and Cory began their daily search for fire wood. Gwen took Anna by the arm. "Oh, I hope we get to stay. I'll just die if we have to go out again. I hope we build cabins."

Cory limped slightly from the snake bite, but her enthusiasm showed through her shining face and sparkling eyes. "I heard Pa say we were staying. He said we were building cabins and staying all summer. We're to tend the fields and cattle for those going to Zion."

"Oh, Cory," exclaimed Gwen. "That would be too good! We can have a dance every night. And boys can come to call every day. We'll have to make new dresses; all mine are in rags."

"I don't know," said Anna. "As we made camp, I saw wagons crossing the river. They're going on. We might have to."

"Well, we'll see," said Cory, obviously offended that Anna had contradicted her. "In any case, I hope Pa can find something to buy to eat. We're almost out! We've had nothing but cornmeal and bread for days and I'm starving. I don't mind keeping thin, but my cheeks are disappearing," and she pointed to her pale cheek. "See that? Soon I'll have no cheeks at all. I'll have nothing to offer young men to kiss."

Gwen laughed. "I heard you never offer your cheek, anyway. You always offer your lips!"

Both Cory and Anna clapped their hands and yelled at Gwen's words. Cory, pleased by the remark, pretended to be offended. "My lips are sacred. They're part of my body's temple and saved for my husband."

"But," asked Anna, "what else is available now? Your cheeks, and certainly your ears."

"Anna!" complained Cory. "I never let a young man kiss my ears... well, almost never. If Billy Irvine wanted to kiss them, I'd have to give in." Billy was Cory's current interest.

Gwen showed a knowing smile. "And what if Billy wanted to kiss your neck?"

Dance at Garden Grove

Suddenly, Anna thought of Brother Martin and pictured him bending over and kissing her on the neck. Her hand reached up to cover the imagined spot as she tried to shake off the idea, her ears tingling from the rush of blood. The thought of Brother Martin holding her, kissing her and touching her, frightened Anna; yet it also did something else. It made her stir inside. When she imagined a kiss from Joey Taylor or one of the other boys, it seemed clumsy and even funny. But not with Brother Martin for he was a grown man while they were mere youngsters. She knew the feelings, the stirrings, weren't wrong. It was the woman in her coming out. Her mother had talked to her and told her about women and men. Abruptly, Anna realized that Gwen and Cory had wandered off in their search for wood and she knew it was time for her to go to work. She gathered a load of dry branches and tree limbs and returned to the camp where Michael had already dug out a fire pit and lined the perimeter with boulders.

When the chores were finally done and supper ready, Anna and Gwen sat down around the fire with the other Sinclairs and eagerly awaited their meal. Mary and Aunt Alice dished up the portions onto tin plates and passed them around. When Anna received hers she was disappointed. On her plate was a small serving of baked beans, greens and a slice of hot, dark bread. That was all! She had eaten only oatmeal for breakfast and a hardtack biscuit at noon, and she had been served beans for two meals the previous day. She looked at Uncle Stan, half expecting a protest, but Uncle Stan meekly sat on a barrel and slowly ate his food. As Anna looked around the fire, she noticed that everyone was quiet, as if they personally were responsible for the poor fare.

As Gwen hurriedly gulped her food, Anna's stomach ached from emptiness and she began to eat, surprised how good the beans tasted. In just a few minutes, everyone was finished and plates were gathered to be washed in water from the Weldon. Uncle Stan stood. "I have an announcement to make." Anna nervously wiggled on her seat. He was announcing whether they were staying at Garden Grove. "At our council," continued Uncle Stan, "Brother Lissman said we would be staying here for awhile."

A sigh of relief came from each of the Sinclairs when they heard his words. "We will be helping in the fields and building some cabins, but then we will be going on to Council Bluffs. The fields will be harvested by others and the cabins used by others."

"Stan?" asked Mary. "How long are we to be here?"

"Several weeks, a month maybe."

"Pa?" interrupted Gwen. "Is there a dance tonight?"

He faced his daughter and grinned. "Yes, but we won't be going."

"But, Pa!"

"We just got here, Gwen, and we have chores to do. The dance will start any minute and no one is dressed. Now, Tuesday there will be another dance and you'll have plenty of time to prepare. Brother Brigham will be here, you'll want to look your best."

"But, Pa!" Gwen continued. "We can get ready fast. And we haven't been to a dance in ages."

Uncle Stan looked at his daughter and a scowl came to his face. "We're not going!" he said. That was it! Uncle Stan had come to speak for both Sinclair families and so no one would go. They would have to wait until Tuesday—four days away!

The next morning, after camp chores, Jason and Jack Jr. left to help with building cabins while Michael and the women went to the fields to help with the planting. Uncle Stan loaded their small oak dining table into a Dearborn wagon and headed for a small settlement on the Missouri border where he would try to sell it for food.

All the Sinclairs had plowed or planted back on the farms in Illinois, so the work was no adventure for them. In fact, Anna soon became bored with walking over the cool, soft earth in her bare feet, throwing out the wheat seed, and her imagination quickly divided on food or how she was going to get a dress ready in time for the dance.

On the day of the dance the sky was clear and blue and the sun warmed the air into the seventies. By evening a gentle breeze from the west was welcome relief. The dance was held outside where a flat patch of ground had been turned over and then stomped by many feet until it turned into a hard dirt surface. Poles supported ropes from which hung decorative pieces of cloth or colored string. A long table held a punch bowl and several cakes, cut into very small pieces to accommodate the hundreds of Saints who gathered around the floor, waiting for Captain Pitt's band to begin. Chairs were placed along two sides of the floor for the Apostles, their wives, the various train captains and other Church officers.

Brother Brigham Young sat in the center of one row with his wife, "Mother Young," by his side. Anna looked down the row of chairs, trying to recognize the others, but she identified only Brother Wheeler and his wife, Sarah, and Brother Lissman. Behind and beside Anna, all the Sinclairs were gathered waiting for the music to begin. They didn't have long to wait as Captain Pitt raised his baton and the band members picked up their instruments. Among the first on the floor were Uncle Stan and Aunt Alice. As they gracefully moved across the floor to a French four, Anna was struck by how handsome Uncle Stan was and how lovely Aunt Alice looked, all fixed up in a clean green dress. The two Sinclairs smiled at each other and Anna saw the sparkle in their eyes. Gwen nudged Anna. "Look at my ma and pa. Don't they make a fine pair!"

"Yes, they really do," replied Anna. She glanced at her mother and wondered if she was thinking of her pa right now, but there was no way of knowing. Her mother was smiling and clapping her hands as she watched the dancers.

Suddenly, Gwen lost interest in the dancing and began searching the crowd. "Where's Joey Taylor? I don't see him anywhere."

Anna put her hand to her mouth. "Oh, Gwen! I thought you knew! Joey had to do guard tonight."

Gwen looked at her cousin in disbelief. "Tonight?" The hint of a tear came to her eye, but Gwen fought it back. "Well, then I'll have to dance with someone else and save some dances for him, won't I! Someone has to guard the herd."

The first dance ended and everyone clapped as the dancers strolled toward the sides of the floor. Anna felt a gentle touch on her right shoulder and turned to find Brother Martin standing by her side. "May I have this dance, Anna?" She glanced about for his wife, Kathleen, but didn't see her. Yet, Anna wasn't confused since it was common for a married man to dance with a single lady at these affairs. "Well?" he asked.

Anna simply nodded, and he took her arm and guided her to the floor. A Virginia reel began. Brother Martin was light on his feet and his touch was surprisingly gentle. At first, Anna was nervous–she had never danced with an older man before, only boys. But, as the music took over, her feet moved with lightness and she smiled at her partner, enjoying herself–proud that Brother Martin had chosen her to dance. Responding to her attention, he smiled back.

As soon as the music stopped and the dance ended, she was nervous again because she didn't know just what was expected of her. He took her elbow and slowly led her back to her place, next to Gwen. "Thank you so much, Anna. I enjoyed that. May we dance again, later?"

She felt powerful and just a little wicked, actually batting her eyelashes at him. "Yes, of course." Smiling, he gave a stiff little bow and left. Anna's heart was racing.

Gwen leaned close and took Anna's arm. "Anna!" she exclaimed in a half hushed voice. "He danced with you before his wife! He's sweet on you. I told you he was, didn't I?"

Anna felt very alive and didn't want the feeling to go away just yet. "Yes, I guess he is. But, he's far too old and, of course, he's married." Saying that he was married gave her another thrill and she smiled again.

Billy Irvine and Cory Tobbs danced by and Cory waved. Gwen and Anna giggled and waved back. A tall boy with a crooked nose stepped up and asked Gwen for a dance. Gwen glanced at Anna, blushed and was gone. For the rest of that dance, Anna watched the others, whirling about in front of her. Uncle Stan and Aunt Alice were still on the floor and Anna saw Brother Martin dancing with his wife. When the dance ended, Luke Allison, a sixteen-year-old Anna had known in Illinois, stopped before her. "Hi, Anna! I didn't know you had arrived."

"Hi, Luke."

"Ya want to dance?"

"Sure." And they went to the floor for a Copenhagen jig.

The band kept up a lively repertory of jigs, reels and waltzes and it seemed that everyone danced. Even Apostle Brigham Young took to the floor with Mother Young and when they finished, everyone gave them hearty applause. When it was late, and Anna knew the dance would soon be over, Brother Martin approached again. He held out his hand and smiled, not speaking a word. Without hesitation, Anna took his hand and they walked out onto the dance floor.

The music began and, to Anna's horror, it was a waltz! Brother Martin would be putting one arm around her waist and holding her in his arms! Square dancing was one thing, but a waltz! She hadn't considered this. She might secretly imagine him holding her, but she wasn't prepared for him to do it, and especially not in public. But it was too late. The blood rushed to her face as he took her hand and slipped an arm about her slender waist. Then they were moving across the floor. At first, he neither smiled nor frowned, but soon just the bare suggestion of a grin

Dance at Garden Grove

stole across his lips. He was flirting with her, and she could hear her heart pounding in her ears.

Once again, the music took over and she was caught up in the thrill of the moment. He was such a good dancer and held her so firmly, yet with proper decorum. They danced across the floor and she held her head up and smiled back at him. Before she knew it, the dance was over and Brother Martin stepped back and gave a little bow. A presence was next to them and Anna turned to be confronted by Brigham Young standing next to Sarah Wheeler.

"Brother Brigham," said Martin. "Let me introduce you to Anna Sinclair."

Brigham Young stepped forward and took Anna's hand. "You, my dear, are the young lady who killed that rattlesnake. Isn't that right?"

She couldn't breathe! Brigham was talking to her and the air was sucked right out of her lungs. She tried to gather her thoughts but only managed a weak nod.

He turned back to Carl Martin. "You'd better be careful, Brother Martin. I'm afraid you've got yourself a wildcat here!"

Brother Martin, Brigham Young and Sarah Wheeler laughed, but Anna didn't. Her ears were ringing and her heart pounding. She wasn't sure what her leader had meant by his remark, but she knew she didn't like it.

* * *

Crocker led Wes down a wooded ravine to a small creek. The mountain man stopped and examined the ground close to where icy water tumbled and fell over rough earth and rocks. Wes huffed and gulped air to catch his breath as he pulled on Jeff's reins, encouraging the horse to share a small spot of ground with Betty, Crocker's mare. "What we looking for?" Wes asked when the air finally found his lungs.

Crocker grunted. "Tracks! Ain't ya never hunted before?"

"What tracks?"

"Animal tracks."

Wes looked about but saw nothing indicating animals had been near the stream. "I don't see nothing!" he proclaimed.

Crocker looked at Wes and sneered. "Well, that's cause we ain't found 'em yet!"

Wes would shut up; Crocker was in another of his moods. Sloan led them up the creek, always keeping his head low and searching the soft mud at the water's edge. As Crocker moved ahead, leading Betty, the horse sensed what her master desired and carefully selected a path so as not to interfere with her master's pursuit. Jeff, on the other hand, was determined to step around the wrong side of every tree and balk at each branch, forcing Wes to turn and waste energy coercing the horse to continue. On the open prairie Jeff was a powerful, spirited mount, but in the woods he needed to learn some manners.

After following the ravine for several hundred yards, Crocker stopped, bent down, and examined something on the ground. Wes knelt down to get a better look and saw the faint impressions of prints in hard mud. "A mink, I'd say," pronounced Wes.

Crocker shook his head. "A skunk!"

They continued up the canyon, and Crocker stopped at another track, which Wes immediately recognized. Two large tooth-shaped imprints, arranged like a partially opened clam shell, were pressed deep into the mud, close to the creek and were, even now, slowly filling with water.

"A deer," whispered Wes.

"Yes, and a big buck, at that," responded Crock.

"How can you tell it's a buck?" demanded Wes.

Crocker pointed to the heel of the prints. "Look how deep it's set and look how the hoofs separate. A big buck and he's already spooked. He's walking up-creek, probably to an opening in the canyon where there's new grass." Crocker looked up through the trees to their right and then straight ahead. "I'd say this gulch turns to the left where it widens. That's probably where he is right now."

Wes was astounded at the depth of information Crocker extracted from the single hoof print. "Well, come on! Let's go get him. I'm hungry."

"Hold on, Farm-boy!" warned Crocker. "Ya go stumbling up there and you'll just scare him away. You'll make so much noise you'll never see him."

"What do we do?"

Dance at Garden Grove

"We'll hitch our horses here. Then you sneak up to the right and get on the ridge. Follow the ridge until it turns left, then find yourself a spot to sit. This hoss will sneak up the ravine on the left and try to get a shot at 'im. If he spooks, he'll probably go over the ridge in front of you and head for the next ravine. Now, remember, if ya get a shot, think of yer ball leaving yer rifle and going straight into his heart. Half the aiming takes place after ya pull the trigger."

"But what if he don't go for the ridge? What if he continues up the canyon?"

"Well," sighed Crocker, "then we'll miss him, ya damn saphead!"

"Ya, you're right! I'll go up to the right and get on the ridge and then I'll go…"

Crocker interrupted by hissing through clinched teeth. "Get the fuck up the hill!"

Wes hurriedly tied Jeff's reins to a branch. "I'm going, I'm going!"

With his Kentuck rifle in hand and his hunting pouch at his side, Wes hurried up and out of the ravine without making any loud noises. Once on the ridge he looked back down the hill but couldn't see Crocker or the horses. He checked the priming in his pan and carefully began walking up the spine of the ridge, keeping an eye on the canyon for any motion. After two hundred yards the ravine turned left, just as Crocker had predicted. Wes found a rock from which he had a good view of the bend in the ridge and sat down, straining to catch sight of the light brown coat of a deer coming out of the ravine.

Many minutes passed without any noise or motion, and Wes became impatient. He considered leaving his rock to go back down into the canyon, but he didn't want to be mistaken for the game they were hunting. Still trying to decide what to do, Wes heard the sound of a footstep and turned to see Crocker right behind him. Crocker sat down beside Wes.

"I thought you was going up the ravine?" whispered Wes.

Crocker grinned. "I did; it turns to the left and just ends. There's a set of springs up there feeding the creek. That buck is up near the bend. I didn't get close enough to see him but I'm sure he's there. We just got to wait until he makes a break for it."

"What makes ya think he's coming up here?"

"He'll head down the canyon and run into the horses. That'll spook him up the ridge. Besides, look over yonder," and Crocker pointed to the side of the ravine where it broke from the trees. Studying the ground, Wes discovered what Crocker was pointing to: a deer trail weaved back and forth up the hill until it disappeared over the top. It would be the natural path for the buck.

"I say we go down there and take it," pronounced Wes. "No use spending all day up here, waiting for it to make the first move."

Crocker looked at Wes and his mouth dropped open. "I'm sorry, Farm-boy, I didn't know ya was in a hurry. Ya got a shin-dig to go to? Someone having a dance? Or is it a birthday party?"

Wes couldn't figure what Crocker was driving at. "There ain't no party."

"Of course not! We got nothing to do all day. If we rush down there, we'll spook that animal and maybe get one quick shot, if we're lucky. If we wait here, we'll get a good shot; one we can pick ourselves. Now don't bother me anymore. Just sit there and keep an eye out."

That was it, then. Crocker was going to sit and wait for the deer. Wes didn't dare defy Crocker and go himself, so he was stuck. He leaned his back against the rock and pulled his hat over his eyes. Suddenly, something was hitting and banging on his head and he opened his eyes to see Crocker beating on him with his hunting pouch. "Ya damned rawheel! Keep an eye out. I don't plan on waking ya when he comes!" Rubbing a stinging cheek, Wes turned around and impatiently began watching for a deer he knew was never coming anyway.

The time dragged and Wes became bored. He itched, and scratching to exterminate the discomfort, would soon find another itch. Each time Wes moved, Crocker gave him a warning stare to be still. It was hard for Wes to concentrate on the peaceful scene before them. His mind wandered back to Illinois and the farm and, soon, he was in a full-fledged daydream of childhood and friends and family. The sun moved from just before noon to mid afternoon. Just when Wes was convinced they were stuck here until the winter snows came to cover them up, he received a sharp jab in the ribs. "Look," whispered Crocker.

Wes glanced at the bottom of the deer trail and, to his great surprise, saw a large five-point whitetail buck slowly turning its majestic head and surveying his surroundings. Satisfied all was secure, the deer walked with great dignity up the trail toward the ridge, which was only seventy yards from the rock and the two hunters. Crocker tapped Wes' gun and pointed toward the deer.

Wes couldn't believe it; Crocker was going to let him take the first shot! With pounding heart and shaking hands, Wes slowly moved his rifle to his shoulder, all the time watching the buck to make sure he wasn't seen. With the rifle stock at his cheek, he gingerly pulled back the cock and waited.

The buck stopped several times on his way up the hill. Each time he looked to both sides, searching for any concealed danger. When he reached the crest of the ridge, he just stopped and held his head high, as if sniffing the wind. To Wes, the buck was a beautiful sight, silhouetted against the skyline, waiting for the hunter to make the first move. Wes pictured the ball leaving the muzzle and going straight to the buck's heart, located behind the front shoulder. He aimed and slowly squeezed the trigger. The cock fell, striking the frizzen and igniting the pan. A half second later, the end of his rifle exploded with blue smoke and the gun kicked against his shoulder.

Wes looked through the smoke at the target. The buck tried walking but stumbled, his tongue hanging out. A mournful bleating reached Wes' ears as he looked at Crocker and saw the mountain man had his Hawken shouldered and ready, but was watching the buck. "I think ya got 'em, Farm-boy!" The deer gave out a final bleat and fell to his knees. "Yes, sir! Ya put 'em under," and Crocker uncocked his rifle and stood. Without warning, the deer regained his feet and, with an explosion of energy, bolted toward a shallow ravine on the right. Crocker shouldered his gun and fired, yet when the smoke cleared, the deer was gone. "Damned rantankerous critter!" mumbled Crock.

"Let's go!" yelled Wes. "Let's get that animal! Ya know it's wounded. I got him, I got him good."

Crocker shook his head. "Just sit down and cool yer heels. Ya ain't going nowhere."

"But we can't just let it go!" whined Wes. "That's meat and we're hungry. Ya saw I shot it!"

"First," said Crocker, "if ya chase that animal, it will just run, then you'll have to chase more. It's wounded, wounded bad. It's going to go somewhere close and lay down. It'll bleed inside 'till it can't get up no more, and then we'll get it. Besides, ya ain't reloaded yer gun yet. This coon ain't going nowhere till my bullthrower's reloaded."

Of course, Crocker was right; he was always right. Wes quickly began reloading his rifle, frequently looking over the ridge where he had last seen the buck. After Crock finished with his gun, he found a comfortable place and sat down. Wes was still impatient. "How long we got to wait?" he asked.

"Not long. Let 'er bleed a bit. If ya want something to do, go fetch the horses and mule." Wes was charged with energy and had to do something, so he dashed off to recover their animals. Returning, he saw, to his great dismay, that Crocker had pulled his hat down over his face and appeared to be sleeping. Wes couldn't stand it. He danced about and made grumbling noises and talked to the horses, but Crocker didn't move. Finally, Wes gave up, sat down on the hard ground and held his rifle and the reins to the horses. He was resigned to wait it out.

When the sun had moved another hour lower in the sky, Crocker stirred and looked up at Wes. "I thought ya wanted to go after that buck? Well, why we sitting around here?"

"God, Crock, I been waiting. You been asleep! That deer is probably run all the way back to the Big Muddy by now. Wolves probably ate it."

"Wolves, rivers! Don't talk, son, just to hear the words. If ya ain't telling me nothing, just shut-up!"

They mounted and rode down into the next ravine. Crocker made no effort to be quiet but talked and whistled as he followed the tracks and the blood left by the deer. As soon as they entered tall grass and bushes in the bottom of the gully, they spotted the buck, laying next to a log, his head and neck up off the ground, his large brown pain-filled eyes staring at them. He didn't even try to get up when they approached. Crocker quickly dismounted and, stepping over the animal, cut its throat.

As Crocker began butchering the deer with his large Green River knife, he paused and pointed it at Wes. "Now I want ya to do this: sit down and think about what happened today. Start when we first found the track and remember everything that happened. Ya got some lessons to learn, Farm-boy, and I don't want to have to repeat them every time we need fresh meat. Learn what ya learned today and don't forget it. Your life may depend on it."

CHAPTER 12

June, 1846

Wild Onions

Wes carried more kindling to the fire and threw it on top of the burning logs. The sun was setting and the sight of sparks racing upward against the pink and red horizon made him stop and stare at the beauty in the sky. Beyond their campground, toward the sunset, was the Big Sioux River. Since the fight in the rumhole, they had traveled north to the American Fur Company trading post at Council Bluffs and then north again to the juncture of the Big Muddy and the Big Sioux.

"God!" exclaimed Crocker. "Do ya have to build that fire so big? Every Injun in a hundred miles will see it!" Wes continued staring at the red sky. "Farm-boy, do ya hear me? I said to dampen down that fire!"

Buffalo Man

Wes grunted and, with a stick, stirred the fire to reduce the flame. "We ain't really seen no Injuns, not hardly–just them poor Pottawattamie and that family of Pawnee."

Crocker was cutting strips from a deer's hindquarter. "You're the one's so keen on killing Injuns. What was wrong with them Pawnee?"

Wes knew Crocker was teasing him again. "Well, there just weren't enough of 'em. My brother, Gunner, is a real Injun fighter. He's been out here before."

Crocker put down the knife and looked up at Wes. "You been awful high on this Gunner fellow. Now you say he fought Injuns? Just what Injuns he fought?"

Wes had to think. "I'm not sure; he didn't say. He was a scout with the army and he got into lots of fights with savages. Told me so himself."

"Oh, he told ya himself, ya say? Well, was he in the Black Hawk War? That was in '32."

"Eighteen-thirty-two? Hell, Gunner was too young for that one, but my Uncle told me all about it."

"Then just where did this Gunner fight and who did he fight? What army did he scout fer?"

"I'm not sure."

"Then, before ya go bragging him up, find out."

Wes was silent as he thought about what Crocker had said. Maybe Wes didn't know exactly the where and who, but, of course, Gunner had been an Injun fighter. Wes had always known it. Gunner wouldn't just make it all up. Suddenly, Wes thought of something else. "Crocker? How did I miss those Jim Crows at the barge? I shot right at 'em."

Crocker smiled as he ran a pointed stick through a deer steak and hung it over the fire. "Now that's a good question. You knew what ya wanted in yer head and in yer eyes, but not in yer body."

Wes sat down before the fire. "I don't understand."

Crocker chuckled. "Yer body has to know what yer eyes see. Now, if ya had really been scared, ya would a aimed right at their hearts, ya would a seen it in your head, your ball going straight into their hearts. But ya weren't scared enough so ya just aimed at their bodies and hoped."

"Hell, Crock, I was scared plenty!"

A dark look came to Crocker's face as his eyes narrowed and his eyebrows lowered. "Ya don't know what 'fraid is, Farm-boy. And hope ya never do!" Crocker was through putting the steaks over the fire and, brushing off his hands on his black buckskin pants, he sat down. "But, to answer yer question, next time make a picture in yer head of yer ball leaving the gun and going straight into his heart. That's how to shoot straight. That's how ya shot that big whitetail."

"But I do all right deer hunting–I can hit a deer."

"Oh Christ, you're a saphead. That's cause them deer ain't shooting back. Wait till a bufler comes charging at ya. Now, get out them eggs and put 'em by the fire."

Wes retrieved a bag filled with grass in which they had buried six small sage hen eggs. "We goin' to eat them all?" asked Wes.

"Sure, no use saving."

Crocker never did like to save for tomorrow what he could eat today, thought Wes. He placed the eggs next to the fire on a small knoll of sand, spreading them out so they all caught the heat of the flames. "Crocker, we still going north or are we going back to Point aux Poules and the trading post? Where we heading for?"

"Well, now, this hoss has a new plan. Why should we sell our meat to them at the trading post at Council Bluffs? They'll just turn around and sell it to the Mormons and make all the money. Them Mormons are going to be reaching Council Bluffs any day and they're strung out all through Iowa Territory. There's nothing to hunt or eat in that place, least not for large parties. Them Mormons must be starving to death! I say we head for the Mormons and make meat on the way. What we get we'll sell directly to the Mormons. What do ya say?"

Wes had never told Crocker that he was wanted for killing a Mormon. "I don't know, Crock. Maybe they don't have no money! Maybe we got to sell to the trading post. Anyway, them Mormonites are heathens. They practice all kinds of depraved things on women and children. Preacher Tammerman told us all about it."

"God Almighty! Don't ya never want to see things fer yourself? This coon ain't going under yet and I want to see them Mormons and all their wives fer myself."

"I don't know, Crocker. Them Mormons might steal our meat and leave us with nothing."

Crocker cocked his head as he stared at Wes. "You seem pressed to stay away from them people. They can't be better or worse than Pawnee and ya been wandering all around their digs. Why this concern with Mormons?"

"Well, they were throwed out of Missouri because they was causing trouble. Then, when they lived in Illinois, they were always trying to take over the government."

"Is that so different than any other group of people? Hell, the Democrats or Whigs is always trying to take over the government."

"But Crocker, they do despicable things."

"Now wait! What the hell is a 'despicable' thing? I'll wager ya don't even know. You're just mouthing what that preacher of yours said. Now ain't that right?"

"Well, they murder and rob and they're counterfeiters. Everybody knows that. That's despicable things. They have lots of wives and they do terrible, sinful things to them in their temples. Things what decent folks can't even repeat or we'll go to hell!"

Crocker was watching Wes, his expression hard, his wrinkles tightening around the eyes. "You ever see any of these things, or did all this come from Preacher Tammerman? From what I hear, your folks did some killing and robbing of them."

Wes' defensiveness was increasing. "But they claim that their prophet, Joe Smith, talked with God. Preacher Tammerman says that's blasphemous. You can go to hell for blasphemy."

"Now ya say this Joe Smith talked to God. We all talk to God when we pray."

"No, I mean that Joe Smith talked face to face with God and he walked in a grove of trees with God and with angels, too. Why would God want to talk to an ignorant fellow like Joe Smith?"

Crocker turned and looked out toward the last of the sunset. "You got a lot to learn, Farm-boy. Maybe Joe Smith talked to God and maybe he didn't. That ain't important. I've heard plenty of preachers claim that God came to them and spoke to them. Don't nobody get upset over that."

"And something else," interrupted Wes, "they say that this Joe Smith found a golden book, a secret book, that was written by the Injuns long ago. He copied down this book and the Mormons use it like holy scripture. That's got to be blasphemous." Wes stared down at his hands. "Now, I ain't perfect. I've done bad things, but I went to church and my ma read to me from the Bible. I believe in God and I know He's not liking lies told about Him. He don't like them Mormons lying about Joe Smith and this golden book. That's why God got the people up against them Mormons and forced them out of the country."

"You seem to know a lot about what's in God's head! Ya talk like God were a man. But, what if, just suppose, He were greater, like the wind or the sky, but bigger than them. The Injuns believe in a Great Spirit. That's God, too. They say this Great Spirit is in everything, the ground, the rivers, the air and clouds. Ain't that a beautiful idea? That God is in everything?"

"But the Bible says God is in heaven. You don't believe in this Great Spirit, do ya?"

Crocker smiled and looked into the fire. "Seems to me everyone is in a great rush to make up their minds about God. They want to point at others and say they's wrong and point to themselves and say how smart they is. It's an important question so it don't hurt to take a bit to think on it." Crocker was silent for a moment as if he were turning something over in his mind. "What I believe is what I believe. Now, Farm-boy, get them steaks and let's eat. We still got to find our sleeping-camp and we'll be doing it in the dark."

"Crocker, are ya still saying we should go south toward the Mormons?"

"I'm a-going and you're welcome to come. I don't force no man to go where he don't want to, but then, no man puts me off from where I'm heading."

* * *

Since leaving Garden Grove, Mary and Alice didn't need to call forgetful children to supper. Walking all day beside a wagon or wrangling stubborn cattle stirred up appetites, and with each succeeding day, the food ration tightened. Of the original fourteen hundred pounds of flour carried by the two Sinclair wagons, seven hundred pounds had been contributed to the Church Commissary and over five hundred pounds consumed. Hunger was a common topic of conversation on the trail. Yet, the Sinclairs considered themselves lucky, for they had more food than most and had lost only Lucy during the three and a half months of living out of a tent in weather ranging from snow to blistering heat. Others weren't as fortunate.

Anna looked down into her bowl of soup, trying to identify the solids. Gwen gave her a nudge. "I don't want to remember everything we put in. I just pretend it was good things like ham and pork and pie."

Anna giggled. "Ya don't put pie in soup."

"I know," sighed Gwen, "but I'd sure like some pie right now. How long since we had a giant piece of apple pie?"

"Please, Gwen, don't talk that way."

Uncle Stan approached the campfire, followed by a woman carrying a baby in her arms and a little boy holding on to her skirt. All the Sinclairs looked up as Stan ushered the women and boy before the fire. "Everybody, I want to introduce sister Louise Pierce. This is her son, Bill, and her daughter, Lou Ann." No one moved or made a sound, knowing that Uncle Stan was about to make a serious pronouncement. Anna glanced at Aunt Alice and the slight nod of her aunt's head told Anna that Alice already knew what was coming.

"Louise has had a tragic loss," continued Stan. "Her husband and older son were killed—drowned and her wagon swept away." Anna looked at Louise's face and recognized the red eyes and hollow cheeks of one who is in mourning. "At our council it was decided that Louise should come and join us for the journey to Zion. Now, I want everyone to come forward and give her a hug and let her know how welcome she is to be with us."

Alice was the first up. She quickly stepped forward, put her arms around the woman and gave her a hug. The Sinclairs smiled and laughed and held the children to make them feel at home. Anna wondered if the others thought the same sinful thoughts that kept creeping into her head. With this woman and her two children, there were three more mouths to feed. That meant everyone else would get less. If a person didn't have enough to eat, they could get sick. Anna smiled harder and tried to force the bad thoughts away, but some of them persisted. She would say an extra prayer tonight and ask God's forgiveness for letting Satan put such thoughts in her head.

Returning to her stump, Anna sat down and picked up her bowl and cup. The soup had been disappointing, but at least one cow was still giving milk and she put the tin cup to her mouth and took a drink. The milk had a sweet, acidic taste. "Maybe" thought Anna, "it's just the soup." She tasted the milk again and found the same flavor. "Ma," she complained, "this milk has a funny taste."

Her mother took the cup and smelled it. "Is it bad?"

"No, just funny."

Her mother tasted the milk and a smile came to her lips.

"What is it, Ma?"

Mary handed the cup back to her daughter. "Never mind. It's all right; you can drink it, but we'll have a surprise for tomorrow."

Anna didn't know what her mother meant, but it didn't matter. She was hungry and the milk had been pronounced fit so she gulped it down.

Early the next morning, after the bread had been set to bake, Anna's mother told Anna they were going on an expedition. It was the first time since her father's death that Anna had seen a twinkle in her mother's eye. They walked back along the trail toward where the cattle were grazing. The sun was bright and the air warm. The prairie was covered in new green grass and flowers of every description gently swayed in a soft breeze. Mary began walking slowly, keeping her head down and looking at the ground.

"What are we looking for?" asked Anna.

"Look for a plant about two feet high with small pink flowers." Anna began searching through the sea of flowers and wild grass. Soon, her mother knelt down on her knees. "Here it is, Anna–come see."

Anna hurried to her mother and knelt down on the cool mat of green. Her mother pointed to a tall plant with broad leaves. She took hold of the base of the stem and pulled. The plant came free from the soil, revealing its white bulb and stringy roots. "It's wild onion, Anna," announced her mother. She then withdrew a small kitchen knife from her apron and, cutting off the roots, she wiped the bulb clean. Biting off half the bulb, she offered the second half to her daughter.

As Anna chewed the bulb, she recognized the taste of onion, but this was a milder taste then the onions she was used to.

"We can use them in soups and stews or just raw," continued her mother. "Even the stem is edible." Mary moved forward on her knees and, finding more wild onions, began pulling them up and placing them in her apron. Anna followed and soon had several pounds gathered. Finally, her mother sat down and looked at Anna. "Your Grandmother MacGillivray taught me how to cook a dish she called 'cock-a-leekie' with chicken and wild onions. When your father and I were first married, we were very poor; he worked for a farmer and I was a maid. I used to cook cock-a-leekie for him because we couldn't afford beef or pork. He loved it, or at least he always said he did. He used to call it our Scottish dowry."

Anna watched her mother as she talked and saw the red had returned to her cheeks and the sparkle to her eyes. Anna felt so relieved she wanted to cry. "You miss Papa, don't you."

Mary smiled. "Yes. When you fall in love, you will learn how it can be between a man and a woman."

"Are you going to marry again?" asked Anna.

"We don't have time to think of that right now. First, we have to get to Zion." She reached out and touched the back of her fingers against Anna's cheek. "You're so grown up. You're almost fifteen. In another year or two, you'll be married and gone. Then maybe I'll think of marriage."

Anna felt a gentle blush flow into her face. "Mama?" asked Anna, uncertain if she should proceed. "Can I tell you something?"

"Why, yes, you know you can."

"When Brother Martin is around me, he acts funny." She looked at her mother and blushed even harder. "You know, he puts a hand on my shoulder or stands close. In Garden Grove he always asked me to dance at least once and sometimes twice in a single night. Somehow, it's different than when other men are about. I know he's married and the captain of our ten wagons, but I think he likes me–likes me as a man likes a woman."

Mary moved closer and put an arm around Anna. "I've noticed that he shows special interest in you. Has he ever said anything about how he feels?"

"No, not really. Maybe it's my imagination."

"Has he ever touched you where he shouldn't?"

"No."

"Now, listen carefully, Anna. Some men, even when they're married, want to be with young girls. Sometimes they want to take you to bed. But you can tell when this is so, just as you sense it about Brother Martin. You have to trust your feelings on something like this. Now, next time Brother Martin is around, you act very formal with him. Let him know you are not returning his interest. Be polite, but be firm. Can you do that?"

"Yes, I'm sure I can. But promise me one thing. Promise me you won't tell Gwen we had this talk. She knows Brother Martin is sweet on me, and she goes on about that plural wife thing and that Martin wants me for another wife."

"Well, don't worry. This will be just between you and I. We know that the plural wife rumors are not true. When it is right for you to love a man, you'll know it. You'll know it's not wrong."

"Ma? There's something else."

Mary nodded for Anna to go on.

"When I found out Louise was going to live with us, I had some bad thoughts. I tried not to think them, but I couldn't help it. I thought that if they came, we would have three more people to feed and we would have less. I know it was wrong, but I couldn't help myself."

Mary gave a little laugh. "You're no different than anyone else. I had the same thoughts. But if sharing were always easy, then there would be no virtue in it. When it's hard, like now, it becomes a true virtue to share with those less fortunate. Do ya see?"

"Yes, I guess so."

"Your thoughts were natural. What's important is you didn't listen to them. Now, come on and let's get these onions back to camp."

As Mary and Anna approached the campground, they saw horsemen riding about and people running from wagon to wagon; something important was happening. Without a word, they both broke into a run and reached their wagon out of breath. Michael was there with Uncle Stan, Jason and Alice.

"Have ya heard the news?" shouted Michael. "We're at war!"

Anna looked at Uncle Stan who nodded in agreement. "It's true, we're at war with Mexico."

Mary sat down and put an arm around Alice. Turning to Uncle Stan she asked: "What does this mean, what does this mean for us?"

Uncle Stan shook his head. "Don't mean nothing. We're not in the United States anymore. We're not at war with Mexico. This changes nothing."

CHAPTER 13

Visiting the Wagon Train

Wes built their breakfast fire as Crocker sniffed at a cut of meat, his method for determining if the meat was still worth eating.

"How is it?" asked Wes.

"Poor bull and getting worse, but we'll eat this and throw the rest away."

"Why don't we eat from that buck?" asked Wes.

"Cause we're selling it to the Mormons and I don't want it all hacked up. Besides, this old doe is still good enough for breakfast. We'll get something better fer supper."

"Don't ya ever get tired of eating meat?" asked Wes.

"Tired of meat? Good God, that's what man was meant to eat! Meat's our natural food. You don't like meat?"

Buffalo Man

    Suddenly, Wes was aware of hoofs pounding and something moving from down the draw. In a flash, Crocker had his Hawken in his hands and was checking his percussion cap on the rifle's nipple. Wes reached for his Kentuck rifle and checked the priming in the pan. Soon three cows crashed through the trees, ran close by the camp, and disappeared up the ravine into a deep side gorge.

    "We should of shot one!" cried Wes.

    "Hell, them was cows! We don't need to shoot 'em; we can just go round 'em up after breakfast. They ain't going nowhere up that gully. Come on, let's eat."

    They put the aging deer meat over the fire and sat down to wait for breakfast to cook. After several minutes they heard the slow clumping of a horse coming up their ravine. Once again Crocker grabbed his Hawken and Wes his Kentuck. Soon a large sorrel appeared with a youth as a rider. "Hi!" he said as he reined in his horse.

    "Howdy," replied Crocker.

    "You men seen a couple of cows come by here?"

    "Yep," replied the mountain man.

    "Well, I'm trying to find 'em. Can ya tell me which way they went?"

    "Yep."

    The youth waited for a moment for more information, but Crocker said nothing.

    "Well, which way did they go?"

    Crocker pointed up the canyon with his thumb, but failed to mention that the cows had turned into a side gorge.

    "Well, thank ya–I'll be going." The youth spurred his horse into a walk and slowly passed the fire. Stopping, he pointed down at the cooking meat. "That venison?"

    Crocker put his gun down and shrugged his shoulders. "Hell Almighty! Get down off that horse and eat some; ya look half starved."

    The youth smiled and looked from Wes back to Crocker. "But I got to fetch them cows."

    "Them cows ain't going nowhere. They'll be there after ya eat."

    The young man continued staring at the venison. "It has been a spell since I had meat. I guess a little would be all right, if it ain't too much of a trouble."

Visiting the Wagon Train

"Trouble!" yelled Crocker. "You farm-boys is always trouble, but someone's got to eat this meat. Now set!"

The youth slid from his horse and tied the rein to a branch. "This is awful kind of ya. I'm Michael."

Crocker stuck out his hand. "I'm Crocker Sloan and this is Farm-boy. Used to call himself Wes."

Michael continued smiling and staring at the sizzling meat as he found a place to sit down. "I been chasing them cows all morning. That lightning last night made the whole herd stampede. We got most of 'em, but these ornery critters just kept running away."

"You have a farm around here? Didn't know Iowa was settled this far out." said Crocker.

"Oh, no, I'm a Mormon. We're headed for Council Bluffs. Our wagon train is just a few miles south of here."

Crocker rocked back on his seat. "Mormonites? My God, we been looking fer ya. We got some meat to sell. See that big four-point buck hanging in the tree over there?" Crocker pointed to a large dark form hanging twenty feet up in a walnut tree. "But, if ya got cows, ya don't need venison."

Michael watched the cooking meat as he talked. "We ain't allowed to butcher our cows cause we'll need them to build our herds when we get to Zion. God, we ain't had real meat in days except for sage hen and rabbit!"

"Zion?" asked Wes. "Ain't that from the Bible?"

"Oh, that's what we call our new home."

"Well," said Crocker. "Where is this Zion?"

"Oh, I don't know, yet. The Apostles haven't told us. But, it's some place in the West: California or maybe Oregon. Maybe someplace else."

"You mean," began Crocker, "that yer all a'going to some place and ya don't know where it is, but yer still going?"

"Somebody knows–I just don't know. When the Lord is ready He'll let us know, or maybe He's told the Apostles already and they just haven't said."

Crocker pulled a large cut of steaming venison off the skewer and dropped it in Michael's lap. "Sounds like yer folks got bufler chips fer brains: taking families clear out here and not knowing where yer going and not eating yer cows but starving."

Wes watched Michael's face and was surprised when the youth just smiled, not offended by Crocker's insult. "I can't say about that. I just trust in the Lord and know He'll take care of us." Without any more formality, Michael carefully picked up the hot meat with his fingers and began eating.

Crocker passed meat to Wes and then selected a piece for himself. The three men ate in silence until all the cooked deer meat was consumed. Wiping his hands on his pants, Wes pointed to the coffee pot. "Michael, ya want some coffee? It's watered cause we're a little low, but it's still got some taste. I'm afraid we're out of sugar."

"Much obliged."

Wes poured Michael a cup and then, turning to Crocker, asked, "Ya want me to put on more meat? Ya still hungry?"

Crocker was wiping his knife on his pants. "Na, we'll get something better fer supper. We gots to sell this deer to the Mormonites. What do ya think, Michael? Ya think yer pa will buy this here meat?"

Michael shrugged his shoulders. "My pa's dead; I'm with my Uncle. I don't think Uncle Stan has any money. Most folks is out of money."

Crocker groaned at the news. "Hell, Farm-boy and I was going to hire out as hunters and get rich. Now ya say no one has money! Well, Farm-boy, you help Michael fetch them cows and I'll load Mule up with the deer and we'll mosey down and pow-wow."

As Crocker broke camp, Wes and Michael rode up the side gorge and found the three cows contently grazing on a little patch of tall June grass. They herded the animals back down the canyon where they joined Crocker, and the three men started for the Mormon camp. As they drove the cows down a small bluff, Wes saw the wagon train on the Iowa prairie: fifty wagons circled with interlocking wheels. In the distance he spotted another large circle of wagons–a second Mormon train.

Wes pointed to the wagons. "How many Mormons are there?" he asked Michael.

Michael smiled and shrugged his shoulders. "I don't really know. We got fifty wagons in our company. We started with one-hundred but broke into two camps. They say some trains are almost to Council Bluffs and we got others still in Sugar Creek on the Mississippi. I guess there is thousands on the way to Zion."

After returning the cows to the herd, they rode to Michael's wagons where everyone stopped their morning chores as Michael and the two strangers rode up. Mary held up a plate. "Come on, Michael, I saved breakfast for you."

Michael dismounted. "I ate already, Ma." He turned to the newcomers. "Ma, this is Crocker Sloan and Farm-boy. They fed me breakfast and helped me find the cows."

The woman put the plate down, walked forward and extended her hand as Wes and Crocker dismounted. "I want to thank you for helping."

Crocker quickly stepped forward and gently took her hand. "We's always proud to help the child of such a lovely lady."

A tall, handsome man with silver hair approached. "I'm Stan Sinclair."

At the mention of his name, the hair on the back of Wes' neck stood up. It was a Sinclair man that he was accused of killing. Could this be a relative? Maybe not, there might be lots of Sinclairs. He would just keep his mouth shut and his ears open.

Stan Sinclair first shook Crocker's hand and then Wes'. "I want to thank you men for helping my nephew find those cattle. I take it you're not Mormons."

"No sir, Mr. Sinclair, we ain't," declared Crocker.

"Well, you men sit down and have a cup of hot coffee and some fresh baked bread."

Crocker, Wes and Stan marched to the fire pit and found seats. "We sure will and we thank ya for your hospitality, but we got business to talk, too," announced Crocker.

Wes looked at the Mormons as they assembled around the two visitors. He could tell they were proud people, dressing neat and clean, but their faces showed they weren't eating properly, shallow cheeks and sunken eyes giving the truth away. As Wes sat next to Crocker, a young girl handed him an empty tin cup and a large slice of dark bread. Taking the cup and bread, he carefully looked at her. Her large blue eyes peered back from a pale white face framed in black hair hanging in curls to her shoulders as her pie-cherry pink lips held a hint of a smile. "Thank you," said Wes, but it came out as a half whisper.

Embarrassed, she looked away from Wes and handed a cup and a slice of bread to Crocker, then left to fetch a big coffee pot. Wes continued watching her as she moved away, her back to him, her hips slightly swaying. He realized she was very young, but he couldn't help himself–he couldn't take his eyes off of her.

Stan Sinclair sat beside Crocker and the mountain man began his bargaining. "Now, Stan, we got this buck and it's only a day shot. It's a scrumptious piece of meat, a four-point buck and has got at least one hundred pounds of meat, maybe one hundred and twenty. I can let ya have it for, say, twelve dollars. How's that sound?"

"Twelve dollars is a lot of money."

"Sure it is, sure it is, but we's talking fresh venison."

Wes continued watching the young dark-haired girl as she returned with the coffee pot and filled their cups. He felt that she knew he was watching her, but now she wouldn't return his look. After pouring the coffee she put down the pot and retreated to stand with the other family members.

Stan Sinclair shook his head. "I'm sorry, Mr. Sloan. I wish I had money to buy your meat. You can see we need it. But, the truth is, we got no money. None of these people in the train have that kind of money. We been selling off furniture to farms we pass just for Injun corn."

Crocker first looked at Stan Sinclair and then at his family and neighbors who had gathered to stare at the strange men. "I'm sorry," continued Stan. "If you want cash for your meat ya got to go to the captain, Brother Lissman. He's the captain of our company. If he wants, he can ask the Church Commissary for the money."

Crocker was silent for a moment and then he waved toward all the wagons in the circle. "He's the boss of all your wagons?"

"These fifty in this circle," responded Stan.

"And if he buys the deer, then he'll divide it between all the wagons?"

"That would be the fair thing to do."

"Hell, Stan! This old bugger thought he was getting rich off you folks by doing your hunting. Now I see it ain't going to work."

"We can make a trade for the deer! We got no more furniture, but we got clothes to trade. I have a good bridle I'm not using and I got a pair of boots that's almost new. They might fit you."

Crocker shook his head. "I only wear moccasins. I don't mean to be unkind, Mr. Sinclair, but I don't think you got anything I want." Crocker stood. "Come on, Farm-boy. We got to get. Thanks much fer the coffee, Sinclair. Good luck to ya."

Stan stood and shook Crock's hand. "I wish I had something to trade."

Crocker shook his head. "Maybe next time." He walked to his horse and swung up into the saddle, Wes hurrying to follow. Once in the saddle,

Visiting the Wagon Train

Crocker pulled Mule up along-side his horse. Withdrawing his knife, he made a quick slice of a rawhide restraining rope and gave a shove. The deer slid from the mule and fell to the ground. Crocker looked at Stan. "I reckon you know what to do with it."

"God bless you, Mr. Sloan," whispered Alice Sinclair. Crocker tapped his heels to his horse and started off when Stan called for him to stop. Crocker reined in.

Stan turned to a young man. "Jason, go fetch that flour in the open sack, and Anna, fetch some coffee and sugar." He turned back to the mountain man. "It ain't much, but maybe it will help. I got no tobacco—gave it up."

Now that Wes was over the shock of what Crocker had done with the deer, he was staring again at the young girl. So, her name was Anna, Anna Sinclair. She was beautiful and each time he saw her face, he half expected that she wouldn't be quite as pretty as he remembered, but each time he looked, she was even more stunning.

Crocker grinned. "Well, thanks. Farm-boy has been telling me all kinds of stories 'bout you folks, but I can now see they was all just bamboozle. He said every man had twenty wives and that ya ate babies and all kinds of terrible things. What do ya say now, Farm-boy?"

Wes felt the blood rush to his ears and knew every eye was on him. He wanted to punch Crocker in the face for saying such a thing, but all he could do was smile and shake his head.

"Now, don't worry, folks." continued Crocker. "Farm-boy can talk, but he's just a bit shy, especially when he sees a pretty girl," and Crocker tipped his old felt hat toward the ladies.

Wes wanted to die. He would just draw his hunting knife and cut his own throat. Anything was better than sitting on his horse and listening to Crocker tell lies. Except somewhere in Wes' brain he knew they weren't lies; Crocker hadn't told one real fib. Yet, none of the Mormons seemed to take offense; they just grinned at Crocker's words.

"Have ya heard the news, Mr. Sloan?" asked Uncle Stan.

"What news? We ain't seen white folks for weeks, since leaving Council Bluffs."

"We're at war. We're at war with Mexico."

"Ho!" yelled Crocker. "Ya mean we're taking on the Bean-Eaters? When this happen?"

"President Polk declared war on May 13th. There's already been fighting down on the Rio Grande."

"Hell!" exclaimed Crocker. "It's June! War might be over now. Them Spaniards ain't big on fighting. Good horsemen, but no stomach for a blow-out."

"I don't know," responded Stan, "we've heard Missouri is calling for volunteers. Might be Old Polk has a mule by the tail."

Crocker rocked back in his saddle and laughed. "Could be, could be!"

The young man, Jason, returned with a sack containing a few pounds of flour while Anna returned with two packages and handed them up to Crocker. "Well," said Crocker, "I do believe we are well provided with possibles to go back to the prairie." He waved and urged Betty on. Wes looked once more at Anna, hoping she would smile or in some way acknowledge him, but she only stared back with large, sad eyes. He touched his heels to Jeff's sides.

They returned the way they had come, riding up the small bluff. Crocker reined in and turned to stare at the wagons. "Ya see, Farm-boy. They didn't rob or kill us–just normal folks."

Wes was still upset at what Crocker had said. "Why did ya say those things about me?"

Crocker chuckled. "They was nervous and I wanted to relax 'em, so I just said 'em. Did I lie?"

"No." Wes was silent for a moment. "You gave the deer away."

A scowl came to Crocker's face. "Yes, I know. Stupid, but those sapheads is starving and it hurt. I'll shoot us a new one tonight. Say, what do ya think about us fighting Mexico?"

"I don't know."

"Well, I guess it don't affect us, none. I'm too old and you're a wanted man. Let's go sell some bufler to them Oregon pioneers." He turned in his saddle and grinned at Wes. "Say, you had yer eye on that little squaw, didn't ya. What was her name? Anna? She's a pretty little thing. Going to break men's hearts in a year or two. You couldn't take your eyes off her."

Wes didn't want to talk about it. "I didn't notice," he lied.

"Ho! Didn't notice? You're blinkers almost popped out of yer head! Everyone saw ya. Ya drooled all over the ground. It was embarrassing. Now, when I introduce ya to some Injun squaws, ya can't just stand there, frozen. Ya got to be able to move yer mouth and yer arms. See, like this,"

Visiting the Wagon Train

and Crocker waved his arms back and forth. "Ya got to show them squaws you're really alive." Wes tried to ignore him.

* * *

As the two strangers rode away from the wagon train, everyone just watched, not really believing what had happened and what lay on the ground before them. Finally, Uncle Stan told Jason to fetch his butchering knives and, when Jason returned, Stan went to work on the deer. It had already been gutted, so all he had to do was skin and quarter it. As he worked, the Sinclairs, Taylors and Wheeler's watched. Alice knelt down beside her husband and whispered in his ear. "You're not giving this over to Brother Lissman?"

Stan stopped work and looked at his wife. "If Mr. Sloan had wanted it that way, he would have sold it to Brother Lissman, but he didn't." Stan looked up at Joey Taylor. "Get a knife, Joey, and take one of the shoulders." He then turned to Sarah Wheeler. "I'll save a hindquarters for you and John."

Sarah Wheeler put a hand to her mouth. "God bless you, Stan."

Gwen quietly stepped beside Anna. "Anna, did you notice how that Farm-boy looked at you?"

Anna felt the rush of blood to her head again, just like when the boy had stared at her with those sad, brown eyes. "I saw him, yes."

"He was cute! How old do ya think he is? Seventeen? Did ya see the way he sat his horse and held his rifle? Anna? Are you listening to me?"

"Gwen, he's not even a Mormon. And besides, we'll never see them again. They're mountain men; they live up in the Rocky Mountains and, besides, they all marry Indians. Cory told me so."

"Ya, but if he was a Mormon and didn't live with Indians, wouldn't you be interested."

Anna hoped that Gwen would give up on her idea about this Farm-boy. "Mr. Sloan said that the Farm-boy said terrible things about us. He probably hates Mormons."

"I think Mr. Sloan was teasing him because he was looking at you."

He had openly watched her, but Anna was embarrassed and dared only covertly glance back at him. From the moment she laid eyes on him, he had occupied the center of her attention, and, yet, she didn't understand why. He wasn't as tall as Uncle Stan, nor as powerful in body as Brother Martin. True, he had broad shoulders and a handsome, if rough, face. But, it wasn't just his shoulders or his face. It was the way he moved–like a cat–smooth and tense, compelling her to watch him. Suddenly, Anna was aware of Gwen standing next to her, waiting for a response. "Well, it don't matter, because we won't see them again and so I'm not going to think of him."

CHAPTER 14

Fego's Cabin

They rode down the slope and entered a stand of willows, Crocker in front and Wes following, riding Jeff and leading Mule. Inside the willows, they moved along a high ledge overlooking the Elkhorn River until they came to an old cabin that faced the River, a slender string of smoke twisting from the chimney and dissipating in the tree branches.

Crocker reined up before a hitching post and slid from the saddle just as the door creaked open and a large, black-haired man stepped out. The man yelled in Spanish at Crocker, who turned and, holding out his arms, yelled back. "Fego, ya old Bean- Eater!" Both men laughed and, rushing forward, threw their arms about each other, giving great bear hugs, each man trying to pick up the other. "God damn, Fego, it's been donkey's years!"

"'*Si, companyero*!" said the stranger in a low, throaty voice. "You have been gone fucking long! Come inside, you stinking *Americano*!"

Wes hurriedly tied up Jeff and Mule and followed the two men, who completely ignored him, into the dimly lit cabin. Inside, tools, clothes and belongings lay about everywhere, on a table, on chairs and on the floor. The only light came from a small fire in the fireplace and two tiny windows covered in scraped and oiled deer skin. The man called Fego lit a lantern and placed it on the rough-cut table. Crock and Fego looked at each other again and gave each other more hugs. "Oh, Fego, this hoss had a cold winter. Beav is gone–no one buying. Price down to nothing. Everyone says beav is gone for good. Bufler robes are now the thing."

Fego pulled up two chairs. "Sit! Sit and we have *aguardiente*." Fego looked at Wes, who still stood in the doorway, and pointed to Crocker. "This best fucking bossloper in all Crow Nation."

Crocker turned toward Wes. "Farm-boy, don't be a saphead–close the door and get in here–get a seat."

Wes quickly found an empty chair as Fego lifted a large jug off the floor and placed it on the table.

"Fego," said Crock. "This here ugly dog is Farm-boy. Found him hatching under a bufler turd. Some old sow-pig was about to eat him so I pulled him out. What do ya think? Did I do wrong?"

Fego looked Wes up and down as Wes stared back at the large man. Fego had coal-black hair, a broad nose and high cheek bones, suggesting Indian or Spanish ancestry. Wes guessed he was in his sixties, a few years older than Crocker. His skin was dark and carried countless wrinkles, but underneath that skin he wore muscles that suggested he was, even at his age, powerful and tough.

Crocker pointed toward Fego. "Farm-boy, met Elfego Rodriguez Baccala. Claims to be half-Spaniard and half-Crow, but I know fer a fact he's half panther piss and half bufler shit. He's the meanest panther this side of the Rio Grande and he hates farm boys so don't tell him where yer from."

Fego laughed and punched Crocker's shoulder. "God, Crock! Take a fucking drink–real Taos Lightning. I make this myself from Big Muddy and good bacca. No St. Louie piss-juice for Fego."

Crocker held the neck of the jug to his nose. "Did ya throw in some skunk juice? Ya always used skunk juice."

Fego's Cabin

Fego winked. "Better–use squaw juice." Both men burst out in laughter, and Wes smiled though he was unsure what they meant.

Crocker tipped the jug to his mouth and took a healthy swallow. "Oh, God!" he moaned. "That's powerful Taos! Here, Farm-boy, learn what a man drinks." Crocker passed the jug to Wes who took it and tipped it to his lips. The moment the liquid filled his mouth, he knew he'd made a terrible mistake. Quickly, he swallowed and then gasped for breath. The taste was vile, his throat burned and his stomach turned over in an attempt to return the whiskey, which he somehow managed to keep down.

The men laughed, their eyes sparkling. "Fego!" yelled Crocker. "Did ya hear? We're at war! We're at war with you!" and he pointed at finger at his friend.

A scowl came to Fego's face. "War? Who? *Americanos* and Crows?"

"Hell, no! The United States and you Spaniards! We're at war with Mexico."

"*Hau! Guerra!* Fego's people will chase *Americanos* to Big Muddy."

"Oh, shit, Fego! They ain't got a chance! Them Dragoons from Fort Leavenworth will make 'em all turn tail. It'll be over in a month if it ain't over already. You Bean-Eaters can't fight, ya take too many *siestas*. Our boys will put 'em under, sure."

Fego's face turned red and Wes braced himself. The Mexican pulled out his hunting knife and stabbed it into the table while a steady stream of Spanish spilled from his mouth.

Crocker slapped his knee. "Ain't you the one! Fego, yer nothing but an old *pelado*. Now tell me the truth, ya really think them Mexicos can hold out against the whole United States?"

Fego thought for a moment and then, as suddenly as it began, his anger was gone and he shrugged his shoulders. "*Quien sabe?*"

"Now, Fego," said Crocker, getting serious, "where's yer squaw? Where's Broken Hand?"

Taking the whiskey from Wes, Fego helped himself to a drink, wiped his mouth on his sleeve, and looked back at Crocker with sorrowful eyes. "'Esposa' is gone!"

"What do ya mean gone? She's gone under?"

"No, gone to see her tribe."

"Oh, God, don't do that! I thought ya meant she died. How long she been gone?"

"Two...three months–up north on Little White, I think." Fego pushed the jug across the table toward Crocker and, pointing at the jug, nodded for his friend to take another drink.

"Hot damn," said Crocker, "let's have a shindy." He picked up the jug and Wes felt his own stomach turn over again.

Fego looked about his cabin. "No food–poor bull! No fucking flour, no biscuit, no *pinole*." He stood up and began rummaging about in a cupboard. "*Capote* cheese. Farm-boy, you like *capote* cheese?" He threw a slice of cheese the size of a foot onto the center of the table where it broke into pieces, demonstrating its age and hardness. Wes picked up a piece and saw the outside was covered in mold. Fego was still looking for something acceptable to eat. "Fego is disgraced–no food. *Darle a uno mucha pena.*" He suddenly drew a long barreled Colt revolver. "Fego will kill Hernandez."

Crocker jumped to his feet and stood before his friend. "God, Fego, ya can't shoot yer horse just to feed us. Hell, that horse is worth more than us two coons, together!"

"But Crocker, we must have meat!"

"Meat? Well, then that cheese came from a goat. Here," and Crocker grabbed the gun, "I'll shoot the damned goat!"

Fego screamed. "*Capote*! No! She is Broken Hand's."

"Aw, hell, you can buy her another," and Crocker was out the door.

Fego ran after, still screaming, "No! *Capote*! No!"

Wes was a little light headed from the whiskey, but his heart was racing from the developing situation for he knew how easily Crocker twisted the slightest misunderstanding into a war. He could hear the two men arguing outside, Crocker insisting a goat was worth shooting and Fego pleading for Crocker to shoot him, instead. Wes decided he wouldn't venture out to witness anything strange that might be going on. Suddenly, a shot rang out, followed by quiet. Wes jumped to his feet. "Oh, God!" he moaned. "Oh, God!" and he danced before the door, not knowing whether to stay put, make a break for it, or go see who was shot. A second shot rang out and then a third. Wes cocked his head and strained his ears but, at first, heard nothing from outside. Finally, a deep voice called out. "*Que mosca te pico?*"

'Oh, shit!' thought Wes, 'Fego has killed Crocker!'

"Fego? Ya hit?" It was Crock.

Fego's Cabin

"*Siempre* no!"

"Well, ya god damned simple Bean-Eater! Ya son-of-bitch! Didn't nobody tell ya not to grab a loaded gun from another coon's hand?" Wes gave out a sigh and slumped back onto a seat. Taking the jug of whiskey, he lifted it to his mouth and downed a mouthful. Once again the liquid burned his throat as he felt it slide all the way to his stomach.

"*Compadre*, you go blind!" said Fego. "Can't shoot!" Both men, laughing, entered the cabin, arms around each other and carrying on like nothing happened.

"To hell with meat, Fego. What else ya got? *Frijoles? Atol?*"

"Ha! Herds have moved west, but Fego knows where *cibola* are!"

"Bufler?" replied Crocker. "Let's go! Come on, Farm-boy, old Fego and I will show ya how it's done. That is, if Fego can still ride a horse." Crocker and Fego began yelling and Fego dashed about the cabin gathering up his gun, powder horn and hunting pouch. Crocker thrust the jug into Wes' arms. "You carry the bug-juice, Farm-boy. If one of us gets a terrible thirst, ya juice us. Ya got that?"

In minutes they were all saddled and mounted, headed down to ford the Elkhorn. Occasionally their progress slowed when Crock or Fego demanded a drink, which immediately prompted the other to follow. When Wes believed his stomach wasn't watching, he took another drink, himself. After crossing the Elkhorn River, they rode up the wooded bank and out onto the prairie, north of the Platte Valley. The land was flat but frequently broken by shallow ravines covered in brush and occasionally by trees. Fego led them northwest. No game was evident and Wes couldn't imagine that beasts as large as buffalo would be hiding out here. Of course, he had never actually seen a buffalo.

Finally Fego led them to a grove of hickory trees. Entering the trees, he took them to a long, gently sloping hill bordered by a broad, shallow valley which was covered in deep grass. From their hiding place in the trees, they saw two dozen buffalo peacefully grazing in the valley.

Crocker chuckled. "This is it, Fego. Sure ya can still shoot that old bullthrower of yours? Let's have another pull on the jug before putting one under." Wes passed them the jug and then took a drink, himself. Both men pulled their rifles from their sheaths and checked their percussion caps. Wes couldn't understand what the preparation was all about for the buffalo were great clumsy beasts, certainly easier to kill than deer.

Buffalo Man

It was going to be nothing for two experienced hunters on good mounts to rush down and kill one of them.

Crocker and Fego pointed their weapons up with their right hands as they held their reins in their left hands. Looking at each other, they smiled and Crocker yelled, "Go!"

To Wes' complete surprise, both men discharged their guns into the air, spooking the buffalo and causing them to stampede. Crocker and Fego spurred their mounts and started down the hill and out of the trees toward the withdrawing herd. Wes urged Jeff on to keep close to the action.

The two hunters galloped through the grass after the buffalo and Wes had to hurry Jeff to keep up. "How are they going to shoot the buffalo if they've already fired their guns?" wondered Wes. Then, as Wes galloped closer, he saw both Crocker and Fego stand in their stirrups, hold their reins in their teeth and begin reloading their rifles! He couldn't believe what he was seeing! At full gallop, they measured powder into their muzzles, followed by lead balls and then ramrods. Fully loaded, they closed on the herd. Passing up several large bulls and two calves, they both selected a medium sized cow and closed in for the kill. Still at full speed, they aimed their guns and fired almost simultaneously. The cow took only two steps before falling to her knees. She momentarily regained her upright position, took several more staggering steps, and then tumbled over.

By the time Wes rode up, Fego and Crocker had returned to their kill and dismounted. "I shot first!" yelled Crocker, reloading his rifle. "I killed it!"

"Fucking *Americano*—you missed! Elfego Baccala has killed another *cibola*."

"Aw, shit, I seen yer ball bite the dust! You Bean-Eaters can't shoot and ya know it."

Fego began cussing again in Spanish.

"Farm-boy!" yelled Crocker. "Get over here and wet our tongues with Taos! We're eating boudins today."

Wes dismounted and handed the jug to Crocker. As the mountain man stood next to the killed buffalo and took a long drink from the jug, Wes saw him in a new light. These weren't just old trappers, out having fun. These were remarkable hunters, and Wes was both humbled and a

Fego's Cabin

little frightened. He had believed that he'd already learned a great deal while with Crocker, but now he realized he had learned very little of what the man knew. Crocker handed his reins to Wes. "Picket the horses and build a fire; we'll butcher the meat."

As Wes worked on the fire, he watched Fego and Crocker roll the cow on her side and open her gut. Laughing, Fego reached in with his knife and both hands and pulled out the cow's large liver. Slicing off a piece of raw flesh he stuffed it in his mouth, and Crocker followed by cutting a piece for himself. Wes only wished he could paint a picture of the two hunters, standing on the open prairie, blood on both arms up to their elbows, eating raw liver and laughing.

Fego pulled out and cut off a section of small intestine. Crocker held several sticks around which Fego wrapped the intestines. Wes couldn't stand the suspense. "What's that for?" he asked.

Crocker carried the sticks to the edge of the fire pit and drove the ends into the ground so the intestines would cook. "Ain't ya never had boudins before?"

"You mean we're going to eat that?" asked a horrified Wes.

"Sure! It's the best part, beside the tongue. Good cow chyme. If ya don't eat boudins, ya don't eat bufler."

While the boudins cooked on the sticks, they sliced the tongue into strips and roasted it over the fire. Wes had enjoyed beef tongue before and now admitted that buffalo tongue was even better. All the while he kept one eye on the buffalo guts roasting on their sticks.

After consuming substantial tongue, they still had to wait for the boudins to cook and so passed the jug of Taos. Wes felt light-headed again but wasn't concerned since the two hunters were getting drunk, too. Finally, when Crocker was satisfied, they stripped the now crisp buffalo intestines from the sticks and began eating them with their fingers. Wes put a piece in his mouth and found it surprisingly light and crunchy. The fatty flavor was strong, but pleasant. He eagerly joined with the other two in feasting on the buffalo guts as the sun slipped below a red horizon.

Later, when the meat was consumed and the liquor gone, Wes stirred the fire with a stick and thought of what he had done that day as Crocker and Fego snored in their drunken slumber. Off to the north a wolf gave a howl, and Wes, looking about the dark landscape, moved a little closer to the fire. Then it struck him—they were camping by their cook-fire, something Crock would never allow. Wes stood and walked to his friend who lay sprawled on the still warm earth. "Come on, Crock!" and he poked at Crocker with the tip of his boot. "Come on, we got to go!" But Crocker didn't stir.

Wes tried to awaken Fego, but the Mexican just kept snoring. The wolf called again and a second animal answered from the west. Wes knew he had to do something. Retrieving Betty, he lifted, pushed and shoved until Crocker was belly down over his saddle. Wes repeated the procedure with Fego, who took considerably longer since he was a heavier man. Wes hated to leave so much meat on the prairie for the wolves, but then discovered that Fego had butchered several cuts from the hindquarters and wrapped them in canvas. Wes tied the bundle on the back of Jeff's saddle and, collecting all the weapons and implements, mounted Jeff and led the other animals away from the fire.

He wasn't sure just where to take them. The forested hillside was too close and the cabin was across the Elkhorn River; too dangerous to cross in the dark with two drunks. He would simply head back toward the cabin until he found a suitable place for the night.

After nearly an hour's ride through the blackness, Wes found a small stand of trees where he cleared a spot on the ground and, unloading his cargo, covered them with their buffalo robes. Picketing the horses and hanging the meat from a tree, he lay down and covered up with his blanket. It had been a long day and he was tired. Just before falling asleep he thought of Anna Sinclair and wondered what she was doing at that moment. He was a little surprised at how clearly he could remember her face, her clear blue eyes and delicately pink lips.

Wes woke with a start and, sitting up, looked around, half expecting some trick by Crocker since he had slept past sunup. But Crocker and Fego were calmly sitting by a small fire, cooking breakfast. Wes quickly looked about his bed, not believing some awful nastiness wasn't waiting for him, yet he found everything in order.

Fego pointed toward him and said something in Spanish to Crocker and they both laughed. Getting up, Wes joined them at the fire. As he sat down, Fego nodded and Crocker smiled. "Yer up, huh?"

"Yes, I guess I overslept." Fego handed Wes a hot cup of coffee. "Thank you, Fego."

Fego's Cabin

Crocker took a sip of his coffee and looked at Wes over the cup's rim. Wes waited for a lecture on his laziness, but, instead, Crocker put his cup down and gently placed a hand on Wes' shoulder. "Ya done all right, Farm-boy. Ya had the sense to move us last night when Fego and me was goners. And to show my appreciation, I'm letting ya change yer name. No more Farm-boy. What do ya think, Fego, has he earned it?"

"I liked 'Farm-boy,'" said the Mexican.

"Well, I do too. After all, this hoss gave him that name. But, he done good and I'm generous. What do ya say, Farm-boy, ya want to be called 'Wes?'"

Wes felt a sea of tenderness sweep over him for the old trapper. He'd secretly hated being called "Farm-boy" for it was a constant reminder he was a rawheel, but now that he had a choice, he wasn't sure he wanted to give it up. "I don't know. I've kind of grown used to it." Wes couldn't believe he was actually saying this. "I guess it's all right for now."

Crocker smiled. "You just say the word, Farm-boy and it's 'Wes' again. Agreed?"

"Agreed."

* * *

As Anna and Gwen walked beside the wagon, they saw a rider hurriedly move up the line. "I don't recognize him, Gwen. Do ya think he's bringing news?"

Gwen kicked at a dirt clod. "I hope so. I'm so bored of this constant walking I could scream. Let's hope it's word to camp early."

An early stop was not made, so they continued walking, yet, as soon as the wagons circled for evening, the rumor was flying from wagon to wagon: the American Army was coming!

Anna and Gwen struggled to put up the tent. "Why are they coming here? We haven't done anything!" complained Gwen.

Suddenly Jason appeared from around the wagon. "Did ya hear?"

"Yes," responded Anna. "We already know the Army's coming. Why are they after us, Jason? We aren't even in the United States anymore."

Jason sat down while the girls continued with the tent. "Oh, I don't think they're after us. It's only a few, anyway: an officer, they say, and some enlisted men. I don't know why they're coming, but it can't be to attack us."

"Maybe they want to arrest someone," offered Gwen.

"Holy Jesus!" shouted Jason. "I didn't even think of that! What if they're coming to arrest Brother Brigham?"

"More likely, it's Brother Rockwell," said Gwen.

"But," interrupted Anna, "if it's only a few men, they can't plan on making arrests, either."

"I don't know," said Jason. "I just don't know. Maybe it's got something to do with the war with Mexico!"

The speculations continued all through supper. No one could imagine why the soldiers were coming, but men checked their rifles and placed them where they would be handy. After the killings and skirmishes in Missouri and Illinois, no one wanted to take a chance on treachery.

The next morning, before the camp broke, the trumpet sounded, signaling everyone to gather at Brother Lissman's wagon. Walking around the outside of the wagons, the Sinclairs joined other families as they swelled into a crowd before their leader's camp. A young man in a military officer's uniform stood next to Lissman up in the front of the wagon.

When all was ready he said a short morning prayer and then gave the news. "Sisters and Brothers, you have been called here to listen to a Captain from the United States Army. He has important news."

Brother Taylor called out from the crowd. "What the hell does he want? We ain't in the United States anymore."

Lissman glanced uneasily at the officer and then addressed the gathering. "He wants to talk to us about volunteering to fight the Mexicans."

Everyone stood in stunned silence. Anna couldn't believe her ears. After fighting the people of the United States and being ejected from their Holy City to wander in the wilderness, they were being asked by this same Government for volunteers to fight a war. How could they dare come and plead for help now?

Mumbling started in the crowd as angers flared up. Brother Taylor raised a clenched fist in the air and shook it. "He can go straight to hell! I ain't going nowhere to fight for them scum!" The adults in the crowd nodded in agreement.

Fego's Cabin

Lissman held out his arms for silence. "Listen, the U.S. Army has already conferred with Apostle Brigham Young. Brother Brigham has agreed to provide five hundred men from our trains."

Michael was standing next to Anna and she saw his face grow red as his hands clenched into fists. "Why should we?" he yelled out. "They killed my pa! I ain't fighting for the sons-of- bitches."

Brother Lissman's face also became red as he held up his arms again. "Now listen here! We won't have none of that talk in my train. Brother Brigham knows what he's doing; he says we're going to raise five hundred and we will. If we fight, the Government will pay us and we're desperate for food for the winter. We can't harvest enough to get half through so we need this. Now, I want everyone to listen to Captain Allen here." Lissman stepped back.

Captain Allen smiled. "Ladies and Gentlemen, I have been sent by the Government to recruit soldiers to march against Mexico. You may be asking, 'why are we at war with Mexico and why should I help?' Well, I want to try and answer these two questions."

Gwen nudged Anna. "Isn't he cute!" she whispered. Anna turned to stare at the soldier. She had to admit that he was very handsome in his uniform and he wasn't very old for an officer. Certainly, he was younger than Brother Martin. "Oh," said Gwen, "if all soldiers are like him, I hope we see lots more!"

"The United States," continued the Captain, "was attacked by the Mexican Government. On the twenty-fifth of April, Mexican soldiers, without provocation, attacked a patrol of General Taylor's men on the Rio Grande. It's obvious the Mexicans want to extend their empire farther into the southwest and that they want to challenge Texas again. The only course of action available to our President was to declare war. If the Mexican armies are allowed north of the Rio Grande, all Texas will lay at their mercy and if we remember what happened at the Alamo, we know what Mexican mercy is! Once Texas falls, they will pour into the Indian Lands, enslave the Redman and build their evil presidios up and down the Missouri River. From there, they can raid Missouri and the Iowa Territory at will. Think of it! Mexicans pushing Americans back from the frontier!"

Anna looked about the crowd and noticed that quite a few of those gathered were nodding in agreement with Captain Allen.

"Now," he continued, "that is why we're at war with Mexico. But why should you Mormons help? Your leader, Brigham Young, has already agreed to provide a battalion of men. As soon as the battalion is ready to march, their first month's pay will be available at Fort Leavenworth. It means supplies and food to get you through the winter. By helping your Government in its time of need, you'll be helping yourselves." He stopped for a moment to look over the crowd. "I have already been to several trains and the recruiting is under way. I hope the men of this train will join their 'brethren' to march with us. Thank you and God save America!"

Several people mumbled "God save America" as Brother Martin jumped up on the wagon. "Listen!" he began. "I know we've been kicked about and that sometimes the Government has been a thorn in our side, but I'm proud to be an American and I can't stand by while a bunch of dirty Spaniards try to kill and rape our fellow Texans. We are in a tight place without enough provisions, but we all know God works in mysterious ways and I say He has given us this chance to make it through. Let me tell you all a story that many of you have heard. One of our daughters was bit by a dirty rattlesnake."

Anna's ears tingled at Brother Martin's words for she knew the story he was about to tell and she knew she was going to die of embarrassment. Two-hundred and fifty Saints were gathered around, listening to every word of Brother Martin's.

"And one of our own young ladies, Anna Sinclair, picked up a stick and killed that rattler. Well, brethren, them Mexicans is like a dirty rattler striking at our sons and daughters and I say we show the same grit as little Anna and strike back!"

The crowd's blood was running strong. They cheered Brother Martin's words and those around Anna reached out and patted her on the back or head. She could feel the blood rushing to her head and only wanted to hide, but there was no place to turn. Brother Lissman stepped forward again. "Now calm down. I don't want no one stepping forward now. Go back to your camps and discuss it. Those men deciding to join are to let me know by prayer time tonight."

The Sinclairs returned to their camp. Anna looked at each face, trying to decide what was going to happen. She was terrified, after seeing the effect Brother Martin's speech had on the Saints, that all the Sinclair

Fego's Cabin

men, Uncle Stan, Jason, Jack Jr. and Michael, would march off to war and all be killed. After losing her father and little Lisa and then Lucy, Anna didn't think she could stand another of her family dying. She noticed the worried looks on the faces of both Aunt Alice and her mother and knew they were having the same thoughts.

Uncle Stan waited until everyone was gathered. Jason, fidgeting, couldn't take the silence. "What we gonna do, pa?"

Stan slowly looked at everyone gathered. "I'm not sure. We've been asked to do a lot already without this. Splitting families up! It don't make sense to me." He looked at Michael. "I suppose everyone should have a say in this. How about you, Michael?"

Michael spit on the ground. "Ya know my feeling. The Government stood by while that Illinois militia came down on Nauvoo. My own pa's been killed by them Gentiles. We don't owe them nothing. Let the Mexicans kick their butts back to Washington."

Stan scowled at his nephew. "Watch yer mouth, Michael. No use saying filth." He turned and nodded toward Jack Jr. "What's your thoughts?"

Jack looked first toward his brother, Michael, and then at his Uncle Stan. "I don't know. I still feel like an American even though we were kicked out of Illinois. I still feel that way. It wasn't most the people of the United States that attacked us, just some folks in Missouri and Illinois. I'm not sure, but if America is being attacked, I think we have to protect her."

Michael milled about, kicking at dirt and sticks and not looking at his uncle. The silence dragged on. Finally, Uncle Stan stood. "Listen," he said. "This has to be a personal decision. No one can be asked to go against their will. If ya don't think ya can fight for the Government or ya don't think ya can leave the train, then that's it. On the other hand, if ya believe ya can't just sit by while America is attacked, then ya go. Agreed?" Uncle Stan was looking at the three Sinclair boys.

Aunt Alice stood and stepped forward. "Now just who do you think you are, Stan Sinclair? You're letting each of these boys make up his own mind, but what about the rest of us? If all of you go marching off to war, what will become of us? You can't break up the family. What about Jack's boys? Look at them sitting there! They've already lost a father! Now ya want them to go and die? For what?"

Buffalo Man

Stan's stern expression didn't change under the barrage from his wife. When she was done, he turned toward Michael. "You first, Michael. What do ya say?"

Michael looked up and just shook his head.

"All right," said Stan. "Michael stays. Jack?"

Jack Jr. slowly stood and turned toward his mother. "I think I've got to go. You understand, don't ya Ma?"

Mary didn't respond, but continued standing with her arms folded in front of her, pain written on her face and her eyes brimming with tears.

"Jack goes," said Stan in a low voice. "How about you, Jason?"

Jason shook his head. "I'm sorry, pa, I don't want to go. I can't see marching off to Mexico when the family needs us here. It's going to be a hard time this winter and I don't want to be a thousand miles off when I'm needed."

"Fair enough–Jason stays." Stan turned toward Alice. "I'm going, Alice. Two will stay and two will go so now you're not being left alone. Michael and Jason will be here and when this little war is over, Jack and I will be back–maybe before winter sets in."

Alice stood with arms straight at her sides and fists balled up. She spoke very softly, but most around the campfire still heard her. "Damn you, Stan! Damn you!"

Three weeks passed before the five-hundred Mormon men left for Fort Leavenworth in what was soon called the Mormon Battalion, and by that time, Lissman's wagon train had reached Council Bluffs. A party was held for the departing recruits and the thousands of Saints who had arrived at Council Bluffs turned out in their finest clothes to wish the men well. Mormon leaders gave many fine speeches and toasts to the battalion's success. Wives and sweethearts cried as the battalion marched away. Anna, standing next to Michael while the new soldiers moved out of sight, let the tears flow down her cheeks and fall to the ground. Would she ever see her brother Jack again? Would she ever see Uncle Stan?

Michael turned away and, putting a hand to his mouth, gave a cough which came from deep in his lungs.

Anna wiped the tears away. "Michael," she warned, "you keep yourself wrapped up That cough sounds bad."

"It's nothing, Anna, nothing."

CHAPTER 15

Council Bluffs

The sun shone brightly, warming the air after a cold night, and a slight breeze kept the horse flies away as Wes and Crocker slowly rode west across the plains, Wes leading Mule. Early July saw the dry season beginning, but a wet spring had left the prairie green and luxuriant.

Approaching a small bare ridge, Crocker reined to a stop, pulled off his hat and wiped a trace of sweat from his brow. "Gonna' get hot 'fore supper," he announced.

Wes reined up beside the mountain man. "Where are we now?" Crocker looked first at the sky and then at the surrounding landscape. "I'd say almost to the Cedar River."

Wes followed Crocker's example and wiped the sweat from his forehead. "Where's these buffalo you was talking about?"

"They're out here; they just go west and north this time of year."

"And I ain't seen no Injuns, neither. I thought you said this was Pawnee Country?"

"It is. Pawnees make their main village at the mouth of the Loup River–southeast of here."

"Then why ain't we seen 'em? I ain't seen nothing out here but weeds and dirt in the last two days."

Crocker turned in his saddle to face Wes. "So what did ya expect? This coon ain't here to entertain ya. Besides, ya don't want to run into Injuns if ya don't have to. And fer the bufler; I told ya they move west with the tribes chasing them during the summer. Now stop yer bellyaching." Crocker turned back to survey the western horizon. "I figure we'll find 'em up at the headwaters of the Calamus or the North Loup. We'll load old Mule with tongues and humprib and take 'er down to the Oregon Trail along the Platte. Maybe them Mormonites didn't have no money, but I'm sure those rawheel pioneers from Missouri will have gold in their pockets."

"Why won't they shoot their own buffalo?" asked Wes.

"Oh, they will, but it won't be easy until they is a ways up the Platte. At first, see, they'll be hungry and not know how simple it is. Then we can unload this meat for supplies or money.

"Why don't we just go after beaver now?"

"God, Farm-boy, I told ya, it's the wrong season. Ya got to go after beav when it's cold, not in the middle of the summer, cause their plews are too thin now. We want the thick, rich winter plew. That's what catches top dollar." Crocker touched his heels to Betty's sides and started down the gentle hill, and Wes followed.

"Seems like we're never going to get rich, Crocker," complained Wes. "Let's at least get a wagon so we can haul buffalo robes."

"I don't like to be slowed down with wagons."

They moved across a small bare valley and up a bluff to find themselves overlooking a steep drop of fifty feet to a creek below. "This Cedar River?" asked Wes.

Crocker looked at the creek and shook his head. "Don't think so, but it drains into it, sure. Come on, let's find a way down this cliff."

They rode northwest along the ridge looking for a place to descend and cross the creek. After ten minutes, they came to a steep, narrow gorge cut into the hill at right angles to the creek bed that provided an entrance to the stream bottom. At the edge of the gorge, Crocker reined up again, stood in his stirrups, and slowly looked around the entire horizon. He seemed to sniff the air as he glanced at the sun.

"What's wrong?" asked Wes.

Crocker shook his head. "Don't know, don't know." Again he looked over the gorge and creek bottom where a small stand of ash lined the creek, a soft breeze stirring their leaves. "Let's go," said Crocker in a casual tone.

Carefully selecting their path, they rode their mounts down the side of the gorge and out to the creek, which was only a few feet wide and no more than six inches deep. They crossed the creek and headed north along its west bank. Approaching more ash, Crocker stopped and looked at the leaves as they turned on their stems, waving like flags in salute. Concerned with Crocker's strange behavior, Wes turned in his saddle and looked at the ridge from which they had just come. Nothing was different.

Suddenly, Crocker pulled off his hat and tilted his head as if listening to something in the wind. Wes looked about, but again saw nothing strange. Replacing his hat, Crocker turned and, glancing at Wes, half whispered. "Come on! Stay close!"

Crocker urged Betty into the trees. With pounding heart, Wes followed. Wes had no idea what Crocker was about, but he knew by now that the old man didn't make many mistakes, and so he would follow the mountain man as closely as possible. The breeze increased, causing the tree branches to gently sway. Crocker led them along the stream until the creek bottom widened and then turned to the west where a deer trail followed the bottom of the cliff. Crocker kept urging his horse on without forcing her from a trot into a gallop.

For several minutes they moved along the deer trail until it intersected a gully entering the stream bottom from the west. Crocker reined to a stop and considered which way to go: farther up the creek or left up the gully. Wes welcomed the stop and removed his hat to wipe his forehead when he happened to glance at the top of the eastern ridge, the ridge they had been on just minutes before. The figures of rider and horse stood motionless on the ridge, and Wes realized at once it was an Indian. He looked at Crocker, but the mountain man was already staring up at the Redman.

Buffalo Man

Wes turned his attention back to the ridge and discovered three Indians and then, suddenly, there were six. They were warriors, their faces painted with black and white splotches, eagle feathers waving in the breeze from their hair and reins. Their hands held lances, shields, and bows and their horses were painted with large black, red and yellow spots. These were not boys playing games; these were men bent on war and ready for combat. Abruptly, Wes felt very small and vulnerable, his Kentuck rifle and single shot pistol little comfort against these savages. The images began to pour into Wes' mind: images of these warriors chasing him down, knocking him from his horse, thrusting a lance through his heart and scalping him. That's what these Indians were out to do, and Wes didn't know if they were now planning to do it to him or not, but he knew he was helpless and his fear grew so intense it occupied his mind and body like a snake occupies a gopher hole. He could taste his fear and knew it wasn't going to go away. "Please God!" he prayed, "take me far away from here and I'll always be good!"

Without warning, the Indians wheeled their ponies and disappeared from the ridge. Wes looked at Crocker. Crock whipped his hat from his head and stared back and at Wes. "Let's get the fuck out of here!" he yelled and slapped his hat against Betty's rump.

This time Crocker didn't hold Betty back, but urged her up the creek bed with whacks from his hat and prodding from his feet. Wes struggled to get both Jeff and old Mule moving, but the two animals didn't want to advance in unison. He kept looking behind him, back down the deer trail, knowing that if the Indians were coming, they were making better time than he and Crocker.

Crock stopped and whirled Betty around. "Good!" thought Wes. "He must know the Indians aren't coming." Crocker slipped from his horse, ran to old Mule and jerked the lead rope from Wes' hand. Pulling the mule down toward the creek, he tied the animal behind several large bushes where he would be hidden from anyone on the trail. Returning to Betty, he mounted. "Don't stop, Farm-boy! Don't stop fer nothing!" and he spurred Betty on and rode back down the trail the way they had come.

Back down the trail–Wes couldn't believe it! Crocker was heading back toward the Indians! Was he going to challenge them? Was he going to attack them? Without thinking, without knowing why, Wes urged Jeff on and followed Crocker.

Council Bluffs

They reached the gully leading west, and Crocker turned and headed away from the creek. Suddenly Wes understood: Crocker had simply hidden Mule so they could outrun the Indians who surely had managed to find a way down the east cliff into the creek bottom by now. Following Crocker and not caring about footing or hidden obstacles, Wes bullied Jeff up the short gully and out onto the open prairie. On the level plain, Wes saw Crocker galloping at full speed due west across the grassland. Surprised at how much distance old Betty had put between them, Wes glanced once more down the gully, saw nothing, and spurred Jeff in the sides to catch up with his partner.

Betty was a strong mare but no match for Jeff, and soon Wes had caught up to Crocker, who didn't slow but continued urging Betty on. The two men rode for a quarter-hour and the horses' sweat turned to white foam on their bodies. Finally, Crocker reined Betty to a stop and wheeled her around to look at the eastern horizon. Wes also stopped and looked back. On the skyline rose a trail of dust. At the base of the dust appeared tiny figures of men on ponies—the Indians were following! Crocker looked about. "Oh shit—we done 'er now! Come on, Farm-boy," and he urged Betty on again, this time heading south.

They rode at a slower gait for a half hour; Crocker was a good horseman and knew better than running his mount into the ground. Wes couldn't help but look back over his shoulder and, each time he did, he saw the dust trail and the riders drawing closer. Across open spaces the two men rode, down shallow gullies and back up the opposite sides. The prairie was treeless with no place for them to hide.

Crocker again turned toward the west and then, after ten minutes, turned south. Finally, they approached another creek bed cut deep into the soft earth and, stopping at the ravine's edge, stared across to the other side. Once more, Crocker tilted his head in that strange, unnerving manner. Suddenly, Wes heard whooping and yelling as two dozen Pawnee warriors rode to the opposite edge of the small canyon and waved their lances in the air at the two Whitemen. Wes spun in his saddle and looked behind him to see the original Pawnee coming closer. He and Crock were now trapped between two parties of warring savages!

"Oh, shit!" repeated Crocker. "Look at them dancing devils! They want this coon's scalp, sure!"

The Indians continued yelling and holding their lances and bows high in the air as their ponies pranced along the edge of the ravine's cliff. "Well," said Crock, "if this hos is going under, he's taking a bunch with him." He withdrew his Hawken and took aim.

Wes couldn't believe what was happening–Crocker was mad! He couldn't fight all these Indians. Wes felt the snake of his fear spring from his stomach and bite off his brain. "WHAT THE FUCK ARE YOU DOING?" he screamed at the mountain man. "RIDE, GOD DAMN IT! RIDE!" and Wes kicked his heels into Jeff's sides. Jeff responded by jumping forward to a gallop. Wes didn't care where he rode, just as long as he got away from those Indians. He rode along the ravine for several minutes until he realized the Indians on the opposite bank were following, so he reined Jeff to the right. He would try to ride away from both groups of warriors. He would ride Jeff until the horse dropped dead and then he would run and no Indian would ever catch him.

As he galloped out across the open prairie, the beast of fear slowly subsided into a ball of pain in his stomach once more. Turning, he found Crock trailing one-hundred yards behind and, behind Crocker, came the Indians. Wes knew he could out distance everyone, but could he do it and lose Crocker? He gently pulled on the reins to slow Jeff.

Crocker gradually overtook him. Riding alongside, the old man waved at Wes to follow and then turned slightly toward the left. Wes relinquished the lead to Crocker, but kept looking over his shoulder to see the pursuing Indians strung out in a line, with the front warriors less than two-hundred yards behind. Wes wanted to cry–he was trapped! There was no place to run and hide and this old man with him was going to get him killed. Why had he come to Indian Territory? Why did he want to bother these people? Why didn't he just stay in Illinois and go to prison where he would be safe?

Crocker turned them away from the open prairie and down a gentle slope into a shallow valley containing a dry stream bed.

Instead of taking the easy path leading up the valley, Crocker led them up a steep incline on the opposite bank. The horses struggled to reach the top, and the two men gave them no rest but urged them on again.

They rode north along the valley and then west again, but the Indians were still close behind. Jeff and Betty were now covered in white foam

Council Bluffs

and Wes prayed one of them didn't trip and fall or just give up! Crocker continued leading them into small gullies and ravines and up their steep banks, always finding the most difficult path. Yet the Indians were in no mind to quit, keeping after the two hunters. The chase continued through the heat of the day, and sweat ran off Wes' face into his eyes, forcing him to frequently wipe them with his shirt sleeve. His hands became cramped and the inside of his thighs rubbed raw.

Finally, Crocker located a particularly distasteful hill of soft sand. The ride up was torturous for the horses and near the top, both men had to dismount and pull their animals the remaining distance. Quickly mounting, they rode off again. After a few minutes, Wes looked back–nothing! He rode alongside his partner and pointed behind. Crocker only grinned and continued on.

Slowing their gait, they continued for a half hour before stopping in a small grove of box elder, the first stand of trees they had found since the ash that morning. Crocker reined in, dismounted and withdrew his Hawken from its scabbard as Wes reined Jeff in and dismounted. The grove of trees was too small to completely hide them, but it was better than being in the open.

Crocker, his face streaked with sweat and dirt, looked at Wes and grinned. "We done 'er, Farm-boy. We tricked them Pawnee. Now, you wipe down these horses while I keep a look-out."

Grateful to be out of the saddle and standing on wobbly legs, Wes removed his shirt and wiped the sweat from the backs and chests of the horses. Crocker leaned his rifle against a log and climbed up one of the trees. From his perch, he scanned the horizon in every direction. Back on the ground, he retrieved his canteen, but rather than drinking from it himself, he watered both horses.

"I could a used a drink!" complained Wes.

"We don't need a drink," responded Crocker. Then grinning he added: "what we need is wings!" He seemed to enjoy his joke, breaking out in laughter.

"Ain't they gone?" whined Wes.

"Hell no! I think they's just regrouping, so we better vamose before they spot us." He slipped a foot into his stirrup and swung up into his saddle. Wes' heart sank–ride again! It would almost be worth it to let the Indians come. But, then thinking on it, he decided it was better to ride. They left the trees and headed southwest, both horses fatigued and Crocker moving them at a trot. Wes kept giving Jeff little pats and words of encouragement for the horse had saved his life and now he felt a special closeness to Jeff: a closeness that can only be felt by those who have brushed with death and come through with each other's help.

Crocker found a ravine with a dry creek bed and led them down a steep cliff to the sandy bottom. The gully was narrow with vertical sides rising ten feet to the prairie above. They now rode southeast until the ravine intersected another, larger gully. Crocker stopped and again repeated the strange ritual of cocking his head and listening, but Wes still wasn't sure what he was listening for. Satisfied, Crocker led them up the larger gully. Wes wasn't sure of their direction anymore, but thought they were heading back toward the Indians.

For half an hour they moved up the ravine, twisting to the left and right as it grew narrower. Suddenly, Crocker stopped and held up a hand. Wes quickly reined in beside Crocker. Crocker slipped from the saddle and led Betty to the near cliff where he pulled his horse close to the vertical clay wall and placed a hand on Betty's nose. Wes, heart pounding, copied the old man's actions.

They stood, neither speaking, the hot sun beating down on men and horses. Then Wes heard the far off sound of pounding hoofs. The sound grew as animals approached the gully and in his heart Wes knew it was the Pawnee. The pounding grew louder until it occupied the very center of Wes' brain. Dust and small dirt clods fell on them from the prairie above as horses rushed along the edge of the gully, right above Wes and Crocker's heads. Wes' heart was pounding so loud he feared those above would hear.

Then it was over, the pounding diminished and then was gone. Wes discovered he had been holding his breath and let out an explosive burst of air. He heard Crocker laugh as the mountain man turned and faced him. "Ain't it great, boy? Ain't it a shining? Them Pawnee are so fucking dumb they make rocks look smart! Now, come on! Let's vamose."

Just before dusk, they came to the Calamus River and, without fire, camped in a grove of willows. Wes, after wiping down and watering the horses, was so exhausted he couldn't keep his eyes open. Crocker said they would have to take turns standing watch and he would take the first watch. Wes rolled up in his blanket and closed his eyes. Drifting off to sleep, he heard Crock speaking low, "Wes?"

Council Bluffs

"Yes."
"Ya know we got to go back for Old Mule, don't ya?"
"Sure."
"Ya done good, Farm-boy. Ya done all right!"

* * *

Anna and Gwen walked from the wagon along the side of the hill toward their dugout that was located in the sparsely settled Council Bluffs settlement. The majority of Saints were camped in Kanesville on the east side of the Missouri River. Alice and Mary had wanted a cabin, but Jason pointed out they didn't have the time to cut and haul the logs for a cabin; a dugout would have to do for now. Michael and Jason toiled almost a week before completing the structure: a twelve by eighteen room with sod walls, a roof of oak beams covered with dirt and a chimney of sod and loose stone. They draped a blanket to divide the dugout into a small room for the women containing only their bed rolls and two trunks and a larger room furnished with a crude fireplace, a table, chairs, a small bureau and a place for Michael and Jason to sleep. The boys also constructed a small window to let in light when the door was closed. After months on the trail, the little cabin seemed like heaven to the Sinclairs.

As Anna and Gwen walked toward the dugout, they were stopped by Brother Martin. "Hello, Sisters," he said in a cheery voice. "I waved to you Anna when you were on the hill, but you didn't wave back, only Gwen."

Anna looked him straight in the eyes. "You didn't go with the Battalion." Anna heard Gwen draw in her breath.

Martin didn't flinch, but stared back with bright blue eyes. "I wanted to, I volunteered, but Apostle Young ordered me to stay. He said that too many captains were volunteering and he needed some to remain here. You must know I wanted to go." It was said in a detached coolness, except for the last comment which sounded to Anna like a plea.

Anna decided not to let it pass. "It must be difficult," she said, "to know those who went will return heroes and will be men honored above all others."

He smiled, but his lips hinted at a slight sneer. "Yes, they will be honored. But to seek out glory in the secular world is vanity, and God does not favor a vain man or woman." He turned slightly to address Gwen. "I prefer to obey God's will and to do His bidding, however difficult that might be."

Gwen nervously smiled and glanced at her cousin. Anna nodded. "Yes, but we must hurry to obey our mothers or no one will eat tonight," and she took Gwen's hand and pulled her along toward their camp.

"How could you talk like that?" demanded Gwen when they were away from Carl Martin. "You were just terrible. He's our captain!"

"He's only the captain of our ten wagons and that's hardly a captain at all. And I don't believe that story about Brother Brigham ordering him to stay. Do you? He can make grand speeches about the flag and our country, but when the men go off, he stays here, where it's safe!"

Gwen snickered. "Does this mean Brother Martin is no longer your favorite?"

"Gwen, he never was! It's just that I'm disappointed he would encourage our men to go and then stay here, himself."

They entered the dugout and sat down on their bed rolls. "When we're settled," said Anna, "I'm asking Ma for material to make a dress; I don't have anything to wear. I appreciate your dress, Gwen, but I really want something different, just for a change."

Just then Cory Tobbs stuck her head around the curtain. "Hi!" she said and slipped into their private apartment. "This is a grand cabin. You should see ours; it's so small!"

"But," objected Anna, "you only have four in your family. We have to crowd six in here and eight when the men return."

"Yes, I know," said Cory as she plopped down. "But it's all so depressing. I pleaded with Pa to build a regular cabin. All the Apostles and captains have them, but he said 'no!' He said it would take too much time and timber. He said we were staying here only through the winter and he was tired of building just to abandon what he builds." Suddenly, Cory remembered something else. "Gwen! Joey Taylor didn't go with the battalion!"

"Of course not," responded Gwen. "Joey's only seventeen."

"Well, many of the men were only seventeen."

"But not everyone needed to go," said Anna. "Luke Allison didn't go either."

Cory smiled. "Yes, and I saw you dancing with him at the last dance. Is he your sweetheart? What happened to Brother Martin?"

"I was never interested in Carl Martin."

"You danced with him enough," responded Gwen.

Cory frowned. "All the really interesting men are gone! It's nothing but boys left." She looked at Gwen with pleading eyes. "Since so many men are gone, Gwen, don't you think it would be nice if Jason asked me to dance the next time one is held?"

Gwen laughed. "So that's what all this is about! Jason is nineteen and, anyway, I think he's interested in someone else. He's always talking about Ellen Munce."

"Ellen Munce!" exclaimed Cory. "But she's so plain! If Jason knew I was interested, don't you think he would ask me to dance?"

Gwen nodded. "I'll tell him, but I can't guarantee he'll want to."

"Of course he will!" declared Cory.

Suddenly, the door opened and the girls heard Aunt Alice's voice. "Are you hiding in there? You girls come out here, I've got something I want to show you." They scrambled out of the cabin and stood before Alice who held a small basket and a sharp stick. "Now I want all three of you to come with me."

"But," objected Cory, "I got to go, Sister Sinclair. My ma will be looking for me." Alice's eyes narrowed as she stared at Cory. "Has your ma showed you how to find mice seeds?"

Cory shook her head.

"Good, then your ma can wait. You come with us." She led them up the hill and out on the grass-covered plain. "Now you girls watch me," she cautioned. Looking at the ground, Alice slowly moved forward and, finding what she wanted, thrust the stick into the ground several times. Finally, she knelt down and, with the stick, dug a hole. Soon she uncovered a cache the size of a robin's egg, filled with black, hard seeds. "You see this," she said. "they're pea-vine seeds, stored here by the field mice. Now to find them, you just look for their trails," and she pointed to the ground markings which identified their tunnels, "and probe with a stick until ya feel the cache."

"But Sister Sinclair!" exclaimed an alarmed Cory, "you can't mean to eat them things! That's mouse food."

"Cory, they're just pea-vine seeds."

"But they've been handled by mice—they're filthy! How can you eat something like that—laying there in the dirt."

Alice frowned and then, with patience, smiled at the fifteen-year-old. "Cory, how long since you've had meat?"

"Well, we..."

"And how much flour does your ma have? Don't you understand that there isn't enough food in the settlement? Don't you understand that we're going to be here for a long time and that winter is coming? Many of us could starve, so we need all the sources of food we can find. Sister Wheeler showed me this. She said the Pottawatamies showed some of our people, and the Indians have been eating these seeds for years. They'll be cooked and, you'll see, they'll be good."

Cory looked at the seeds Alice held in her hand. "I don't know."

"You gather some and take them to your ma. If she doesn't want them, I'll take them. All right?"

Anna was fidgeting to get started. "Come on, Cory. It'll be fun. It's better than sitting around the cabin. Come on, let's get some sticks."

Gwen nodded. "Come on, Cory."

"All right, but I'm not saying I'm eating them."

They found sticks and sharpened the ends and then headed out to find tunnels belonging to the field mice. The first cache was difficult to locate and yielded only a few seeds, however the next was easier and soon the girls were busily finding them, one after another.

Later, Anna and Gwen returned to their cabin with their prizes twisted up in their aprons. Entering the cabin, Anna discovered Michael under his blanket, shivering as if it were the middle of winter instead of July. "Michael," asked Anna, "what's wrong?"

He looked at her with dark, sunken eyes. "I'm sick, Anna. I'm real sick."

CHAPTER 16

August, 1846

Red Eagle's Camp

Horse flies and gnats swarmed about their heads as fine dust slowly settled on both riders and horses. Wes looked at the sky, and the sun glared back from directly overhead. Hot and uncomfortable, he wondered why they were traveling instead of finding some cool shade to hide under. He looked at Crocker, but the mountain man's chin rested on his chest and his body swayed in a manner suggesting he was asleep. For several minutes Wes watched Crocker, looking for any sign that the old man was faking. Catching Crock asleep was just too good an opportunity for Wes to pass up.

Riding through a field of long-stemmed knotweed, Wes reached down as far as he could and, grabbing the stem of one of the plants, pulled it up and into his lap. Breaking off the roots and holding the stem, he thrust the prickly bulb down behind the cinch on Betty's tender belly.

Wes' action produced the desired result. Betty gave a snort and a buck, and Cocker, his siesta rudely interrupted, grabbed at his saddle horn and jerked up straight. "Wha! What in hell! Where are they?" he shouted.

Wes laughed until Crocker withdrew his six-shooter and, cocking it, swung it about. "Where are they? Come out, I say!" yelled the mountain man.

Wes lay flat on his mount. "God! Don't! It was a joke!"

"What?" said Crocker. "A joke? That was you, Farm-boy?" Crocker put the gun away as his face turned red. "I wasn't asleep–I knowed it was you all the time."

"Crocker, why are we out in this heat? Why don't we just lie low for awhile?"

Crocker looked about to get his bearings. "I thought we'd find some friends. I think Red Eagle is out here, somewhere."

"Injuns? You want to find Injuns?"

"Not just Injuns. How many times I got to tell ya: there's Injuns and there's Injuns. I'm looking for Red Eagle–he's Sioux. He and his people should be in these parts, if we're where I think."

"But you told me a person shouldn't deliberately try to find Injuns–that's what ya said."

"I know, but this is Red Eagle. He's a chief and he's Sioux–that's different."

"But why go looking for them? Why don't we kill some more buffalo for the pioneers?"

"Cause we already sold bufler to them rawhorns and it's time we move on. We got flour, coffee, sugar–we're fixed fer a time."

"Then why look fer Injuns?"

Crocker turned in his saddle and scowled at Wes. "Damn it, Farm-boy! How old are you, anyway? Ya got anything between your legs? Don't ya ever want a woman?"

Wes couldn't believe what Crocker was saying. "You mean you're going to sleep with Injuns? Ya can't do that; they're so filthy and they're ugly."

"You have such a refined way of talking of the sweet lovin' of a gentle squaw."

"But Crocker, ya can't sleep with a squaw. Preacher Tammerman says Injuns are heathens and their women are whores cause they sell their bodies for beads. Anyway, they're so dirty, how can ya get close to 'em?"

Red Eagle's Camp

Crocker smiled. "You still got a lot to learn, Farm-boy. Now, my second wife was a squaw–a Sioux, in fact. Are you saying my second wife, God rest her soul, was a whore?"

"NO! Of course not, I didn't mean it that way."

"Now let me tell ya something: ya want to have some fun and put yer pole in a warm, dark place, what do ya do? Well, if ya go fer one of them pale, sickly white women, ya got to chase her and tell her awful lies and act a fool and then most times she clamps her legs closed, anyway. But, with a young Injun maiden, it's different cause they like having fun, too. Ya don't have to chase and lie and carry on. When yer done, ya give her a little foofuraw to show ya enjoyed yourself and that yer a gentleman. What's wrong with that?"

"Well, I don't..." began Wes.

"And another thing," interrupted Crocker. "This here Tammerman fellow don't know what he's talking about. He's never been with Injuns and never had a squaw wife, so forget him."

Wes thought about what Crocker said and had to admit the old man's description sounded more civilized. "Well, what about how dirty they are? And ugly, too!"

"Now, there ya have me. Each hoss has his own tastes and what's fetching to me, might turn your stomach. So, I'll say this: when we find old Red Eagle and go to his village, you take a look around and if yer staff don't get hard and beg for a place to play hide and seek, then I'll admit you're right."

"It's a deal, but you're going to lose. Nothing is going to get me up next to a savage."

Crock chuckled. "This old griz knows one squaw you'd jump on: that little Anna Sinclair! Now ain't this coon shootin' center? Don't yer balls ache when ya think of her?"

Wes felt the blood rushing to his face, for Crocker was right–he did think of her and he did think of touching her, holding her. But Crocker's words sounded offensive and crude. "I don't know what yer talking about. Who is this Anna? I'm not whoring around until I'm married." Suddenly, he realized what he had said and blushed even harder as Crocker slapped his knee and hooted in his merriment.

They continued moving over the prairie; a prairie that days of sunshine had turned from the green of spring into the brown of summer.

Buffalo Man

Wes tried thinking of other things but his mind kept wandering back to the Indians they were seeking. He prayed the Sioux behaved more peaceful and civilized than the Pawnee because the memory of being chased by the wild Pawnee warriors still caused him to flinch in fear and look over his shoulder. They moved west beyond the headwaters of the tributary streams feeding the Loup River to a large open plain south of the highest reaches of the Niobrara River. Twice they spotted Indians at a distance, but both times Crocker made no effort to contact them, since the first was a family of Oglala and the second a hunting party of Cheyenne.

Finally, on a warm afternoon, when the air was still and the flies were especially bothersome, they spotted a young half-naked brave sitting on a horse on a far off ridge. Crocker raised his hand with two fingers held together and extended. The brave watched for a moment and then copied the gesture.

"What was that?" asked Wes. "What did ya do?"

"That's sign," replied Crocker. "I give him the sign fer 'friend,' and he signed back. You best learn sign for ya can't learn all the Injun tongues, but they all talk with their hands."

Wes turned to look at the Indian again, but he was gone. "Where'd he go?"

Crocker laughed. "Gone to report us to the tribe, I reckon. He's Sioux, but I'm not sure what tribe."

"You mean he's gone to bring more after us?"

"They ain't after us. He weren't all painted up fer war! Get a hold on yerself. All Injuns ain't out to scalp ya."

They continued and soon a half dozen young men, barely Wes' age, arrived on fleet-footed ponies. They yelled and hollered as they rode around the two Whitemen, doing fancy tricks on their horses. "Look at 'em show off!" said Crocker. "Ain't they rambunctious critters? But don't be fooled, cause they're mighty caballeros, ain't better riders north of Mexico. Look at 'em go!"

Finally, when the youths were satisfied they had demonstrated their skills, they whooped and rode off. Crocker pointed after them. "That's where we'll find old Red Eagle."

"How'd ya knew it's Red Eagle?"

"I recognized some of them boys."

Red Eagle's Camp

They walked their horses up a gentle hill and on the crest saw an Indian village of a dozen tipis spread in a half circle next to a spring and, beyond the spring, a herd of horses. Crocker led them to the center of the tipis as Indians appeared from everywhere and gathered around the two visitors. Wes tried taking in everything at once as this was his first Indian village and he was amazed at the varied and sophisticated activities in evidence. The tipis stood sixteen to eighteen feet high, each covered with a dozen hairless buffalo skins sewn together. The lodge entries faced east, with the bottom of the tipi covers rolled up to let in fresh air, a open flap in the tipi's top allowing the fire's smoke to escape. Inside the tipi, Wes saw the Indians' personal belongings and small cooking fire.

Close to a hundred people gathered around them, but the dogs easily outnumbered the Indians as they dashed between the humans' legs and howled their greeting. Wes realized the Sioux had been hunting buffalo because the Indians had fashioned a work area beside each tipi where hides were scraped to remove the fat and hair or rubbed with a messy substance that Wes later learned was fresh buffalo brains. The Indian children yelled and reached up to touch Crocker's pants, and older Indians called greetings, which Crocker heartily returned. Wes watched it all with apprehension for he knew savages could act very unpredictable. How could one be sure what they were going to do from one moment to the next? Crocker reined in before the center tipi and dismounted. At once braves and squaws stepped forward and gave him hugs or grasped his hand, all jabbering away in a strange tongue, which Wes knew would be impossible to learn. Yet, Crocker seemed comfortable with all the attention as he returned their greetings in the Sioux language. Finally, Crocker turned to Wes. "Come on down here, Farm-boy. Meet these folks."

Wes slowly dismounted and stepped next to Crocker.

"That's better," said the mountain man. He put an arm around a middle-aged woman. "This here is Crazy Owl, Red Eagle's first wife and a special friend to this hoss." He gave her an affectionate hug and she grinned back at him, showing several missing front teeth. Crocker pointed to a tall, dark brave with scars over his face. "This here is Swift Fox, Red Eagle's oldest son." Crocker continued introducing the Indians, and Wes soon lost track of the names, most of which contained the name of some animal. Yet, he was impressed by the fact that Crocker knew so many of the Indians.

Buffalo Man

Suddenly, they heard a yell and all turned as a large Indian rode up on a black pony. The crowd moved back as the brave reined to a stop and gracefully slid from the horse's back to land before Crocker. In his forties, he was tall with broad shoulders, wearing only a breechcloth around his waist and a brass band on his upper arm. His eyes sparkled as he looked at Crocker. "*Mahtola!*" he called as he opened his arms wide and flung them around his friend. "*Mahtola!*" he said again, pulling free but holding onto Crocker's arms. "*Mahtola* come back!"

Crocker laughed. "Yes, Red Eagle, this hos is back. And I've got a friend." Crocker pointed to Wes. "This here coon is Farm-boy. He travels with me."

Red Eagle nodded and began jabbering in Sioux. Crocker laughed and slapped the Chief on the back. They turned and, drawing aside the covering to the tipi opening, slipped inside. Wes didn't know what to do. The adult Indians were wandering away while the children stood and stared at him. Soon the flap opened again and Crocker's head came out. "What the hell ya doing? Get in here!" and he disappeared inside again.

Wes looked for someplace to tie up Jeff, but a young boy gently took the reins from Wes' hand and smiled up at him with large brown eyes. Wes nodded and, letting go of the reins, entered the tipi. The inside was filled with smoke, and through the haze Wes saw Red Eagle and Crocker sitting at the tipi's other end. "Get over here, Farm-boy. You're holding us up." Wes maneuvered around a small fire in the tipi's center and gingerly stepped over the Indians' sleeping furs and clothing to sit beside his partner.

The lodge's inside was larger than Wes expected, but Red Eagle's family had collected a variety of items which left little free space. Rawhide boxes rested beside the tipi's walls, and fur bedrolls showed that at least a half dozen people lived here. A short horizontal pole, resting on two vertical sticks, held feathers, several pipes and small pouches. Hanging from the tipi's ash support poles were buckskin shirts and dresses, fur covered quivers full of arrows, ladles made from animal horns, and several shields. Iron tipped lances leaned against the wall and a small pile of firewood sat next to the door.

Once in the tipi Red Eagle appeared even larger; his face round and full and his eyes almost black. His hair, black and shiny, fell straight to his shoulders, and his grin showed a set of perfect, if somewhat stained, teeth. Red Eagle retrieved a bundle wrapped in soft deerskin and, unwrapping it, revealed a long-stemmed pipe. Speaking rapidly, he picked up a pouch of tobacco and began filling the pipe. "*Waste bacca, Mahtola.* No *kinnik-kinnik*," he said and held a burning stick to the bowl.

"Why does he call you *Mahtola?*" asked Wes.

"Cause it's my name. Means 'little bear' or 'bear cub.'"

"What did he just say?"

"He said that the bacca was good, not *kinnik-kinnik* which is what the Injuns use when they can't get real bacca. It's the inner bark of the red willow. Not too bad."

Red Eagle took a deep drag from his pipe and, holding the pipe up over his head, blew out the smoke and uttered something in Sioux. He then solemnly handed the pipe to Crocker. Crock repeated Red Eagle's gestures; taking in the smoke, blowing it out and speaking. As Crocker handed him the pipe, Wes shook his head. "I don't know what to say!"

"Don't say nothing. Just take a lung full and nod like it sets well with ya. A hos must always smoke the peace pipe with these Injuns cause they put much stake in it. Ain't that right, Red Eagle?"

Red Eagle nodded and smiled. Wes took the pipe and sucked in the heavy pungent smoke. Then, feeling as if he were on a stage, he decided to show Crocker he could act the part. He held the pipe over his head, blew out the smoke and spoke in a low voice. "I say there should always be peace between the Redman and the Whiteman. Let the lance and bow never be raised between us." Smiling, he lowered the pipe and looked at Crocker.

The mountain man let out a howl and slapped Wes on the back. "That was pretty, Farm-boy. You're gonna make an Injun yet!" Crocker took the pipe from Wes and returned it to their host. Then Crocker and Red Eagle got down to serious business, but since they spoke only in Sioux, Wes was left on his own.

Wes looked about and noticed that a woman, the one named Crazy Owl, had entered the tipi along with a young, fierce looking brave and a girl of eight or nine. Crazy Owl was busy with some chore and kept after the little girl to help, but the child kept stopping to stare at Wes. The young man just scowled at Wes as he sat cross-legged, holding an old musket in his arms. Wes looked behind him for something to lean on, and Crazy Owl, noticing, gave a command to the child who scurried about the lodge and gathered up four white-bleached rawhide pillows. She scooted over to Wes and stuffed them behind him, encouraging him to lean back and be comfortable. "Thank you," said Wes, pleased with all the attention.

"That's *pila maye*, Farm-boy. That's how ya say 'thank you,'" said Crocker.

Wes turned back toward the little girl. "*Pila maye*," he said, and she put a hand to her mouth and giggled. Crazy Owl snapped out another order and the girl hurried to fetch three wooden bowls and place them next to Red Eagle, Crocker and Wes. The flap opened and Red Eagle's son, Swift Fox, entered and, stepping around and over the others, made his way to the side of his father. Red Eagle gestured for his son to sit and join them. Soon, the two Indians and Crocker were deep in conversation again, leaving Wes to be stared at by the young brave.

Crazy Owl left and, gone for several minutes, returned, accompanied by an Indian maiden Wes judged to be his age or a little younger who carried a small black iron pot. Placing the pot on the ground before the men, the young maiden ladled up large pieces of meat in a clear hot liquid. When she filled Wes' bowl she looked at him with round brown eyes and batted her long, black eyelashes. Wes felt the blood rush to his head as something stirred between his legs.

"Now," said Crocker, turning toward Wes, "that's Little Frog, Red Eagle's daughter. Ain't she pretty?" He nudged Wes in the ribs. "How about it? Your balls swelling just a mite?"

Wes knew he was blushing and knew the Indians were watching, but he wasn't sure how much they understood. "She's very nice. Yes, she's very pretty." The Indians all smiled and nodded as if they knew perfectly what was meant. Wes noticed that the others were eating with their fingers so he just waded right in and picked up a piece of meat and put it in his mouth. It was delicious! "What is this? Buffalo?"

Crocker grinned. "No. In honor of our visit she cooked a dog. Good, ain't it! I love dog." And he went back to jabbering with Red Eagle and stuffing his mouth with food. Wes looked into his bowl with its vile contents to check how much meat remained. Could he just ignore it and put the bowl down or would that offend everyone? He decided to try finishing what was left and, taking hold of each piece, he popped it into his mouth and swallowed without chewing, praying it would stay down.

Red Eagle's Camp

Finished with the dog meat, he felt very pleased with himself. But, without warning, Little Frog snuck over and refilled his bowl along with the bowls of the others. Wes looked down in dismay at his bowl, brimming again with the detestable flesh. The first time wasn't too bad, maybe he could get by again. This time, he allowed himself the luxury of chewing and tasting just a bit.

When the second bowl was empty, he decided what he'd heard about dog meat wasn't true. While he pondered the good taste in his mouth and the pleasant state of his stomach, Little Frog refilled his bowl.

Crocker leaned close to Wes. "As long as your bowl is upright, they keep filling it. To show you're done, turn the empty bowl upside down."

After his third helping of dog meat, Wes decided he'd consumed enough—one shouldn't take advantage of hosts—and he turned his bowl over and smiled at Crazy Owl. *"Pila maye,"* he said. Crazy Owl laughed and clapped her hands together, causing her husband to rebuke her. Chastised, she turned away from her husband, but gave Wes a shy, teasing look.

Little Frog placed a reed serving tray of brown pancake-shaped cakes before the men and then enticed Wes to try one. He eagerly picked it up and, nodding, took a big bite—it was awful! A sour, vile taste quickly spread throughout his mouth as he tried to withdraw his tongue to its farthest reaches. He made a strenuous effort to remain calm and dignified, but noted, with sinking heart, that he was being watched by Crazy Owl, Little Frog, the little girl and the scowling brave. He would have no chance to secretly expel the poison so, resolving himself to a slow, painful death, he chewed what was in his mouth and, somehow, swallowed. Suddenly, the effort was over, and he wanted to gasp for breath and drink a river of water, but he would remain the gentleman. Smiling, he nodded toward his hosts. *"Pila maye."*

Crocker laughed as he pointed at the rest of the cake in Wes' hand. "Ya better eat that or they'll be offended. Nasty, ain't it! Made from berries, meat and grease, but I'm 'fraid the grease sometimes get's putrefied and takes the upper hand. Now, be a good Farm-boy and gobble it down."

Mustering all his self control, Wes put the rest of the cake in his mouth and, chewing as little as possible, swallowed. When he was done, Crocker laughed again. "I like mine this way," and he picked up a cake, rolled it about a piece of meat in his bowl while letting the broth soak in, and began chewing on it. "Ya get used to it. It's fat cow when you're starving in the winter snows."

As the braves and the Whitemen ate and talked, more Indians stole into the tipi, one at a time. Soon Wes counted fifteen people in the lodge, most sitting quietly, smiling from time to time and watching with large brown eyes.

Since first entering the tipi, Wes had notice a slightly rancid odor and now it had increased in strength. He leaned closer to his partner. "Crock?" he said in a low voice. "What's that I smell?"

The old man sniffed the air, then sniffed himself and then Wes. "Well, Farm-boy, we ain't had a real bath in some time."

Wes sniffed under his armpit and recognized the sweaty body odor he gave off, but knew it wasn't what he now detected in the tipi. "No, not us! I mean that smell I been smelling since I came in here."

Crocker sniffed and looked about again and then the look of recognition came to his face. "Boy, it's funny how a coon gets used to things. You're smelling the Injuns. It's rancid grease. They slick down their hair and rub it on their bodies sometimes. Ya get used to it. Makes their hair look nice, don't ya think?"

Crazy Owl, Little Frog and the girl-child left and returned with more food. First they were served slices of buffalo tongue. Next came a tender cut of buffalo meat, which Crocker said was taken from the spine and hump of the buffalo. Again, Little Frog served cakes, but Crocker let Wes know they were baked from corn-maize traded from other tribes. Although these new cakes tasted rather bland, they represented a great improvement over the previous ones.

After supper, the Indians again refilled their pipes and the talking continued, but Wes, not understanding Sioux, had no idea what was said. When it was late, Red Eagle stood and, giving a command, clapped his hands. In seconds, the tipi emptied of all Indians except Red Eagle's family. Crocker stood and prepared to leave, and so Wes stood also, but Crocker put a hand on Wes' shoulder. "You're staying here in Red Eagle's tipi tonight, Farm-boy. I'm going to visit a little Injun maid and I don't need you looking over my shoulder."

Wes hadn't considered that he would be required to stay all night in the lodge. "In here? Alone?"

Red Eagle's Camp

Crocker laughed. "No, you'll be with Red Eagle and his family. They'll treat ya good, don't worry. I'll see ya before sunup. Don't forget to have a drink. I've sent a boy for your bedroll."

Wes nodded and slouched back down on the pillows. Crocker hurried out of the tipi and, suddenly, Wes felt deserted. The same young boy who took care of Jeff entered with Wes' bedroll. Crazy Owl scurried around, moving things so Wes would have room.

Red Eagle's family, including Crazy Owl, Little Frog, Swift Fox, the sulking youth, the little boy and little girl, seven in all, began preparing their robes for the night. They laid their bedding out so their feet pointed toward the fire and their heads toward the tipi wall. The sulking youth rolled the tipi's skin covering all the way to the ground and securely staked it down. Wes pulled off his boots and slipped under his blanket, feeling naked without his Kentuck rifle at his side, but the gun was with Jeff, wherever that was. When Wes was settled, Red Eagle approached and laid a beautiful bleached white buffalo robe over him and said something in Sioux. Wes nodded. *"Pila maye, pila maye,"* Everyone was pleased and, nodding their heads, grinned back at Wes.

As Wes watched, Crazy Owl dampened the fire and adjusted the flap at the apex of the lodge. Wes' heart gave a jump when Little Frog adjusted her robes across the fire from him and then, kneeling, pulled her rawhide dress over her head to reveal her soft naked skin underneath. Just before wiggling under her robe, she smiled at Wes and batted her eyes again. Tongue-tied, Wes could only smile back. At last, the fire glowing with only a few red coals, everyone was tucked under their buffalo robes. Wes felt very full and satisfied, the smell of the cured buffalo hide replacing the odor of rancid grease. He closed his eyes and, giving a sigh, began thinking of Little Frog, kneeling naked on the buffalo robe, but, as he drifted off to sleep, her image was replaced with that of Anna Sinclair.

* * *

Anna pulled the cover from the window, trying to increase the air circulation in the small cabin and then, returning to Michael's bedside, she fanned him with a homemade rush fan. He looked at her and smiled but soon his eyes closed as fatigue overtook him. "How are ya feeling, today, Michael? Is it any better?" she asked.

He opened his eyes again and, reaching down, pulled the sheet from his feet and legs. "How do they look?" he asked, not rising up to see for himself.

Anna looked down at his puffed and blackish legs and feet. They appeared no better than the day before. "They look fine," she lied. "Do they still hurt?" She reached down and gently stroked his leg.

He struggled up on one elbow and looked at the lower part of his body. "Oh, God–it's worse," and he plopped down on his back.

"No, it's not, Michael. Yesterday they were much more swollen. You have to have hope–you're getting better."

A scowl came to his face. "Then how come when I try to stand, I get dizzy and how come I can hardly walk? My cough's gone but now this."

"Don't worry, Ma's making soup with wild horseradish. Brother Taylor said it worked wonders on Sister Taylor."

Gwen walked into the cabin and sat down on a small stool made from a tree trunk. "Goodness, it's hot! Sarah Wheeler says it's over ninety-five. Can you imagine–ninety-five! Look at my dress, it's ruined. All this sweat just ruins my clothes."

"How's Cory?" asked Anna.

Gwen shook her head. "Cory's sick, real sick. Brother Lissman says it's pleurisy. She coughs and can hardly breathe." Just then a cough came from behind the curtain dividing the cabin. Gwen nodded toward the curtain. "How's Ma?" she whispered.

Anna shrugged. "She's been asleep."

Gwen stood and cautiously looked behind the divider and then returned to her stool. "She's still sleeping. God, I wish all this fever and sickness would go away. You can't walk in Winter Quarters anywhere without running into the sick."

Michael struggled up on one elbow again. "Have you been to the cemetery? Jason says there's new graves every day."

"Don't talk like that when we got sick folks of our own," demanded Anna. "God is watching, remember that, Michael." Immediately she felt regret for scolding her older brother. "I'm sorry," she said. "I didn't mean it."

He slid onto his back again. "It's all right."

Mary entered carrying a small steaming kettle while little Billy Pierce ran in after her and grabbed at her dress hem. Mary placed the kettle on the hook over the fireplace. "There," she announced. "Nice hot soup. As soon as it cools, you're to have some, Michael. It's all seasoned up with salt and has beans and horse radish and peas. It'll be good for you, son."

Anna felt her stomach grumble at the mention of food. "Do we get some, Ma?"

"No, Anna, this is for your brother and for your Aunt Alice. There isn't enough for everyone. You'll have to wait for supper. Now, I want you and Gwen to go out and look for seeds or artichokes. Michael and Alice can't get well if you two are always hanging around the cabin."

"But Ma!" complained Anna. "We're always out looking. I told Louise I'd watch Billy."

Mary shook her head. "Well, you're not doing much watching. I'll look after him; you go with Gwen." Resigned to her fate, Anna grunted at her cousin and the two girls left the cabin for their foraging fields.

Anna and Gwen walked along a creek bank, poking into various hiding places, looking for artichokes or wild onions. The chore was done with little enthusiasm since they each confessed they were tired of the constant diet based on wild plants with little meat or bread to add flavor and substance to their meals. Finding few plants, Gwen sat on a log and chewed on a blade of grass. "I wish Ma would get better," she said, half to Anna and half to herself. "I wish Ma and Michael and Cory would get better and I wish they would come into camp with a wagon train of food with all kinds of good things to eat and that the Battalion would get back."

Anna sat on the log and, putting an arm around her cousin's shoulder, drew Gwen's head down on her own shoulder. "I know, I wish for all the same things."

"But it's so tiring," continued Gwen. "I know we're supposed to be tested by God, but can't we be tested all at once and get it over? Does this have to go on, day after day, with no break, no fun? Sometimes I get so hungry I could eat the bark off trees or my shoes. Everyone is getting so thin! Look at me, Anna, look at how stringy I'm becoming. By the time some boy does look at me, he'll see right past me to someone else."

"I know, Gwen, each night I pray for the Battalion to return and for more food in camp and to be on our way to Zion. How long can this go on?"

They both heard a rustling in the shrubs behind them and turned to see what was there. From the bushes came a call. "Hello!" It was said in a male's voice but was slurred to sound far away.

"Who's there?" demanded Anna. "You'd better come out!"

For a moment they heard nothing, then the voice spoke again. "This is God speaking. I've heard your prayers, Anna Sinclair."

Gwen giggled. "Who is that?"

"I've also heard your wishes, Gwen Sinclair, and I'm going to grant you the wish you want most."

Both girls now giggled. "You in there!" called Anna. "You better come out. I've got a gun and I'm shooting it into the bushes."

"Don't you want to know your greatest wish, Gwen?" said the voice.

"Oh yes, Lord, tell me what it is!"

Joey Taylor jumped from behind the bush. "It's me! I'm your greatest wish." All three of them laughed as Joey joined them on the log. "What are you two doing?" he asked.

Gwen tried not to smile or bat her eyelashes. "We're having a private conversation, and you've no right to listen in."

"Aw, girls are all the same–always talking. That's where men are different."

"I suppose you consider yourself a man?" inquired Anna.

"Well, course I do. Don't I go hunting and guard the cattle and build cabins? Ain't that the work of a man. Out here, a body has to grow up fast." He feigned seriousness. "I tell ya, ladies, it's a rough country, with Injuns and Missourians and them Spaniards going to war, not to mention the fever and rattlers. Ya got to be tough–women, too."

"Joey," interrupted Anna. "You don't have to remind us of how hard it is; we know. But it's much harder for women. We're responsible for feeding you men and with no food in all of Winter Quarters, how are we to do that? You men are supposed to keep us supplied with fresh meat and all ya bring in is skinny little sage hens not fit to feed a scarecrow."

Joey smiled and his eyes twinkled. "Ya say we don't provide enough meat? My mouth smacks for something else right now. What would be the one thing you'd want to taste if you could taste anything?"

Red Eagle's Camp

Anna replied at once. "Meat, a pile of...no, ice cream."

"Yes," cried Gwen. "Ice cream."

"Not me," said Joey. "I'd go for chocolate." He stopped speaking and looked at the girls.

In unison, they both screamed and Gwen grabbed him by the arm. "You have chocolate?"

He grinned as he shook his head. "I don't know, you girls don't think us men provide very well."

Gwen hit him on the shoulder. "Joey, stop that! Do you have chocolate? Tell me!"

"Luke Allison traded some from a teamster up from Independence. He's waiting right now, over at the boulder. He's also got another surprise, if ya can handle two."

Gwen and Anna both jumped up. "Come on," said Gwen.

The three youths hurried up the bank of the small creek until coming to a stand of willow trees surrounding a large smooth boulder ten feet high. Joey led them to a place in the rock where a crevice gave sufficient footholds for them to climb. The boulder top was a secret hiding place for young people when they didn't want to be found by their elders.

Climbing up, they found Luke Allison waiting at the top, sitting cross-legged with a jug and a package between his legs. He smiled at them as if he had just completed the most astounding feat imaginable. Anna, Gwen and Joey quickly sat down. "Guess what, Luke," said Joey. "We don't have to share because they said we don't provide enough food."

"We did not!" protested Gwen. "And anyway, that was before we knew ya had chocolate."

"Look at this," said Luke, as he unwrapped the small package to reveal a bar of rich, brown chocolate. "Got it from a fellow up from Independence, a Gentile. Had to trade an old clock but it's worth it."

Joey was scrutinizing the bar. "You already had some?" he asked.

Anna nudged him. "Who cares? Let's have some now."

Luke brushed his blond hair aside and reached into his pocket for his knife. Opening the blade, he wiped it on his pants and began to carve up the bar.

"Oh God!" said Gwen. "I haven't had so much fun in ages. How much can we eat? Can we eat it all?"

"No," said Luke. "I got to save some for my little brother and I'm saving some for my ma's birthday. But we can eat the rest."

Anna shook her head. "Oh, no! Let's not eat it all right now. Figure how much we have and then divide it in two. We'll eat half now and half later. That way it will last twice as long!"

Everyone agreed. Luke carved off a piece for his little brother and mother and then the rest he divided in two. Removing one piece from the wrapping, he retied the package. "There," he said. "Now, we won't be tempted to cheat."

"Come on!" said Gwen.

Luke cut the piece into four equal parts and passed one part to each friend. The four of them sat still, holding their treasure, not knowing who should go first. Gwen couldn't take it any longer and, carefully biting off a piece, began savoring it with audible groans. Each of the others quickly followed. They were silent except for moans and grunts for the first few moments, enjoying the rich flavor they had missed since setting out on the trail in February.

"This is just too good," said Anna. "Luke, I don't care what anyone says, you're the most handsome, bravest, smartest boy I've ever known." Luke smiled and showed his chocolate covered teeth.

"I wonder," said Gwen. "Is there chocolate in Heaven? What if there isn't any food?"

"Sure there's food in Heaven," replied Joey. "Eating's one of the best things, so naturally God would have food."

Gwen turned to Joey, her chocolate almost gone. "Joey, you said Luke had another surprise. What's in the jug?"

Luke leaned forward and lowered his voice. "I also got this from that Gentile fellow. It's real corn whiskey! How 'bout that?"

"Ugh!" exclaimed Gwen. "Who'd want it?"

"Luke," warned Anna, "you know you're not supposed to be drinking whiskey. Your pa catches you with that and he'll tan ya good."

"First of all," countered a hurt Luke, "my pa don't give me lickings no more cause I'm too big. Second, Miss 'Pure as Water,' the Brethren have a nip now and again. I know, cause I've seen 'em."

"But Brother Brigham said that whiskey was the Devil's own tea and that Saints shouldn't partake of it."

Red Eagle's Camp

Joey picked up the jug. "We know! We know! We've heard the same sermons as you. But the Apostles even have a drink once in a while, even Brother Brigham."

"Aw, come on, Anna," said Gwen. "Let's try it."

Luke pointed to the jug. "Even late at night, while riding the herd, a fellow will pass a jug and give us a sip. It ain't the first time we've had whiskey, huh, Joey?"

"Now watch me," said Joey. He tipped the jug up and took a mouthful of spirits and quickly swallowed. Screwing up his face for several seconds, he gasped for air. "See, that weren't so hard, and it feels good going down."

"Now it's my turn," said Luke as he took the jug. The liquid produced the same result on young Allison.

Gwen looked at Anna. "If I try it, you won't tell, will ya?"

Anna felt the excitement rush through her. "No, I won't tell. Promise!"

Gwen took the jug and, wiping its mouth with her hand, cautiously lifted it to her lips. There she hesitated, uncertain whether to proceed or not. "Come, on," said Joey, "it ain't going to poison ya."

Satisfied, she tipped the jug and let some of the whiskey slip into her mouth. At once she swallowed and gagged, trying to spit out the remaining alcohol. "Augh! That was awful."

Luke and Joey both laughed and soon Anna joined them. "Ya did it all wrong!" declared Luke. "Ya got to swallow and then blow out." He took another drink to demonstrate his knowledge.

"Oh, it's vile. How can ya drink that?" asked Gwen.

Anna giggled again. "It can't be that bad."

"Then you try it," said her cousin.

"Ya, come on, Anna," challenged Luke. "You try."

Anna shrugged her shoulders. "All right, it's just one drink. Let me have the jug." Without hesitation, she held it to her lips and took a swallow, blowing out afterward as Luke had shown them. "There," she said, "that wasn't too bad." Everyone was grinning at her and she felt very naughty, but happy too. "I could even do it again."

"All right," announced Gwen. "We'll all take one more."

After the second drink, everything they said suddenly became funny and they all were soon laughing and holding their sides. Empty stomachs and strong spirits produced quick results on the uninitiated. Before a half hour was up, Anna realized she was in trouble. "I think I'm gonna be sick," she announced.

Gwen looked at her. "Sick? What's wrong with…" Abruptly, Gwen placed a hand over her mouth and quickly turned to one side as she began retching. At first Luke and Joey laughed but their laughter soon died away as it became apparent that Gwen couldn't stop throwing up. Anna couldn't stand watching her cousin and there was no way to get off the rock in time. It started in the depth of her stomach and rushed up like a stampeding herd of cattle. She turned away so the boys wouldn't see and tried not to make a mess on her dress.

Luke looked at Joey. "Maybe we overdid it! They ain't never had hard stuff before, ya know. What's wrong, Joey? Ya look a little green!"

When it was over, the girls tidied up and said their excuses to the boys who were in every way gentlemen and very understanding. Anna felt queasy and realized she was still acting under the influence of the whiskey because her head was light and her legs shaky. Luke promised to save the second half of the chocolate and to guard it with his life. Gwen and Anna didn't want to discuss chocolate just then; they said goodbye and climbed down from the boulder.

Before returning home, they stopped at the creek and washed their hands and faces. Still unsteady, they helped each other out of the stream bed, over a small hill and down to their cabin.

As soon as they turned the corner and saw a buggy and several horses tied up before the dugout, they knew at once what had happened. Gwen let out a hurtful moan and ran to the door, pulling it open, Anna hurrying right behind her. Inside stood Brother Lissman, Brother Martin, Brother Taylor, besides Mary, Jason, Michael and Louise Pierce. The curtain was pulled back, and on her bedroll lay Alice Sinclair, a small bouquet of flowers in her clasped hands, her eyes closed, her body cold in death.

CHAPTER 17

December, 1846

Trapping Beaver

Wes' only clear sensation was cold. It was always cold, always had been cold and always would be cold. Cold remained the single force in the universe and, no matter how Wes tried to fight against it, cold would continue to rule his life. He dragged the sapling poles and forced his way through the knee deep snow as he struggled to keep up with Crocker, twenty yards in front, headed for the beaver pond. Only a light wind blew, but the stinging air froze Wes' breath to his scarf, forming a crust of ice. His legs ached from the climb through the stand of alders and each intake of air pained his lungs. "God!" he thought. "If he keeps going at this rate, I'll just fall down. I'll just fall and freeze and let the snow drift over me!"

Looking up, Wes saw that Crocker had reached the top of the hill and then turned to see what was keeping his assistant. The mountain man stood unintimidated against the wind, dressed from head to foot in animal skins, metal traps hanging over his shoulder, bait pegs and castoreum pouch hanging from his belt, his moist breath condensing in the air. "Come on, Farm-boy. We got beav down there."

"I'm coming. God, why ya have to go so fast?"

Crocker waited until Wes made the hill. Below them lay a large frozen pond, the banks cleared of trees by the industrious beaver. Crocker pointed at snow covered mounds out on the ice. "See there at the other end? That's a lodge, and down here are two more. We'll set at all three." They moved down the hill and through a thin stand of trees to the pond's bank. Crocker examined the ice as he walked along the pond's edge and, finding the place he wanted, held out his hand to Wes.

Wes dropped the poles and, withdrawing a hand ax from his belt, handed it to Crocker. The mountain man walked out on the frozen pond to a point several feet from shore, knelt down and began hacking away at the ice. Wes plopped down in the snow to rest.

"Ya see this?" said Crocker. "I'm cutting a hole in the ice."

"Yes," thought Wes. "Ya show me every time like it's the first. I know how to do it."

"When ya got 'er big enough," continued Crock, "about three feet round, ya have to check out the depth." Crocker removed his fur-lined mitten, pulled up his coat's sleeve and reached down into the icy water with his hand. "Now ya want it 'bout a half foot deep, but next to a drop-off." Feeling around with his hand, he stuck his tongue out and twisted up his face. "Damn! Ain't no ledge, water's too shallow." He stood, shook water off his arm and hand and replaced his mitten. "We'll try over to the left."

Wes knew what was next: it was his turn to dig a hole. He watched Crocker walk the bank until he was satisfied he'd located an underwater ledge. Wes then struggled out of the snow and walked out on the pond to chop at the ice; hard work, but at least he would get warm. After Wes cut the hole, Crocker called out for him to stop. "Now, ya want me to check it or can you?"

Wes hesitated. If he said "no" then he'd have to reach down in the cold water, and if he said "yes" Crocker would lecture him about being a slow learner. Better to reach into the icy depths. Removing his mitten, he pulled back his sleeve and flexed his poor, about to be tortured, hand. "Come on," yelled his partner. "Get humping!"

Wes reached down and felt the pond's bottom eight inches under the surface. The water was painful, taking his breath away. He reached farther under the ice and found the ledge which dropped off into deeper water. It was perfect.

Wes pulled out his arm. "It's good. Nice drop-off."

"All right," said Crock. "Let's do 'er." He carried one of the poles, which measured two inches at its trunk, out onto the ice. They had trimmed its branches, leaving one to two inch long spikes all along the main stem. Crocker pushed the pole into the hole, forcing the top into deep water and sliding a ring over the large end. The ring was attached to a beaver trap by a chain. He secured the pole with a second chain to the pond's muddy bottom and then set the trap, placing it below the pole and covering it with a thin layer of mud. He rolled a bait peg in his castoreum pouch and drove the peg into the mud next to the trap. Standing, he kicked snow over the hole to cover it.

The process was simple: the beaver scented the castoreum and became attracted to the aspen pole. Wishing to secure the pole, it attempted gnawing through the sapling, stepping on the trap. With the trap tightly holding the beaver's leg, the animal instinctively dove into the deep water, and the ring attached to the trap chain slid down the pole and over the spikes. The beaver, diving to deep water and unable to return to the shallows, drowned, the frigid water preserving the fur and animal until the trapper's return.

After an hour, they had set all three traps at the three beaver lodges, and Wes' arms were soaked to the elbows. "Farm-boy, roll yer sleeves up so ya don't get wet. Look at ya! Your shirt and coat are gonna freeze. Come on, let's check them other traps and get back to camp." With resignation, Wes followed the older man out of the little valley and up the snow covered ridges leading to another trap line. At the second pond, none of the four traps had been sprung.

"Damn!" cussed Crocker. "Them beav is gettin' smarter. We'll give 'em one more day and then re-set."

"Maybe," said Wes, "they's all dead. Maybe the lodges are empty." It was the wrong thing to say.

"Jesus Christ Almighty!" yelled the old man. "Gone? Can't be! Hell, all them beav can't be gone under. What's a trapper to do? An old raccoon like me can't make a living any more. Jesus, you'd think someone would still want beav, but no, they want them awful bufler robes now. Hell, any hos can shoot a bufler and skin it. Look at a bufler robe—it ain't nothing. But a plew, now that's real fur; best fur in the world and nobody wants it!"

Wes was sorry he'd irritated Crocker into protesting again, for Crock could complain for hours about the injustice of it all. Yet, Wes couldn't see what all the fuss was about. Setting traps in the middle of the winter wasn't fun, while hunting bufler, or hunting anything for that matter, was exciting. "Going fer beav," as Crocker called it, was just hard, uncomfortable work with little reward. "Let's go," interrupted Wes, "I want to get a fire going and get me dried out 'fore we go out again."

For eight days they checked the two ponds and their seven traps, but at the end of that time they had only two more beavers to show for their efforts. Crocker was visibly depressed over their lack of success and, as they sat before a small fire, drying moccasins and mittens, he pointed toward their bundle of plews. "Look at that, Farm-boy. Only fifty! Fifty plews to show for our work. Most years I'd have a hundred by now, maybe one hundred and fifty. You know what a hundred plews be worth back in thirty-two? A thousand dollars, maybe even twelve hundred. A coon could get a good stake. But now they're a dollar a pound! We got less than a hundred dollars there and that barely buys possibles."

Wes was holding his moccasins over the flame, trying to dry them out. "What we gonna do?"

Crocker threw away the bait peg he had been whittling. "Hell, we're 'bout out of coffee, bacca's low—sugar is plumb gone! We got to go fer possibles or we'll be up in these Rockies until spring."

"Where we going?"

Crocker rubbed his new, short beard. "Only one place to go—down the North Platte to Fort Laramie."

Wes felt very weary all of a sudden. "How far is that?"

"Well, if we could get over them-there mountains," and Crocker pointed toward the east, "we could do 'er in a little over a hundred miles. But we can't go that way cause the passes are closed. We got a hundred and fifty down the North Platte to the junction of the Sweetwater, then another hundred and fifty to the Fort."

Trapping Beaver

"God!" moaned Wes. "Three hundred miles! Why did we ever come up here?"

"For beav, boy, for beav."

"Then where?"

"Don't know. Why do ya always have to know where we're going? Ain't it enough that we're going? If we make good time we can return for spring trapping. If something else comes up, we'll do that. How 'bout living a spell with Red Eagle?"

Wes fell back in the snow. "I just want to be warm. I want a fire and I want a big steak of beef and baked potatoes and apple pie and I want some whiskey."

"Farm-boy! This hoss is hurt! The way you're talking, anyone would think ya ain't having fun. Hell, this is a shinin'. I can remember bad times, times when the snow was over the tree tops and the Injuns were all crazy fer topknot. This is sweet summer compared to them days."

Wes was quiet for several minutes, staring into the gray sky. Finally, he turned toward Crocker. "Say, can I ask ya something?"

"Sure, what?"

"Remember when them Pawnee was chasing us? How did ya know they were there? Ya had us on the run before they came in sight. How did ya know?" He watched the old man's face as Crocker considered the question.

At first Crocker was serious, but then a grin crept across his lips. "I just knowed, just a guess."

Wes sensed Crocker was holding back. "Buffalo crap! That ain't good enough. You knew!"

"I just smelled 'em. You know how Injuns smell."

"That won't do cause I know you're so used to Injun smell ya don't notice now. Come on, Crock, tell me."

Crocker was serious again. "There are things still to learn out here. Things that don't come easy just because ya ask. Some rawheels never learn and others do. If it's right for you, then you'll learn. If not, well, my telling won't make sense."

Now Wes' curiosity was bubbling over. "Please, Crocker, just give me a hint, just a hint and I won't ask again."

Crocker turned to face Wes and put down his coffee cup. "All right. I'll just say this and then ya got to stop asking. Ya got to think in Injun ways. These mountains and deserts are powerful dangerous places. Injuns been living here for a long time and they've learned 'bout living with danger. So start to learn their ways and maybe, if you're lucky, you'll come to understand."

"It was an Injun trick! That was it, wasn't it?"

Crocker just looked at Wes and scowled.

"All right," said Wes, "I'll be quiet. But I'll figure it out, you'll see."

"If you're so keen on figuring, then figure how we're getting them horses and Mule through the deep snow and down to the headwaters of the North Platte."

* * *

Gunner pulled his coat tight around him and looked down the road, desperately hoping to see some haven in which to escape the storm as the icy wind bit into his face. He felt stupid to have left St. Louis for Independence in the dead of winter when he could have hid out where he was. St. Louis was a big city, plenty of places to hide. He turned in the saddle to see Roland Palmer with his head down, trying to keep his face from freezing in the bitter cold. Gunner shook his head as he turned his attention back down the road. He never should have taken Roland with him, should have left him in Illinois. The man had no brains; just a half-witted pickpocket was all he would ever be. Gunner needed companions with intelligence and imagination and guts: men who could think ahead and plan for the big take; not these little robbers who steal and then drink everything away.

Of course, Gunner ignored the fact that it was his drinking and fighting in St. Louis that caused them to leave the City on short notice. Roland's petty thieveries hadn't been noticed by the sheriff, but when Gunner killed an unarmed fourteen-year-old boy outside a tavern the sheriff did take notice, and it was only the warning given by a local whore that allowed them to leave town in time. But Independence would be a new place, a new start. He would get a little money and open his own tavern; maybe keep some whores and do a few jobs on the side, just to keep a hand in. He knew the West was ripe in opportunity for a man like himself, a man not afraid to use a gun or knife and smart enough to take advantage. And he knew it was only time before that big break would come.

Roland poked his nose out of his coat. "Where are we?" he whined.

"How the fuck should I know?"

"I'm 'bout froze, Gunner. We got to find someplace and find it soon or we'll die!"

"Shit, don't ya think I know it? Just shut your trap and leave it to me."

"But ya ain't never been here!" complained Roland. Gunner only grunted, and Roland drew his nose back into his coat and remained quiet. They slowly continued, their horses plowing through snow as heavy flakes pelted both riders and animals.

As the sky grew dark in the late afternoon, Gunner reined up before a sign nailed to a tree. "Lodging and Whiskey," he read aloud. "Come on, Roland, before our tits freeze and fall off." They rode down a path leading to a small boat-house on the Missouri River and, hitching their mounts, hurried into the shelter.

Inside, a few oil lanterns gave insufficient light to clearly see through the smoke. The little room held a bar and a bench built into one wall plus two small tables. Gunner made out an old man at the bench, a child sitting on a wooden keg, and an ugly woman behind the bar. Gunner knew the woman. "Mary McNaughton, you old whore! What you doing here? Last summer you were on the Mississippi!"

Mary looked through the haze at the newcomers. "Is that you, Gunner Hamlin? Jesus Christ, where did you come from? Who's that with you? Roland Palmer! I though you was dead."

"God, Mary, give us a drink," said Gunner. "That storm just about done us in. We're freezing!" He walked to the bar and removed his coat, Roland following.

"You boys got money?" asked a suspicious Mary.

"Hell, yes, we got enough to buy whiskey. Come on, now, give us the good stuff. No blue-ruin or watered corn mix."

She reached down, found a bottle, and poured whiskey into two glasses. "What you boys doing in this storm? No one travels in weather like this."

Gunner took a drink before answering. "God, we left St. Louie and the weather was fine. We hoped to make it to Independence without trouble. How'd we know a storm was coming? Say, how far is Independence?"

"About sixty miles. You're at the last big bend of the River here. Independence is straight west."

Palmer reached out, took his drink and gulped it down. "Hell, Mary," he said, "we liked to die. Give me another shot. Ya got any women? I could sure use a woman."

"Oh God, Roland, my whore went and died! Got the cramps and just died on me. No one's gonna stop if'n I ain't got a whore. Business will just dry up."

Gunner pointed toward the child on the keg. "Who's that?"

"Oh, no," said Mary. "That's Lisa–she's only six. Can't use her yet."

"She yours?" asked Gunner, still looking at the girl.

"No, just adopted. Parents are dead and I'm taking care of her."

"Yeah," chuckled Roland, "so she can take care of you later!" The three adults laughed.

"Now, Roland," said Mary. "Don't be unkind. I got to get my investment back, don't I?"

"Where's that fucking-ugly half-wit ya call a son?" asked Gunner.

"Toby? He ain't a half-wit, Gunner. That's uncalled for! He's asleep: he don't do well in cold weather. Jake's in the galley making supper. You boys can afford supper, can't ya?"

"Sure," replied Roland. "We got money."

Gunner motioned for another drink. "Say, Mary, you need a new whore. How about this: when this storm is over, Roland and me will go to Independence and get ya another and bring her back. How about that?"

Her eyes narrowed. "Why send you? Why not just send Toby?"

Gunner smiled. "Cause ya know that Toby will bring back some sick thing that's ugly enough to kill a blind ox. Now you let me go. I'll bring back some pretty little thing that will have the rawheels in here begging for her. You can double yer whiskey price and they'll love ya for it."

She smiled back at Gunner. "If I had that many customers, I could use two whores."

"Well, hell, I'll bring back two then."

"And what do you want for this little favor?"

Trapping Beaver

Gunner pointed to Roland. "Palmer and me? Hell, we don't want nothing really. Just a part of the whores will do. Maybe half."

Mary rocked back on her heels and let out a deep laugh. "You got to be crazy, Gunner. I feed 'em and I house 'em and you get paid for 'em. I'll give ya ten percent for the first six months. That will be a bundle, I'll tell ya, if ya get pretty ones."

"Half for a full year."

"You're crazy. I can go to Independence myself when the storm is over and get my own women. Why should I throw money away on you?"

"I know my whores, Mary. You go there, and ya got to get one away from a tavern there, and what kind of woman wants to leave a real city to come out here? I'll tell ya, the old and sick ones. The young one's are making too much money there. What are ya gonna do, kidnap 'em?"

She continued smiling at him and her eyes flickered in the lantern light. "It won't be the first time," she said in a quiet voice.

Gunner chuckled. "I'll bet. Now, do we have a deal?"

"I'll give you twenty-five percent for nine months, but only if they're young and they got to be beauties. Otherwise, you can hustle them right back to Independence."

"A full year!"

She shook her head. "Nine months."

"Agreed." He held out his hand and she took it.

"Now," said Mary, "let's get some grub. I'm deducting your stay from your profits, Gunner. Business is business."

Gunner stopped by the child and reached down to stroke her cheek with his finger. "This one will do fine in a few years. Six years old ya say?"

"Yes, six."

CHAPTER 18

February, 1847

A Gift of Elk

The storm blew snow over the bare landscape and off the cliffs overlooking the Missouri at Council Bluffs. Crocker and Wes stopped at the American Fur Company's trading post eight miles south of the Mormon settlement of Winter Quarters to deliver mail they had contracted to transport from Fort Laramie. Then, pulling their buffalo coats tightly about them, they rode north toward Winter Quarters, moving through the storm as snow pelted them and stuck to their clothing, turning their windward sides into snowmen. To visit the Mormons and check up on how the Sinclairs were doing was Crocker's idea. Yet, they had no assurance the Sinclairs had made it as far as Council Bluffs; many Mormon trains were still on the trail in Iowa.

Riding around a bend to discover seven hundred cabins and dugouts surrounded by a stockade, the two trappers reined in to gape at the sight. They had visited Council Bluffs just the previous summer before the Mormons arrived and at that time the only civilization was the trading post at the Pottawatamie Village and the ferry. Now a town lay before them complete with grist mill and log tabernacle.

They asked directions at several cabins before learning the Sinclairs' dugout sat on a hill overlooking the main settlement. Arriving at the dugout, they dismounted and tied their horses to a small hitching post. They saw no one outside, but a wisp of smoke blown from the chimney by the wind told them someone must be home. Stomping their feet and brushing the snow from their bodies, they stood before the door as Crocker knocked. After a few moments, the door opened wide and a youth called for the visitors to enter quickly. Wes and Crocker stepped inside while the door was closed behind them.

Wes needed a moment to recover from the snow blindness and adjust to the dim light, yet he could tell the cabin was small and crowded with people and belongings. The inhabitants stared at the newcomers, but Wes didn't recognize them. The youth who closed the door stepped before them and looked into their faces, trying to recognize who they were. Wes realized the Sinclairs had expected Mormon guests and, now that strangers stood before them, were uncomfortable and confused. "Can I help you?" asked the youth.

Crocker pulled off his otter cap and his mitten and thrust out his hand. "Howdy! I'm Crocker Sloan. This is Farm-boy. We met ya last summer." The young man took Crocker's hand but his face showed he was still struggling to remember.

A woman stepped forward from the shadows. "Oh, my goodness! I recognize you, I recognize you both! I'm Mary Sinclair." She pointed to chairs by a tiny table. "Please, sit down, take off those coats. This is my son, Michael." She turned toward her boy. "Don't you remember, Michael? These are the men who left the deer. Remember?"

Suddenly, the light shone in Michael's face as he grabbed Wes' mitten-covered hand and gave it a hearty shake. "Oh, yes, I do remember now: you gave us the meat. We're so sorry, we didn't realize it was you. It's been so long."

The two trappers removed their outer garments with the help of Michael and Mary and sat at the table. Mary ordered someone to fetch coffee cups. "Let me introduce everyone," she said. "This is Michael, of course; he's my youngest son. Jack, my other son, went with his Uncle in the Mormon Battalion."

Crocker cocked his head to one side. "Yes, we heard at Fort Laramie that your people sent men to fight the Bean-Eaters."

Mary nodded as she pulled up a chair to the table. "Yes, both my brother-in-law, Stan, and Jack went."

"Stan is the white-haired man?" asked Wes.

"Yes," said Mary, "that's right."

From the corner of his eye, Wes saw Anna Sinclair approach the table and place tin cups before the two men. As she withdrew, her eyes met Wes', and he knew she recognized him from her shy smile. His heart began pounding and he had to look away, embarrassed that someone would notice.

Mary continued with the introductions. "This is Anna, my daughter, and over here is Gwen, my niece. Step forward Gwen so they can get a look at you." Next, Mary gestured to a young plain woman sitting on a box. "This is our friend, Louise Pierce, and that's her boy, Billy, by the window. Her baby daughter, Lou Ann, is asleep. Well, I guess that's all of us."

Crocker looked straight into Mary's eyes. "I remember another woman, a blond woman."

Mary smiled and her eyes became watery. "Yes, that was my sister-in-law, Alice, Stan's wife." She was silent for just a moment as she cleared her throat. When she spoke, her voice was slightly lower. "Alice died last summer."

"I'm sorry," said Crocker. He leaned an inch closer to Mary. "You've lost many on the trail?"

Mary nodded, but turned to Anna. "Sweetheart, get the men some coffee." She turned back to face Crocker. "Many died last summer from fever. It was very bad. Many of us came down with sickness. Now the sickness is gone but it is still hard."

Suddenly Gwen stepped forward. "You wouldn't believe it, Mr. Sloan, it's been terrible. My uncle Jack was shot." Wes had been trying to sneak another look at Anna, but when he heard that Gwen's uncle had been shot and his name was Jack, Jack Sinclair, the hair on the back of his neck stood on end and a pressure pushed on his chest, forcing out the wind. This was the family of Jack Sinclair, the man he was accused of shooting! Yet, no one else seemed to notice his consternation as Gwen continued. "And then my little sister, Lucy, died and my cousin, Lisa, was lost. It's just..."

"That will be enough," Mary gently interrupted. "I'm sure that Mr. Sloan doesn't want to hear all our troubles." Anna leaned over the table and filled both cups with steaming coffee. Wes barely noticed, his mind still swimming with the realization he was sitting among the very people who might be after him for murder.

Mary smiled as she addressed Crocker. "Now, tell me, Mr. Sloan, what have you and your boy been doing since we saw you last summer? Have you been hunting?"

Crocker grinned and pointed at Wes. "Oh, Farm-boy ain't my son. He's Wes Tucker, from Illinois. He's wanted by the law for killing a man." Wes' ears were on fire from Crocker's words, and his heart skipped a beat as he realized he was about to be undone by his own partner. "He says he didn't do it, and this coon believes him, cause we've shot bufler and trapped beav and I know the lad. He's a good boy."

Mary reached over and lightly placed her hand on Wes' knee. "Don't you worry none, Wes. You're among friends here. We know what it's like to be accused of false crimes and chased from our homes. The law and the people behind that law can be blind and mean at times. I'm sure you'll be cleared of this trouble someday."

Wes struggled to gather his wits. "Yes, ma'am, I suppose you're right." In an attempt to act casual, he picked up his coffee cup and sipped the steaming liquid only to discover it was so watered the taste of coffee was barely discernible.

Mary, catching his reaction, frowned. "I'm sorry about the coffee. We have very little left, and I'm afraid we've grown used to making it a bit weak. But you must be hungry! How about some nice soup. Anna, bring them some soup."

Crocker held up his hand. "There's no need. We just come by to see how ya was doing. We don't want to eat ya out of house and home."

"Nonsense," replied Mary. "You're our guests. Now tell us what you've been doing."

Michael pulled up a large piece of kindling and, using it as a stool, sat down next to Wes. "You been hunting beaver?" he asked, his eyes wide.

Wes nodded, relieved his crime was still undiscovered. "We've been trapping up in the Parks, but it weren't too good."

A Gift of Elk

"Where's the 'Parks?'" asked Michael.

"The Parks is in the Rocky Mountains. We went up Laramie River to its headwaters..." Anna approached and placed a wooden soup bowl in front of Wes. He stopped talking and just watched her, not caring anymore if someone saw him stare. She looked so pale! He remembered her with color in her cheeks and glossy black hair. Now, dark circles ringed her eyes and her hair had lost it luster. She looked sick, and Wes' heart ached in alarm that she was ill. He looked at her brother, Michael, and recognized the same characteristics—a listlessness and hollowness, dark rings around the eyes, pale skin.

Suddenly, Wes was aware of Crocker. "Yes, ma'am, this here is scrumptious soup. Best this hos has crammed in his breadbasket in days. What ya say, Farm-boy, ain't this fat cow?"

Mary was embarrassed. "It's nothing, just potatoes and wild onions."

"Potatoes, huh?" exclaimed the mountain man. "We call them 'murphys' up in the Rockies." Crocker gestured toward the little boy, Billy. "Come here, sonny, and let old Crock give ya a piece of murphy." Bill stood and, with wild eyes fixed on Crocker's plate, took several steps forward.

Mary shook her head. "No, Bill's had dinner. He don't want no more. He just ate."

"Nonsense," retorted Crocker. "Boys is always hungry. Farm-boy once shot a bufler and ate it all before I could get off my horse. Ate the whole thing plumb down!" Billy slipped up to Crocker and, with fingers pressed on the table and eyes peering over the edge, stared at the strange wild man. Crocker speared a piece of potato with his fork and offered it to Bill. The boy took it without hesitation and gulped it down.

"Now, Bill," said Mary. "That's enough. You let Mr. Sloan eat his soup."

Crocker pushed the half finished bowl away. "Can't! Too full. Before we came here, Farm-boy and I just finished a feed of fresh venison." Wes stopped eating and looked at his partner—they hadn't eaten all day! Crocker was lying. "Come on, Farm-boy, time to get going. We've bothered these fine folks long enough. We just dropped in to see how ya was all coming along. I'm powerful sorry 'bout your sister-in-law."

"Thank you, Mr. Sloan," said Mary as she stood up. "And thank you, too, Wes. I'm so glad ya both came by. Drop in whenever you're close."

Crocker was already up and pulling on his buffalo coat as Wes hurried to finish his soup and catch up. Fully dressed for the storm they moved toward the door. Michael looked out the window and then at his mother. "Ma, it's a big blow outside. Why don't we have Mr. Sloan and Wes spend the night here?"

Mary stepped forward and took Crocker's arm. "That's a grand idea! The storm should be gone by morning and you can tell us all about your adventures."

Crocker shook his head. "Can't. We'd love to sit and jaw awhile, but we got important business. Ain't that right, Farm-boy?"

Wes simply nodded, still unaware of what his partner was up to.

"Well," said Mary, "you're welcome anytime. Be careful and good luck."

Crocker opened the door. "Thank you Mrs. Sinclair. Come on, Farm-boy."

Once outside, the door was quickly closed behind them to prevent the cold and wind from entering the little dugout. The two men unhitched and mounted their horses. Wes leaned close so Crocker could hear in the wind. "What the hell is going on? Why didn't we stay? This is growing into a blizzard."

"Didn't ya see them?" responded the old man. "Don't ya recognize that look? They're starving! They're starving and they give us their food. Now ain't that the damndest thing ya ever saw?"

Wes felt sick inside–Crocker had confirmed his suspicions. "What can we do?"

"We're going hunting, that's what we can do. Now let's vamose."

They followed the Big Muddy up river until they found a place to sit out the worst of the storm. The next morning the wind was down and the snow had stopped falling. Taking Mule, they left their camp and began looking for tracks. The area around Winter Quarters had been cleared of game by the Mormons and it took three days of skilled tracking before they found a small herd of elk seeking shelter at the foot of a bluff on the Elkhorn River. They dropped a large cow, gutted it and packed it on Mule. Their return to Council Bluffs was slow, the deep snow forcing them to detour often.

Just before dinner time of the fourth day they arrived at the Sinclair dugout. As the sun peeked from under a cloud, causing the snow to

A Gift of Elk

reflect a brilliant white, they knocked on the door. Gwen Sinclair opened the door and then just stood, staring at Crocker and Wes. Mary Sinclair's voice came from the darkened cabin. "Who's there, Gwen?"

"It's Mr. Sloan and Farm-boy."

Mary was at the door in seconds. "My goodness, we didn't expect you two back so soon. Come in, come in."

Crocker pointed to Mule. "We was just passing through and had this animal we brought down this morning and we didn't want to drag it around so we wondered if you might put it to use."

Mary stepped out the door to look where Crocker was pointing. As she stared at the elk on Mule's back, she put a hand before her mouth. "Oh, my God! An elk!"

Wes felt so proud he thought he would burst. "Ya, we want you to have it. We sometimes shoot too many, so if you'd take it off our hands, we'd be much obliged."

Mary continued looking at the meat and holding her hands over her mouth, but tears streamed down her cheeks and her shoulders shook from sobbing. Wes became embarrassed and turned to see Crocker fidgeting, too. The other Sinclairs slowly came out of the cabin, moving like prisoners just freed after years of imprisonment, to stare at the dead animal.

Mary tried to stop her crying as she put a hand on Wes' arm. "God bless you, God bless you both." She quickly turned and ran back into the cabin.

Michael stepped up to the elk. "This is for us?" he said as if it couldn't be true.

Wes laughed, glad that Mrs. Sinclair's crying had stopped although he noticed tears on the cheeks of both Gwen and Anna. "Come on, let's get it off old Mule. We'll hang it somewhere."

Mary appeared at the door, her eyes wiped clean and her composure back. "Michael, help Mr. Tucker with the deer."

"Elk, mother."

"Yes, elk. Mr. Sloan, you and Wes must stay for a meal. We'll cook elk and make a party of it. Say you'll stay."

Wes smiled to see Crocker blush. "Oh, all right. Guess we can stay fer one feed, but nothing fancy. Just elk, now. That's all!"

The Sinclairs and the two visitors entered the cabin except for Jason and Michael who stayed outside to butcher the animal. Against Crocker's objections, Mary sent both Gwen and Anna out to neighbors' cabins to fetch coffee, flour and sugar. Wes was disappointed when he saw that Anna was about to leave and almost asked if he could go with her, but caught himself in time.

Soon, a nice fire burned in the fireplace. Crocker and Wes sipped hot coffee with sugar, and biscuits baked in a homemade oven. From where Wes sat, he could see out the little window and he noticed that Michael kept making trips down the hill with bundles under his arm. They were sending gifts of meat to their neighbors.

Mary placed large cuts of elk meat over the fire, and Louise made a thick, dark gravy to cover fresh, hot biscuits. When all was ready and the Sinclairs found places to sit, Anna sat down at the little table next to Wes. With her so close, he could hardly eat, afraid to look at her with more than just a glance, yet afraid he'd make a mistake and draw her attention. But he could look at her hands, hands which moved with a gentle grace, small hands which reminded him of his grandmother. Anna spoke little during the meal, leaving the conversation to her mother, brother and Gwen. Yet, when she did speak it was generally addressed to Wes. "Have you been a trapper long, Mr. Tucker?" she asked.

"No," responded Wes. "I just hitched up with Crock last summer."

"And where have you been during the winter?"

"Oh, we've been at the Parks. We were at North Parks at the head of the Laramie River."

Jason stopped eating and looked up. "Where's that? I've never heard of the Park."

Suddenly, Wes felt very experienced and knowledgeable. "Well, ya see, there are these three valleys or plateaus in the Rocky Mountains: the North Park, Middle Park and Bayou Salade."

"Now, boys," commanded Mary, "let Mr. Tucker eat his dinner."

They finished dinner and, as Gwen and Louise cleared the table, Crocker asked permission to light up his pipe. "Of course, Mr. Sloan, go right ahead–we don't mind."

"Mrs. Sinclair, just call me 'Crocker.'"

"All right, but you must call me 'Mary.'"

Little Bill mysteriously appeared at Crocker's side. "Did you fight Injuns?"

A Gift of Elk

Crocker looked down and, for the first time, took real notice of the child. "Well, who do we have here? Is this the hombre, Bill?"

"Did ya live with Injuns?"

Crocker picked up the five-year-old and placed him on his lap, and Wes almost laughed to see the rough mountain man with a child on his knee, smoking a pipe and telling about Indians. "Oh, yes, this hos has lived with the Injuns, lived with Crow and Sioux. They call themselves 'Lakota.' My second wife was a Sioux. Good woman."

Bill's eyes grew as large as saucers and everyone stopped their conversations to listen to Crocker.

"You were married to an Injun? Weren't ya afraid she would scalp ya?" asked the boy.

"Lord, no! She was my wife. Bore me two sons and a daughter." Suddenly, Wes was sitting up, taking notice for he hadn't known Crocker was a father. "One boy died and the girl, too, but one boy lived. He's back East in school, but some day he'll come back to visit. He's name is Running Elk. Gave him the name, myself."

"And ya saw Injun fights?" asked Bill.

"Oh, God Almighty, I seen fights I can't even talk about– too terrible, just too terrible! The Injun is a fierce warrior, especially them Sioux and the Bug's Boys."

"Who are the Bug's Boys?" asked Anna, her chin in her hands, her elbows on the table.

"Oh them Bug's Boys is the Blackfeet. Meanest Injuns on God's green earth. Great warriors and hates the Whiteman. Everyone's 'fraid of the Bug's Boys. But this hos is safe." Crocker reached down in his shirt and pulled out a small leather medicine pouch that hung about his neck. Wes was amazed; he had seen the little herb pouches the Indians wore for protection, but after living all this time with Crocker, he had never realized his partner wore one.

Crocker took the pouch from around his neck and held it in his hand so Bill could see it. "Now them Injuns have secret clubs, ya see. They have the Badger Society. That's a warrior club. It's secret and only the bravest Injuns get in, see. They also have the Fox Society, another warrior club. Well, all the medicine men got together and made a secret club. The Medicine Man Club and the head medicine man made this here good luck pouch. I wear it to protect me from them Bug's Boys. They can't hurt me long as I wear this."

Bill's eyes were so large Wes was afraid they were going to pop out. "Gosh, the head medicine man made it for you?" He reached his hand as if to touch it, but didn't dare.

"Go ahead," said Crocker. "Go ahead and touch it."

Bill gently stroked the soft leather.

"Here," said Crocker. "Cause you're my special friend and cause you're going to see the Injuns while you're going to your Zion, you can have it." He quickly looped the rawhide strap over Bill's head and laid the pouch on the boy's stomach.

"Gosh, for me? Holy Ghost! This is the best thing I ever got!"

"You take care of it and them Bug's Boys will never get ya."

Wes felt a slight pressure and turned to find Anna's hand laying gently on his arm. "Wes, have you lived with the Indians?"

He was petrified they would notice his blush, but there was nothing he could do. "Last summer we stayed with Red Eagle, he's a Sioux chief. His tribe is just a little one, part of the Broken Arrows. That's a sub-tribe of the Sioux."

She smiled and cocked her head slightly to one side and a coal-black curl fell over her cheek. "And you actually lived with them? I mean in their tipis?"

"Oh, yes, I was in Red Eagle's tipi. They're really very warm and comfortable."

"But," continued Anna, "weren't you afraid they would scalp you while you slept?"

Again, Wes felt very brave and strong. "No, they wouldn't do that. There are all kinds of Injuns. Some are good and some are bad, just like the Whiteman. Red Eagle's people are good Injuns. I wish you could meet them."

The Mormons kept asking questions, especially of the lands to the west, lands they might have to pass through on their way to Zion. Crocker answered the questions with a depth of knowledge that surprised even Wes. Late in the afternoon, Wes and Crocker drank one last cup of coffee and then said their goodbyes. The Sinclairs begged them to spend the night, but Crocker was adamant they must go. Wes was disappointed, but knew Crocker didn't want the Sinclairs to borrow more coffee and sugar from their neighbors just for them.

Before they mounted their horses, Mary Sinclair walked to Betty's side with Crocker and spoke to him, but she spoke so softly that Wes

A Gift of Elk

couldn't hear what she said. Mounted, Wes and Crocker waved, and the Sinclairs, all standing in the snow in front of their dugout, waved back. Wes took one last, long look at Anna Sinclair and, to his great gratification, found she was smiling at him.

They headed west toward the Elkhorn, but Wes didn't even think to ask Crocker where they were going. Before dusk, they reined in on a snow swept ridge. As Crocker looked about, he seemed to be feeling for something on his chest.

"That was quite a tale about the pouch," said Wes.

Crocker didn't look at him but continued to scan the horizon. "Just a make-believe, just pretend."

"You mean ya didn't get the pouch from the head medicine man?"

"Nope, just made it up."

Yet, as Wes watched his friend, he wasn't convinced it was all made up. "Why don't we go visit Red Eagle," offered Wes.

Finally, Crocker turned and smiled at him. "Now, that's an idea that agrees with this old badger. No more of this silly civilization! Let's vamose."

* * *

Anna snuggled down under her warm blanket with a full stomach for the first time since she could remember. That evening they had prepared a splendid supper and all ate until they could eat no more. The cow elk provided so much meat they were able to send large cuts to their neighbors: the Taylors, the Wheelers, the Tobbs, and even the Martins.

Before drifting off to sleep Anna thought of Wes Tucker and how he appeared much taller and older than the boy she remembered from the summer before. His voice was deeper and he carried himself more confidently. While he was visiting, Anna couldn't help but sit down beside him at dinner, and when sitting by him wasn't enough, she had placed her hand on his arm, and then he'd turned to look at her and her heart skipped a beat. He was so handsome and the memory of his face was so clear to her now! She felt a pleasing tickling between her legs and smiled to herself. Yet, she had to remember it would be unlikely she'd see Wes Tucker again. He was a mountain man and probably was returning to live with the Indians.

CHAPTER 19

July, 1847

The Buffalo Hunt

After a quick visit with Fego on the Elkhorn, Wes and Crocker headed for Middle Parks to trap beaver, returning to Red Eagle's village when the summer weather made beaver trapping unprofitable. There they joined the Sioux as the Indians moved west, chasing the buffalo herds. Crocker was restless, continuously asking the Sioux the whereabouts of an old Crow medicine man called *Osota Wicasa*, Smoke Man. When Wes asked Crocker why he was so interested in this Indian, Crocker only shook his head and walked off.

One evening Wes and Crocker sat before their tent and watched the sunset, Crocker nibbling on a rib as he searched for the last morsel of buffalo flesh. "I like panther," he said, "and I like dog, but bufler is still best. Beav is good, but bufler is best." Wes only nodded as he leaned on one elbow and enjoyed a smoke from Crocker's pipe. "Ya know," said the mountain man, "that little Sinclair girl and her family is probably somewhere along the North Platte right now. They say one of them Mormon wagon trains has already gone through South Pass."

"Where they going?" asked Wes.

"Nobody knows: this Brigham fellow has everyone guessing. He might go to California or Oregon or maybe someplace else. Another bunch of Mormon trains are strung out along the Platte. Plenty other pioneers besides the Mormons going west. The Mormons stay on the north side of the Platte and them others use a road on the south. Guess it keeps 'em from fighting! Most them other wagons are bound for Oregon."

Wes took another deep drag. "Well, it don't make any difference to me."

Crocker threw the rib in the fire. "It ain't none of this coon's business, but I know ya got an itch fer that Sinclair girl. Every time we're around them Sinclairs, ya can't keep your eyes off her. Why don't ya just admit it to yerself? Ya got a hankering for her. Why don't we just mosey on down there and have a visit."

Wes glanced at Crocker through the tobacco smoke. He had known the man for over a year and felt that a bond of trust had grown between them. "Crock, I can't go. You don't understand, there's things that can't be overcome."

"What? That she's a Mormon and you're not? I wouldn't let that stop me. What difference does it make if you believe in a Christian God or a Mormon God? They're all the same. Ya get along with these Injuns don't ya? They believe in the Great Spirit."

"But I'm not married to an Injun, and besides, that's not it."

"Not it? What is it then? What could possibly keep a young buck like you from riding down and kidnapping her off to some preacher's house? I know yer not a coward. What's keeping ya?"

Wes gave a heavy sigh. He didn't want to dig up all the unpleasant memories, but he guessed it was time. "Ya know I'm wanted in Illinois."

"Yeah, I knowed that."

"Well, it's kind of involved. It started when I went to fetch a mule for my brother, Bert." Wes told the story slowly and left nothing out. Crocker just listened the whole time. Finally, when Wes was finished, they both lay back on the warm ground and watched the red and purple western sky.

The Buffalo Hunt

After a few minutes, Crocker rolled on his side to face Wes. "Ya mean that if she finds out you're the one wanted fer killing her pa, she'll hate ya and not go off with ya? But ya didn't do it!"

"What does that matter? The Sinclairs believe I shot him, and my saying different won't change their minds. Even if she wanted to believe me, my being around would remind her of it all, and I'm not too sure her brothers and cousins wouldn't stretch my neck with a rope."

Crocker was silent for a moment as he considered the problem. "Well," he said, "I can see your troubles. Say, why don't ya just steal her away and take her up to some lost and forgotten spot in the Rocky Mountains. That would do 'er. Once she had yer children, she'd stick around."

Wes had to laugh. "I couldn't do that. She'd always hate me. She'd hate me for killing her pa and for taking her away from her religion. It just won't work." Wes took another drag from the pipe. "Besides, there's got to be more women in the world than Anna Sinclair. I'll forget her. Hell, I've only seen her a couple of times. This feeling can't last long."

Crocker took the pipe from Wes and knocked out the spent ash. "Yes, you're probably right. Ya hitch up with them religious women and they make your life hell-fire. Always nagging and making ya do things ya don't want to. They make ya dress all up and go to church and ya can't never cuss and drink whiskey. What kind of life is that?"

"That's just what I'm a-thinking," replied Wes.

Crocker lit his pipe and took a slow drag. "Then there's this other thing."

"What other thing?" asked Wes.

"Well, ya know that love is blind. It don't matter whether it's a fat old Injun or a sweet young Mormon girl. When love strikes, makes no difference who it is, you're a goner. You'll do any old fool thing just to be around your sweetheart. Men become blamed sapheads and act like donkeys. If it didn't feel so good, it won't be worth it. And what makes it worse, ya can't make it go away just wishing. It either goes or it don't. I knew a coon that saw a woman only once and from that day..."

"Crock!" interrupted Wes. "I thought you were trying to help me."

"I am," said Crock defensively.

Just then a young brave rode into camp and stopped before Red Eagle's tipi. As he dismounted, Red Eagle came out of his lodge and listened to what the brave was telling him. Wes had been around the Sioux long enough to pick up some of their language, but the brave spoke too fast and was too far away for him to know what was said. When the brave finished, Wes turned to Crocker. "What did he say? Could ya tell?"

"He's from Man Without Hair's tribe. They're just over the hill, come to join up with Red Eagle."

"More Injuns? Are they Sioux?"

"Oh, sure, they're Sioux: another sub-tribe of the Burnt-woods. From what I can gather, once they join up, we'll be moving west again fer another rendezvous. Injuns like doing that; they join together fer the big bufler hunts and to get reacquainted."

After a half hour, when the sky was turning dark, the newcomers arrived. All Red Eagle's people went out to welcome them and the Indians yelled and hollered as friends and relatives greeted each other. Red Eagle's people pitched in to help raise the tipis in the village circle, after which they lit a large bonfire in the circle's center. Squaws relit the cooking fires and dancing began as the Indians displayed their open and sincere joy at seeing friends.

Early the next morning as Wes and Crocker cooked breakfast, a tall, skinny Indian with pox marks on his face came to visit them. He sat on his haunches and looked about their little camp while Crocker prepared the pipe. After the three of them completed the pipe ceremony, Crocker and the Indian held a long conversation that was lost on Wes, even though he tried hard to follow. The only words he did manage to get were *Osota Wicasa*. After the brave left, Crocker acted nervous, lighting and relighting his pipe and looking around. Finally Wes couldn't take it any longer. "What's wrong with you? What'd that Injun say?"

Crocker sat down next to Wes. "I got to take a trip. That brave said old *Osota Wicasa* is up on Antelope Creek. That's not far from here."

Wes was alarmed. "I'm going with ya, ain't I? You're not leaving me?"

"Son, I got to go and do this alone. I can't explain it, but I got to see old *Osota*. Hell, I'll only be gone a few days and then I'll be back. You won't even know this hos is gone."

"It's got something to do with that pouch ya gave that boy, Bill, don't it!"

Crocker's face knotted in pain. "I never should of done that. I wanted to help them, but I shouldn't have done that."

The Buffalo Hunt

Wes was not only frightened at being left alone with the Sioux, but was hurt that Crocker wouldn't share with him. "I told ya about Jack Sinclair!"

The furrows deepened in Crock's forehead. "I know, boy, I know. Maybe someday I can tell ya about this, but just now I can't. I've got to go. I'll leave the tent and the possibles and Mule. I don't need nothing, I'll be traveling light. You just tag along with Red Eagle and everything will be all right."

Wes felt somewhat relieved for if Crocker were leaving all the belongings, he obviously planned on coming back. But what if something happened to the old mountain man while he was gone? What if he was killed? Wes nodded to his friend. "Take yer Hawken and yer six-shooter."

Crocker smiled. "Thanks, Wes. You'll see, this old coyote will be back soon." He went right to work packing a few belongings and saddling Betty. After a quick council with Red Eagle, Crocker was ready. He mounted Betty and reached down, placing his pipe in Wes' hand. "Don't forget to use the pipe. Injuns is fun—you'll have a shining, Farm-boy." With that he tapped his horse in the ribs and moved off. Within minutes he was out on the prairie and out of sight.

Wes sat down before the fire and turned the pipe over in his hands. Looking up, he saw dozens of Indians moving about the camp, preparing for the day's hunt or working buffalo hides. He didn't even speak their language and felt very alone, wishing he were with Crock. Not knowing just what to do, he watched the sky lighten with the coming sun and began practicing those few Sioux words he did know. Soon he heard the 'weh weh weh' of the squaws calling for their dogs. Wes rolled on his side to face the tipi circle and discovered the squaws dismantling the lodges, preparing to move the village. Wes jumped to his feet to clean up his camp.

The squaws disassembled twenty-seven tipis, folded and packed the buffalo hides, used the ash poles in travois' or neatly tied them on top, and packed all their belongings. Even dogs pulled small loads on miniature travois'. Before the sun was two hands high, the women had packed the village and were ready to travel. With belongings piled high on travois' and small children sitting on top, the column moved; braves leading, women and children following.

Wes wasn't sure where he fit in the column so he followed the women. Soon dust stirred up, forcing him to one side of the trail to avoid being choked. The Sioux moved west until late afternoon when the men selected a campsite and the women went to work putting the tipis back up as young braves moved the horses to pasture. Wes put up his own tent and built his cooking fire. At least staying with the Sioux, he won't have to move his camp after eating supper.

As Wes sat before his fire and cooked strips of buffalo meat, he was ignored by the Indians and suddenly he felt even lonelier. Would he have to tag along without any company until Crocker came back? He could just slip off, but he didn't really want to be alone on the prairie; what if other Indians should find him?

Early the next morning, the tribe moved west again. All day they travelled until reaching a tree-covered hill leading down to a stream that wound through a grass covered valley. A village of at least fifty tipis was pitched along the stream. As Red Eagle's column moved into the village, hundreds of Indians ran from their camps to greet them. Before Wes knew what had happened, dozens of jabbering young children walked at Jeff's side and pointed at the Whiteman. Wes waited until he saw squaws erecting tipi poles before he chose a spot for his little tent. Then, as he prepared his fire-pit, another column of Indians joined the village. As the sun set, Wes looked about and tried to estimate the number of lodges: at least one-hundred and maybe more. With as many as ten Indians per lodge, the village could hold a thousand Redmen. The hair on Wes' neck began to tingle.

Before dark, Swift Fox, Red Eagle's son, appeared at Wes' fire and gestured for Wes to follow him. Feeling nervous, Wes picked up his rifle, but Swift Fox shook his head and motioned for Wes to drop the gun and to pick up a buffalo robe.

Complying, Wes put down the weapon, grabbed his robe and, with pounding heart, followed the Indian. They moved through two rows of lodges to an opening in the center of the village where a bonfire blazed away and dozens of Indians sat on robes and passed the peace pipe. Swift Fox escorted Wes next to Red Eagle and motioned for him to sit.

Wes gave a sigh: at least they weren't going to throw him on the fire or hang him from a pole just yet. He spread out his robe and sat down, yet no one spoke to him since the pipe ceremony was under way. Soon an intricately carved long-stemmed pipe came to him. He took a long drag, held the pipe up in his hands, blew out the smoke and uttered his

The Buffalo Hunt

oath. "May the Lakota and Whiteman live in peace." He choose to make it simple and fast, not really expecting anyone to understand. Finished, he passed the pipe to the man on his right. When the pipe ceremony was concluded, the same Indian turned to Wes and spoke. "That was good, *wasicun*. We should live in peace."

Such clear English spoken by the Indian shocked Wes. "Excuse me," he said, "you speak American!"

The Indian nodded. "Yes, I learned your English at the White Man's trading post. I speak well, do I not?"

"Yes, you speak very well."

"Good. I asked Red Eagle to allow me to sit next to you. I talk English when I can, when Whitemen come or when other Lakota speak English. I am part white; my grandfather was white. My mother sent me to the trading post because I am part white. She said that I must learn to speak your language."

Wes didn't feel quite so alone anymore. "I'm glad you do speak English because I know very little Lakota. I'm Wes Tucker." Wes held out his hand for the Indian.

The man smiled and shook Wes' hand. He was large with skin which, to Wes, appeared no lighter than the other Indians. He dressed in the Indian fashion and in every way looked Indian.

"I'm Black Face." he announced. "Do you know why I call myself 'Black Face?'" Wes shook his head.

"Because when I go into battle, I cover all my face in black. That is to show that in here," he pointed toward his chest, "in my heart, I am all Lakota–I am all Indian. It is not good for a man to be two men, half Indian and half White. A man should be one complete man–all Indian or all Whiteman. Do you agree?"

Wes shrugged his shoulders. "I don't know, I've never thought about it."

Black Face nodded and smiled. "That is because you are all Whiteman. If you were a half-breed, you would agree with me. But tell me, why do you use a Whiteman name here with us? Wes Tucker is a Whiteman name."

"Oh, my partner, Crocker Sloan..." Wes noticed that Black Face was frowning. "I mean, *Mahtola*, *Mahtola* is what your people call him."

"Yes, I know *Mahtola*."

"Well, he calls me 'Farm-boy' because I come from a farm."

"Farm-boy is a Whiteman name. I will speak to Red Eagle. You must have a Lakota name. Maybe after you hunt the *pte* or you raid with us, we will know what to call you."

Black Face's formal style of speaking was unnerving and now the mention of an Indian raid made Wes squirm. "The Lakota are planning to raid?"

"Not now–all these lodges gather for the hunt. We will go in the morning and kill many *pte*. You must come: you will ride with me. You can use your gun and I will use my lance and we will see who kills the most *pte*. Do you have whiskey?"

The last comment caught Wes off guard. "Well...no, I don't. We usually don't carry whiskey." Wes didn't want to reveal the real reason they had no whiskey: Crocker always drank up their supply by the time they were a few days out on the prairie.

Black Face smiled. "That is good. Whitemen should not give whiskey to the Lakota. Whiskey is bad. It is a good thing that you do not have whiskey." Black Face momentarily turned and made a hand signal to someone behind him. "But I talk too much. We must eat. We must have a feast so we will be strong for tomorrow."

Women served boiled meat in wooden bowls as the men continued their conversations. Those Indians on the inner circle with Wes were older: the elders of the Lakota tribes. Younger men sat behind them and then came the women and children. As the first braves finished their meals, the drummers took out their drums and the braves started a dance to celebrate the hunt.

Wes had never seen this many Indians together at one time and wished he could melt into the background for he was painfully aware of his differences from the Sioux. Yet, he felt excitement surging through him, for he knew that few Whitemen had ever seen the sights he was seeing this very night. And tomorrow? Tomorrow he would ride out onto the prairie with perhaps three hundred Sioux hunters and they would chase the buffalo. "A shining!" he thought. "This is a shining!"

The next morning Wes woke before sunup, when just a silver ribbon showed on the eastern horizon, and dressed before Black Face came for him. The Indian squaws were already up, preparing their breakfast fires. Next the young braves who assisted the hunters came from the tipis

The Buffalo Hunt

to wrangle the ponies; an important job since each hunter used several horses. Finally, when the sun was above the horizon, the braves came out of their tipis all armed for the hunt. Black Face approached Wes' fire. "Good," he said, "you are ready. Bring your horse and follow me."

Wes trailed after Black Face to the Indian's tipi where half a dozen other Sioux hunters prepared their equipment. A youth handed Black Face the reins to a pony and Black Face swiftly mounted. Wes swung up on Jeff. The youth handed an iron tipped lance to Black Face who held it out for Wes to see. "I will use the lance. I have a gun, but I use the lance because it is the Lakota way. You use your gun. We will see who kills the most *pte*." Wes didn't like the way this hunt was turning into a personal contest between him and Black Face.

They moved out of the village toward the southwest, and Wes saw other hunters already on their way. Black Face pointed toward an Indian who carried a long club across his lap as he rode along. "That is our *akicita* who will punish you if you start the hunt too soon."

"What is an *akicita*?" asked Wes.

"*Akicita*? This is one who punishes if you do wrong. He is like the Whiteman sheriff. The hunt's *Wakicun* will say when the hunt begins–he is the decider. If we do not wait for the *Wakicun's* signal, the *akicita* will punish us. Do you understand?"

Wes nodded. "Sure. Who is the *Wakicun*?"

"He is with the *pte* now. You wait for me. When I begin, you begin."

They rode for an hour before coming to the buffalo herd where the Indian hunters spread out in a great circle to surround the giant beasts. Waiting for the hunt to begin, Wes and Black Face sat on their mounts on a slight hill and gazed out over a herd of several thousand animals. Behind them two youths cared for Black Face's other ponies and several women and children waited to butcher the fallen *pte*. "Remember," warned Black Face, "it is the cow we wish. The bull's hide is tough and hard to work and the cow has the best flesh for eating."

Wes nodded. Crocker had taught him which were the cows and which were the bulls. He only wished the hunt would begin because he was getting nervous. On several occasions he had tried to reload while riding like Crocker, but he hadn't mastered the art and he feared he would now have to stop and reload each time he fired his gun thus falling behind in the hunt.

Buffalo Man

Finally the signal came as Indians in all directions raised their weapons and gave a chilling yell. Black Face raised his lance and, calling out with the others, urged his pony to dash off toward the waiting buffalo. Wes tapped Jeff in the ribs and bounded after the large Indian. The buffalo spooked from the Indians' yelling, but since the hunters attacked from all sides, the beasts ran forward and then turned back in confusion. Soon, Indians and buffalo were mixed together in one great dusty whirlwind. Wes picked out a nice fat cow but before he could get close, she turned and disappeared. He heard the sounds of shots fired and remembered that many Indians owned guns, mostly old English or French muskets.

The dust grew thicker, and Wes had difficulty finding the buffalo. Each time he picked out an animal to ride down, it was turned by Sioux coming from the other direction and lost in the mayhem. Finally he caught a young cow by herself and closed in. Standing in the stirrups, with reins between his teeth, he aimed his Kentuck and fired at the small bald spot behind the cow's front leg: the killing mark Crocker had shown him. The smoke from the gun blew away at once, but the cow disappeared too! Wes turned and looked back but saw she hadn't dropped behind him. He glanced around and finally spotted her running off as if nothing had happened.

Wes felt foolish and angry with himself. Certainly the first shot should have bagged the animal. Yet, he wouldn't let her get away and, besides, she might be wounded. He spurred Jeff on and, standing in the stirrups, attempted reloading while chasing her. It proved disastrous! He spilled powder, dropped the ball and then the ramrod, forcing him to stop and return to retrieve it, by which time the cow completely escaped. After he reloaded and was ready to hunt, the immediate field was cleared of both hunters and game with only the large lumps of fallen buffalo to mark where a kill had taken place. Women and children hurried among the beasts to begin the butchering.

Wes quickly mounted Jeff and rode off in the direction of the most dust, assuming that's where he would find the most buffalo. His next attempt was more successful. Riding down a cow, he waited until he was sure of his shot before pulling the trigger. This animal ran only a few paces before falling. Watching it take its last breath, Wes quickly reloaded before dashing off to catch up to the herd, knowing that squaws

The Buffalo Hunt

and children would soon find the cow and claim the prize. At least he had put one *pte* under.

As he caught up to the hunt, he saw Indians still chasing buffalo and scattering them in all directions. Finding a good cow was now more difficult, but finally Wes spotted two cows and a calf in a slight shallow and charged down on them. One cow split off and Jeff quickly overtook her. As Wes pulled up alongside and aimed his rifle, Jeff stumbled and, abruptly, Wes was flying through the air to land hard on his back. His first sensation was that he couldn't breathe. He tried sucking air into his lungs, but his chest wouldn't obey. He struggled harder and everything began spinning. With every ounce of will he fought to get air into his lungs and finally succeeded, his chest swelling and the life force rushing in. Now he felt a pain in his back. Carefully rolling on one side and continuing to catch his breath, he propped himself up on an elbow. His back wasn't broken, but he was in pain.

Two Sioux boys rode up and, pointing down at him, laughed. In a flash of anger, Wes threw a handful of dirt at them, but the struggle to do so only pained him more, making the boys laugh with renewed vigor.

Suddenly Wes remembered that Jeff had stumbled and quickly looked around for his horse, praying he wouldn't discover him limping. Jeff grazed near by, apparently unaffected by the incident. Wes struggled to stand and felt a stabbing pain in his left wrist. Feeling the bone with his fingers he decided it was only sprained. In pain and with bruised dignity, he picked up his dust-coated rifle and limped back to his horse.

By the time he overtook the herd and the hunting, the animals were scattered all over the prairie. He tried finding a cow to ride down, but his heart wasn't in it. By midday the Sioux stopped hunting and headed back to the village. With the hunt over, Wes had only one animal to his credit.

At the village the activity was intense: women and children cut meat and stretched hides to dry while many of the men helped with the butchering. A favorite treat consisted of thinly sliced liver or tongue eaten raw, and many hunters sat before their tipis, eating raw meat and telling of the day's adventure as they enjoyed a pipe of tobacco. Wes returned directly to his tent and gingerly lay down to recover from his fall, his back and wrist still sore. Without warning, Black Face rode up to his camp and reined to a quick halt. "Black Face has killed four *pte*, four *pte* in one day! I did it with this lance, without a gun. How many?"

Buffalo Man

Wes looked up at the Sioux and saw a powerfully muscled man holding a bloody spear and sitting on a sweat-covered pony. The look in Black Face's eyes and the smile on his face told Wes that the man felt a great triumph.

"I shot one," said Wes.

Black Face leaned back on his mount and roared with laughter. "Only one? With a gun you killed only one?" Then he caught himself. "That is good–you are still young. When you are older, old like *Mahtola*, you will kill more. But now you must be proud of killing one. We will celebrate tonight and you will sit next to me, we will eat together. You have earned your new name. Now I will go and your name will be told to me." He urged his pony on and was gone. Wes didn't want to do anything right now but lay back and mend his wounds. Maybe by tonight he would feel like celebrating.

That evening Wes sat before the bonfire with Black Face at his side. First, they smoked the pipe and then the squaws distributed bowls of boiled meat. Black Face questioned Wes regarding what had happened to him during the hunt and when told of the fall, he hooted with pleasure. Then he proceeded to tell anyone who would listen about his hunting and the Whiteman's hunting. Wes felt he was on exhibit for Black Face's entertainment.

After eating, they smoked again and then the story telling began. Brave after brave stood and told of his adventures complete with gestures and mimicked sounds. In the pit of Wes' stomach he knew that Black Face waited for just the right time to stand. When he finally did, Wes wanted to hide under the robe he sat on. Black Face must have told a funny story of Wes for all the Indians laughed and those behind him reached forward and patted Wes on his head or back.

Black Face looked down at Wes. "Now it is time for your new name. Your name will be *Wasicun Takpe*, the Whiteman That Kills. Is this not a good name?" He turned toward the audience and pronounced Wes' new name.

"The Whiteman That Kills," thought Wes. "That's not too bad! Better than Bear Cub!" Suddenly Wes became aware that, while some of the audience of Sioux nodded in agreement, others shook their heads or covered their faces with a corner of their robes, a sign of displeasure. Red Eagle stood and spoke before Black Face sat down. Wes couldn't

The Buffalo Hunt

understand what was happening. After Red Eagle spoke, the crowd nodded in agreement, except for Black Face who just stood and glared at Red Eagle. Red Eagle walked to Wes as Wes quickly got to his feet. The Sioux chief placed a hand on Wes' shoulder. "Name not *Wasicun Takpe*! Name is *Wicasa Ozu*. This is name given by *Mahtola*."

Wes felt flattered with all this attention, but was confused why Black Face's name wasn't acceptable. "What does *Wicasa Ozu* mean?" he asked.

Red Eagle patted his shoulder. "*Wicasa Ozu* is 'Man Who Plants.' This is *Mahtola* name for you."

Of course, Farm-boy and Man Who Plants. But why couldn't he have the name Black Face offered? Whiteman Who Kills! That was much better. Man Who Plants? Who wanted such a name? Red Eagle patted him again and repeated the name and then returned to his seat. Black Face gave a little growl and left the inner circle. Wes wondered if the Indian's pride had been hurt. Oh, well, *Wicasa Ozu* it was!

After the story telling, the dancing began. First, hunters danced around the fire to honor the fallen *pte*, then the women and children joined in. Swift Fox pulled on Wes' arm forcing Wes to stand and, following the lead of the others, stomped about the blaze in time to the drums. It was great fun. However, the Sioux were in no hurry to end the festivities and the dancing and singing continued until Wes was ready to drop. Tired from both the day's hunt and the hours of dancing, Wes excused himself and returned to his darkened tent.

Once back at his camp, Wes slipped into his tent and, removing his boots, snuggled under the robes. Before he even had a chance to close his eyes, he heard a scratching at his tent flap, the Indian's way of knocking. Thinking he was wanted back at the bonfire, he hurried to the flap and threw it back, sticking out his head to see who was there. The night was dark, but he saw a woman or girl bent down, her head close to his. She said something in Sioux that Wes didn't understand.

"What is it?" he asked. "Am I wanted back at the dancing?"

Giggling, she knelt down so her face was level with his and jabbered again, but still he didn't understand. "Does someone want me back at the fire? Does Red Eagle want to see me?" He felt frustrated.

She reached out and, taking hold of his right hand, placed it on her breast. With her other hand she reached down and gently stroked his groin. She now whispered, and Wes still didn't understand the words but the meaning was clear. He was shocked and pulled back, even though her stroking was having an effect on his manhood.

She interpreted his withdrawing into the tent as an invitation and quickly followed him inside.

"You don't understand," he began as he heard her pulling her rawhide dress over her head. Even in the almost complete darkness of the tent, Wes saw her outline and her firm round breasts. His staff grew even more. She reached forward and, releasing his constrained desire from his pants, stroked him. His resistance crumbled. Laying back, he reached out and caressed her firm, willing body.

The next morning she was gone, and Wes realized he didn't even know her name! His first experience with a woman and he would never know who she was unless she stepped forward. Remembering the night before, excitement surged in his groin.

Just then, Swift Fox came by and commanded him to follow. *"Wicasa Ozu hakamya upo,"* he said. Wes started to obey, but Swift Fox shook his head and pointed toward Jeff and Wes' gun. Wes understood and gathered his hunting equipment; today he was hunting with Red Eagle and Swift Fox.

This day the buffalo were scattered over the prairie and the Sioux, with Wes tagging along, rode far from the village before they made their first kill. Yet, Wes didn't really mind for, in the company of Red Eagle and his son, he enjoyed the riding and hunting. Toward the end of the day, a young brave approached Red Eagle and delivered a message. When the brave had left, the Sioux chief spoke to Wes. "At the Whiteman fort, many wagons come."

"You mean Fort Laramie?" asked Wes.

Red Eagle nodded his head. "Yes, Fort Laramie. These Whitemen are followed by other Whitemen."

"The Mormons?"

"Yes, some wagons pass the Fort; others are not there."

Wes looked south, in the direction of Fort Laramie. Was Anna Sinclair with the Mormon wagons?

Red Eagle pointed his rifle toward the south. *"Wicasa Ozu* goes to see?"

"You know, Red Eagle, I just might do that."

The Indian smiled. *"Mahtola* tell Red Eagle–*Wicasa Ozu* look for squaw down there," and he pointed again toward the south.

The Buffalo Hunt

* * *

Breaking away from his dreams, Gunner slowly became aware of a pounding noise. He opened his eyes and, seeing the raw, rough-cut lumber, realized the sun was well up and that someone was knocking on the bedroom door. He rolled over, trying to ignore Sally who was still softly snoring. "Who's there?" he yelled.

"Mary's sick." It was little Lisa's voice.

"So what?" called back Gunner.

"Mary wants ya, Gunner." Gunner heard the little girl's clopping feet as she hurried away.

He let his head fall back on the dirty pillow, not wanting to get up yet. He had a headache—too much whiskey from the night before. Besides, it was just too depressing to get up and face another day. Working whores for Mary hadn't turned out to be the easy life he'd imagined. Mary kept those damned books and wrote in them every time he slept with someone or took a drink. She charged him for everything and by the end of each month, he was broke. Roland was always getting drunk and wandering off, usually to Independence. Gunner had to keep the girls in line himself and what did he end up with? Nothing!

A sharp pricking struck Gunner's inner thigh and he quickly scratched, cussing the lice. Damn it, he was awake now! Might as well get up and see what the problem was. He slowly maneuvered to the edge of the bed, pulled on his pants, shirt and boots and stumbled out of the tiny room.

Gunner walked to the front of the barge and down steep stairs to Mary's room where he found the fat women in bed, Lisa sitting on a stool at the head of the bed, holding a wet cloth in her hand. A smoky oil lamp gave off a dull, flickering light. Gunner walked toward the bed as Lisa stood and quickly backed away. Stopping, he looked down and snarled at the little girl, but she only stared back with large fearful eyes. She was a beautiful child, but something about her annoyed him; it was a look in her eyes or a particular twist in her lips that made him feel ashamed or dirty and he hated her for making him feel that way. With an unwashed hand he reached out and roughly pushed her away, causing her to stumble and fall.

"Gunner," said Mary in a weak, strained voice, "don't bother that child."

"How ya doing, Mary? Ya look awful."

"I'm sick, Gunner. I'm powerful sick."

"What can I get for ya?"

"Jake will have to run things. Toby's the oldest, but ya know how he is; he can't take care like Jake. You've got to help Jake. He's still young and will need your help. You do that while I'm sick, Gunner, and I won't charge ya for a thing until I'm better. All right?"

As a putrid odor rose up to stifle him, he looked down through the dim light at the fat heap sweating under the stained blanket. Yet, as much as he was repulsed by Mary McNaughton and these miserable surroundings, he smiled and nodded his head. "Sure, Mary. Sure, Old Gunner will help Jake run things. We'll make a bundle, you'll see."

She smiled, but her eyes were dull. "Thank you, Gunner. I'll make it up to you, soon as I'm well."

"Mary, does Jake know I'm to help?"

"I told him that he was to charge you nothing as long as I was sick."

Gunner smiled and nodded again. "You just get well in a hurry, sweetie! We'll take care of everything."

Gunner hurried back up the stairs, breathing in the fresh air once on deck. He found Jake in the galley, baking bread. "You talk to yer ma?" demanded Gunner.

Jake, tall and skinny, wiped his hands on his apron and brushed a lock of black hair from his forehead. "Yeah. She said I shouldn't make ya pay for anything if you agreed to help out."

"Well, I agreed, so no charging. Now how about breakfast, I'm starved."

"Ya got to help, ya got to stay around and watch them whores and collect the money and turn it in to me. And if there's trouble, ya got to handle it."

"Shit, I know that! I already do all that. Don't I always take care of trouble? You just do your part and we'll get along fine." Gunner looked about. "Where's that fucking brother of yours?"

"Toby's still asleep."

"Did ya send for the doctor?"

"Ya, Roland, but I don't think he's gone yet."

The Buffalo Hunt

Gunner sniffed about the galley for a minute more and then returned to the bar where he found Roland Palmer drinking a glass of whiskey. Seeing his friend, Gunner just grunted, stepped behind the bar and bent down to look into a dark low shelf.

"What ya looking for?" asked Roland.

"Nothing."

Roland took another drink. "I got to go fer a doctor. Ain't no doctor coming all the way out here. Don't make sense. We're two days from Independence. That's the closest doctor." Gunner didn't answer, but continued looking. "What ya looking for? Maybe I can help."

Gunner stood up and spit out between his teeth. "Fuck!" He leaned over the bar toward his friend and spoke in a low voice. "Where's that rat poison?"

Roland grinned and whispered back. "Who ya gonna poison?"

Gunner reached over and grabbed Roland's throat, squeezing until Roland dropped his glass. "Don't ya never say that again! Now ya tell me where it is and then you forget I ever asked or I'll take my Arkansas toothpick and shove it up your ass!"

CHAPTER 20

Love on the Trail

On April 17, 1847 Brigham Young and a wagon train of one-hundred and forty-four men, three women and two children left Winter Quarters on the Missouri and began the long trek up the Platte Valley toward their final destination in the Great Salt Lake Basin. These were the first Mormons to enter Salt Lake Valley, the vanguard to the Mormon immigration. On June 15, 1847, when Brigham's train was beyond Fort Laramie and at the headwaters of the North Platte River, another company of Mormons gathered at Liberty Pole, eleven miles from the Elkhorn Ferry. This wagon train was called "Big Company" and consisted of five-hundred and sixty-six wagons and approximately sixteen hundred Saints. Brigham Young was not aware of the formation of Big Company and did not realize until later that they intended following his wagon train west that summer.

Anna, Gwen and Billy walked along a small stream that flowed into the Platte River. Their wagon train, one of the many comprising Big Company, had stopped on the east bank of the stream while the men double-teamed the wagons across the mud and sand to the west bank. This interruption gave the women and children time to relax for a few minutes before the arduous trek began again. As the girls and Billy walked along, enjoying the freshness of the morning breeze, Brother Carl Martin rode up on his large palomino, reined to a halt and dismounted on the opposite bank. "Have you heard the news?" he asked the girls.

They stopped and turned toward Brother Martin. "What news?" asked Gwen.

"The Battalion is due to be discharged this month."

"What?" exclaimed Anna.

Gwen clapped her hands and jumped about. "You mean they're coming home?"

"Yes," responded Carl. "A small party has met Brigham's train and is headed this way; about a dozen men, I think."

Gwen couldn't believe it. "Who's in the party? Is my father there?"

"No," said Brother Martin. "Your father and Jack Jr. are probably still in California. In fact, none of the men coming down the Platte are from our company. But at least the Battalion is going to be discharged and coming home. No telling when we'll be seeing them."

"How do you know this?" asked a suspicious Anna.

Martin stuck out his chin. "Because several soldiers from General Kearny's command arrived just minutes ago. The Battalion men are accompanying the General and Colonel John Fremont."

"Who cares!" said Gwen. "At last, the Battalion is coming back!" Billy, who had been patiently listening and holding a small rock, threw the rock into the stream, splashing water on Brother Martin's pant leg.

"Ho! What's this? A little trouble-maker, is it?" yelled Martin as he grinned at the child. Billy picked up another rock and threw it.

"Billy!" yelled Anna. "Stop that!"

"We'll see about this!" said Martin as he picked up a rock and tossed it into the water, splashing both Billy and Gwen.

Billy squealed with delight as Gwen jumped back. All of them laughed as they looked about for more rocks. Soon, Anna, Gwen and Billy were throwing rocks and stones, trying to get Brother Martin wet and Brother

Love on the Trail

Martin ran back and forth to make their work more difficult. Occasionally, he stopped to throw his own large rock, which splashed a wave of water on the youngsters. They continued playing and laughing until everyone was at least partially wet from the game. Finally, Martin held up his hands. "Enough! Enough! I give up. We've got to stop: we're all wet. Here," he stepped close to the stream's bank and held out a hand, "I'll help you across."

First, they passed Billy and then Martin assisted Gwen and finally Anna across to his bank. "Come," he said, "I'll walk back to the wagons with you girls. We all need dry clothes." They strolled along, Carl leading his horse, and let the sun dry their skin as their clothes clung to their bodies. Little Billy pulled at his shirt.

"I want my shirt off! It's all wet!" He unbuttoned the last button and pulled it from his shoulders.

Brother Martin suddenly stopped Billy and turned the boy to face him. "What's this?" he demanded, pointing to the small rawhide pouch hanging around Billy's neck on a string.

"Oh, that!" explained Anna, "That's just a good luck charm. Mr. Sloan gave it to Billy. It's Indian."

"Mr. Sloan, the mountain man, the one who left you the elk?"

"Yes," said Anna.

Carl's face flushed in anger. "Don't you know what this is?"

"What?" asked Gwen.

Anna couldn't understand what the fuss was all about. "It's just an herb pouch. The Indians wear them for good luck."

Carl shook his head. "They're medicine pouches—it's their religion! They put spells on these things. It's the work of the Devil!" He quickly slipped the string over Billy's head and stood, holding the pouch tightly in his fist.

Billy jumped up and down. "That's mine!" he yelled. "That's mine! I want it back!"

"See!" said Carl. "See what it does! Those savages cast spells on these things and the Devil's spirits can live in them. Don't ya know the Ten Commandments? 'Thou shalt place no other gods before Me.' This is the Devil's work."

Billy stared at the pouch in Carl's hand and began crying. Anna couldn't believe what she was hearing. "Don't be silly, Carl. That's nothing but a good luck charm and you know it. It doesn't mean anything."

"Doesn't mean anything?" he retorted. "That's just how Satan works; he gets into little things like this and soon he's in control. Charms and magic are the Devil's work and you know it. Satan's spirits are all about and when we weaken, when we let our guard down, they can get inside and take control of our bodies. You want that? You want a devil to get into Little Billy's body and destroy him? You're supposed to protect him."

Anna couldn't argue with him. She had heard the same sermons and what he said she had heard in church. Yet, she felt he was just over reacting. The pouch meant nothing—just a gift from a kind man. Anna suspected its being a present from a Gentile was causing Carl's strong reaction. She took Billy's hand. "Come on, Billy. He's just a mean old man. Come on, I'll make you a top, all right? Now stop crying."

Martin, holding his horse's reins in one hand and the pouch in the other, stood and watched with a menacing stare as the two girls and Billy continued walking toward the wagons.

"Oh, Anna," said Gwen, "do you think he's right? Do you think devils can hide in those pouches?"

Anna was a little annoyed at her cousin for not helping her stand up to Brother Martin. "No, I don't. If a devil were to live in something, it would be ugly and awful, not something nice, like the pouch. Besides, Mr. Sloan wouldn't give us something that would be hurtful."

"But, Mr. Sloan isn't a Saint. He doesn't know what we know."

"I suspect Mr. Sloan knows a lot more than anyone gives him credit for."

When they reached the wagons, the incident with the pouch was forgotten, except for Billy, because the wagon train was swept with the news of the Mormon Battalion. Fathers, sons and brothers would soon be returning and everyone was excited by the prospect. As Anna walked to her wagon she was surprised to see Sheriff Taylor Hawes talking to her mother. It had been a year since she'd seen the Sheriff and she'd supposed he had returned to Illinois. Her heart started pounding, for his presence here meant only one of two things: Lisa was rescued or her father's killer had been arrested!

"Anna," called her mother, "come and say hello to Mr. Hawes. He's just arrived from the East."

Anna rushed forward. "Is it Lisa? Have you found her?"

Frowning, he shook his head. "I'm sorry, Anna, we never did find your sister. My men looked hard, they really tried. We did come up with one possibility. I was just explaining to your mother that a family of Jim Crows by the name of McNaughton ran a rumhole on the River bottoms a few miles below Nauvoo. It was discovered that they took in a little girl not long after Lisa disappeared. The description fits your sister."

Without thinking, Anna reached out and took Taylor Hawes by the arm. "You've got to go see. You've got to see if it's Lisa!"

He frowned again. "It's not that simple. When we went to the River bottoms, the rumhole was abandoned and the family gone. We have no idea where they've gone or even if the little girl was your sister. I've sent notices as far south as St. Louis, but there's been no word. The best we can hope is that the McNaughtons do have Lisa and that she's well treated."

Now Anna was confused as to why Hawes was here. "Then what is it, Sheriff? Is it my father's killer; have you caught Weston Hamlin?"

He laughed and his eyes sparkled. "No, nothing like that. I'm not here on official business; I'm not sheriff anymore. I gave that up and I'm on my way to Oregon Territory. I just stopped to say hello."

Anna was disappointed for she'd hoped that her sister was saved, and if not that, then at least that her father's murderer was under arrest. But she smiled and shook Hawes's hand. "Well, I'm glad to see you, anyway."

"Thank you, Anna." He laughed again and looked at Mary. "Your daughter has sure growed into a pretty young woman, Mrs. Sinclair. I'll bet the young boys are always gathering around and pestering her."

Mary's smile was strained. "I'm sure they would, except they're all away in the Battalion."

"Yes, of course," replied Hawes.

"But enough of this," said Mary. "You must stay for supper."

"Well, thank you very much, Mrs. Sinclair. I would like that." He turned again toward Anna. "I understand from your mother that all of you were the beneficiary of a real mountain man last winter. Is that right? A Mr. Sloan?"

"Yes," Anna responded. "They gave us an elk. Actually, they left us meat twice."

"They?"

"Mr. Sloan and his partner, Wes Tucker."

"Tucker? I knew a Tucker back in Illinois. He was kind of a mountain man, but I think his first name was Wallace. He was about forty."

"Oh no," said Mary. "Wes is much younger. Eighteen, maybe."

Taylor Hawes stroked his chin. "Wes, Wes Tucker," he said, half to himself.

The next morning, Taylor Hawes left the Mormon wagon train, and the Sinclairs' two wagons continued in the third train of fifty of Big Company under the stewardship of Captain Lissman. That evening, Mary came down with fever and Michael fell from his horse and broke his foot. In the early morning of a clear, blue day, Anna built the breakfast fire while Gwen prepared dough for baking bread. The circle of wagons was alive with activity as the Saints prepared for another day on the dry, dusty trail. Sarah Wheeler called to them from her own campfire. "Anna! How's yer ma? Is she feeling better today?"

Anna shrugged her shoulders. "About the same."

Sarah frowned. "I'll be over in a while, dear, to see what I can do." Sister Wheeler turned back to making breakfast for her son, Paul.

When the fire was burning, generating the coals necessary for baking, Anna decided to check on Michael. She climbed up into the wagon box, held back the canvas flap and peeked in to find Michael half dressed, sitting with his back to the wagon's side. With pain written on his face, he was attempting to pull on his pants.

"What are you doing!" scolded Anna. "You can't get that pant leg over the splint."

He looked at her and gritted his teeth. "How in hell am I going to get dressed if I don't get these damn pants on?"

She climbed up into the small space in the front of the wagon. "You don't have to swear. You know you're not supposed to swear and, besides, I didn't break your foot, so don't be mad at me!" She took hold of the pants leg to see how to put it on.

"I'm sorry, Anna. It's just that it hurts."

She carefully examined the bandage and splint. "It looks swollen! Does the bandage need to be retied?"

Moaning, Michael leaned back. "Oh, Christ!" he complained. "It hurts just to look at it. It's funny, last night when I broke it, and even after the splint was put on, it didn't hurt that much. But this morning it's killing me."

Love on the Trail

Anna looked at her brother, frustrated because she didn't know what she should do. "Do you want some breakfast before we start?"

"Anna, if I don't get my pants on, I can't ride my horse and if I have to ride in this wagon, the banging around is going to kill me. Help me get on my horse!"

"But Jason says you're to stay here until he gets back."

"Where's he going?"

"To round up the oxen; the wolves chased them off again."

"Anna, cut my pants open so I can get my leg in. I can't ride in this wagon all day."

The flap drew back and Jason poked his head in. "Hi! How ya feeling?"

"It hurts!" responded Michael. "Did you find the oxen?"

"No, they ran down the trail. I'm going now with some of the boys to look. Don't go anywhere because we're staying here today."

"Is the train staying?" asked Anna.

"No," said Jason, "just us. I looked in on Ma. She needs the rest. Another day bouncing around in the back of that wagon will make her worse. I told Brother Martin we would stay here today and pick up with one of the later trains."

Michael seemed relieved. "What did Martin say?"

Jason laughed. "What do ya think? He was mad as hell! Said we shouldn't break away from Lissman's train. I told him it weren't his mother sick and needing rest."

Jason rode off with three other men to look for the lost oxen while Louise came out of the wagon to help with breakfast. Anna took her place at her mother's side. At first, Mary was asleep, but after a few minutes she opened her eyes. "Hi, sweetheart. Could I have a little drink?"

Anna helped her mother swallow several mouthfuls of water. "How ya feeling, Ma?"

"I'm better, Anna. Don't I look better?"

"Sure," lied Anna, forcing a smile to her lips. Studying her mother's face she recognized the signs of advanced fever: sunken, dark eyes and pale clammy skin. "You're looking just fine. You get a rest today; we're staying here."

Worry showed on Mary's face. "Not because of me?"

"No, it's Michael–his broken foot. He just needs a day to rest. We'll hitch up with a later train."

Mary lay back down, beginning a coughing spell that lasted almost a minute, requiring Anna to hold her as the coughs shook her weakened body. "You all right, now?" Anna asked. Her mother just nodded and smiled as Anna continued. "Carl Martin is mad because we're staying and Jason's gone down the trail again to look for the oxen; the wolves chased them again last night. Did you know we're only a few days from the Platte Ferry? After that we'll leave the Platte River and go up the Sweetwater. I hope we get out of all this awful alkali dust; it covers everything." She looked down to see her mother's closed eyes and knew she was sleeping again.

After Anna and Gwen served breakfast of oatmeal and corn meal mush, Jason returned with only two of the three missing oxen and was soon arguing with Brother Martin about waiting for the upcoming trains. When the other teamsters hitched their animals to their wagons, Jason just watched, for the two Sinclair wagons would stay. Jason walked back and forth as the Lissman train pulled out onto the trail and disappeared around a bend.

"What's wrong?" asked Anna. "Do you think we should have gone?"

Jason shook his head. "No, Aunt Mary needs the time, but I should go look for the other animal and I don't dare leave here. Michael's no good, all banged up. I'm afraid Injuns might come by and steal our oxen. Then where would we be?"

"Jason, leave yer rifle with me and Gwen. We can shoot."

He looked at her and smiled warmly. "I believe you would, too. You'd blow down any Injun that came by. But, if some braves thought no men were about, it might give them ideas. If a man is here with a gun in his arms, then they pass by."

"But, Jason, we've had no Indian trouble on the trip. I haven't even seen any Indians in the last few days."

"Well," he said. "We'll see. I'll just stick around for awhile and have another cup of coffee."

Anna made tea for the women and then she, Jason, Michael, Gwen and little Billy sat around their fire and talked. Anna felt guilty to be relaxing so, feeling she should be out doing something useful. Jason was as nervous as a cat, wiggling about and looking first down the trail and then up the trail, as if the lost animal was going to appear by magic. A wind from the northwest stirred up the dust and made the wagons' canvas tops flap back and forth.

Just as the heat and dust were beginning to make Anna uncomfortable, Jason stood and pointed up the trail. "I see someone coming."

Michael laughed. "Probably Brother Martin coming to see if we've been scalped by the Injuns yet."

"No," said Jason, "it's a rider leading a mule. It's a trapper, I think."

Now everyone except Michael stood and looked west at the dust covered trail. Anna squinted to see better and was the first to recognize Wes Tucker as he rode into their camp. "Howdy! I was up on Salt Creek with a village of Sioux and heard you were moving west. I thought I'd come see fer myself."

At first, no one moved, finding it hard to believe Wes had appeared seemingly out of nowhere. Finally, Jason found his tongue. "Wes Tucker! My God, it's really you!" He extended his hand toward Wes. "Get down off that horse and have some coffee. We got tea, too." Suddenly, everyone scurried about to find Wes a seat and a cup of coffee.

Even though he was in pain, Michael was excited by the visit. "How did you find us? You were living with Injuns? They didn't scalp ya!"

Wes laughed. "No, not Red Eagle's people. They're good Injuns. Now, the Pawnee are mad at the Whites so ya got to watch yer step around 'em. But you're already west of their hunting ground."

Anna stared at Wes, thrilled to see him sitting next to her, his worn, black rawhide clothes and long hair giving him a look of strength and wildness. "Are you married to an Indian?" she asked. The words were out before she'd considered what she was saying and they couldn't be taken back. As the others stared at her, she put her hands in front of her face.

"Well!" said Gwen. "You sure get to the point, don't ya, Anna?" They all laughed, especially Wes, and Anna lowered her hands.

"I'm sorry," she said. "I didn't mean it to sound like that."

"No, I'm not a squaw-man, that's what they call a trapper that takes a squaw. Now, my friend Crocker has been married to two Injuns–his second and third wives."

"God," swore Jason. "How many wives has he had?"

"I'm not sure," responded Wes. "They seem to die on him, poor man. Only his first wife is alive. She lives back East and is remarried to a fisherman."

"Yes," said Anna, "I remember you said something about that the last time we saw you." With no warning, Wes and Anna began staring at each other as the rest of the Sinclairs watched.

Finally, Jason gave a deliberate little cough to catch their attention. "Wes, would you do us a favor?"

"Sure."

"We're staying here today 'cause my Aunt Mary is sick. One of my oxen ran off and I got to get 'er. You can see Michael's got a broke foot. Could you stay around here while I go down the trail again and try to find it? I'd be awful obliged."

"My pleasure," he answered, truly meaning it and needing an excuse to hang around Anna.

"Thanks," said Jason as he jumped up. "You got a rifle, so I'll take mine with me. We ain't had no trouble but I'm afraid Injuns might come by, you know."

Wes nodded. "I understand, but the Sioux around here won't do more that maybe steal a few horses. A horse is a great temptation to a young brave. These Sioux is good Injuns and if they run off with anything, I'll fetch it back." Suddenly Wes felt very proud of himself.

Jason re-saddled his horse and was soon gone. Michael, still complaining about the pain, hobbled back up into a wagon for a nap. Louise sat in the back of the second wagon with Mary and baby Lou Ann. This left Anna, Gwen, and little Billy to visit with Wes. The three young people, now by themselves, could relax and talk without an adult looking over their shoulders.

Anna sliced bread for Wes as Gwen refilled his coffee cup. "What's it like in an Indian village?" asked Gwen. "Do they scalp their captives? Do they eat raw meat? Come on, tell us what it's like."

Wes leaned back, sipped his coffee and looked at the two attractive girls crowding close to hear his episodes. "It ain't much different than us. I never saw them kill a captive. In fact, I never saw them with a captive. Sometimes they eat raw meat, but it ain't bad."

Anna's eyes grew large and round. "You've tried it?"

"Sure. When ya kill a bufler," he used Crocker's word for buffalo, "ya slice off a piece of tongue or liver and pop it in yer mouth. It's good!"

"Ugh! Sounds awful," said Gwen.

"Oh," he continued, "that ain't the half of it. What we mountain men like best is boudins. Ya know what that is?"

Both girls shook their heads in unison.

"Well, ya cut a length of bufler gut and ya wrap it around a stick."

The girls sat entranced, and Billy suddenly poked his head around Gwen. "Buffalo guts? Did you say buffalo guts?"

"Ya, and we cook 'em up good, so they're nice and crisp."

"You're funnin' us, aren't ya," said Gwen.

Wes shook his head. "I'm telling God's awful truth. We cook 'em up and eat 'em. They're good!"

Anna decided to change the subject. "What are the Sioux girls like? Are they pretty?"

He smiled. "Yes, they're pretty, but Injun girls marry early, fourteen or so. By the time they're our age, they have a baby or two."

Gwen nudged Anna. "Anna's only fifteen and she already has a suitor."

Anna felt the blush rush to her face. "I'm almost sixteen–sixteen this fall, and I don't have any suitor."

But Gwen wasn't to be put off. "Wes, at every dance, Anna dances at least once with Brother Martin and he's the one that asks her! Now, that's a suitor."

"You have dances?" he asked.

Anna nodded. "Whenever we get the chance, we hold a dance. We have our own band–Captain Pitt's Brass Band. Of course, it's difficult to have one while we're on the trail, but once we get to Zion, we'll have plenty."

Wes was intrigued. "Where is Zion?"

"We're not sure," said Gwen. "It's someplace southwest of Fort Bridger. It's by a great salty lake."

"The Great Basin!" Wes couldn't believe it! There was nothing around the salt lake–it was all desert. "Are you sure?"

"Yes," answered Anna. "Is something wrong?"

He decided that either they were mistaken or it would be improper of him to dash cold water on their expectations. "No, I was just curious."

Anna placed a delicate hand affectionately on Wes' leg. "When we get there, you should come and visit. We could all go to a dance together. You'd like it. We do all the dances: the Copenhagen jig, the Paul Jones, French Four, Virginia reel."

He felt alive with her hand touching him and wished he could be at a dance with her and hold her. "Yes, I'd like that. I'm not much of a dancer."

"Oh," exclaimed Gwen, "we'll teach you. You should really come. There are always more girls than boys. It's no fun to go to a dance when there aren't enough boys to dance with."

"But, Gwen," corrected Anna, "you're always dancing with Joey Taylor!" It was Anna's turn to tease.

Gwen blushed. "I like Joey."

Anna turned back to Wes. "How long can you stay? Are you going back to live with the Indians?" She casually withdrew her hand.

"I'll stay until the next wagons come up the trail. You'll be going then. I'll go back to Red Eagle's village and wait for Crocker; he's off visiting some old medicine man."

Anna was interested. "Does he believe in the Indian god– The Great Spirit?"

"I'm not sure, but I think so. It's really much more involved than just believing in some Great Spirit. He talks about it, but it's sometimes hard to understand."

"Wes," said Gwen, with a smile on her lips, "why don't you come to one of our church meetings? You'd like it. We sing songs and have a sermon and afterward we sometimes have dinner at a neighbor's. Won't you come?"

He shrugged his shoulders, not wanting to get in a religious discussion. "I might. Maybe when you're all settled in Zion."

The three young people visited all morning. In the early afternoon, after dinner, they were joined by Michael. Still, Jason did not return and no wagon train came up the trail. When Anna checked on her mother, she found her sitting up, drinking hot tea and visiting with Louise. It was the best Anna had seen her mother looking in days. As the sun drew closer to the western horizon, dark clouds gathered in the sky and the wind grew in strength, blowing alkali dust over the campsite and the wagons.

Wes covered his eyes against an especially dusty gust of wind. "I think it's going to be a bad storm."

Gwen looked at the flapping wagon tops and frowned. "I hope it doesn't get worse. I hate these storms. It'll be miserable all night." As she spoke, the wind kicked up more dust and a few rain drops fell as if to confirm her fears.

Wes stood and looked about, but by now he could only see a hundred paces from the wagons because of the great clouds of dust. He pointed toward the north. "I think I saw a rock up there just where a small gully begins."

Love on the Trail

Anna first looked north into the haze and then back at Wes. "Do you really think we should move? What if a train comes?"

"Any train caught in this will corral for the night. If they aren't here now, they won't come until this is over. We need something to block the wind."

Michael struggled to get up. "Wes is right. We don't want to spend the night out here in the open. I'll drive one wagon and he can drive the other."

Wes shook his head and talked louder to be heard over the increasing whistle of the wind. "No, you get back in the wagon. You said Louise has been driving? She can drive one and Anna and Gwen can drive the other." He turned to Anna. "Have you handled a team before?"

"Of course! Gwen and I can do it. You just lead the way."

As quickly as possible, they cleaned up their campsite and loaded the wagons, Louise helping to hitch the oxen. One animal was still missing, but three could easily pull the second wagon the short distance they were moving. When ready, Wes walked in front of the first wagon to ensure the way was level and to make sure they reached their destination without getting lost.

Within just a few minutes they found the tall, jagged outcropping and pulled the wagons up close to the southern face so it blocked the storm. Large rain drops fell, signaling the worst was about to come. Sheltered from the wind by the rock, the Sinclairs and Wes could now easily hear each other and didn't have to yell. "Thank you," Louise said to Wes. "We couldn't have found this without you." She turned to Gwen. "Do you think you can start a fire? I'd like to get some warm soup into Mary. She's doing so much better."

Anna pointed toward the edge of the rock where a small overhang provided even more shelter from the wind and rain. "Look, Louise, we can build it right here and sit against the rock. It's perfect."

Wes went back into the storm to retrieve his animals and find more firewood while the women prepared supper. By the time it was dark, the rain came down in torrents, but the protection of the rock and the wagons made their own little world cozy and dry if not draft free. After supper, they continued their visit with Wes explaining all he had learned about the wild Sioux Indians and beaver trapping. Soon Billy and Lou Ann fell asleep and Louise put them in a bed made up in a wagon and then retired to the wagon with Mary. Michael, Gwen, Anna and Wes were alone again and decided to take turns telling ghost stories with the prize finally going to Gwen. Michael's foot looked better when he climbed back into the wagon for the night.

Gwen's eyes grew heavy and she excused herself to crawl up into the wagon and curl up with Billy and Lou Ann. "Now, when you're ready, Anna, just come up with us. Wes, you can put your bedroll right here by the fire."

"Good night, Gwen," said Wes.

"Good night, Gwen. I'll be up soon," offered Anna.

Now alone, Anna and Wes watched the fire die down and listened to the wind and rain. Wes unrolled his buffalo robe and draped it about his shoulders. "Are you cold?" he asked.

She shook her head. "No, not really." Picking up a stick, she stirred the fire's hot coals. "What are you going to do? Are you always going to be a trapper with your friend, Sloan?"

"No, I don't think so. There's no money in trapping beaver anymore. Most the mountain men are retired or acting as guides for the pioneers or taking buffalo hides."

"What about the Indians?"

"It's fun living with them. In some ways it's just a long party, going out to hunt all day and then eating and dancing at night."

"You've been to the Indian dances?"

"Oh, yes, they're great fun. All you do is get up and hoop around to the drumming, you don't dance with partners. You'd love it. But, I know I can't live all my life with the Sioux."

"What else would you like to do? Do you want to farm?"

"No," he said after a little thought. "I grew up on a farm, but I know now that farming isn't for me. I just don't take to the soil like my brother does. But, I do have an idea."

"What's that?" she said as she scooted a little closer. He opened his robe and offered her the seat next to him. She looked at him and the robe and then decided it was all right. Moving beside him, she sat down and, without planning to, snuggled up against his side. He enveloped her with the great warm robe, putting his arm around her shoulder. She felt safe, warm and natural next to him. Heaving a sigh, she looked up into his face. "You were going to tell me your idea?" For a moment she thought she detected a slight tremble in his side and arm.

"I have Jeff, my horse. You won't find a stronger or faster stallion in the West. I've been thinking, I could get a few mares and start a small horse ranch. The West needs good horses. Jeff would make a perfect stud. I've seen some beautiful places out here where a man could build a house and barn, where there is plenty of good feed all year round. Doesn't it sound grand? I would be out here and free. I don't want to return East– it's too crowded, and besides, out here is a kind of smell or feel that you don't have back East. It has something to do with the mountains."

She was slowly drifting in the comfort of his arms, his dream of a ranch sounding like paradise to her. "It's a grand idea and I know you'll do it." She snuggled even closer. "Tell me more about the mountains."

"Oh, the mountains! You've seen Laramie Peak to the west, but that's just one mountain. Soon you'll see some of the most beautiful mountains in the world. When you go through South Pass you're at the southern base of the Wind River Range. To be in the middle of the Wind River Mountains this time of year is an experience one can never forget. I've seen deep valleys with great granite walls which have broken off in giant blocks to tumble to the valley floor as if some monster kicked them all down. Up in the Parks, the mountains are pointed and sharp."

"What about where we're going?" asked Anna in a near whisper.

"The Great Basin? To the southeast of the Great Salt Lake a range of mountains rises up in tall gray towers. Their strength is unbelievable. You can feel their strength, it gets right into you. Right under your skin. Oh, Anna! Living in these Rocky Mountains changes ya for life! You're never the same because the mountains have a power of their own. It sneaks inside and changes you forever."

She could feel his excitement and his trembling and wanted to share in his vision. Knowing it was wrong, but not allowing herself time to think about it, she moved away just enough to raise her face toward his. At the same time, she reached up with her left hand and, placing it on the back of his neck, drew him down to her. His lips were firm and dry and she felt them quiver as she pressed hers against them. Her own body began to quiver as he reached his arms around her and pressed her close to him. They kissed again and again.

Her body was on fire and she thought she would die if he didn't put his hands on her, didn't caress her, yet she would never let him and somehow she knew he wouldn't force her. They kissed again and she heard his slight involuntary moan. She couldn't stop kissing him, but the barrier protecting her virginity was too strong, forged from strong bands of devotion by her family and her church. She knew all about sex and she'd talked to her mother about the love feeling, but nowhere in her deepest dreams had she known that the desire would be so sweet–so strong!

He was holding her in his arms, kissing her and shaking with the desire to have her, and all the time his past life and identity screamed in the back of his mind. Would she tremble so at his touch if she knew he was Weston Hamlin, accused murderer of her father? How could he do this, how could he kiss her and hold her, knowing he could never have her for his own? She was a Mormon and would soon be swallowed up again into the depths of her strange church. Yet, if he only held her this once, then he would kiss her again and again until she stopped him. He bent down, and her willing lips were there to meet his.

She kissed him again, but this time she felt the wetness on his cheek. Pulling back, she reached up and touched his face and realized they were tears! He had been silently crying as he loved her! "You're crying!" she whispered.

"No," he said, the lie so obvious it forced her to stop her probing.

He was so strange, so wild and strong, yet he cried to kiss her! He was at once hard, yet yielding. Her desire swirled about and came out a hunger. Reaching up again, she pulled his head down and pressed her lips to his and tasted the saltiness of his tears.

Early the next morning, Wes awakened with a start and felt her warm body still curled next to his. A faint hint of light showed along the horizon. The storm had passed and now the air was sweet and renewed and the sky was clear. He pulled the robe back just enough to see the outline of her face. Reaching down, he gently stroked her cheek until her eyes opened. "Anna," he whispered, "you have to get up into a wagon before anyone wakes up."

She closed her eyes and put her arms around him, snuggling closer. He bent down and kissed her cheek. "Anna, you must get up."

She gave a little morning moan and struggled to sit up beside him. Moving forward in the half-dark, she kissed him on the lips, her breath warm and full of life. "You'll come to Zion? You promise?"

"Yes, I'll come. Not right away, but I'll come. I promise."

She gave him another quick kiss and then hurried to find her place in one of the wagons.

Wes couldn't go back to sleep, so he gathered firewood and started a small fire to heat his coffee. After the better part of an hour, he heard stirring in one of the wagons and soon Louise climbed down and joined him at the fire. The others got up and prepared breakfast. After eating they hitched the oxen to the wagons and drove back to the previous day's campsite. Wes packed Mule and prepared to go, only waiting for another wagon train to come up the trail. When Anna finished with her chores she came and stood with him, holding his arm with her hand, but not speaking.

Standing in the morning sunlight, watching the trail, Wes wanted to put his arms around her, wanted to repeat the endearments he'd spoken the night before, yet he felt constrained by the presence of her family. Before mid-morning, the first riders appeared and were soon followed by wagons. Jason rode up and dismounted and Anna released her hold on Wes.

Her Church and family had returned to claim her, and Wes knew it was time to go. He said his goodbyes and mounted Jeff. Before riding off, Anna reached up and took his hand.

He was tempted to kiss her once more but decided against it. "I don't think anyone knows you were with me last night," he whispered.

"I don't care if they do," she said. Squeezing his hand, she looked up into his eyes. "You promised!"

"I'll come."

Late the next day, Wes arrived back in Red Eagle's village and found Crocker hadn't returned. He made camp and settled in to wait for his friend.

Early the next day, as Wes heated his morning coffee, Crocker stormed into camp. "Ho, Farm-boy, this griz is back!" He slipped from Betty's back and picked up a tin coffee cup. "That coffee ready? I been riding since before sun up and ain't ate yet. Ya got biscuits? God, I'm hungry. Unsaddle Betty, will ya, while I get me a cup of coffee."

Wes hurried to unsaddle and hobble Betty and returned to the fire where Crocker was preparing meat over the flame. "God!" exclaimed Wes. "I'm sure glad you're back. Did ya find that old medicine man?"

Crocker nodded, "Sure did!"

Wes looked to see if Crocker wore a new good luck pouch and the rawhide strap around Crocker's neck told Wes he was. "Ya ever see so many Injuns?" asked Wes.

"It's a big village, all right, but they won't stay together all summer. They'll hunt and party and then split up again. I stopped at Red Eagle's tipi before coming here. He said ya got a new name—*Wicasa Ozu*! Now how'd that come about? Injuns don't generally bestow new names unless something special happens."

As the mountain man ate, Wes told him all about the hunt and the feast afterward. When Wes was finished, Crocker lit up his pipe and leaned back. "You sure get into things on yer own, don't ya! Now, did ya get lucky with the ladies? Any young squaw been sneaking around?"

Wes felt himself blush as he remembered the night with Anna. He averted his eyes from the older man. Crocker slapped his hand against his leg and let out a holler. "God Almighty, it's true, you been bedded. I can tell from yer face! Congratulations, Farm-boy, you've degraded yourself to laying with savages. Must have been awful! She tie ya down and threaten ya with a knife?"

Wes shook his head. "I wasn't with an Injun girl. I took a few days and went down to the Oregon Trail."

Crocker gave Wes a knowing look. "Did ya find that little Anna Sinclair?"

"Yes, I found them in a wagon train going to the Great Basin."

"And what happened?"

"Nothing. Nothing happened."

Crocker watched his friend for a few moments. "But ya still got a hankering fer her, don't ya?"

Wes was silent for a moment as he tried to understand how he felt about Anna Sinclair and sensed the whirlwind of emotion starting up in his gut. "Ya, I guess I do."

CHAPTER 21

October, 1847

The Battalion Returns

Wes and Crocker rose early and took the ferry across the Mississippi River to a landing just three miles below the Hamlin farm, and, before the sun was barely up, they reined Jeff and Betty to a stop before the Hamlin farmhouse. Wes was so excited he could hardly tie Jeff's reins to the hitching post. "Come on, Crock," he urged as he hopped up the two steps to the front porch and then waited before the door as his friend hurried to catch up. Just then the door opened and a young woman peered out.

"Can I help you?" she asked cautiously.

Confused because he had never seen her before and wondering what was she doing in his house, Wes stared at her. "I'm Wes," he stammered. "I'm Wes Hamlin."

"Oh, my God!" she said as she backed up and opened the door wide. Wes and Crocker slowly stepped into the small front room while the woman turned and called over her shoulder. "Bert! It's Wes!" She looked back at the two men. "Please, come in. I'm so sorry—you don't know me."

Just then, Bert rushed in and, spotting his brother, stopped suddenly. "God Almighty! Wes!" he yelled. Stepping forward, he threw his arms around his brother. "Oh, God, I thought you was dead!"

Wes hugged back, tears welling up. "Oh, Bert!"

Bert pulled away to look Wes in the face. "You've changed! You've growed." His cheeks glowed wet with tears and his eyes shined. He pulled Wes close again, and they gave each other another bear hug.

Pulling back, Wes saw his mother standing in the kitchen door, holding a dish of steaming sliced ham. "Oh," she whimpered and dropped the dish, breaking it and scattering the ham on the floor. "Oh, Wes!" she cried, hurrying to him and taking him in her arms, moaning and hugging as if he were still a child.

He cried and patted her back. "It's all right, Ma, I'm back. It's me, I'm back."

When she finally let him go, he pointed toward Crocker who stood with hat in hand, a shy grin on his face. "This here is Crocker Sloan. He's the meanest, most ornery, hardest mountain man alive and he's my partner."

Bert quickly shook Crocker's hand and his ma took Crock's hand and gave the back of it a little kiss. "Thank you, Mr. Sloan, thank you for bringing him home."

Crocker was embarrassed and blushed as he stammered. "Aw, it was him. He come back on his own. This coon just tagged along."

"My God!" yelled Bert. "I almost forgot." He tenderly pulled the young woman forward by her arm. "This here is Lacy, she's my wife!"

Wes awkwardly stepped forward and, putting his arms around her, gave her a hug. "Wife? Jesus!"

"Come on," commanded Wes' mother, "let's go into the kitchen. You look to need a good breakfast. Now, come on everybody."

Retiring to the kitchen table, the men drank coffee as Ma and Lacy prepared their meal. Every few minutes, Wes' mother stopped what she was doing and, walking to her youngest son, put an arm around his shoulders and gave him a peck on the head or cheek.

Bert shook his head. "We thought you was dead, we really did. We didn't hear from ya in St. Louie so Ma wrote to her cousin, Butterworth, and a woman wrote back he was dead. Then we figured you would write on your own, but ya didn't. Then that Sheriff Hawes said he went all over looking for ya, even to St. Louie, and never did find ya. We just figured ya got yourself killed."

Wes put his coffee cup down. "I meant to write after I found out Butterworth was dead, I really did, but things were kind of all mixed up. I left St. Louie and hitched up with Crocker, here."

"Hitched up!" bellowed Crocker. "Ya tagged along so a man couldn't do nothing without ya dogging him."

"Did ya hear about the Sheriff?" asked Wes' ma. "He's gone. He quit the sheriffing business and went out West."

"Probably after me!" complained Wes.

"No," said Bert. "He really did quit. You can come back now; no one will bother ya. We got a new top sheriff in Hancock County, and I've already talked to him. He says if ya come back, ya won't be charged. There was too much killing on both sides and we got to put all that behind us and start building again."

"But," Wes objected, "I didn't do it—I'm innocent!"

"It don't matter—no one cares—it was a Mormon. Lots were killed and lots of us got killed. It was only that crazy Hawes. He was the one wanted ya so bad."

"But, Bert, it matters to me: I'm not the killer. What about Gunner? Didn't ya talk to Gunner? He can clear me. He and his friends were the ones there. He knows I didn't do it."

Bert and Wes' ma gave each other embarrassed looks and Bert shook his head. "I talked to Gunner, Wes." He looked down into his coffee cup. "Gunner said ya did it." Bert said the words in a low voice, almost as if he were fearful his brother would hear.

Wes couldn't believe his ears. Gunner accusing him of shooting Jack Sinclair! "I don't believe you. Gunner wouldn't say that!"

Bert looked up at his brother. "It's true. He said he saw you fire the gun at that Sinclair fellow. He even told Sheriff Hawes that he saw ya. Everyone believes ya did it. But don't ya see? It don't matter now, cause that was the Mormon War and it's over."

Wes felt sick inside and, glancing at Crocker, flushed in embarrassment. "Gunner really said that?" he whispered. Bert only nodded. "Gunner's my brother. Why'd he lie?" groaned Wes.

Wes' ma sat down next to him. "You have to face it, son. Gunner lied to protect himself. He or one of his friends shot that Mormon and then claimed it was you to get out of it themselves. Gunner ain't the man ya grew up thinking he was– Gunner's mean."

"Then I got to go see him. I got to talk to him face to face and clear this up. He'll have to confess. If it don't matter now, he'll tell the truth."

Bert shook his head. "Ya can't–Gunner's gone. That Roland Palmer's gone too. And Cyrus Maggio–he's dead. Someone shot him and left him at the River."

"Where's Gunner gone?"

"I don't know, no one does. Maybe he's dead. The sheriff wanted to talk to Gunner about a merchant killed down at a rumhole, but Gunner had already disappeared."

Much later in the day, when the sun had set and supper was over, Crocker sat in a straight-backed chair on the front porch, smoked his pipe and watched the western sky darken to a blood red. Hearing footsteps, he turned to see Wes' mother step out on the porch. Crocker started to get up, but she held up her hand. "No, don't get up, ya just ate. Here, I'll sit down with ya." She quickly pulled an old rocker next to the mountain man and eased into the chair.

"Scrumptious meal, ma'am. Fat cow, it was."

"Thank you, Mr. Sloan."

"Beautiful sunset, ma'am."

"Yes, it is. Mr. Sloan, I want to thank you for bringing my boy back home. You can't understand how a mother suffers when she don't know the whereabouts of her child. You've taken a great burden from me and I'm ever grateful."

"Weren't nothing, ma'am. Truth is, ya got quite a boy there. Saved my life a few times, he did. Ya know, he's been living out with the Injuns– the Sioux."

"Yes, he's very proud of that, and of your friendship, too. But, I know what you're saying: he isn't a child anymore. I can tell that just looking at him."

Crocker's face screwed up in wrinkles as he thought out his words. "It's a bit more than that. True, he's growed some. Yet, down at rock-bottom, he came back cause he wants to clear his name. It's important to him."

"But, don't ya see, Mr. Sloan? It doesn't matter now because no one is after him. He can stay and take up his life again and fear nothing." Crocker was quiet for a few minutes as he watched the sky. Mrs. Hamlin reached over and gently touched his arm. "Mr. Sloan, you're thinking something else. Please share it with me, if it's about Wes."

"Well, ma'am, your boy has been out and seen other parts of this Country and now I'm not sure he intends to be a farmer in Illinois. That's one thing I'm thinking. Then there's this other problem. Ya see, he met the Sinclairs, he met that Mormon family that's related to the man he was supposed to have shot. In fact, he met Jack Sinclair's daughter–prettiest little thing this side of the Alleghenys. He's quite taken with her. Oh, he won't let on, but I know it's true. She don't know who he is, cause he uses the name Tucker out West. He's scared when she finds out he's Wes Hamlin, she'll hate him and he can't stand the thought of that."

"You mean my son is in love with this woman, this girl?"

"Yes, ma'am, he's been struck right between the eyes."

"But if he can't clear himself then he'll have to stay here. He can't go back to her."

"That seems partly true. He daresn't openly court her, but I'm afraid he'll keep wandering about out West where he can be close to her."

She was now silent for a moment. "Where do you think Wes will be going?"

"Can't say."

"What about you, Mr. Sloan?"

"Oh, I'll just mosey up to the Parks to trap for the winter beav or maybe I'll wander up closer to them Bug's Boys. I've heard it said that them Blackfooters are guarding a valley where the beav grow big as horses."

"And the land of these Bug's Boys, it is a dangerous place?"

"Yes, Mrs. Hamlin, it's dangerous. Most places west of the Big Muddy are dangerous places."

"Do you think Wes will go with you?"

"Now, I don't plan on inviting him, but if he asks to go, I won't stop him."

Her voice was very soft. "You will take care of him, won't you Mr. Sloan?"

"I will do that, ma'am. I'm a mite fond of yer boy."

* * *

The first Mormons, Erastus Snow and Orson Pratt, reached the Salt Lake Valley on July 21, 1847. Brigham Young's advance party arrived soon afterward and by the end of July, ground for crops had been broken and a dam built across City Creek. The potatoes, corn and peas planted during 1847 never matured. By the second of October, all of the individual companies from Big Company had made it to the Valley. That first winter of 1847-48 saw over two thousand Saints gathered in what would become Salt Lake City.

Anna and Billy worked carrying rocks out of the newly plowed field and dumping them in a pile. South, at the field's other extreme, Anna saw Michael walking behind a plow. Billy pulled at her dress. "Is it dinner time, yet?" he asked.

"No, Billy. Not until the sun is straight up."

He shielded his eyes and stared up. "It looks straight to me."

She gently punched his stomach. "Come on, you lazy-bug, keep working!"

He laughed and stumbled back over the clods of freshly turned earth, looking for rocks. Anna absentmindedly kicked at the ground. The soil was sandy and alkali; not dark and rich, like the soil on their farm in Illinois. How were they ever going to grow anything here? She shielded her eyes against the sun and looked out over the treeless valley where only sagebrush and withered grass grew in the thin soil, where Rattlesnakes and big black crickets could easily be found under the hard knotted sage. She simply couldn't understand why the Apostles had stopped at this desolate place when reports from Oregon Territory claimed the soil was black and three feet deep; that trees grew with

The Battalion Returns

trunks as big as cabins. Why wouldn't the Apostles choose to go on to Oregon?

"Come on," said Billy, "you have to work, too!"

Anna stopped her daydreaming and began searching for boulders. After several minutes she straightened up and wiped the sweat from her forehead and, as she did, glanced at The Fort, the log and adobe collection of cabins which was their temporary lodging until homes were built. Even at this distance she saw people run from cabins and tents and men jump on mounts to ride off. Anna turned and yelled at her brother. He stopped his plowing, and she pointed toward The Fort.

While she continued to watch the excitement, Michael abandoned his ox and plow to join her. "What is it? Why did ya call?" he asked.

"Look! Something's happening back at The Fort. Can you see?"

He strained to get a better look.

"What's happening?" she asked.

"I don't know. We'd better go see."

Anna and Michael trudged over the field, with Billy running to catch up. They climbed over the new fences and reached the beginning of the city lots, then walked down a newly marked off road toward The Fort. At their tent, pitched beside the Fort's outer wall, they found Mary looking toward the northwest, beyond City Creek.

"What is it, Ma?" asked Anna.

Her mother turned, and Anna recognized the joy on her mother's face. "They're here–the Battalion! They've come back. Look, look over there!" She pointed to a column of walking men led by several horsemen. They had been expected from Fort Hall for the last week and here they were!

Anna couldn't help herself as she jumped up and down and grabbed Michael's sleeve. "Come on, let's go!"

Michael scooped up Billy and, along with dozens of other Saints, ran to meet the returning men. As the Saints approached, the returning soldiers gave a cheer, waved, and threw their hats into the air. Drawing close, Anna recognized individual men including Brother Wheeler and Brother Taylor. But they were in such rags: not one of them wore a decent set of clothes. She scanned faces looking for her uncle and brother and almost stumbled over Gwen. "Where are they?" she shouted to be heard over the din of the crowd. Gwen shook her head and continued pushing forward through the throng of men.

All at once Anna heard her name and spun around to face Jack Jr. in a torn, dirty shirt and patched pants, his face streaked with dust from the day's march. He lunged forward and swept her up in his arms. "Oh, Anna, we're back!"

She hugged her brother and the tears began to flow. Suddenly Ma was there and Jack let Anna go to throw his arms around his mother. Uncle Stan appeared with Gwen under one arm and, stepping forward, put his other arm around Anna. "Ho, my girls! Look how big you've grown. We've gotten smaller and you've grown bigger." He let go of Anna to hug Mary. "Where's Alice?" he asked, looking around for his wife.

Abruptly the mood dampened as the Sinclairs glanced at each other and then at the ground. Mary put an arm around Uncle Stan's waist. "I wrote you, when I heard you had reached California, I wrote."

He shook his head. "We've received nothing."

Mary stood on her tip toes and, with her arms around Stan's neck she spoke into his ear. "She's gone, Stan, Alice is gone. She became very ill and there was nothing we could do. She's with our Lord Jesus."

Stan's arms circled around his sister-in-law and held her tight. He shut his eyes and his shoulders heaved. Anna felt Jack's arm around her shoulders. She looked up into her brother's face and, with a great knot in her throat, repeated her Ma's words. "Aunt Alice is dead, Jack–she died."

As they walked to the Sinclair's tent, they all cried. For Jack Jr. and Stan it was a new pain and for the others, an old one relived. Once at the tent, Anna started a fresh fire and put the coffee on. Michael borrowed a bottle of whiskey to lace Uncle Stan's coffee. No one spoke, the sorrow too sharp to overcome just yet.

The men of the battalion milled about The Fort, greeting loved ones. Someone broke out in song:

Although in woods and tents we dwell,
Shout! shout! O Camp of Israel:
Others took up the trail song and soon the Sinclairs joined in.
No 'Christian' mobs on earth can bind
Our thoughts, or steal our peace of mind,
Lo, a mighty host of Jacob,
Tented on the western shore

Of the noble Mississippi,
They had crossed to cross no more.

The next morning, Uncle Stan, Jason, Jack Jr. and Anna walked to the Sinclair city lot to examine the work accomplished on the new Sinclair home. Each city block occupied ten acres divided into eight lots. Every family received a lot on which to build a house while, at this time, the farm land was held in common. The home Jason was building was ten feet by fourteen feet, consisting of a dirt floor, poles at the four corners and walls of adobe and rock which Jason had managed to raise to a height of three feet. Both Stan and Jack examined Jason's work but said little. As they completed their review, Jason grew nervous. "I know it ain't much, Pa, but it's late and I was afraid the snow would come before I got it done."

Uncle Stan nodded his head. "I can see your thinking, but son, it just won't do. It's too small and we need a home of real logs. I know you was doing your best and that ya had to work alone. Now, Jack and I are here to help."

Jason squinted his eyes and Anna saw the pain in her cousin's face. "Where are we going to get the logs?"

Stan looked toward the eastern mountains. "We'll fetch logs and lay a solid foundation. We'll take one of the wagons up a canyon and cut pine or fir. Now, we can't all work on it all the time 'cause the Church has other duties for us. But, with luck, we can get at least a one, maybe a two room cabin done before the cold weather."

"But, Pa!" complained Jason. "What if the snows come while we're up the canyon trying to get the logs down? It's the middle of October!"

"You're right, son. We'll take the box off one of the wagons and put it down here next to your sod house. You finish what you've started and we can live in the wagon and your room while we start on the other. If the snow comes, we'll at least have this for shelter." He turned toward the south in the direction of the fields. "Tell me, Jason, what is the soil hereabouts like? Is it rich?"

"Pa," responded his son. "I'm afraid there ain't no soil around like in Illinois. It's all dry and alkali and very thin. I don't see how we're going to plant crops. When Brother Brigham's party arrived, they tried to plow, but couldn't–the ground was just too hard. That's why they dammed up City Creek. They had to flood the ground to soften it up before they could turn it over. That's what we've been doing ever since. I swear I spend half my time fooling around with watering the field."

The look on Uncle Stan's face was one of pain as he bit his lip and again looked toward the south. "I'm sure the Lord will provide," he said in a low voice.

"Pa?" spoke up Jack.

"Yes?"

"Is Louise and her kids going to live with us?"

Uncle Stan tilted his head as he looked at his nephew. "Why shouldn't they?"

"Well, we took them in for the trip, but I thought that maybe they would have their own place once we reached Zion."

"But who is going to build this place? Who's going to feed them and cut wood for them if we don't? We can't just turn them out!"

Jack became defensive. "I didn't mean that. I just thought the Church had other plans."

A horseman came down the road, and the Sinclairs turned to see Brother Wheeler hurriedly riding by. "Hello, John!" called Uncle Stan. Brother Wheeler neither looked to the left or right, but just kept going as if no one had called. "Now, what's wrong with John this morning?" asked Stan.

Anna put a hand to her mouth. "Uncle Stan, haven't you heard?"

"Heard what, Anna? This is only my second day home. What haven't I heard?"

Jason scratched behind his ear and smiled in a secretive manner. "Sarah Wheeler run off. She run off with a man."

Uncle Stan's mouth dropped open as he looked first at Jason and then at Anna. "She ran off with another man? My God, I marched half way around the world with poor old John and now he comes home to find his wife gone." Suddenly everyone was reminded of the fact that Alice had died, leaving Uncle Stan alone. Stan frowned and kicked at a clod. "Hell of a thing to do. Who was it? Who'd she run off with?"

Anna couldn't constrain herself. "Oh, you won't believe it! It wasn't even a Mormon–she run off with that Taylor Hawes!"

"You mean Sheriff Hawes?" exclaimed Jack.

"Yes, but he isn't a sheriff now–just an ordinary man," said Anna. "We met him on the Platte and then he showed up a few days after we got to the valley. When he left, Sarah disappeared! Someone saw them riding together up north beyond the hot springs. Guess he took her to Oregon."

Uncle Stan shook his head. "Didn't no one go after them? Maybe he kidnapped her!"

"Not likely," replied Jason. "She left a letter for her husband with Paul. Paul went ahead and opened his Ma's letter and read it. She said how she loved this Hawes and was going off with him."

Stan ran his fingers through his silver hair and looked after John Wheeler who was still riding away. "Funny, ain't it? Funny how things change in ways ya don't expect." He put an arm around Anna's shoulders. "I wonder why Sarah Wheeler run off with Taylor Hawes? Don't that seem funny?"

Anna looked up into her Uncle's face and noticed how he had aged since the previous summer. Was it the news of Alice or was it the long march he had made? Maybe it was both, but he looked years older now. "Ya know, Uncle Stan, I think they was in love before he came here, because how could they fall in love in just a few days? I think they was in love back in Illinois. He knew the Wheelers then."

Stan gave her a squeeze. "You're probably right, honey. It takes time to fall in love. It don't happen in one or two days. It takes a time. Ya got to let the other person grow on ya."

CHAPTER 22

November 1847

The Hot Springs

Following the Oregon Trail, Wes and Crocker traversed the Bear River Divide and moved down the Bear River to Soda Springs. There they dammed a hot spring, creating a pool of steaming water in which to bathe. As they languished in the splendor of the hot bath, Wes looked at the sky and tried to smell the wind. "You know," he said, "it's late—snow could trap us."

Crocker's entire body was under the water except for his face. Keeping his eyes closed he smiled. "Weather don't dare bother this old hos."

"But Crock, we can't stay here all winter."

"We ain't, we're going on. But can't ya let a body take in a bit of this heat!"

"Where we going from here?"

"We'll continue along the Trail to Fort Hall."

"I ain't never been there."

"Course not, ya ain't never been nowhere, ya dumb rawheel."

"Then where?"

Crocker pushed himself up until his head was out of the water, and Wes saw a glint in the old man's eyes. "Well, this coon has heard fer years 'bout them Bug's Boys way north of Fort Hall. Saying goes, they're guarding a secret valley, a valley with beav big as mules. Think of it, Wes! Giant beav! One plew would be worth fifty...maybe a hundred dollars."

"But them Bug's Boys don't let Whitemen into their territory. You told me that—you said the Blackfeet never give an inch. How we going up there without getting scalped?"

"I figure it this way, Farm-boy. The Blackfooters will be wintering and won't be about. If we do run into them, we'll say you're a half-breed. We'll say your mama was a Blackfooter, but ya don't know nothing 'bout Blackfeet cause ya was raised in a mission. How's that?"

"My God, ya can't be serious! I don't look at all like an Injun. They'll find me out right away!"

"Hell, who does look Injun? You're as good as anyone. It'll work fine."

"But I don't even have black hair; my hair's brown."

"Yeah, but that's cause yer a half-breed."

"I'm not going to do it," announced Wes as he stood and walked to his waiting clothes. "It's too crazy—we'll be scalped. I don't care how much talking ya do, I'm no half-breed." He glanced back to see that his partner had again slipped down under the water until only Crock's face showed, his eyes closed.

"Now this is how I see it," said Crocker. "We'll find the biggest chief of them Bug's Boys and tell him yer looking for your mama. That she left ya at a mission, and you're just trying to get home. You then tell 'em ya remember yer ma telling ya about her home in this valley with giant beav. That'll convince 'em, see."

Wes looked down and saw Crocker's clothes laying on a bush. He was tempted to laugh, but controlled himself, not wanting to alert his partner. As the mountain man talked away about the giant beaver, Wes quietly gathered up all his clothes and tiptoed into the brush to a spot where he could watch the pool without being seen. He didn't have long to wait for the excitement to begin. Soon, Crocker opened his eyes and looked about.

"Farm-boy? Where'd ya go, Farm-boy?" He sat up and took a good look around. "Where'd ya go?" He stood up and walked toward the bush that once held his pants and shirt, but stopped short when he saw the bush was bare. "God damn, this ain't funny, now, Farm-boy! Where's my clothes?" Crocker looked about, trying to determine which way Wes had gone. "Come on, ya dirty sneak. I'll tan yer hide when I get my hands on ya." A slight breeze stirred up, bringing a chill with it, and Crocker wrapped his arms about his body. "God Damn, it's almost December, Farm-boy–have a heart!" Crocker moved through the bushes and drew closer to Wes' hiding place, so Wes cautiously backed up. He was tempted to call out and taunt Crocker, but didn't want to give his position away yet. As Crocker moved closer, Wes muted his laughing and continued stepping backward.

Wes heard twigs break in the bushes behind him. As he turned he heard a growl–a growl that was only a few feet away. He spun about to face a towering grizzly bear; not just any grizzly bear, but the papa grizzly, the grandpa grizzly of all. Standing ten feet tall, the bear looked at Wes from a distance of fifteen feet. "HOLY SHIT!" screamed Wes, as the grizzly turned its head, opened its mouth and gave a blood-curdling roar. There was no time to think, no time to weigh the alternatives and make a choice. Wes turned and ran away as fast as his feet would carry him.

As Wes passed his naked partner, he yelled out one word: "GRIZ!" And he didn't look back to see if Crocker understood, but kept going, heading for where his Kentuck rifle rested next to a granite boulder. Reaching the rock, he grabbed for his gun just as Crocker joined him.

"Bear?" asked Crocker. "Did you say bear? A griz?" As Wes fumbled with his pan, trying to prime it, Crocker held up a hand. They heard the crashing of the brush as the large animal closed on them. "Oh Jesus!" yelled Crocker as he grabbed his gun and desperately tried to extract a primer from the brass box set in the stock.

They were both armed and cocking their weapons as the grizzly broke from the bushes and came straight at them. Wes shouldered his gun, aimed, and fired in one sweeping motion. Then a second explosion told him that Crocker had fired. In the next second the grizzly was at them and they both jumped out of its way.

Buffalo Man

Wes landed hard on his side, but rolled over to see his single shot pistol on the ground next to his hunting pouch. He scrambled to his knees and, scurrying to the gun, picked it up. Turning, he saw the bear on all fours, wild eyes open and tongue hanging out. It made several nerve-wrenching moans and turned to face Crocker who scrambled to his feet on the other side of the animal and, spotting Wes with the pistol, yelled to him. "Shoot, for Christ's sake! It's still alive!" Wes aimed at the beast's head but Crocker's voice stopped him. "Not the head, Shoot here," and he pointed to a place on the side of his own chest.

Wes aimed at the grizzly's side and pulled the trigger. The gun's muzzle exploded and, through the blue smoke, Wes saw the bear turn and look at him. The beast let out a terrible roar and began a slow walk toward Wes who held only an empty pistol in his hand. This was it! They hadn't killed the bear and now it was the bear's turn. Fear overwhelmed Wes as he struggled backward.

Abruptly, Crocker was on the bear with his six-shooter, firing point blank at the animal. Expending all six rounds, he dropped the gun and jumped away. The bear, in great pain, opened its mouth and let out a deafening roar before falling onto its chest. Unable to stand and with its head on the ground, it gave out great breaths, which stirred up small clouds of dust. Soon it closed its eyes and stopped breathing.

Crocker, still naked, stumbled beside Wes and crashed to the ground. "Holy Christ in Heaven above! Jesus, Jesus—was that close!" He rubbed his weathered hands over his face. "God, Wes, we about met our Maker today. These close calls can wear a coon down."

* * *

Five of them sat at a round table in the McNaughton house boat, which served as a tavern: Gunner, Roland, two whores named Sally and Tamla, and a short, stocky, dark-complexioned man who called himself Friendship Brown. The only customer sat at a small table in the corner, his head on his arm, sleeping off the alcohol. Toby McNaughton stood behind the bar, blindfolded and barefoot, attempting to pour whiskey into glasses before him. Gunner, his friends, and the whores watched the fat man with delight.

"Come on," yelled Roland. "Get them drinks over here, Toby. We got a thirst."

Toby nervously smiled. "I'm doing it, I'm coming." He placed a finger in one of the glasses and felt the liquid level rise as he poured in the whiskey.

"Now remember," warned Gunner, "ya got to get over here without spilling. Ya got that, Toby?"

Toby filled the last of five glasses. "Ya, sure, I know, Gunner. Here I come!" He picked up each glass and, carefully feeling a tray with his fingers, placed the glass on the tray. When ready, he grinned and picked up the tray. "Here comes Toby."

"Shit," whispered Brown, "I bet he don't make it! I bet five dollars he spills." No one seemed interested in taking the bet, all eyes were on the hulk as he staggered out from behind the bar.

"Here I come!" He took two steps and walked into a chair resting next to an empty table. Gunner and the others burst out laughing.

"Oh, shit!" said Toby. "Did I spill?"

Sally stopped laughing long enough to answer. "No, Tob, you're fine. Just keep coming."

He took a turn in the wrong direction and walked into the table, overturning one of the glasses on the tray. "Oh, shit, I know I spilled–Toby knows."

"Just one," said Sally. "Keep coming."

"We got to make this more interesting," announced Gunner. He picked up an empty glass from the table and threw it onto the floor between Toby and Gunner's table. The glass broke and the pieces scattered across the floor.

"What was that?" asked Toby.

"Nothing," answered Roland. "It wasn't nothing. Just keep coming."

Tamla looked at Gunner and spoke in a quiet voice. "That ain't fair, Gunner. He'll cut his feet."

Gunner's voice was low, almost a growl. "Shut yer fucking mouth, Tamla or I'll put you out there."

"Come on," encouraged Friendship Brown. "Get a move on."

Toby weaved across the floor toward their table and somehow, as he took each step with his bare feet, he miraculously missed all the sharp slivers of broken glass. "Am I close?" he asked as he stopped before their table.

Tamla clapped her hands. "That was wonderful, Toby. Ya didn't step on the glass once?"

"The glass?"

Gunner frowned as he withdrew his six-shooter, cocked it, and pointed it at Toby's foot. "Ya know what that is, Fat-boy?"

"Ya, Gunner, it's a gun. I can hear—it's your gun."

"That's right, and it's pointed at yer foot. If ya spill one drop putting that tray down, I'm gonna shoot off yer big toe. Ya got that?"

"Ya, Gunner, don't worry, I won't." He carefully felt for the table before slowly putting the tray down. Not a drop was lost from the remaining four glasses.

Gunner frowned again as both Sally and Tamla clapped their hands and congratulated the fat man. Gunner reached forward and, with the barrel of his gun, tipped three glasses over, spilling the contents onto the tray. The last glass he picked up and began to sip.

Sally pointed toward the tray, which was now covered in a quarter-inch of whiskey. "That weren't fair, Gunner."

Gunner jammed the barrel of his gun into Toby's groin. "Now listen here, ya fat tub of shit. You spilt whiskey on that tray and ya got to lap it up. Now get yer head down there and get lapping."

Tamla shook her head as Toby bent down to the tray and lapped up the whiskey. "That's unfair, Gunner. He's already had too much. You'll make him sick."

Gunner removed the gun from Toby's groin and pointed it at Tamla's temple. "All right, then I'll shoot you if he don't suck it all up! Ya got that, ya dirty whore? If he don't suck up every fucking drop, I'm pulling the trigger and blowing a hole in yer fucking head."

Tamla's face paled and her eyes grew round as silver dollars as she stared first at Gunner and then at Toby. "Come on," she whispered, "you can do it, Toby."

Toby worked for several minutes, trying to lap up the spilled whiskey, but finally, he stood upright. "I can't! I'm sick."

Friendship jumped up. "Don't quit," he laughed. "Ya almost got it." Walking around the table, he put a hand on the back of Toby's neck and forced the big man's face back down into the tray. "Now drink, ya slob.

The Hot Springs

Drink it all up." As Friendship held him, Toby went back to drinking the spirits. "Look at that!" said Friendship to Roland. "Ain't that the worst sight ya ever saw?"

Finally, Toby could take it no longer. He tried to straighten up again, but Friendship held his neck so the fat man stepped back from the table, breaking from Friendship's grasp. "I can't drink no more! I'm gonna be sick." Toby slumped to the floor and leaned over. "I'm gonna be sick," he moaned just before he threw up.

Gunner was disgusted. "God damn it, Toby, look what you've done!" He turned and yelled toward the galley. "Lisa! Lisa, are you out there? Get in here and clean this up!"

Sally looked away from the mess on the floor. "Why don't ya have Toby clean it up, Lisa didn't do it. Why ya picking on her? She's just a little kid."

Gunner snapped at the whore. "Cause he's too drunk and I don't want to look at it. Lisa! Get the fuck in here before I come out there and whip yer ass."

No one came out of the galley door. Roland looked at Gunner. "Maybe she's in her bunk. Maybe she's sick. Maybe she's out looking fer vegetables."

"Vegetables?" yelled Gunner. "Where's she getting vegetables this time of year? You're drunk, Roland. Maybe you should go get her. Get her ass up here right now, do ya hear me?"

Roland slowly stood and steadied himself against the table. "Ya, sure, send old Roland. I'll fetch that little shit." He staggered off to the galley door.

Gunner looked down at Toby. "Get out of here and clean yourself up. You're a pig, ya understand, a pig! Now get out!" He turned toward Tamla. "I'm getting hungry. Go fix me something to eat."

Tamla pouted. "Where's Jake? Why don't he fix us all something?"

"I don't know where Jake is. Go fetch him and have him cook something. I don't care, but just get off yer ass and get going." Pouting again, Tamla stood and walked out of the barroom. Gunner shook his head and looked at Friendship. "I just don't know, Brown. Sometimes these people are just deadwood. If I had some real people around me, we wouldn't have to live on this shitty barge and take in pennies from the few strangers that come by." He lifted his glass and drained the last of the whiskey. "I tell ya, with a real bunch, I could open a place out in the Territories and make real money. With high class whores and good gambling equipment, we would make real money."

Roland entered the barroom and, stepping behind the bar, selected a bottle of whiskey and poured himself a drink. "Well," demanded Gunner. "Where is that little shit?"

"Ain't here." announced Roland.

"What do ya mean?"

"Ain't here! I looked everywhere. No place ya can hide on this boat. She's gone and so is Jake. They took his horse."

Gunner stood up, knocking over his chair. "Gone? They's run off? Jake's taken that girl and run off?"

Roland stared at Gunner, his face twisting up in confusion. "Ya didn't send them to Independence for nothing?"

"No, I did not! I don't never send the two of them off like that. Not since Jake's mama died. Now, we got to go after them. Ya hear me?"

"Sure, Gunner," said Roland. "Let's go!"

"I'll go too," offered Friendship. "They can't get far. We'll overtake them."

The three men stumbled from the bar, across the gangplank and to the lean-to where they kept their horses. As they struggled to put saddle blankets on their mounts, Gunner stopped them. "Hold on, you two. We can't go now, we're too drunk. We'll wait until tomorrow and then we'll go to Independence and fetch them back."

The other two men were more than willing to abandon the chase. Dropping their blankets to the ground, they stumbled back into the tavern.

Late that night Gunner lay in his bed, half unconscious from illness induced by his drinking binge. All at once, he was fully awake, his nose full of the strong smell of smoke. He heard a crackling noise from somewhere in the boat. Kicking Sally out of bed and onto the floor where she fell with a heavy thud, he slipped out of bed and felt for his pants in the darkness. Sally moaned as she pulled herself off the floor. "What's wrong. Why'd ya do that?"

"The fucking boat's on fire, ya dumb bitch! Get dressed and get out!"

"On fire?"

The Hot Springs

"Yes, God damn it!" Gunner opened the door and a wall of warm air rushed in accompanied by black smoke, the hall lit by a red glow. "Go on!" Yelled Gunner, pushing her through the door even though she was still naked. "Get the fuck off the boat!"

She hesitated as if to return to the little cabin, then glancing in the direction of the fire, turned and ran off. Gunner pulled on his pants and then, kneeing down on the floor, felt with his hands until he found a loose board in the wall located under the bed. He pushed the board aside and reached into the wall. Finding a leather pouch, he pulled it out and then hurried from the cabin.

Once on the River's bank, Gunner looked around to see if everyone was accounted for. He spotted Roland and Friendship and Toby and both Sally and Tamla. Everyone had escaped. Looking back he saw the boat engulfed in flame.

Toby was on his knees. "Oh, God, look, look! Our home's gone!"

Gunner felt numb from the close call. "It was Jake! I know it! That fucking Jake tried to kill us all!"

"No," yelled Toby. "He won't kill me! I'm his brother!"

"He tried to kill us all, Toby. He probably killed yer mother and was going to kill us so he could run off with the little girl. But we'll show him. We'll catch that son-of-a-bitch and we'll teach him to set fire to our place." Gunner stroked his pouch of money. At least he could start over. Once he settled with Jake and got Lisa back, he would start over.

CHAPTER 23

March, 1848

A Second Wife

Crocker led the way across the snow field as Wes followed, riding Jeff and leading Mule. The sun shone brightly, and Wes put his hand over his eyes to clearly see his partner up ahead. Even though the sun was out, the day was cold with gusts of wind blowing from the north. Crocker stopped at the snow's edge and surveyed the timberline ahead as Wes reined to a stop beside him. "Christ, ya think they're coming after us?" groaned Wes.

Crocker turned in his saddle and glanced at Wes before turning back to look over the snow field they had just crossed. "Don't know, just don't know." He faced front and again stared at the tree line. "I ain't giving up these plews. They can ride after me to Mexico and back but I ain't giving them up."

Wes removed his hat and adjusted the scarf covering his ears. "Ya never should a-said that about the princess. They were never going to believe my ma was an Injun, let alone a princess."

Crocker wasn't smiling as he looked over his shoulder. "Hell, I could see my first lie wasn't working, so I just thought I'd throw that princess thing in. Shit–them Injuns weren't supposed to be there anyway; they's all supposed to be tucked away in their lodges until spring."

"Crocker, this is spring–it's March!"

"Spring? Look at the snow! This ain't spring, it's winter."

"Well, you tell that to the Blackfeet. Tell them it's winter and we's sorry we killed their beaver and we'll just mosey back up the Gallatin and leave them alone."

"Quit yer bellyaching, ya ain't scalped yet." Crocker withdrew his six-shooter and checked it. "We got to get ya a better pistol, Farm-boy. That pea-shooter of yours just ain't doing the job."

Wes felt an itchiness, an uneasiness in his back and spine. The wind had died, but now a light breeze came up from over the snow and stirred the pine needles not covered with snow. Crocker cocked his head to one side and listened. Wes knew the behavior well and his heart pounded. "Ya hear 'em?" he whispered.

Betty nervously shifted her weight, taking several steps forward, and Crocker held up a hand for Wes to be silent as he continued listening. Wes looked down at his rifle resting in the sheath and, pulling it half out, checked the priming in the pan. Finally Crocker turned toward Wes, deep furrows showing in his forehead. "They're out there, Wes. This might get sticky. Come on." He urged Betty forward. Wes followed.

Crocker led them through the timber and farther up the canyon but he moved slowly, and Wes realized the mountain man wasn't sure where the Indians were. As Wes tugged on the lead rope forcing Mule to keep up, he cussed under his breath at their predicament. How had he let Crocker talk him into this crazy scheme? After Fort Hall they had moved north, crossing the Bitterroot Mountains to the headwaters of Beaverhead River, down the Beaverhead to the Gallatin, over mountains and across a plateau to the Musselshell River. They worked their way north toward old Fort Mackensie, looking for that secret valley with the giant beaver. The valley was never found, but ordinary beaver were plentiful, and now Mule was loaded with plew. The winter brought deep snow; Crocker just laughed and assured Wes the Blackfeet were all snuggled down in timbered valleys to sit out the cold weather, making it safe to move about and trap.

Just that morning, on their way to check a trap line at a beaver dam, they ran across a dozen young braves bathing in the pond. "Jesus!" thought Wes. "Playing in the water while patches of ice still float on it!" The naked savages stopped their playing when the two Whitemen accidentally rode in on them. Crocker, trying to buy time, told the lie about Wes being a half-breed, but even Wes saw the Indians didn't believe it. Then Crocker gave the little speech about Wes' mother, the princess. That was the last insult. The Indians dashed for their breechcloths and weapons as Wes and Crocker lit out. Now, Wes wasn't sure whether they were being hunted or not, but he was positive the Blackfeet were not about to accept two strange trappers in their territory.

Crocker stopped and Wes pulled up alongside. "What is it?" asked Wes. Crocker pointed through the pines. Ahead, Wes saw a solid granite wall where the canyon ended "What we gonna do, Crock?"

"We'll have to go back down. No time to look fer a passage."

"God, Crock, you can bet those Blackfeet know this canyon."

Crocker was angry. "Now what the hell does that mean? I told ya I only been up in Blackfooter land once before and that was in Thirty. I ain't never been in these particular parts. Christ, probably no Whiteman has."

Wes had never seen Crocker this unnerved and it increased his own fear. "If we head back down, those braves could be waiting! Why don't we stay here and try sneaking out tonight?"

Crocker pulled off his mittens and blew on his hands. "Cause if this canyon don't have an exit up here, them braves will get the whole tribe out to block the way. We best act now, before they get things figured out. Let's cache these plews."

"Jesus, Crock, that means we got to come back for them."

"Yeah, maybe tonight, or in a couple of days." Crocker urged Betty on and moved up next to the granite cliff. They inched along the rock wall, hoping to find an easy passage, but without luck. Finally, Crocker found two fallen pines surrounded by spring ferns. Unloading the plews from Mule, they hid them between the two trees, covering them with dead leaves, and then carefully covered their tracks to the trees. "That should do it," said Crock. "Now we'll take Mule down trail and picket her. With any luck they'll miss her and we'll recover both the plews and Mule."

Wes' spine tingled again. "Well, let's hurry. No use sitting around here."

They carefully rode back down the canyon, trying to avoid the deeper patches of snow. At a sheltered spot close to the cliff, Crocker tied Mule. Free of the pack animal, they could now move faster. Near the open end of the canyon, they entered a large forest of tall pines with deep snow between their trunks. Crocker inched forward, stopping frequently to listen. At one stop Wes saw the mountain man sit up straight in his saddle, and then Wes heard it, too—the sound of a large animal plowing through snow and brushing against pine tree branches.

Crocker quietly dismounted and waved for Wes to follow. On foot, they led their horses slowly through the woods. Wes bent low and looked for horses' legs showing below the lowest pine branches. They moved toward the right where the trees ended at the bank of a mountain stream, swollen by spring runoff. Crocker led them right down the stream bank and into the fast moving water. From their position, they could look up and peek over the top of the snow and through the tree trunks.

The ice water flowed up to Wes' knees and filled his boots. He had been in ice cold water before while setting traps but at those times, he knew he could leave the water when he wanted. Now, being trapped in the stream made the pain intense and he couldn't understand how Crocker stood so still as the water swirled about his upper legs. Wes knew it wouldn't last long before the numbness came, but he bit down on Jeff's reins to keep from making any noise. Slowly, the pain diminished, but Wes didn't care now, for he was watching horses move between the pines, seeing just enough of the ponies to catch a glimpse of Indians' leather-covered legs. For several minutes the Indians moved up the canyon toward Mule and the cache. How many, Wes didn't dare guess but more than they had stumbled on in the pond. Was it the whole tribe out to find them?

Wes felt the fear—fear like when he was chased by the Pawnee—a great hideous snake that uncoiled from his stomach and reached up to wrap around his heart and bite his brain. If the Indians should come to the stream bank and look down, he and Crocker would be trapped.

A Second Wife

Crocker slowly turned to look at his partner, his face covered in deep furrows of worry, but, seeing Wes, he smiled and silently mimicked laughter. Eyes flashing, Crocker made an obscene gesture toward the Indians and then silently laughed again. He removed his pistol and pointed it at his own temple, stuck out his tongue and rolled his eyes. "He's crazy!" concluded Wes. "He's plumb, fucking crazy and I'm a dead man!"

When the Indians were out of sight, Crocker motioned Wes on. They continued down stream, Wes walking Jeff along the edge of the creek, being careful not to trip for his legs were so numb they felt like logs tied to his knees. They moved down stream until encountering a deep pool and a steep bank. Here, they left the creek and moved up into the pines once again. Walking through the snow, Wes' boots and pant legs froze solid, but he didn't care, he was watching over his shoulder to make sure the Indians weren't coming back down the canyon. The snow thinned and open patches of ground appeared, covered with new growth of ferns and grass. They mounted their horses and urged them forward at a trot. Turning east and breaking out of the trees, they reined up before a small grassy field. At the opposite end of the field rode three braves, faces blacked for war, eagle feathers fluttering from lances, ponies painted red and black. The Indians reined to a stop and stared at the two Whitemen.

"Oh, shit!" moaned Crocker. "Let's ride!" They reined their mounts about and thrust their heels into the horses' bellies. Wes looked back for just a second to see the Indians holding their lances high as they rode after them through the field. War whoops reached Wes' ears and he slapped the end of the reins against Jeff's rump.

They rode back into the woods and, reaching the stream, plunged in, hurrying their animals across. Free of the creek, they galloped back into timber where they encountered enough snow-free ground to ride with a frenzied swiftness between the trees. They had no time to look back, the trees and logs came too fast and required every bit of concentration from horses and riders. With abandoned recklessness, Crocker led them down a steep wooded hill. Wes prayed Jeff wouldn't stumble. At the foot of the hill the trees thinned, and Wes saw a broad, open valley ahead–a chance to let Jeff go and outrun the pursuers.

They were almost out of the forest when Wes encountered the dead branch, hanging low and aimed straight at him making it difficult to spot. He didn't see it until it slammed into his shoulder. Wes was knocked back, twisted and then pushed from Jeff's back. He crashed hard on the ground and, in a flash, remembered the buffalo hunt when he'd fallen. Knowing he couldn't breathe, that the wind was gone from his lungs, he struggled up and made a lunge for Jeff who had stopped a few yards away. The woods spun and he sensed himself falling as the black came rushing in.

He was warm and comfortable as he floated through the blackness. Suddenly, a terrible noise made him jump and open his eyes. Crocker sat on Betty, shouldering his rifle, blue smoke drifting away from the muzzle. Crocker sheathed the Hawken and drew his pistol, aimed it and fired again. Then he moved to dismount. "Don't!" yelled Wes as he struggled to turn on his side and stand up. "I'm up!" he said. Crocker fired again at something down the trail through which they had just passed. Wes, spotting Jeff, half ran and half limped to his horse. "I'm good! I'm coming!" He yelled. He mounted and they again galloped down toward the open valley.

Somehow, Betty slipped ahead of Jeff before they reached the valley, but once in the open space, Jeff quickly overtook the smaller horse. With no time to pick their path, with the Blackfeet still coming, they had to force the horses on as fast as they would go. As Jeff passed her, Wes saw Betty go down, her leg caught in some animal's burrow: the nightmare of every horseman–his animal stepping into a hole at full gallop. Wes stood in the stirrups and reined in with such force he almost turned Jeff on his side with the effort. He grabbed his gun, slipped from Jeff's back and ran back to Crocker who was sprawled face down on the ground–motionless.

Wes looked toward the trees and saw two Blackfeet coming at full gallop. Kneeling down, he gently rolled Crocker over. Crock's face was covered with dirt, and blood began running from his nose and mouth as he opened his eyes and smiled up at Wes. "Howdy Farm-boy! Am I gone under?"

Wes shook his head. "Not yet, you ain't." He stood, shouldered his rifle and carefully took aim at the leading Indian.

"Take yer time, Farm-boy," whispered Crocker. Wes waited and forced his concentration on the target. He imagined a magic line extending from his gun's muzzle to the Indian's breast and saw the ball leave the rifle, fly through the air and strike it's mark. Wes tracked the path of the oncoming Indian and slowly squeezed the trigger. The cock fell and

A Second Wife

the flint ignited the pan. The rifle's stock slammed his shoulder and the smoke exploded from the barrel.

The Indian's pony galloped on without its rider, and Wes lowered his gun. He had assumed that the second Indian, seeing his friend shot out of the saddle, would stop and turn back, but he didn't! He just came on. "Oh Christ!" mumbled Wes and he tried to get into his pouch to reload.

"Use yer pea-shooter!" said Crocker who had managed to sit up and lean on one arm. "He's coming—use the pistol!"

Wes dropped the rifle and drew out his handgun. It would have to be one shot from close range. He took the gun in both hands and aimed. The Indian was yards away, coming at full speed with his lance raised high to plunge down into the Whiteman enemy. Wes waited until the last moment before pulling the trigger. The brave threw his weapon before falling from his pony, the lance flying harmlessly over Wes' head.

"Draw yer knife," warned Crocker.

Wes withdrew his knife and walked toward the Indian who lay on his back, legs sprawled over a low bush, arms spread out. Wes carefully approached and, when near, saw that the brave was still alive, his chest heaving and his eyes open. With each breath, blood bubbled from a large hole in the brave's chest. Wes stood over the Indian and looked into his face. The brave's eyes were glassy but locked onto Wes, and Wes was jarred by the hatred he saw in them.

Wes felt like crying; he hadn't planned on killing any Indians, he was just trying to leave their territory. "I'm sorry," he whispered. The brave opened his mouth to say something, but in the next instant he was still. "I'm sorry," Wes whispered again. He wanted to kneel down and shake the Indian so he'd come back. He wanted to patch up the wound in his breast and stop the bleeding, but it was too late.

"Farm-boy!" yelled Crocker. "Where are ya?"

Wes replaced his knife and walked back to where Crocker waited. The mountain man had made it to his hands and knees and was searching about the ground. "Wes, help me find my six-shooter. We got to get—there'll be more."

Wes knelt down. "You all right? Aren't ya hurt?"

Crocker looked at Wes, and Wes saw that Crock had tried to wipe the blood and dirt from his face. "Hell yes! I broke my nose and lost some teeth, but this coon ain't going down unless you've decided to make camp here where the Blackfooters will be any second. Now help me find my gun and then check that other Injun."

The six-shooter was quickly found and the second Indian was dead, a hole in his chest. Wes kept glancing at the tree line, expecting any moment to see hundreds of savages pour into the valley. Poor Betty was moaning and grunting as she lay on her side, her front left leg snapped in two. "God! God! God!" cussed Crocker as he stood over his horse and held the pistol at the animal's head.

"You want me to do that?" asked Wes.

Crocker grimaced, and Wes saw tears in his partner's eyes. "Fuck no!" He pulled the trigger and blew a hole in Betty's head. "Come on!" he yelled at Wes. "Let's get the hell out of here!"

They doubled up on Jeff, and Wes thanked all the gods in heaven that Jeff was such a big, strong horse. They moved north through the valley and disappeared into the forest.

* * *

In the midst of their hunger, Uncle Stan announced they were going to have a party. He didn't say why, but to Anna a party seemed a delightful idea; something to take everyone's mind off their empty stomachs. But Uncle Stan didn't want just a plain party–he insisted they have a feast. Half starved, where were they supposed to find enough food for a feast? Yet, to Anna's surprise, they managed to secure a variety of edible items, which were now carefully laid out on the table before their partially completed cabin. Of course, they had boiled Sego Lily roots and thistle tops; but these constituted too much of the Sinclairs' diets to be considered treats. Receiving a small ration of oats from the Church Commissary, Mary baked three loaves of hot oatmeal bread and procured dried potatoes and corn. However, the real prize was the badger Michael killed. Anna boiled the meat off the bones and used the potatoes and corn to make a thick, creamy stew. As she and Gwen stood at the table and looked at the fare before them, their mouths watered in anticipation of the meal to come.

Uncle Stan stepped onto the porch. "Already, are we?"

A Second Wife

Anna turned to see the Taylors approaching, Brother Taylor carrying a cake pan, and she prayed that a moist, rich cake was inside, unable to remember the last time she'd tasted cake. Behind the Taylors, came the Martins, and from out of the cabin came Louise with Lou Ann and Billy. Soon everyone was assembled; over twenty Saints, the Sinclair family and their neighbors and close friends gathered for a celebration.

No one touched the food, for they knew a prayer was needed. Uncle Stan stood in the door and held out his arms. "We're all here, but before we begin, let us pray." The men removed their hats and everyone bowed their heads as Stan delivered the invocation.

When Stan had finished and before anyone could begin the meal, he waved his arms again. "Listen everyone. I know you're anxious to start, but you must know we didn't call you all here just to eat!" Anna was intrigued; her uncle was about to make some announcement. Stan motioned for Mary to step next to him. "As you know, Mary lost her husband, my brother Jack, back at Nauvoo. And I lost my Alice last year to the fever. Well..." he put an arm around Mary and gave her a squeeze. "I would like to announce that Mary and I have decided to be husband and wife."

Anna's heart skipped a beat as she placed her hand to her mouth. It couldn't be, but it was! Her uncle and her mother were to marry! Warmth flowed over her as tears came to her eyes. What a wonderful union. She loved her Uncle Stan almost as much as she'd loved her father and she had worried that her mother would marry a stranger and Anna would have to live in a stranger's home. Now, this was perfect.

The assembled Saints applauded and then filed by the betrothed to shake their hands. Anna slipped up beside Gwen. "Oh, Gwen, isn't this exciting! We're going to be sisters."

Gwen turned and smiled as she put an affectionate arm around Anna's shoulder. "Yes," she said, "it is very wonderful. There's no one I'd rather have as a sister."

Anna sensed something was wrong; her cousin seemed withdrawn. "Is something the matter?" she whispered.

Gwen smiled and shook her head. "No, nothing's wrong."

Anna slipped her arm around Gwen's waist. "Come on, you can tell me. Don't you like the idea of my mother marrying your pa?"

Gwen gently pulled away as she faced Anna. "Really, I'm glad they're marrying. You have to believe me. It's not that; it's something else."

"What?"

Gwen shook her head again. "I can't say." She gave a weak little smile and walked away.

Anna was hurt. Gwen was her best friend and for her not to be overjoyed at the news confused Anna. Was it really something else? If so, what? And why wouldn't Gwen share it with her? She wanted to rush after her cousin and make her confess what the secret was, but decided she had better wait at least until the party was over.

Uncle Stan and Mary walked about, their arms around each other's waists, smiles on their faces as friends and family congratulated them and toasted to their future bliss. Anna saw the sparkle in her mother's eyes and knew she was happy. Thinking back over the last months, Anna now realized what had been happening. Her mother and Uncle Stan had spent time together, talking and sharing experiences, yet Anna had always thought it was just because they were family and friends. She hadn't realized something else had been growing between them.

Before evening, when the shadows grew long and the food was consumed, the neighbors bid their goodbyes and returned to their own homes as Louise cleaned up the table. Mary came out of the cabin and took Anna's hand. "Let's go for a walk, Anna. We can talk."

They walked from the family lot and down the dirt road toward the fields being plowed and prepared for planting. Finding a large sandstone boulder at the corner of a field, they sat down and faced the western mountains to watch the sun set.

"Are you happy for me, Anna?" asked her mother.

"Oh, yes," replied Anna. "I can't imagine a better thing. We'll all stay one family. Gwen will be my sister."

"And Jason will be your brother."

"Yes, that's right."

"I'm so pleased that you approve. Of course I always thought you would. That's why we didn't say anything sooner."

"I think it's going to be wonderful, Mama. I really can't see you married to anyone else, now." It occurred to Anna to mention Gwen's strange reaction, but decided it would spoil the moment.

A Second Wife

Mary put a comforting arm around Anna. "I only wish everyone was as lucky as I am." Anna thought it a strange statement considering that her mother had lost her husband and youngest daughter and suffered starvation and disease during the last two years. "Do you know what I mean?" asked Mary.

"I'm not sure. You mean you're lucky to be a Latter-day-Saint?"

"Yes, that's part of it, but mostly I mean that I'm lucky to have your Uncle Stan. There are so many women, especially young women, who have no one."

"Like Louise?"

Mary hesitated as she looked at her daughter. "Yes, like Louise. She deserves to have a husband. She's still young, not much older than Gwen. There are so many Mormon women who don't have a husband, who can't have one because there aren't enough men. That's really not fair, is it?"

"No, I guess not."

"Now you know, Anna, that the Lord hates unfairness and because He hates injustice He always has a solution to any problem. We must always believe that, even when we see a problem that looks impossible. God knows how to solve it."

In the back of Anna's mind an alarm went up—this talk was no accident; her mother was getting ready to tell her something. She looked into her mother's eyes. "What is it?"

Mary hugged Anna closer. "Sometimes we are asked to help God solve his problems and it's difficult—it's so difficult. But if we believe and have faith in the Lord, it will work out. Do you believe that, Anna?"

"Yes, of course."

"Well, God sees that we Saints have a problem here in Zion. He knows we have too many women and not enough men. So He's given us a solution. Now, Anna, what I am about to tell you, you must swear to never tell another living soul until you have permission. Do you agree?"

Anna wanted to object. Why did she have to make such a commitment? Couldn't her mother just tell her? "All right, I agree."

"The Lord has given us many secret blessings; you know that. He's given us the keys to the priesthood here on earth. In ancient times, the prophets had a custom that was blessed by God to help them. It was when a man took more than one wife. Not because he wanted to, but because he needed to, to do God's work. God knows we have a difficult situation here in Zion. He has, once again, given us the blessing of Celestial Marriage to help us through the hard times. With this blessing, no woman is forced to be without a husband. It is her choice to marry if she so desires. Do you see how this works?"

Mary waited for Anna to respond, but Anna didn't know what to say. She had heard the rumors of plural marriage, but had always been told that the rumors were lies circulated by their enemies to discredit the Mormons. Now, it was true!

"I know," continued her mother, "that it is hard to understand what this all means. I know we've been taught that it is a sin for a man to have more than one wife. But it wasn't a sin in biblical days, and so it can't really be a sin today. Life doesn't always work out the way we want it to. Sometimes we must make sacrifices to make it through."

Anna felt like crying, but didn't understand why. She looked at her mother's face again and saw the tears forming in her mother's eyes. "What sacrifice do we have to make?" Anna whispered.

Her mother's voice was strained as the tears flowed onto her cheeks. "We...I have been asked by the Lord to help. Louise has no one. So, we are taking her into our family."

Now Anna knew the whole truth. She knew why Gwen had been so cold and secretive–Gwen had known. "Uncle Stan is going to marry Louise, too!"

Mary pulled her daughter close to her breast and whispered. "Your Uncle Stan has already married Louise. I will be his second wife."

The pain welled up in Anna's chest as her mother held her tight. She didn't want to cry, she wanted to be strong for her mother, but she couldn't help it. She began to sob and her mother gently rocked her back and forth and sang a soothing lullaby from the days in Illinois.

CHAPTER 24

June, 1848

The Crickets

The first crickets appeared as individual insects, hiding under young shoots of wheat—just pests. However, as the crop ripened, their numbers grew until they swelled to be millions and were not just pests—they were the enemy. Coming from the canyons and mountains they swarmed over the wheat, devouring the precious kernels of grain. The Saints burned, crushed, buried and drowned the large black crickets, but always more came to take their place.

Anna worked in the wheat field's northeast corner where a ditch intersected the big canal that carried water from Big Cottonwood Creek. She, Gwen, Michael and Carl Martin fanned out into the field, each assigned to protect a portion of the wheat, and feverishly struggled to stem the tide of crickets that came to destroy their crop. Anna carried a short length of rope as she walked through the ripening wheat, trying to keep to the same path, trying not to trample the grain unnecessarily. As she walked, she swung the rope through the tops of the wheat, knocking off the crickets that clung to the precious kernels.

At first swinging the rope wasn't difficult, but the continuous activity soon tired her arms, and they ached in protest. Yet, she couldn't stop–her assigned area was large and when she completed her circuit through the field, it was time to begin again, for the crickets always came back. Each time they returned, fewer grains of wheat remained on the plants' stems. By slow, agonizing degrees the insects stripped the plants of their seeds.

After she lost count of the times she'd passed through the field and the countless steps she'd walked, the sun set low over the Strawberry Range, casting a red glow in the sky. She turned toward the south and saw the other defenders of the wheat giving up for the day. Anna limped to the canal and sat down on the bank, dropping her rope to the ground. Looking at her section of the field and the black bugs swarming on the plants, she realized this part of their crop would be gone by tomorrow.

Carl waved to her. "Come on, let's go clean up. We can't do more here." He turned and headed for home.

Anna watched the others walk back toward town and wished she had enough energy to move, but decided it just wasn't worth it. Looking over the valley, she saw smoke from the fires used to incinerate the insect army. They had tried fire and water and clubs, yet nothing really worked. If they stopped the crickets from entering a field on one side, the battle was already lost on the other. She lay back, not caring if an insect were under her or not. By now, she was used to them, no longer revolted by their black prickly legs or hard bodies. Anna wiggled her feet and felt a sharp pain. Raising her bare feet to see, she examined them in the fading light and discovered that her soles were covered with scratches and several large blisters.

She wanted to cry, but gritted her teeth and held back. She was always crying for some reason or other and was tired of it, swearing she'd not succumb to childish emotion again. Why weren't there more things to be happy for? When were the good times going to come? Gwen had announced her upcoming marriage to Joey Taylor. Such news should have caused her both joy and excitement for Gwen was her best friend. But Anna knew that after they were married, Gwen

The Crickets

and Joey planned moving to the new settlement north of Salt Lake called Bountiful. With Gwen gone from the Sinclair home, who would Anna talk to? Who would she share her secrets with? Maybe Gwen wouldn't go to Bountiful. If the crickets devoured all their crops, the Latter-Day-Saints would have to leave the Valley. They might go on to California or Oregon and start over.

Anna sat up and groaned at the soreness in her back. Wiping the dirt from her hands she examined them, tenderly touching a broken blister. The tears wanted to return, but she wouldn't let them. Rather, she dusted off her dress and prepared to stand when she noticed Carl returning to the field and carrying something in his hands. As he drew closer, she saw he held a bowl of water and carried a clean cloth draped over his arm.

Approaching, he smiled and knelt down. "When you didn't come out of the field, I figured you could use a little help." He gently took her hands and, turning them palms up, examined them. Next, he reached down, took hold of her foot and, looking at her sole, shook his head. "Why didn't you say something?" he asked.

"I'm all right."

"Well, we'll see." With tenderness, he soaked her feet in the bowl of warm water before carefully washing and drying them. When he was done, he withdrew a small blue bottle from his pocket. "Kathleen uses this when her hands are sore." He removed the cap and poured a measure onto his palm. Taking her feet, he gently rubbed the lotion into her skin.

She was touched by his caring and felt a loving warmth for him flow through her. Most of the time Carl acted like an overbearing autocrat, bent on everyone following the same strict rules he followed, yet now he was so gentle and kind, she didn't know what to think. "Thank you," she said in a half-whisper.

Finished with his administering, he wiped his hands and sat down beside her on the canal bank. "You know," he said, "Kathleen is very fond of you. She suggested the lotion when I said I was coming here."

Anna looked at him, not knowing whether to believe him. At each dance, Carl danced at least once with Anna, and at such times she felt Kathleen jealously watching her. Could Kathleen really feel fondness for her now?

"You don't believe me," he said, looking into her face.

"If you say so, I do."

He nodded and smiled. For several minutes they sat and watched the last of the sunset. Finally, he turned toward her again. "Are you pleased about Gwen?"

Anna shrugged. "I suppose."

"You're upset she's moving."

"Yes, of course. She's my best friend."

"I know. When you're young, friends are very important, but, as you get older, you marry and your family becomes more important."

She smiled and decided to tease him. "Are you saying I'm still a child?"

"No, I think you've become a young woman. But what I am saying is that it's time you think of getting married, yourself. I have seen you with Billy and Lou Ann and I know you've grown to love them. Now you should begin thinking of having your own children."

"Oh, I would, if only there was someone to marry, but all the eligible men are gone on missions or already married. I suppose I'll just have to be an old maid."

"You're teasing me."

"Maybe."

"Has your mother accepted Louise, yet?"

She stared at him, not knowing how much he knew or how much she should admit. After all, she had been sworn to secrecy.

He smiled and a twinkle came to his eyes. "I know you've been told about Celestial Marriage and I know that both Louise and your mother are married to Stan." Suddenly he changed the subject. "Did you know I'm to be made second counselor in the Seventh Ward?"

She hadn't heard but was impressed. Smiling, she touched his arm. "Carl, that's wonderful! Second counselor–that's almost bishop."

He nervously looked at the ground between his feet and cleared his throat. "The bishop suggested that it is time for me to consider another wife."

Anna knew now what was coming and she both dreaded it, yet found it exciting. "You're asking me to be your second wife?"

He nodded and placed a hand on her hand. "Anna, you must know I love you; you've known it for a long time. God has given us the bless-

The Crickets

ing of Celestial Marriage and I have been asked to partake in it. I love Kathleen, but I also love you. Does that sound impossible?"

He was so sweet, like a little puppy dog. She didn't want to hurt him, yet she had to be honest. "Yes, I think it's possible to love two people at the same time. But, Carl, I have to tell you that, even though I'm fond of you, I don't love you."

He gave her hand a little squeeze and she thought she caught sight of a tear in his eye. "I know that, Anna, but you admit you're fond of me. And, sometimes, that's how it starts. First, you're fond of someone, and then it grows until it's love. Not everyone is madly in love when they marry. Sometimes it's just a fondness."

"But Carl, even if it were more than a fondness, I don't want to be anyone's second wife. When I marry I want to be the first and only wife. That might seem selfish to you, but it's the only way I'll be happy."

A frown came to his face. "But you know how plural marriage works. You've seen it work with your own mother. I know you care for Louise."

"Yes, I do—I'm very fond of Louise. Yet I still wish mother was Stan's only wife. You can't believe mother desires to be his second wife."

"You mean she regrets her marriage?"

"No, she loves Uncle Stan, but you have to see this from a woman's point of view. We're the one's being asked to share a husband. How would you like it if I were already married and asked you to marry me."

Without warning, he drew her hands to his lips and gently kissed them. "For you, Anna, I would do it! If God told me it was right, and you would have me, I would marry you tomorrow. But God has decided how Celestial Marriage is to work. He has told us that it is necessary for some men to take more than one wife so no woman has to be without a husband. I've often wondered if it were reversed, if there were more men than women, if God would have commanded the women to take multiple husbands. Yet, it doesn't really matter. The only thing that matters is that God has spoken through His true prophet and, in turn, has told me I should marry again. And I love you! If I must do this, then you are the only one I want."

As much as the idea of being a second wife displeased her, she found herself moved by his declaration of love and for just a moment wished he were not already married so she could seriously consider his proposal. "I'm sorry, Carl. I do care for you. We've had our differences, but you've always been a good neighbor and a good friend. Can't we just go on that way? If I felt differently, I'd tell you, but I don't."

He slowly withdrew his hand. "Please don't give a definite answer now, that's all I ask. Don't say yes and don't say no. Just think it over and give it a little more time."

She stood up and brushed the dirt from her poor patched dress. "All right, but I'm afraid time won't change things."

He quickly stood and took her arm to walk her back to town. "That's all I ask–a little time. You'll see; in time it will make more sense. It just takes a little getting used to, that's all."

They slowly walked from the field. "You know," she said, wrinkles crossing her forehead, "there might not be a chance for marriage or for Gwen to go to Bountiful. If we can't stop these crickets our crop will be eaten and we'll all have to go from this valley."

"No!" he responded. "That will never happen. I know God chose this valley for us and He'll show us how to deal with these pests–you'll see."

Shaking her head, she looked up at him as they moved down the path. "You have such faith! The crickets are overrunning everything and yet you still think we'll win."

"You must come to have this faith, too, Anna. It's a beautiful thing– absolute faith in our Lord. I carry it like a protector and friend that is always with me and never lets me down. Nothing can ever really hurt me as long as I have my faith."

She thought about what he said and felt a twinge of jealously at not having such a deep faith herself.

That night the mood was grim at the large Sinclair cabin. The men sat at the rough-cut pine table as the women prepared a small meal. The cooking fire lit the kitchen area and a small lantern sat on the end of the table and threw out enough light for those seated to see each others' faces.

"God!" cussed Jack Jr. "I wish I had me a cup of coffee!"

"Don't use profanity," ordered Stan.

"Sorry. I just wish we weren't always out of coffee."

Uncle Stan turned to Michael. "How did it go where you were?"

Michael shook his head. "I don't know. They stripped a lot away and some of the wheat is so bare it won't be worth harvesting."

Stan rubbed his hands over his face. "We've got to keep trying. I know it looks bad, but we have to keep working."

The Crickets

Jason sat next to his father, yet didn't turn to look at him when he spoke. "We've been fighting them for three weeks. Every day we lose more and they gain more. We have to admit it—we're beat!" Uncle Stan made no move to stop Jason's speech. "I've talked to Ernie Fontana," Jason continued. "He said his pa has decided they're leaving for California."

The Sinclairs sat quietly as each considered Jason's words. Finally Uncle Stan broke the silence. "We can't just make an arbitrary decision to go. We're Latter-Day-Saints and we have to follow the leadership of the Church. If the Lord wants us to stay here, then we'll stay here! We must have faith."

Nervous feet shuffled under the table, yet none of the others dared contradict Uncle Stan.

Later, as Anna lay on her bed in the loft that served as her and Gwen's bedroom, she couldn't help wonder what more they could do to show their faith to God. They had left comfortable homes in Illinois and suffered two years in the wilderness. They had been tested by fever, starvation and freezing weather. During the last winter they had survived on Sego Lilies and thistle tops. Now, when their wheat was ripening they were being driven out by the crickets. Yet, the Saints preferred to stay and fight. What more could the Lord ask of them?

She drifted off to sleep and, sometime during the night, she began to dream. It was not the first time she had dreamed this dream, but she never remembered it upon waking. It began with her standing on the bank of the Mississippi River by the little dock at the Sinclair farm. She sees a boat drift slowly past with Lisa inside. She calls for her sister to stop, to come ashore, but there is nothing the child can do. Anna yells and runs along the bank. Suddenly, the dream changes with Lisa in one boat and Anna in a second. Anna continues calling out to her sister as Lisa cries, holding out her arms to be rescued by her big sister.

The current carries the boats along with Lisa's boat in the lead. First Anna tries to find oars, but there are none. Next she tries rowing with her hands, yet, no matter what she does she can't get her boat closer to her sister. Then, to Anna's horror, a strange man is in the boat with Lisa. He is looking at Lisa and laughing. Anna knows the man is planning to remove Lisa's dress, but she dares not yell to her sister or the man will move to complete the act at once. Instead, Anna tells her sister that everything is all right and that Lisa should jump into the water and Anna will get her.

Lisa moves toward the edge of the boat, but the stranger grabs her and pulls at the little girl's dress. Anna can't stand it. She screams at the man to stop and for Lisa to jump into the water. She screams over and over for him to stop as Lisa's boat drifts off into the darkness.

Someone shook Anna and she opened her eyes. It was night and Anna knew she was still in the loft as Gwen held her tight. "Don't, Anna," soothed Gwen. "Don't, sweetheart. It's all right, now. Just a dream, just a dream."

Anna, unable to remember her dream, felt fatigue sweep over her, yet she was afraid to close her eyes. Instead, she'd let Gwen hold her and rock her for just a minute more.

The next morning, Louise woke Gwen and Anna before a sliver of light showed on the eastern horizon. They must eat and get to the fields before the light to be ready for the crickets who would come out from their evil hiding places with the first rays of the sun. By the time the two girls washed and made their way to the kitchen, the others were already assembled; Uncle Stan, Louise, Mary, Jack, Jason, Michael, Billy and little Lou Ann. Everyone would go to the fields except Louise and Lou Ann for she must stay behind to cook and tend the baby. Everyone else would spend the entire day in the fields or working the canals or digging ditches.

As the Sinclairs shuffled out of the cabin into the dim light, Anna saw fatigue on their faces—they all appeared to have aged in the last three weeks. Walking to the fields, Anna looked up at the sky and saw not a single cloud. It was going to be a hot day, which would make her task even harder. Her feet were still sore and she carried part of a burlap bag she intended to wrap them with if the blisters broke open. She arrived at her corner of the wheat field just as the eastern sky turned a pale blue and, looking out over Big Field, saw many others taking their places, preparing for the battle. Brother Martin walked to his part of the field and waved to her. She waved back.

As the sun came up over the Wasatch Mountain Range, sunlight struck the tops of the Strawberry Mountains on the opposite side of the valley, making them came alive with color. Anna was dazzled by the beauty. At this moment she felt a pang of regret at the certainty they would have to leave this place, this hideout in the Rocky Mountains where they were safe from the outside world. Slowly the line of sunlight

The Crickets

moved down the western mountains and across the valley floor until Big Field became ablaze in the rich color of ripening wheat. As Anna watched, her dread returned when thousands upon thousands of black specks came out of the ground and attacked her wheat. It was time to begin her ritual. With rope in hand she started her rounds.

Anna made half-a-dozen circuits of her assigned patch of wheat, and the sun crept higher in the sky as the crickets multiplied in every direction. A few white birds drifted overhead, their wings held still as they caught the air and floated in great circles. Some of them closed their wings and dove toward the earth. More birds arrived and Anna stopped to take a closer look. The birds were seagulls, great white and gray birds with sharp yellow beaks. She looked toward the northwest in the direction of the Great Salt Lake and saw thousands of seagulls in the air, headed for the wheat fields.

Anna couldn't believe it! First the crickets came to eat their food and now the seagulls were coming to finish what the crickets had missed. It would be certain to everyone now—the Mormons were doomed here in the Valley of the Great Salt Lake. She fell to her knees and then fell on her back into the wheat. She was through, finished, defeated. "Let them come, they can have it all," she thought. She was too angry to cry.

"Anna! Anna!" It was Michael calling her. Anna slowly struggled to her feet and looked about for her brother. The birds were now everywhere, swooping down into the wheat. Michael ran toward her waving his rope over his head. "It's a miracle!" He ran up to her and grabbed her by the arms. "It's God's miracle!" he announced. "Don't you see?"

She couldn't understand what he was saying. "Michael, the birds have come to finish off the wheat!"

"No!" he yelled. "Look—look at what they're doing! They're eating the crickets—not the wheat!"

She turned and looked out into the field. He was right! The seagulls were eating the crickets right off the wheat stems. She couldn't believe her eyes. It was a miracle, a miracle sent by God as a sign. The love and warmth she'd felt for her church before returned in a great wave. "Oh, Michael," she half moaned. "God is doing this?"

"Yes, Anna, it's God's work."

She knelt down and tightly clasped her hands together before her breast, Michael quickly joining her. She closed her eyes and began her prayer. She would never doubt again; Carl Martin had been right, Uncle Stan–Father–had been right, the Church elders had all been right. God was on their side. He had sent them to this valley and He would stand by them and protect them as long as they followed His Word. She was so thankful, so grateful to God and to her Church. She was a Latter-Day-Saint–a Mormon–and she was the luckiest person on the face of the earth.

CHAPTER 25

July, 1848

A Visit to Salt Lake City

Anna had just finished weeding the cabbage and peas, and was washing in a basin at the side of the house when she spotted the two riders coming down the street toward the Sinclair's cabin. Immediately she recognized their distinctive dress, and, with heart pounding, realized Wes Tucker and Crocker Sloan were coming for a visit. Wearing their customary buckskins and black felt hats and carrying their long rifles across their saddles, they reined in before the Sinclair's hitching post and dismounted.

Anna ran into the house. "Ma, guess who's here?"

"Anna!" scolded her mother in a low voice. "Not so loud, you'll wake Lou Ann. I just put her down for a nap."

"But, Ma," said Anna in a more controlled tone, "it's Wes Tucker and Crocker Sloan! They just rode up."

"Oh, my heavens!" exclaimed Mary as she rushed toward the door. "I never expected to see them again."

Louise entered from the cabin's other room. "Who's here?"

"It's those two mountain men who gave us the elk," said Mary.

Just as the three women stepped out on the small porch, Crocker and Wes approached along the path. "Howdy," said Wes. Anna stood and stared at him, tongue tied. He seemed so much taller than she remembered and he'd aged; he was a man now, no longer a boy. How long had it been since she'd see him? Only nine months, yet it seemed like a lifetime.

Mary extended her hand toward Crocker. "Welcome, Mr. Sloan, and you too, Mr. Tucker. Please, come in. You remember my daughter, Anna, and this is our friend, Louise."

After shaking hands, the women led them into the cabin and offered them seats at the table while Louise put on water for coffee. Billy came running into the cabin. "Crocker!" he yelled, running right up to the mountain man. "Crocker, where ya been?"

"Well," exclaimed Crock, "if it ain't little Billy, but ya ain't so little now, are ya? Ya growed a mite."

"Crock–ya been with the Injuns?"

"Billy," commanded Mary, "run and fetch Stan and the boys. Hurry now, you can ask your questions later."

Without argument, Billy turned and dashed from the cabin. "Boy's growed," said Crocker.

Anna sat down next to Wes. "Where have you been trapping?"

Her mother wasn't about to let Anna sit idle. "Anna, go to the Commissary and fetch some flour." Next Mary turned to Louise. "Louise, dear, can you see if Sister Taylor has some coffee?" Louise shyly nodded and left the cabin.

Crock held up his hand. "Now, don't go getting nothing fer us. We just ate this morning on a whitetail doe we took up one of the canyons. We're full to the top. Ain't that right, Wes?"

Mary's eyes flashed and she pointed a scolding finger at Crocker. "Mr. Sloan, please, I was going to send her for that flour anyway. Might as well get it now so we can have biscuits with our coffee. Now tell us where you've been."

"Oh, it's been a long time, Mrs. Sinclair. We been all over, from Illinois to the upper Missouri. We been beav trapping and bufler hunting and even guided some rawheels west. But what I can't believe, ma'am, is what you people have done here! Wes ain't been here before so he don't know what's changed, but I seen the valley when there was nothing here but sage and rattlers. You've build hundreds of homes and you've planted the whole valley. It's a miracle! Ain't seen nothing like it."

Mary placed tin cups before the two men. "You're right, there has been a miracle. It's all just too incredible! You can't believe last winter. We almost starved; lived on Sego Lilies and thistles."

Just then Stan entered the cabin followed by Michael and Anna, carrying a sack of flour. Stan held out his big, rough hand as Crocker and Wes stood. "I understand," he began, "that we owe you two gentlemen a great deal. In fact, I understand ya may have saved the lives of my family with that elk." They shook hands and Wes recognized the sincere gratitude in the Mormon's eyes and the welcome in his handshake.

"Weren't nothing," said Crocker as they all sat down except Anna who delivered the floor to her mother. "We just had this here old cow elk and thought your people could use it. But I hear you and yer nephew marched all the way to California and back. Now that must 'a been an adventure."

"Well, can't say as I'd want to take such a walk again. But, please, not 'Mr. Sinclair'–just 'Stan.' All right?" Stan leaned over to Michael. "Run over to Brother Allison's and fetch a drop of drinking whiskey."

"Don't bother," said Wes, "we don't want ya to go to any extra trouble."

Crocker glared at Wes. "Farm-boy, don't interfere with a man and his family."

"Hurry now," ordered Stan. "These men need to cut the dust from their mouths."

The men sat about the table, drinking coffee with occasional sips of whiskey and eating hot rolls covered with fresh butter while the women prepared supper. At one point Crocker looked about. "Say, I remember another young lady."

Stan shined with pride. "That's Gwen, my daughter. She's married now and lives in Bountiful–that's to the north. Jason here, is planning on getting hitched next month to a fine young lady, Ellen Munce. My family's all growing up."

Crocker nodded toward Anna. "This one ain't married yet?"

Stan laughed. "No, not yet, but I'd reckon soon. She's too much of a beauty to go single long." Anna blushed as everyone looked at her.

After supper, when the plates had been cleared from the table and Stan had produced the whiskey once again, Anna decided it was time to take action. Without giving herself time to consider what she was about to do, she gently placed a hand on Wes' sleeve. "Wes, would you like to see the fields?" As she spoke the words, she knew the question didn't make much sense; of course he wouldn't want to look at their fields. And she was also aware that, in the confinement of the cabin, everybody had heard her question and understood what she really meant. The Sinclairs sat in silence and, with knowing smiles, watched the two young people.

Wes looked at Anna as if he hadn't comprehended the question. Quickly recovering, he nodded and spoke in a shy voice. "Sure." Wes and Anna stood, and Anna led the way outside. Once away from everyone's knowing looks, Anna felt better and relaxed. They walked to the street and then down toward Big Field. She wanted to take his arm, but didn't dare. Reaching the first fence line, she found an old log and they sat, facing west to watch the sun set.

"What do you think of our fields?" she asked.

He turned and looked past the fence. "They're fine, really. I grew up on a farm in Illinois. The soil here is rocky, but you've done wonders."

"Yes, we irrigate. It's the only way to soften the ground so that something will grow." For the next few moments they were silent as they watched the red glow over the Strawberry Mountains. Suddenly she remembered and turned to him. "Did you hear about the seagulls?"

"No."

"Oh, you won't believe what happened. The crickets came by the millions and they were eating our wheat. They would have eaten it all– we couldn't stop them. But, just when we were ready to give up, God sent thousands of seagulls and they devoured the crickets. It was beautiful! I was standing right over there," and she pointed to a place in the field, "and the sky was full of birds. It was a miracle." Noticing he was staring at her, she blushed. "Do you believe in miracles?"

"I don't know, I never though much about it. Crocker believes everything is a miracle. He believes in the Injun's Great Spirit."

"I remember," she said, "you told me back on the trail." Building up her courage, she slipped a hand under his arm, and he adjusted his weight on the log to sit a little closer to her. As he again stared at the blazing red sky, she looked at his face. Since the last time she had seen him, it had hardened and the hardness made him even more handsome. He now carried himself with a quiet self confidence, which she found terribly attractive. "Sometimes," she said, "sitting and watching the sunset, I wish the moment would go on forever. It's so beautiful."

"Yes, I know. These mountains seem to have a power, a strength that can flow right into you. Without having been here and seen them, it's difficult to understand."

"You told me that, but I didn't understand it then. Now I think I do. Do you think it makes us different?" she asked. "I mean, having lived in the Rocky Mountains, does it make us different from the people in the East?"

He grinned down at her. "Yes, I suppose it does. I think Crocker believes a special spirit lives in the Rockies." His expression became serious and his voice dropped to a whisper. "I thought by now you would be married."

Surprised by his directness, she shook her head. "There really aren't that many prospects for a girl here. There are more women than men and some of the men are gone on missions, which just makes it worse. But it's all necessary if we're to build up the Church. What about you? Do you have an Indian wife?"

He laughed. "A squaw? No. The Injuns take marriage a bit more casual then we do, and, of course, many Whitemen take Injun wives. I think I told you about Crocker's two squaws. He has a half-breed son back East in school." He openly stared at her as she stared back. "You're..." he had difficulty finishing the sentence. "...you're very becoming. I can't believe you haven't received offers."

She smiled and squeezed his arm. "Maybe I have and maybe I've refused." She noticed he was nervously fidgeting as he sat on the log. Suddenly she remembered something. "Do you remember Sarah Wheeler? She was on a wagon in our company."

He thought a moment and then shook his head.

"She ran off with a sheriff from Illinois. She just ran off and left her husband. She must have been very much in love with this Hawes, don't you think? He was the sheriff who was looking for my father's murderer and my lost sister." She saw his jaw harden at the mention of her father and sister.

"Your sister?"

"Yes, my sister, Lisa, was lost. It happened the day my father was shot by Weston Hamlin." Suddenly, she found herself telling of that day, a day she hadn't talked about in almost two and a half years. "We were getting ready to go to Nauvoo in a boat. We had loaded the boat when Hamlin and some others rode up and started shooting." She told the entire story and when done, tears streamed down her cheeks. He sat stiff and straight as he looked at her, and, even though his face was almost without expression, she saw pain in his eyes. A flood of affection swept over her as she realized he was feeling her pain. She wanted to lean forward and kiss him, but he turned his head and looked again at the sunset.

"You know," she said, squeezing his arm, and speaking in a bare whisper, "I love my Church. I could never leave the Church, like Sarah Wheeler did. I'm required to marry someone within my religion."

He continued looking at the red sky, but tenderly took her hand in his and nodded his head. As they sat, watching the last of the sunset, she wanted him to put his arm around her, to hold her tightly and to kiss her again on the mouth, just as he had kissed her that night on the trail. She didn't care if he wasn't a Mormon and she didn't care if he had lived with the Indians and she didn't even care if she knew almost nothing about him. At this moment, she wanted him more than the breath of life that flowed in her own breast. Her desire was a sweet ache deep inside, yet she didn't move or say anything, afraid the moment would be over and he would be gone. As time passed they only sat and held onto each other, fearful that their togetherness would end.

Wes and Crocker pitched their tent by the side of the Sinclair's cabin that night and the next morning, after a generous breakfast, left Salt Lake City for Fort Bridger. As they rode up Emigration Canyon, Wes was silent, but Crocker kept trying to get him to open up. "Now, Farm-boy, ya look awful. Tell old Crock what happened. You and that little Sinclair girl was out in them wheat fields half the night. Tell this old coon what happened?"

"Nothing happened!"

"I don't mean that! I mean, did ya tell her who ya was?"

"No. I couldn't."

"God Almighty, boy! Ya got this thing in yer craw and ya got to get it out before ya choke on it. Now you know yer innocent and so do I and yer not going to rest till ya tell her who ya are and that ya didn't shoot her pa."

"She hates Wes Hamlin; not only for shooting her father, but for her sister. Did ya know she lost her little sister, Lisa?"

Crocker nodded. "Yeah, Stan Sinclair told me all about it last night."

Wes spun about in the saddle. "You didn't say who I was did ya? You didn't give me away?"

"No, no, I won't do that! You can trust me."

"Well, Anna blames me for losing her sister and she also blames herself fer not going out in the River after her. If she found out who I was, she'd just hate me. Besides, she's going to marry some Mormon."

"You mean she's engaged?"

"No, I mean she can't marry someone like me, a non-Mormon."

"Hell, Farm-boy, no problem there. Christ, just become a Mormon. What difference does it make if ya pray to the Mormon God, or the Great Spirit or Muhammad?"

Confused, Wes shook his head. "I don't know, I don't know anything anymore."

"I got it!" exclaimed Crocker. "What ya need is to go see someone that's wise with such things We'll go see old *Osota Wicasa*. He'll do a fortune on ya."

"The Crow medicine man?"

"That's him. But he ain't just any old medicine man; he's my medicine man. He's got great powers. You'll see, Farm-boy, you'll see."

CHAPTER 26

September, 1848

Celestial Marriage

Wes and Crocker travelled first to Fort Bridger and then through South Pass, down the Sweetwater and Platte and then northeast to the Niobrari River where they found Red Eagle's camp. But Red Eagle had no clue to the whereabouts of the Crow medicine man, *Osota Wicasa*. Riding north again, they located Fego in a small Crow village on the South Fork of Cheyenne River.

Early on a clear September morning, Crocker, Fego and Wes sat before a tipi, eating buffalo tongue. "*Osota Wicasa?*" asked the Mexican. "The Smoke Man? Fego knows where he is. But you two do not want to go there. *Osota Wicasa* is on Clarks Fork of the Yellowstone. That is far from here and it is where the Bug's Boys are!"

Wes groaned at Fego's words. "The Bug's Boys! Hell, we don't want to run into them. I don't think we'll be welcome in Blackfoot Country. Where's the Yellowstone? Up by the Musselshell?"

"South of Musselshell," answered Crocker. "Yep, that's Blackfooter land. What's he doing up there, Fego?"

The half-breed swallowed his buffalo meat. "He was asked there by the Bug's Boys. They need his medicine."

Wes was confused. "I thought *Osota Wicasa* was Crow. Why do the Blackfeet want him?"

Fego gave a secretive glance toward Crocker and then quickly looked back at Wes. "Smoke Man has powerful medicine. Many tribes seek his blessing."

"Well," said Wes. "He must be some powerful Injun cause he's never where ya want him. Crock, why do we have to see him? Why don't we just see the local medicine man?"

Crocker shrugged his shoulders. "I thought you was the one with the broken heart and the sad eyes. *Osota* is the best I know. I thought he could tell yer fortune and help ya out, that's all. But if ya want to see someone else, there's plenty to choose from."

Wes shook his head. "God, Crock, I just don't know. Sure I want to see this-here *Wicasa* fellow, buy those Bug's Boys scare me. I don't want them chasing me again."

Fego turned and called to his squaw, but Wes was unsure what he said, not understanding Crow. The woman came out of their lodge and hurried off. Fego pointed after her. "Fego sent squaw for *Gnuska*—Grasshopper. She was born Blackfoot, but raised by Lakota. The Crow took her from the Lakota."

After several minutes, Fego's wife returned leading a young woman in her twenties with long straight black hair and large black eyes. Wes stared at her for she was the prettiest Indian he had seen, with a narrow face and a straight, thin nose, and when she smiled, showing straight, bright teeth, he was even more enchanted. He felt a nudge from Crocker as the older man leaned closer. "A beauty, huh? Don't tell me ya won't jump on her bones!"

The woman, *Gnuska*, sat down between Fego and Wes. Fego pointed to Wes as he spoke to her. "We will talk in Lakota because *Wicasa Ozu* speaks a little Lakota." She nodded her head and Fego continued. "You were born to a Blackfoot mother?" She nodded. "You remember the Blackfeet, you know the chiefs?"

She nodded again and spoke in a soft, lyrical voice. "Yes, I was young, but I remember. I was nine winters when the Lakota came and took me."

"*Wicasa Ozu* and *Mahtola* wish to go to the Yellowstone, but there is bad blood between these *wasicun* and your people. They wish to go to the Yellowstone in peace to visit the Smoke Man. They do not want to blacken their faces against your people."

As Fego talked, the smile left *Gnuska's* lips. Replying, she gestured with her hands to add emphasis to her words. "My people blacken their faces against all *wasicun*. No Whiteman may come into their hunting lands. They have fought hard to keep their land and do not want outsiders."

Fego nodded. "But, *Gnuska*, these *wasicun* only want to see *Osota Wicasa*. The Smoke Man helps your people now and these men need his help. They should go in peace."

She smiled. "You want *Gnuska* to take them. You want *Gnuska* to keep them free."

"Yes," said Fego.

Then *Gnuska* did something that completely baffled Wes. She leaned far over and placed a hand on Crocker's chest. "He is not *Mahtola*! He is..." but Fego put a finger to his lips, and seeing this, she didn't finish her statement, but leaned back. "I will take you to see *Osota Wicasa* but nothing else. My people may come and kill the *wasicun*, for I do not speak for my people. But *Gnuska* will go with them and if the warriors come, I will speak to them."

Early the next morning, Wes, Crocker and *Gnuska* started for Clarks Fork, over three hundred miles to the northwest of her village on the South Fork of the Cheyenne. She led them slowly and carefully through the Black Hills, across the Powder and Tongue Rivers to the Bighorn River.

The weather was warm for a fall day on the Bighorn. Since leaving Red Eagle, they had run into a few bands of Sioux and Crow but no Bug's Boys, and Wes was very grateful. Now back in Blackfoot Territory, he wondered what was so important about seeing this old medicine man, yet his partner seemed even more determined that Wes should meet this particular Indian.

Gnuska led them down the Bighorn, looking for a place to ford as the afternoon sun reflected off the clear river water, occasionally blinding them. Suddenly *Gnuska* reined to a stop and spoke to Crocker, and then both the mountain man and the Indian cocked their heads and listened. Wes' heart skipped a beat as he spun about in his saddle, looking in every direction. *Gnuska* turned her horse about and led them back up the River, the way they had just come. "This is it," thought Wes. "The Bug's Boys are coming!"

They rode at a trot up river until coming to a bend where *Gnuska* urged her mount up a small hill and reined to a stop. Before either Wes or Crocker made the crest, she turned about and galloped back down. "Blackfeet!" she said as she rode past them. As they hurried back down river, Wes spotted Indians, dressed for war, on the opposite bank, high on a bluff. Without warning, Indians swarmed over the countryside, coming up river and from the bluff above while others crossed the River–all to surround the three travelers.

Crocker thrust out his hand in the gesture for "friend," but the warriors, faces painted and carrying war lances, didn't return his sign. *Gnuska* pointed to Crocker and Wes and spoke in Blackfoot. Wes didn't understand her words, but she didn't stop talking as the young braves gathered about and listened. Suddenly the Indians reined back and allowed another, older Indian to approach the travelers. He was obviously a chief for he wore a large war bonnet and carried a percussion rifle. He pointed the rifle at Crocker and yelled a command. Braves slipped from their ponies and, running to Crocker and Wes, pulled the Whitemen from their animals and held them by their arms.

Wes couldn't believe this was happening. He knew the chief would never believe *Gnuska* and that he would be killed and scalped on the spot. He clenched his teeth and tried to control his shaky legs.

Gnuska tried speaking again, but the chief yelled at her and two Indians pulled her from her pony. She struggled to get free as she continued an uninterrupted stream of speech, but the chief wasn't listening. He walked before Crocker, looked the mountain man up and down and then took Crocker's six-shooter and turned it over in his hands before slipping it into his own belt. Next, he stepped before Wes.

Gnuska broke free and dashed in front of Crocker. The chief turned toward her, anger written on his face, but she placed a hand on Crocker's chest and spoke rapidly. As she spoke, she pounded Crocker's chest with her fist several times. The chief, his face no longer showing anger, stepped before Crocker and, reaching with his fingers, withdrew the medicine pouch from under Crocker's rawhide shirt. He studied the pouch and the buffalo horn painted on its leather surface for several seconds. Stepping back, he spoke to *Gnuska* before giving Crocker back his six-shooter. The chief raised his hand and gave another command, and the Blackfeet began leaving. The chief mounted and rode after his warriors and, in seconds, the three travelers were alone next to the Bighorn River.

Wes shook so violently he could hardly walk, yet he managed to move to the edge of the water where he sat down and placed his hands over his face. "Oh God!" he groaned. "I will never, never come back here again, God, if only you let me live through today."

Wes heard Crocker behind him. "Holy Mother of Jesus! God-in-Heaven-above! Them coons 'bout did us in." Crocker walked to Wes' side and slapped him on the back. "We did 'er, Farm-boy. We fooled them Bug's Boys, we did."

Wes looked at his partner. "What happened? Why'd they leave?"

Gnuska stepped into the water and, bending at the waist, splashed the cool liquid on her face. "They say we can go to *Osota Wicasa* and then we must leave."

"Where is he?" asked Wes.

She walked back on shore and sat by Wes' side. "*Gnuska* has great fear. Did *Wicasa Ozu* have fear? *Gnuska* thought they would kill us." She placed a comforting arm around his shoulder.

Wes turned and her face was only inches away, her smile dazzling and her eyes dancing. A moment ago he thought he would be sick, but her closeness made him feel better. "*Wicasa Ozu* was scared to death! I thought my hair was gone for sure. Look at me shake!" He held out his hand so *Gnuska* could see.

She laughed and held out her own shaking hand. "*Wicasa Ozu* was brave."

Crocker stepped in front of Wes and *Gnuska*. "Come on, you two. This ain't no time to be fooling around. We got to vamoose."

"Where we going?" asked Wes as they retrieved their horses.

Gnuska pointed west. "On the Clarks Fork–not far, one day or less."

"What did that chief say?" asked Wes.

Gnuska's face was grave. "He said to go to Smoke Man and then leave. If he ever catches you or *Mahtola* here again, he will kill you." She lowered her voice. "He is a chief and he has said this. Now, if you return, he will have to kill you. Do you understand?"

Wes nodded.

They traveled southwest and, late the next day, came to a small tipi pitched all alone in a little draw leading to Clarks Fork. They dismounted and hitched their horses. *Gnuska* stayed on her animal. "*Gnuska*!" said Crocker. "Aren't you coming?"

"I cannot." she announced. "I am not permitted to stay or I will be killed–punishment for bringing you. I must return at once."

Wes didn't understand. "But what about us? How are we to leave?"

"My people will not harm you on your return."

"Where are you going?"

She held out her closed fist. "Come here, Man Who Plants."

Wes stepped forward, and she took his hand and placed a large white tooth in his palm. "It will keep off danger. I go back to the Crows. If I please you, come when you are done here." She reined her pony around and started back down the draw.

Wes looked at the tooth in his hand as Crocker approached and looked over Wes' shoulder. "Well!" exclaimed the mountain man. "She takes a fancy to you, don't she! That's a bear tooth, good medicine. You could do worse than hook up with a little squaw like that. She ain't just any woman, ya know. She's got spirit."

"What did she mean, 'come when you are done here?' Doesn't she have a man?"

"*Gnuska*? No, her brave was Gray Pony, but he went under and she must find a man soon. I think she has an eye on you, Farm-boy. Oh well, let's see if Smoke Man is home." Crocker walked to the tipi's flap and scratched on the skin. After a moment an old Indian peeked out. "*Mahtola*!" was all he said before waving for the two Whitemen to enter.

Inside, the tipi was crowded with personal belongings and a small fire burned in the center of the floor. Smoke Man was an old, wrinkled Indian with a dark complexion and narrow set eyes, dressed in only a breechcloth for clothing, but wearing a medicine pouch around his neck. He gestured for the two men to sit with him at the far end of the tipi. Wes sat with *Osota Wicasa* on his right and Crocker on his left.

Crocker pointed toward Wes. "This is *Wicasa Ozu*. He speaks only Lakota, so we must speak so. How are you, *Osota Wicasa?*"

Smoke Man smiled, showing his tobacco stained teeth, his eyes twinkling. "Good, I am good, *Mahtola*. It is good to see you again so soon. Why didn't the Blackfeet kill you? Did the Spirit protect you?"

"The Great Spirit always protects *Mahtola*, Smoke Man, and the Blackfooters don't dare touch me. But I am here for my friend–*Ozu* has a sick heart."

Wes, watching Smoke Man's face and his simple smile, was reminded of a neighbor in Illinois–a neighbor everyone said was only half-witted. Smoke Man had that same look to his face, and Wes wondered how he could be a powerful medicine man.

"My friend," continued Crocker, "has been stung by the bee. He has seen the face of a young maiden and now he can't get free from her magic. He cannot have her, but cannot get her out of his heart."

Smoke Man stopped smiling. "Oh, this is bad magic. But we can do nothing until we smoke." He selected a pipe and, extracting his cutting board, chopped tobacco and filled the pipe. The three men took their time smoking the bowl until the tobacco was gone, no one breaking the silence until the ceremony was done. Putting down the pipe, Smoke Man playfully pinched Wes' tit. "A maiden, huh? She was like the badger and burrowed into you and there her spirit lives and you are not free. This is common, but it is still very painful. We must do something. I will ask the spirits about you, *Ozu*. If they are not lazy, they will speak to us, and then we will know what to do. Sometimes, the spirits play and we are their game."

Smoke Man turned and rummaged around for something behind him. Satisfied he had what he wanted, he turned and displayed a finely worked rawhide pouch. He looked up into the fire's smoke and gave a chant that was meaningless to Wes. Done, Smoke Man opened the pouch and extracted thin dried twigs. Next, he unwrapped a second pipe, one covered with small animal designs, dropped the twigs into the fire and, when they burst into flame, held the pipe in the smoke and gave another chant. Preparing more tobacco, the medicine man filled the second pipe, lit it and offered it to Wes. "Smoke this deep into your body so the spirits can see inside."

Wes glanced quickly at Crocker who looked back with wide eyes reflecting the light of the fire. Wes took the pipe and sucked in the pungent smoke. *Osota Wicasa* smiled. "Good. Keep smoking until it is all gone. I must smoke also, but not *Mahtola*." The medicine man selected a third pipe, filled it and began smoking along with Wes, drawing in the smoke and, after holding it for a moment, blowing it up into the tipi. Wes followed his actions.

Before Wes' pipe was half gone, he felt numb in his arms and legs and his head was light–not an unpleasant sensation. He heard Smoke Man laugh and it sounded as if the Indian were sitting at some considerable distance, while, in fact, he was only inches away. "It sounds funny." said Wes and was amused that his own voice sounded far off.

When both *Osota Wicasa* and Wes finished their pipes, the medicine man gently took Wes' right hand and, with a small sharp knife, made a quick cut in Wes' palm. The action and resulting pain made Wes jump, but he did not pull his hand away. After blood oozed from the wound, Smoke Man rubbed Wes' palm onto his own palm, smearing the blood onto his hand. Letting go of Wes' hand, he stared at his palm. The three men sat still for many minutes while Smoke Man stared at his palm. Finally, Smoke Man looked up and spoke something unintelligible to Wes.

"In Lakota, *Osota Wicasa*," reminded Crocker.

Smoke Man reached up and tenderly stroked Wes' cheek. "Many deer trails lead to the water hole, some are long and some are short, some are hard and some are easy."

"Smoke Man," interrupted Crocker, "get to the point!"

The medicine man looked at Crocker and scowled. "You are in a hurry? You are going somewhere tonight and not staying with Smoke Man? Smoke Man has these words inside and *Mahtola* does not want to hear them?"

Crocker raised his hands in defeat. "Have it your way."

Smoke Man turned back to Wes. "If I could remove this arrow from your heart, I would. I cannot. I do not believe it can be removed. But you can turn the pain to joy. You must go far, *Ozu*, and you must enter a lodge. To find this lodge is hard–*Ozu* must go on a *ihambleiciyapi*. Do you understand?"

Wes shook his head and turned to Crocker. The mountain man had lost his high spirits and looked with a solemn face at his friend. "*Ihambleiciyapi* is a vision-quest," he whispered. "You must go on a vision-quest. What do you see in his quest, Smoke Man?"

Osota Wicasa looked again at his bloody palm. "I see *Ozu wocinpi* and *istima* and *tanka waziya* and at the end of the path..." Smoke Man smiled and made a sign.

Crocker turned toward Wes. "He says your quest will include starving and sleeping and the north wind. It will be cold."

"What is this quest? What do I have to do?"

"I've told you," said Crocker, "about when young boys go out into the wilderness and starve themselves until they have a vision. The vision gives them direction for their lives. That is what Smoke Man says you must do. You must go out and have a vision."

While Wes and Crocker spoke, Smoke Man filled another pipe and handed it to Wes. "Smoke. Smoke and then lay down."

Wes was still light headed from the previous pipe but he took it and began to draw in the smoke, soon becoming tired. Smoke Man took the pipe from his hand, and Wes stretched out on the ground and closed his eyes. Just before drifting off to sleep he heard Crocker's voice. "And *woksapa* too?"

"Yes," replied Smoke Man, "*waksapa* too."

* * *

On this Sunday the Great Salt Lake Valley was beautiful—filled with sunshine and a rich blue reflecting off of the Great Salt Lake. The Saints enjoyed a mild September breeze as they attended church services in the Bowery, a large covered patio used for meetings. Afterward, the Sinclairs accepted an invitation for Sunday dinner at the Martins. Food had not been plentiful for many months, but now conditions were better with half the Saints' wheat saved by the seagulls and the vegetable gardens proving bountiful, plus wagons were arriving from the East with commodities not grown in the valley such as coffee and tea. The Martin dinner table included beef and barley stew plus several steaming dishes of vegetables while the air was full of the sweet smell of newly baked bread. Everyone ate until they were full and then laughed at their bulging stomachs.

After dinner Kathleen Martin cleared away the dishes while most of the Sinclairs and Martins walked out toward the fields to relax and enjoy the sun on this day of rest. As Anna stood to follow, Carl Martin touched her arm. "Would you stay a moment?" he asked.

She shrugged her shoulders. "Of course." He was probably going to propose again, and she would have to gently tell him no. She sat back down and smiled at Uncle Stan who sat at the other side of the table, and he smiled back. Only four of them remained in the Martin's cabin: Carl and his wife Kathleen, Anna and Uncle Stan.

Carl nervously shuffled his feet. "How was the meal, Stan? Did you enjoy it?"

Stan nodded. "Very good," he declared.

"Kathleen is an excellent cook," said Carl. He turned and nervously smiled at Anna as he changed the subject. "Your mother tells me your friend, Luke Allison, is engaged."

Anna nodded. "Yes, he's to marry at the end of the month."

Carl nodded in return and then smiled again at Stan and Kathleen. The awkwardness of the situation was so evident that Anna knew something had been cooked up by Carl Martin, and she didn't have to wait long to find out what. The four of them turned toward the door in unison as the sound of a carriage reached their ears. "My," said Carl, "I wonder who that could be?" He stood and went to the door.

Anna looked to Stan who smiled, but Kathleen didn't smile, glancing away from Anna's look. The door opened and Bishop Lissman and Brother Wheeler entered. "Good day," said Bishop Lissman.

Uncle Stan stood and shook the visitors' hands. "Good to see you, Bishop Lissman. And you, too, Brother Wheeler. Please, have a seat."

The bishop nodded to both Kathleen and Anna. "Good day, ladies. We thought we'd drop by. It's such a lovely day and I don't always get the chance to visit my friends." Both he and Brother Wheeler found a seat at the table.

Carl quickly closed the door and sat down. "We're always glad to have you gentlemen come to visit."

Lissman nodded and glanced about. "You folks have just had your dinner. Good. My wife and I just ate. I must say, it's different than a few months ago. We were starving then, but the Lord has been good to us." The Bishop laid a copy of the Book of Mormon and a small stack of papers on the table. "You know," he continued, "it always amazes me when I visit different homes how we Saints thirst for the Word of the Lord. But, before we talk, let's pray. Prayer is always the proper way to begin a social event, don't you agree?" Everyone around the table nodded in unison. "Good," he continued. "Brother Wheeler, would you do us the honor?"

Wheeler bowed his head and the rest followed. "Almighty God, let Your Spirit be with us today in this humble abode. Give us the strength to divine Your word and understand Your teaching as revealed by the Prophets, Joseph Smith and Brigham Young. Ever remind us, as we administer to the Sinclairs and the Martins, that our covenant needs continual renewal. Help us to give Your word to the young ones, especially Anna Sinclair who sits here with us. Thank You, Oh Lord, for Your many blessings. Thank You for returning our Prophet, Brigham Young, to us from Winter Quarters. We say these things in the name of the Father, the Son and the Holy Ghost, Amen."

Anna leaned back and relaxed, anticipating that Bishop Lissman was about to deliver a sermon, and she might as well get comfortable. She wondered if his message would be a continuation of Brigham Young's lecture from the morning church service at the Bowery.

"I'm so pleased that the Prophet is back with us," continued Lissman. "When he's gone, we're just a lost collection of sinners, but when he's with us, we're God's own children. A people need a head, a leader to guide them through the difficult times. Don't you agree, Brother Wheeler?"

Anna watched carefully as John Wheeler's dark eyes flashed about. Ever since Sarah's desertion, he had been acting in a most peculiar manner. "Yes," he said, "we must have a leader. And in the family, too; there can only be one leader in the family—the father. God has commanded it so."

Bishop Lissman's voice lowered and he leaned toward Anna, addressing her with his next remarks. "I understand, Anna, that you have been made aware of the Lord's blessing of Celestial Marriage. That you are aware that your father, Stan, has taken both Louise and your mother as his wives." The Bishop waited for her response.

She felt her heart pounding and the flush rush to her cheeks. So that's what all this was about: a sermon directed toward her about plural marriage, and it could only be with Carl's proposal in mind. She felt the anger but fought to control it. "Yes, my mother told me." She had meant to say it with force and energy, but her voice was weak.

The Bishop leaned back, smiled and nodded. "Good. Now that you know, it is only fitting that you know the whole truth. If you are aware of only half-truths, you might inadvertently create some harm for the Priesthood by your misunderstanding. It is better that you become one of the blessed family who know everything. That's why we're here today. We all love you, Anna, and the Lord loves you. We want your happiness, but we know that this happiness is dependent on your obeying the Lord and receiving His blessing. You understand, don't you?"

Her anger suddenly gone, she felt a tinge of pride that the ward's Bishop and First Counselor had come just to deliver a lesson for her. "Yes, I understand."

"Good," said Lissman, all humor gone from his face. "Then listen carefully. Many years ago, when our Prophet Joseph Smith was conversing with the Lord, he wondered why ancient prophets took more than one wife. He asked the Lord and received the knowledge of Celestial Marriage. In receiving this knowledge, he was obliged to obey its law. The Lord ordered Joseph to fulfill the law and take another wife. The Prophet was brought up in a good Christian home and he was adverse to doing something that, on the surface, appeared to be unnatural to righteous living, even though God commanded it. For years he put off fulfilling this obligation to the Lord.

Finally he could put it off no longer and on July 12, 1843 he asked again of the Lord and received the following revelation. Now, Anna, you will not find this revelation in the Book of Commandments since it came after the book was printed and because it is still a secret doctrine of the Church." Bishop Lissman moved his Book of Mormon to uncover a page of printed material. "Remember," he said, "that the following is the voice of God!" He then bent forward and began reading.

> 1. Verily, thus saith the Lord unto you my servant Joseph, that inasmuch as you have inquired of my hand to know and understand wherein I, the Lord, justified my servants Abraham, Isaac, and Jacob, as also Moses, David and Solomon, my servants, as touching the

principle and doctrine of their having many wives and
concubines–
2. Behold, and lo, I am the Lord thy God, and will
answer thee as touching this matter.
3. Therefore, prepare thy heart to receive and obey the
instructions which I am about to give unto you; for all
those who have this law revealed unto them must obey
the same.

Bishop Lissman stopped reading and looked at Anna, his eyes burning into her. She felt, once again, the Spirit of the Lord enter the cabin and cover her in a blanket of love. She was hearing, with her own ears, the unadulterated words of God as spoken to her Prophet–holy words that only a small handful of Saints had heard.

Lissman tilted his head as he continued to stare at her. "Let me repeat the last line, Anna. '...all those who have this law revealed unto them must obey the same.' What does that mean? Does it mean that if you hear this law of God, that you must take additional wives if you're a man or that you must enter a plural marriage if you're a woman? No. But it does mean that once you know of Celestial Marriage, you must, as a Latter-Day-Saint, obey the laws of Celestial Marriage." He bent his head back down to the revelation.

4. For behold, I reveal unto you a new and an
everlasting covenant; and if ye abide not that
covenant, then are ye damned; for no one can reject
this covenant and be permitted to enter into my glory.

Anna was tempted to look away from the Bishop at Uncle Stan and Kathleen, but dared not. Instead she continued concentrating on the Bishop's words, on understanding what the Lord wanted of her. She knew she was going through an initiation rite that had been performed for her mother and for others.

15. Therefore, if a man marry him a wife in the world,
and he marry her not by me nor by my word, and he

covenant with her so long as he is in the world and she
with him, their covenant and marriage are not of force
when they are dead, and when they are out of the world;
therefore, they are not bound by any law when they are
out of the world.

Lissman stopped reading again. "Do you see that, Anna? When you have just a worldly marriage, it is over when you die. But God's Celestial Marriage, whether it is one man and one wife or one man and many wives, will last for all eternity. If you love your husband, you don't want to be without him in the afterlife! With God's law, you are bound to each other through all eternity. That is what Celestial Marriage is all about. This thing about plural wives is only incidental. The real issue is whether you will live forever with the man you love." He continued reading.

16. Therefore, when they are out of the world they
neither marry nor are given in marriage; but are
appointed angels in heaven; which angels are
ministering servants, to minister for those who are
worthy of a far more, and an exceeding, and an eternal
weight of glory.

Bishop Lissman looked up again and as he spoke his voice was filled with gentleness. "It is a very simple law, this Celestial Marriage. If you marry without it, your marriage ends with your death and in the afterlife you are just a ministering servant to those with more glory–those who did partake in Celestial Marriage. If you marry in God's law, you are married forever and you go on to greater glory. Anna! Can't you see what a great blessing Celestial Marriage is? God has told us to marry and multiply. To marry, in God's eyes, is to partake in Celestial Marriage which is a covenant given in God's name, by God's Servant, Joseph Smith. This is God's gift to us–our path to everlasting glory and union with our loved ones." He leaned slightly closer to Anna and lowered his voice again. "Children born to a Celestial Marriage are bound forever to their parents. Think about it!"

Bishop Lissman read again from the revelation, but this time it was about those who participated in Celestial Marriage.

20. Then shall they be gods, because they have no end; therefore shall they be from everlasting to everlasting, because they continue; then shall they be above all, because all things are subject unto them. Then shall they be gods, because they have all power, and the angels are subject unto them.

"In this verse," he said, "God tells us we will be gods—think of it Anna—gods! But it is through his law. Now, what have we learned? First, Celestial Marriage is about eternal marriage, not necessarily plural marriage. Once we know of it, we must follow it. If we do, we are married forever and go on to the greatest glory—to be gods ourselves." Lissman smiled and pushed the papers away from him. "Now you know. Do you have any questions?"

Anna looked at the others around the table. They looked back with smiles, as if they had shared a great secret with her. Anna felt very humble, very privileged to be included in this inner circle of the Saints. Now she did understand the issue better. Celestial Marriage was far more complex then the seedy rumors circulated among the bored Saints while on the long trek West. It had to do with God's gift of glory and eternal bonds between family members. Clearing her throat she looked at the Bishop. "If I marry under God's law and I am the only wife, are my husband and I married forever?"

Lissman smiled and nodded. "Of course—that's what it is really all about."

She smiled, realizing she didn't have to marry into a plural family to have God's blessing. She saw her father wipe away a tear and looked at Kathleen who smiled back with sincere warmth. They weren't trying to trick her—they were telling her the truth.

Bishop Lissman gestured toward Carl. "Now, let's consider the situation at hand. I, as Bishop of the Seventh Ward, have told Carl that it is time he consider taking another wife. This is because there are too many women and not enough men. He's not compelled to do it, but he's requested to help out in this manner. He says he loves you, Anna, and wants you for his wife. I know Carl; there isn't a finer man in Zion. If you marry him, he will love, care for and cherish you for all eternity. But, before he can take a second wife, his first wife must agree. That is part of God's law. Kathleen, what do you say? Should Carl take Anna for his wife?"

Anna couldn't believe what she was hearing. It was like some drama she would play out in her own head, but one that could never really transpire. Yet, here they were—talking as if heads of cattle or sacks of wheat were being considered.

Kathleen slowly reached over and touched Anna's arm. "We have been trail companions and neighbors for some time. I have grown very fond of you and I think you know this. I do approve of Carl taking another wife and of all the women in Zion, I especially approve of you, Anna. I know we will be great friends. I know I can share my home with you and make you happy."

For Kathleen, Carl's one and only wife, to say such a thing touched Anna deeply. Anna couldn't help but respond as she reached over with her free hand and laid it on Kathleen's. "Thank you," she whispered.

"Well, now," said Lissman, leaning back and obviously proud of himself. "We have almost everything in place. We have God's Will, and Celestial Marriage, and Carl's love for Anna, and Kathleen's acceptance. All we need now, Anna, is your approval. If you say yes, you and Carl can marry for all eternity and your children will be sealed to you forever. You will have glory as gods. What do you say? Shall we set a date?"

It was moving just too fast! She wanted to say yes, she wanted their approval and God's approval. Carl was a nice man, but could she be married to him forever? It was a breath-taking idea. "I'm fond of Carl," she said.

John Wheeler finally spoke up. "That's it! That's how married people start out. No one begins madly in love. Love is something that has to grow and it always begins with fondness. Take my word for it, Anna, fondness is the beginning...and respect, too. You have to have respect. Then comes loyalty. Without loyalty, all is gone. God loves loyalty. I have a theory that..."

Anna heard Bishop Lissman give a low, polite cough, but she continued to listen to John.

"Anna," said John Wheeler, "don't let God see disloyalty. For I know that the attribute of loyalty is a pure manifestation of God's power. It came to me..."

"Excuse me," interrupted Lissman, "but we covered that, John. Remember? We covered that this morning!"

John sat back and looked at Lissman. "We did?"

"Yes, John. We're talking about Anna Sinclair marrying Carl Martin, now."

"We are?"

Uncle Stan looked at Anna and his brow knotted up. "Anna, you know how I love you. You're my brother's own child and my daughter by marriage and I couldn't love you more. We're not here to pressure you or deceive you. We want you to make up your own mind. I love your mother and I love Louise. I didn't at first–John is right–it does start with fondness. But I can honestly say that now I love these two women beyond anything I ever dreamed and I cry thanks to God each night that I will remain married to them forever. But that is me–not you! You must decide if you want to marry Carl. If you can't say so now, then just say you need more time."

"God bless you, Uncle Stan," thought Anna. Somehow, he had taken the urgency out of the situation and given her a chance to collect her thoughts. She turned and addressed Carl. "I care for you, Carl, but all this is so new to me. I need some time to sort it all out. Can you accept that?"

Pain danced across his face. "Anna, does that mean you're not saying no? That you will consider it?"

She nodded. "Yes, I'll consider it."

He beamed in joy. "You'll see. God will show you the way."

CHAPTER 27

Casting Out Demons

Wes and Crocker left Smoke Man on Clarks Fork and moved on to Fort Laramie by way of the Sweetwater and Platte. All the way to the Fort, Wes complained to Crocker. "I don't know why we went up there and risked our scalps just to talk to that crazy old Injun. I mean, what did he tell us? Nothing! Just some hornswoggle about going on a fast and having bad dreams."

Crock and Wes sat before their tent inside the walls of the Fort next to a comfortable fire, roasting buffalo boudins and sipping watered-down whiskey. Crocker turned the boudins on their sticks so the raw side faced the fire. "It ain't bad dreams, Farm-boy—it's a vision-quest. Course, if'n ya don't want to go, ignore it. You're right, *Osota* is just a crazy Injun. But we did have fun with them Blackfooters, didn't we? We showed them a thing or two."

Buffalo Man

Not knowing if Crock was teasing, Wes turned and suspiciously looked at his partner. "That what you been telling everyone? You been bragging how ya scared 'em off, when ya know they was going to kill us before *Gnuska* saved us–*Gnuska* and that silly herb pouch."

"Now, Wes! That ain't exactly true. Them Blackfooters was put off by seeing me and knowing this hos has kilt many a savage bent on being rowdy. They saw the killing glint in my eye and it made their blood run colder than an icy blizzard."

"You're full of it! We ain't never come that close before and you're just making light. But what puts me off is that it was fer nothing."

"Sure," responded the mountain man, "nothing."

"'Cause I ain't going off somewhere to get cold and starve. How long these quests supposed to last? A week? Two?"

Crocker leaned forward and smiled as he tested the boudins. "Well, now, that's a question, ain't it? How long? Normal, fer a young brave, would be one or maybe two weeks at the most. If he ain't starved by then, he's probably gone under."

"Well, that's something, at least. It don't require a man to be gone his whole life."

"But that ain't you," said Crocker. "*Osota* said *tanka waziya*. Ya know what that means, don't ya?"

"'Big' something, 'big wind' I think."

"Yep, means 'big north wind.' North wind blows in the winter and ya got to go on the quest during a cold winter. Yours is a special quest– some are like that. Means you're a special coon. Ya got to go up in them mountains for a winter by yerself."

Wes was staring at Crocker, not believing what he heard. "You have to be crazy. You want me to go up into the Rocky Mountains for the winter, during which time I'm to starve myself so I can see visions of some animal? I ought to go be a God-damned Mormon. That'd make more sense."

"Yep."

"You want me to be alone all winter in mountains covered with snow? Ya want me to starve and possibly die?"

"Well, not me, Farm-boy–it's *Osota Wicasa*."

"Hell!" said Wes, taking another drink of whiskey. "I won't do it! It's the most rawheel, stupidest thing I ever heard and I'm not doing it. I'd die! Hell, ya can't go all winter without food."

"Now that's the fun of 'er, see! Of course ya don't go without food all winter. Ya take some meat and the cold keeps it. Ya try to figure it so it doesn't quite last all winter, leaves ya low fer a couple of weeks. That's when the vision comes. Takes a heap of cold to make a good vision for *tanka waziya*."

"Well, don't go countin' yer toes, yet, 'cause I'm not going. I'm staying here in the Fort where it's warm and where there's whiskey and maybe, just maybe, we can go for beav for just a couple of weeks at first snow."

"Sounds good," said Crock as he slipped the roasted buffalo guts from the stick onto his lap. "Let's not talk again of this *ihambleiciyapi*. It's a dead subject."

"Absolutely! No more north winds or quests, that's the last of it."

It was late in the fall and both men recognized the signs of an early, severe winter. One crisp, cloudy morning, Crocker woke to find Wes packing his possibles sack. Crocker put on a pot of coffee as he watched his young friend prepare. "Ya got time fer coffee?" he asked.

Crocker's casual remark made Wes feel easier. "Sure, got plenty of time."

"Take lots of DuPont and Galena–winter's a long time."

"I will. Ya got any idea where a good place would be?"

"Hum...if it were this coon, I'd go to the Wind River Mountains. You know where they are–go through South Pass and up the Green River and then enter them from the west. Game will still be plentiful and if ya hurry, ya can build yerself a small cabin. No one will bother ya up there."

"Makes sense."

"And cut plenty of wood. Ya can't have enough wood cause ya got to melt the snow fer water every day. No wood will put ya under 'fore no meat."

Suddenly Wes though of something. "What about Jeff? I can't keep Jeff in those mountains all winter. He'll starve, or I'll end up eating him."

"You're right. After South Pass, when on the Green, look fer a band of Shoshoni. They'll take ya up into the mountains and keep Jeff for ya until spring. They's good people."

For most of the morning, they talked about survival and drank coffee as Wes prepared. Before noon, he was ready and Crocker walked with him outside the Fort's gate. Before mounting Jeff, Wes quickly stepped forward and gave Crocker an awkward hug. The old mountain man pounded his friend on the back. "See ya next spring, Farm-boy."

"Where will I find ya?" asked Wes.

"See Fego on the Elkhorn or find Red Eagle. They'll know. I won't be far."

Wes swung up into the saddle. *"Tecihila, Mahtola."*

Crocker waved. *"Tecihila, Wicasa Ozu."*

Wes followed Crocker's directions and rode up the Oregon Trail until he came to the Green River. On the second day of travel up the Green he found a family of Shoshoni, just as Crocker had said. Wes traded two plugs of tobacco and a blanket to the Indians who led him up into the Wind River Mountains, already their peaks covered in snow. The Indians left him by a high mountain lake in a great forest of lodge-pole pine. Wes went to work at once, hurrying to beat the deep snow, cutting down trees to build a small ten foot by twelve foot cabin and to stack a large supply of wood.

During the first week of November, a savage storm dumped three feet of snow on his little home; winter had come to stay. Each morning he set out through the deep drifts to hunt deer, moose and elk. Before the snow completely locked him to the side of the nameless lake, he had cut and frozen several hundred pounds of meat. Now, all Wes had to do was wait out the cold weather until spring. By his calculations, he could ration his meat and other supplies until late February. All would go well if he didn't run out of logs with which to melt his drinking water and cook. *Ihambleiciyapi?* Was this really going to work? In the farthest stretches of his mind, could he conceive that this Indian ritual would solve his problems?

* * *

The winter of 1848 began early in the Valley of the Great Salt Lake with cold and snow coming in late October. The Mormon settlers were aware that the foods collected in the summer harvest and the goods freighted in from the East would not last all winter and they were faced with another year of deprivation. Brigham Young, quick to understand their desperate situation, instituted rationing early. This move would save many lives.

The Church's Prophet also understood that they could not tolerate allowing the poor to starve while those better off survived. Therefore, he ordered most foods held in common by the Church Commissary. In addition, Brigham Young started the Saints on a campaign to collect large quantities of Sego Lily bulbs, camas bulbs and thistle tops before the snows came.

Anna and Billy trudged over the ground, gathering Sego Lily roots in an old burlap bag. Billy worked eagerly until a rabbit or robin distracted him, and his distractions were many. Anna spent half her time calling him back to work and then chasing him after he failed to respond. They crossed Big Canal and worked the foothills leading to the low mountains that bordered the northeast corner of the Valley.

Anna walked over the top of a hill and found Billy jamming a stick into a badger hole. "Think I can get this badger, Anna?"

"Billy, I think that badger is long gone. Let's work."

"But, Anna, if I catch me a badger, we can eat it tonight. I like badger."

Looking down, Anna noticed someone had already dug for Sego Lily on this hillside so she slumped down next to the boy. "Go ahead. If you catch one, I'll even skin it."

"That's a deal!" he exclaimed and returned to his probing and jabbing.

As Anna watched Billy struggle for his prize, she thought of the upcoming Sunday. She would surely receive another invitation from Carl for Sunday supper, and, if she accepted, he would press for an answer to his proposal. But if she refused, he would spend the entire week moping about, asking if she'd found someone else; it was an impossible situation. Besides, how could she find anyone else? The young men were always off on a mission or some other errand for the Church, at least any that showed an interest in her, and the older men were already married. Somehow it didn't seem fair. She had turned seventeen, and for a strange reason, seventeen was a magic year when other women wondered about a girl if she were not already engaged or at least had a beau. Was Carl Martin her beau?

Billy quit his digging and probing. "I guess he's gone!" The boy sat down next to Anna. "Do we have to look for more roots?"

She put an arm around him and pulled him closer. He was seven now, but still let her cuddle him. "No, not just yet. We'll sit awhile."

This satisfied Billy as he poked at his bare feet with the stick. "Are we getting shoes for winter? I'd like a pair of shoes." He playfully tapped her foot with the stick. "You need shoes, too."

Anna sighed. "I certainly do! If I have to borrow Ma's shoes one more time to go to a dance, I'll die. They're too big for me. Maybe shoes will be coming in before winter closes the trail."

Billy frowned. "We always say that!"

"Say what?"

"When we want something we can't have, we say 'maybe when the next wagon comes,' or 'it will be coming before winter.' I get tired of that!"

"I do too, Billy."

"You had another nightmare last night."

Anna felt the gloom descend as she remembered the night before and her waking in blackness. Gwen was no longer available to comfort her, but her mother had moved into the loft to hold her when the dreams made her cry out. "I know, Billy–I remember."

"Pa doesn't like Aunt Mary sleeping in the loft with you. He says you should be old enough to sleep alone."

"I know," she responded as she brushed a tear from her eye, fighting the hurt inside. "But I have bad dreams."

"Ma says ya dream of your lost sister."

"That's right, Billy–I dream of Lisa."

"How old was Lisa when she was lost?"

"Just five. The same age as you when you and your ma came to live with us. Do you remember that, Billy?"

"Sure, that was after my first pa died. We came to live with you and now I have a new pa and he's your pa, too. Ain't that right?"

She gave him another hug. "That's right! We're brother and sister now."

"Ma says that the Bishop says you might have demons inside you. Do you have demons inside you? What do they feel like?"

This wasn't the first time she had heard Bishop Lissman's views, yet she felt her heart pounding at the suggestion she was possessed. Could it be true? She had heard countless stories of Saints who made some minor transgression only to have Satan's devils take that opportunity to jump in and occupy the sinner's body. The Church elders had to cast out the demons to save the Saint. What had been her transgression? She could think of no specific act like lying or stealing. Of course, she remembered the time she and the others climbed the boulder and drank whiskey, but that seemed like only a little sin; they had only broken the Word of Wisdom.

Yet, even as she searched her past, the possible sin was right before her, but she was reluctant to face it. If sin had allowed demons to occupy her, then her sin was thinking of Wes Tucker, the mountain man. Thoughts could be sins, she had been taught that many times. And late at night as she lay under her blanket, she pictured his face and thought of him holding her and touching her–kissing her, and she felt that special stirring deep inside, that special stirring which needed to be relieved. At the time, her sexual fantasies seemed so beautiful and innocent, yet, they must be the transgressions that now put her soul in jeopardy. How could the ache she felt for Wes Tucker be a sin since her dreams of him could never be fulfilled? He would probably never return to the Salt Lake Valley. She was sure the rumors of her nightmares were circulated by John Wheeler because he was always talking about demons and possession and carrying on ever since Sarah ran off with Hawes. But why did Anna have to suffer because Brother Wheeler's wife ran off with another man?

Anna felt Billy poking at her. "Anna, what's it feel like to have devils inside?"

She poked him back. "Maybe I don't have demons inside. Maybe I just miss my sister."

"Sometimes I have bad dreams of when my first pa died. It makes me cry. It is like that?"

"Yes, just like that."

When Anna and Billy returned home from their bulb gathering, Stan put a gentle hand on Anna's shoulder and spoke in a low voice. "After supper, put on yer ma's fancy dress. We're going to visit the Bishop."

She looked at her father with alarm. "Is it a bishop's court?"

His brows came together as he cocked his head to one side. "No–why would you think that?" She shrugged her shoulders. "Well," he continued. "We're just going to look into this nightmare business, that's all. You do want to be rid of them, don't you?"

After supper, Anna and Stan walked the four blocks to Bishop Lissman's log and adobe house which was constructed with a large parlor in which the Bishop could hold meetings and perform necessary ward business. As Anna and her father walked up the path to the front door, Anna saw through a window that Lissman wasn't alone. In addition to the Bishop were Brother Wheeler and Carl Martin sitting on straight backed chairs. Why would the ward's bishop and two counselors take this time out of their busy schedules if it weren't important?

The men greeted Stan and Anna and found them chairs to sit on. The Bishop didn't waste any time getting to the point. "We've heard, Anna, that you have terrible nightmares. Is this correct?"

They all watched her, and she felt a blush come to her face and hoped that they couldn't see it in the dim light of the lantern. "I have dreams, sometimes, but they're not that bad."

Bishop Lissman lowered his voice and smiled warmly. "I understand that you wake up screaming!"

She glanced at her hands, afraid to look into his face. "Sometimes."

Stan cleared his throat. "She has nightmares once or twice a week. Mary has to sleep with her in the loft so she'll be there when Anna wakes up. I think it's become worse since Gwen married and moved away."

"Have you ever considered," began Brother Wheeler, "that you are possessed by demons and that it is your soul fighting the demons while you sleep that cause these nightmares? It wouldn't be the first time. I have personally seen Saints who were possessed and I have seen them blessed by the word of the Priesthood, casting the devils from their bodies."

The Bishop gave Wheeler a sour look. "We haven't determined whether she's possessed as yet." He turned back to Anna. "Can you tell us what these nightmares are about? That's surely the key."

Anna relaxed slightly and leaned back. "I don't remember them when I wake up. I think it's the same dream each time and I know it has something to do with my sister, Lisa."

"Your sister was lost back at Nauvoo–is that correct?" asked Lissman.

"Yes, lost in a boat."

"That's it," said Wheeler, his eyes flashing. "The demon has taken the shape of her lost sister and lives in Anna, disguised. When Anna dreams, she sees it. That's why the dream is a nightmare–the demon scares her."

Anna had to fight back the tears. "It isn't Lisa that's frightening."

Stan looked at her with surprise. "There's more? You remember more?"

Casting Out Demons

She didn't want to remember but, suddenly, there were more bits and pieces. "There is a man, an evil man."

"Ah hah!" exclaimed Wheeler. "That's it! Don't you see? It's not the vision of her sister, Lisa, which is the devil, but this man—he is the devil in her."

"John!" cautioned the Bishop. "Calm down. We're just getting to the bottom of this. Now, Anna, who is this man? What does he do?"

She began wringing her hands. Thoughts of the dream always made her feel bad and right now she felt awful. She wanted to curl up in a little ball and close her eyes, but she couldn't. "I don't know who he is. I don't know what he does."

Stan leaned a little closer. "Does he do something bad? Does he do it to you or to Lisa?"

The tears forced their way out as she shook her head. "I don't know. Yes—something bad, something evil, but I don't know."

John Wheeler nodded, his eyes darting about the room. "That's it! The man is a demon and performs unspeakable acts in her mind. She can't tell us because the demon casts a spell over her memory so she can't repeat them."

Bishop Lissman was very solemn as he addressed Stan. "We must consider the possibility that your daughter is possessed by one of Satan's demons."

The pain was written all over Stan's face. "But if she were possessed, wouldn't she do bad things? I mean, wouldn't there be other things to tell us?"

"Not necessarily," replied the Bishop. "If the possession were recent, then a battle might be going on inside Anna. As the demon wins more control then these other manifestations will appear. The fact that Anna is so well behaved is credit to her goodness and her faith. Yet, her soul, at this very moment, could be fighting this demonic power."

As the men talked, Anna felt like she were on display; that she was a prize cow they were debating about. Why didn't they speak directly to her when discussing her?

"What do you think, Carl?" asked Lissman. "You haven't said a word."

Anna looked up to see Carl staring at her and she recognized the love on his face. "You all know," he began, "that I have asked Anna to be my wife, and she is considering my proposal. I love Anna and would do anything for her. I don't know if she is possessed or not, but I think these nightmares are scaring her and making her unhappy. I think this stands in the way of her considering my proposal for marriage. Whether it's a demon or something else, God has the power to lay His healing hand on her and cast out the sickness and make her whole."

"Yes," interrupted Wheeler, "but what sin did she commit to open the door for possession? Devils can't get inside us unless we let them, unless we commit a sin so they can get control. We must know what sin Anna has done to let this happen." John Wheeler was breathing hard and his face was flushed as he kept looking from Anna to Lissman.

Lissman appeared to be looking in Anna's direction but his eyes were focused somewhere beyond her. For several long minutes he continued in his trance as the others quietly watched. Finally, he smiled at Anna. "If she is possessed because of some sin, then God knows the sin. If Anna knows what it is and wishes to tell us, she will. We've all known her for a long time and we all know that she is one of our shining stars in Zion. I still remember the day she killed the snake and at that time I thought she would become one of the Church's finest mothers. I'm sure I'm correct in that assessment now." He turned toward Stan. "I believe a blessing is in order, Brother Sinclair. It doesn't matter if she is possessed–a blessing is always a good thing." He stood and the other men followed his example.

John smiled at the Bishop. "We must cast out demons. We must do that in the blessing."

"Yes," replied the Bishop. "We will do a casting out." He placed a chair in the middle of the floor. "Anna, would you like to sit here?"

Her heart pounded and her legs shook, but she stood and, walking to the chair, sat down. The four men, Stan, Carl, John Wheeler and Bishop Lissman, stood around her and placed their hands on her head. At the moment of their touch, Anna felt a warmth, a comfort, come to her and she knew she was safe; these men loved her and wanted to protect her and they all held the sacred Priesthood and could call God to perform miracles.

"Dear God," began the Bishop, "the God of Moses and Solomon and the God of Joseph Smith, our Prophet, we ask You to hear our prayer. In the name of the Melchizedek Priesthood we ask You to cast out the demons in this sister of Zion, Anna Sinclair. For the devils inside her, we command you, in the name of God, Christ and the Holy Ghost, to leave her body at once. We command you, in the name of God, to be gone and never return. God, we ask You to bless Anna Sinclair. Let her look into her heart and find the love that is surely there for Brother Martin. Show her that Yours is the way to righteousness. Give her the understanding that Celestial Marriage is the way to eternal glory that binds wives to husbands and children to parents. Let her understand the love that Your Church has for all Your children. Give her the faith she will need to be a soldier of Zion and bless her with many children, for children are the special reward for women of pure heart. These things we ask in the name of the Father, the Son and the Holy Ghost, Amen."

Anna had felt the spirit of God enter the house as Bishop Lissman blessed her and now she was filled with that spirit. The bad feelings were all gone. She was in safe and secure hands, for how could any harm come to her when she was protected by men who stood so close to God?

* * *

Gunner stepped back into the muddy wagon trail and looked at their handiwork. "What ya think, Winston?" he said, addressing Roland Palmer.

Roland stepped back beside his friend. "Looks good, Gunner."

"Damn!" cussed Gunner. "I told you to call me Sam—Sam Gruber! Now, how many times I got to tell ya that?"

Palmer was hurt. "But, we're alone! What difference does it make now? Can't no one hear us."

"It matters. We got to practice all the time. You make that mistake at the wrong moment and the authorities will be down on us. Now, I'm Sam Gruber and you're Winston Smith."

"What about Friendship? He didn't change his name."

"You dumb shit! He ain't wanted by the law. God, I got to explain everything to ya."

Palmer looked back at the building front they had just erected, deciding not to pursue the current conversation. "It looks grand, Sam, it does. Can't hardly see the back is a tent."

"It ain't a tent!" corrected Gunner. "It's a building of tent material. That's the difference." The two men stood and stared at the false fronted saloon and grinned. "When the money comes rolling in, we'll build it all of wood, maybe brick! I always wanted a brick whorehouse." From the corner of his eye, Gunner saw Nancy exit from her side tent and march toward the two men.

Before she even reached them, Nancy started in. "Where is that little shit? You seen that little fucker? I told her an hour ago to get my coffee and she just disappeared. What you two looking at?" She stopped beside them and looked at the false saloon front, her dirty pink nightgown trailing in the mud and her large breasts straining against the gown's material. She was a large woman, but none dared claim she was overweight. "Full-bodied" was the term used in her presence. "Looks nice, Sam. I told ya it would look good, didn't I. Now, weren't I right again? You wait and see, we'll have a proper place here soon."

Gunner put an arm around Nancy's shoulders. "Yessir, it's a beautiful sight. Say, where's Sally and Tamla?"

"Still sleeping," said Nancy. "Sam, ya got to do something about that little shit–she won't mind. Even when I smack her up aside the head she runs off and don't listen."

Just then Lisa stepped out the front door of the tavern, spotted Nancy and jumped back inside. Nancy, seeing her, took several steps toward the door and screamed. "You little fucker! You get your ass out here or I'll turn Toby on ya! Do–you–hear–me? I said get yer ass out here!" No one came from the saloon, and Nancy shook her head and walked back to the two men. "Ya see, Sam? See what I mean? She's impossible. I tell ya it's time to turn her. After working a few weeks with my girls..." Gunner turned on her with a frightening scowl on his face. "...I mean OUR girls, she'll get in line."

"She's too young," said Gunner.

"She's eight years old. Hell, I know children started younger than that! I tell ya, it will be worth a bundle. We'll auction her off. I'll pass the word back in Independence that we got an eight-year-old virgin. Them business men are just perverts, you'll see. They'll bid their heads off and we'll rake it in."

"What ya figure she's worth?" asked Gunner.

"I'll bet we can get two-hundred! Ya, two-hundred! And that ain't all, cause the word will go out. Others will show up and we'll just tell

Casting Out Demons

'em we got another virgin. They ain't gonna know. We might do it a half dozen times before they catch on. Even then she'll be worth a small fortune. She's got that curly black hair and those dark, pretty eyes. You'll see, she'll bring 'em in."

Palmer looked at Gunner and then Nancy. "What about the law? Whores is one thing, but little girls?"

Nancy squared off against Roland. "Now that's your job. You and Sam keep the law out and keep the crowds in line and me and the girls will roll on our backs and fuck us a fortune. Hell, who's gonna bother us out here? We're in Injun Territory. That fucking Sheriff Hillman can't touch us."

"We got to be careful," said Gunner. "The blue-bellies from Fort Leavenworth can burn us out anytime they want. We can't give 'em an excuse. That's why we ain't gonna rob no soldier–you got that, Nancy? No robbing soldiers. I want them blue-bellies to have fun every time they come. Take on them Santa Fe teamsters, but leave the soldiers alone."

"Honey!" she said with false passion, "I ain't dumb!" She reached down and gently took hold of his testicles. "You just keep packing them guns." She gave him a little squeeze.

He pushed her hand away. "Not out here, ya fucking whore– Jesus!" He started walking toward the tavern.

The anger flashed across Nancy's face. "Who ya calling a whore, God damn it!" she yelled after him. He didn't turn around, so she bent down and picked up a hand full of mud and cocked her arm, preparing to throw it.

Roland stepped by her side and whispered. "I wouldn't do that, Nan. I once saw him shoot a woman fer no reason at all. Just fer the fun of it."

Nancy looked at Roland and the anger on her face was replaced first with confusion and then resignation. "Oh, shit, guess I am just a fucking whore, huh, Roland?" She grabbed for his testicles, but he laughed and backed out of her reach.

Inside the big tent, which served as the tavern and dance hall, Friendship Brown and two other men sat at one of the large round tables. Lisa entered from a back tent, carrying a large cup of steaming coffee, and headed for an empty table. She put the coffee on the table just as Toby followed her into the room. "Nancy's gonna whack yer ass, Lisa!" he said and laughed. "I heard her say it. You better take that coffee out to her or she's gonna whack yer ass!" And he laughed again as he walked toward her, wiping a bloody knife on a filthy cook's apron.

"Get away from me, ya fat tub." yelled Lisa and she dashed around him and back into the kitchen.

"You wait," called a hurt Toby. "You wait. Gunner says I get ya. You just wait."

Lisa ran through the kitchen and entered another tent that served as a storeroom. Behind a large barrel of whiskey she knelt down and, in the dim light, pulled up a loose plank from the wooden floor. With just enough space for her body, she slithered down under the floor and carefully replaced the plank above her head.

Laying under the floor, in the dark, she was safe. At least she was safe for now. Just the night before, Sally had told her again that Nancy was going to let men lay on Lisa and put their things up inside her body. They called it fucking. She couldn't understand why it was called that! Every time one of them got mad they called everything "fucking" this and "fucking" that.

But Lisa wasn't going to let it happen. She would run away first. She didn't care if Gunner did come after her and kill her or, as he always threatened, give her to Toby. She already knew Toby wanted to put his thing in her. He'd already tried to get her dress off and his fingers in her, but she always managed to outwit him. Yes, she would run away first.

In the dark, she began crying, but the crying wasn't bad, because it made the hurt go away. To put away all the bad of her present world, she daydreamed of her other world. The world back on the banks of the Mississippi River in a place called Illinois. She remembered it well and she pictured each of their faces: Mama, Papa, Anna, Michael and Jack Jr. "Yes, Mama," she said, talking to herself, "I'll not use those words again. I'm sorry. Yes, I'll say my prayers. God, help me get away and send someone to kill Gunner and kill Roland and kill Friendship and kill Nancy and especially kill Toby. Say these things in the name of Father and Son and Rolly Ghost."

CHAPTER 28

A Vision-Quest

Winter settled in on Wes as the white cold blanket of snow on the high peaks surrounding the valley moved down, covering the frozen lake and Wes' cabin. Only the pines stood against the deep snow, and Wes found it impossible to travel farther than a few hundred yards from his cabin. He tried keeping busy, rebuilding his crude fireplace and chimney and making a pair of snowshoes. The supply of firewood kept his little home warm, and the meat, frozen and hanging from tree branches, assured him of a meal, yet the nights were long and he had trouble filling all the empty hours with meaningful tasks.

He had never spent a long stretch of time all alone and now he began feeling the estrangement associated with solitude. He remembered his family in Illinois and his old friends and neighbors. He remembered Samual Davidson at the Newtown Mill and Melvin Ingertal. He thought of his cousin, Jimmy Dixon and wondered what Jimmy was doing now. He remembered small, inconsequential things about his father, things he hadn't remembered for years and was surprised that the old scenes survived in him now, like some old faithful dog, come to lay at his feet. He had been young when his father died and now he realized how much he missed him. With loving affection, he remembered his mother and his brother, Bert, and wondered if Bert's wife had given birth to her baby and if so, was it a boy or girl? He was jolted by the possibility he might be an uncle! In the quiet of the high mountain valley, he began talking to his family and friends just to hear the sound of a voice. At night, especially at night, he thought of Anna Sinclair and wondered if she was married, yet.

Inside his cabin the air was dark, warm and full of odors, but outside, on a sunny day with brilliant sunlight covering the valley, the air was cold–bitter cold, making Wes' nostrils tingle and freeze with each breath. Wes carved notches on the log over the door to mark the passage of time, and, as the number of notches grew, he talked to the people populating his memory. He held long conversations with Crocker, then Fego, and, finally, Wes talked by the hour to Smoke Man. "Now is it cold enough? Look! Look outside! The sun's out, but I can see ice crystals floating in the air. You wanted a big north wind, didn't ya? Well, that out there is the biggest, damndest north wind the world has ever seen!" Suddenly Wes heard himself talking and stopped.

Planning to walk to the lake's shore where he would clear the snow and chop ice for drinking water, he strapped on his snow shows and stood up. "Look at that, Crock," he said to himself. "Look at those snowshoes! They're beautiful. I made them myself without any help from you. What do ya think of that?" He opened the door and, kicking away snow, slowly stepped out of his cabin. Mounds of the frozen white fluff stood guard on each side of the door, leaving a narrow path leading to the lake. He pulled his buffalo coat tight about his neck to keep out the wind.

"Come on, Crock, no use standing here and freezing. Let's get the ice," he said as he shuffled along the path. At the edge of the lake he extracted a small hatchet and began chopping. "Sure, Smoke Man, you're warm and nice in your lodge up on Clarks Fork, protected by those Blackfooters. I'm here on this God-awful lake!" Suddenly Wes stood and stared blankly into space with his realization. Did *Osota Wicasa* live alone? That couldn't be, no one could live alone like this for years–you would go insane. Everyone needed someone to be with, to talk to. How could a man survive alone in a tipi in the wilderness? No, Smoke Man must have a woman.

He cut out a nice piece of ice and, picking it up, slowly returned to the cabin. "Always move slow," he thought. "That's the key. If you go too fast, you freeze your lungs or you sweat and the sweat freezes on your body. Always go slow and you won't make mistakes."

That night he dreamed, and in his dream he awoke and opened his cabin door to find the snow covering even the trees. All he saw was a level snow plain extending to the mountains' peaks; no lake, not trees, no trail–nothing! When he really did awake, it was day, yet he still believed his dream to be true. Jumping from under his blankets into the frigid morning air, he ran and pulled open the door. There, before him, stood the trees, covered with great hunks of snow, but trees, nonetheless. Suddenly he realized it had all been a dream. Yet, it had been so real! Only the evidence that now met his eyes confirmed this picture before him to be the real world and his dream to be of the dream world. "If the trees disappear, where will I get meat? It will be buried under mountains of snow. Don't scare my like that, *Osota*. You have the upper hand since I've never done this before. You shouldn't play tricks on me."

He decided to start his fire, dress and then go outside to cut off the first piece of meat from the last deer carcass. One more animal to consume before his fasting begins. When ready, he left the cabin and made his way to the large pine that held the frozen deer. At the base of the tree he looked up and saw the canvas bag hanging far up the tree, secured by the restraining rope, which was itself tied to a high branch. Yet something was wrong–the bag looked too thin! The snow at the base of the pine was high, allowing him to climb directly into the lowest of the tree's branches. Alarmed, he reached the restraining rope, withdrew his knife and cut it. An empty game bag fell to the ground!

"Oh, Christ!" yelled Wes. "Oh, my God, what have you done!" He scurried down the tree and ran to the canvas. Examining the bag he discovered some animal had eaten out the bottom and managed to carry off the entire deer. Whether it was done all at once or just a small piece at a time, he couldn't say. "Oh God!" he moaned again, his numbed brain coming alive with the dreadful possibilities that awaited him. He ran as fast as he could to the cabin and quickly counted off the notches over the

Buffalo Man

door. January 12th! Today was only January 12th and he was all but out of food! He would never survive until the middle of February—that was over a month away. What if the snow trapped him until March? Over six weeks without food!

"Oh God! God! God!" he repeated over and over as he slipped to the cabin floor. He was a dead man! There was no game this high in the mountains this time of year and even if there were, he couldn't get more than a quarter mile from the cabin in all this snow—he was trapped! "God damn you, Crocker! You did this—you and that fucking Smoke Man." Why hadn't he checked all his meat every week—no, every other day? Why had he let this happen to him? No one could be this stupid! He put his hands to his face and began crying; he was already dead—he just didn't know it yet!

After wallowing in self pity for an hour he noticed the cold. Closing the door, he put another log on the fire. "Maybe this isn't so bad, Smoke Man. Let's take stock before we give up." From outside he retrieved a small bag hanging beside the door. Carrying it into the cabin, he opened it and counted six deer ribs that he'd planned to throw away. In his frying pan, he found left-over meat surrounded by cold, hard grease. He would save it all—the ribs, the meat, the grease. He would boil the ribs in soup and then crack them open for the marrow. But that wasn't much more than a single meal!

"Crock, what about these skins? I'll boil and eat my buffalo robe! Sure, I've heard other coons doing it. And I still have a pound or two of flour and salt. I'll put it all together and ration it out. You'll see, it'll have to last." In the back of his mind he knew it wouldn't.

During the next two days he carefully scrounged and prepared every piece of food he could locate. He even found where he'd thrown the bones from his previous carcasses and discovered the cold had preserved them. Cracking them open, he extracted the precious marrow. Yet, after two days, he possessed only a poor soup broth, which he decided to ration at a cup a day. And he was famished! With buffalo robe and hatchet, he trudged to the lake and cleared the snow from the ice. For over two hours he chopped at the ice before opening a hole to the water below. With string and a bone hook, he fished. By the time dark approached, he was stiff from the cold and still didn't have a single fish to show for his efforts. Were the fish frozen in the ice or just not hungry? Vowing to return, he shuffled to his cabin and consumed his day's cup of soup.

A Vision-Quest

That night, his dreams were of cold and hunger and when he awoke, he didn't feel rested. "Might as well sleep in and conserve my energy" he thought. By early afternoon he was back at his fishing hole. This time he was lucky—he caught a fish four inches long. It would go into the soup.

The days managed to unwind into nights and the dreams of night ended with the coming of day. He occasionally caught a fish, which he cooked in his soup, convinced that the broth trapped any nourishment that was cooked out of the meat. He couldn't afford to waste anything. On one fortunate day, he shot a small owl, but his ball blasted away the better part of the bird. The remains, less the feathers, he dropped in the soup. One day, when counting the notches, he realized it was the first of February! He's survived almost two and one half weeks on a few fish and an owl plus many strips of boiled buffalo robe. And during all this time, he lived with gnawing hunger, the kind of hunger that sits in the stomach and eats on the nerves. "I have been told, Smoke Man, that when people starve they stop feeling hunger after two or three days, but this isn't happening to me! I'm always hungry." He removed his shirt and examined his chest. His ribs stuck out—he was starving!

How long could he last? Another week? He slept the better part of each day in addition to the entire night and had little energy for the job of walking to the lake and sitting at the fishing hole. He felt a sense of separation between himself and his surroundings, especially when outside in the cold and knew he needed a strong infusion of meat but had no idea where food was coming from. Should he cut up the rest of his buffalo coat, rub off the hair and add it to his soup? There seemed no alternative.

The job took most of the day and part of the night and when he was done, the resulting broth was thick and gooey with a taste that made him gag. Even salt didn't improve its palatability, but his hunger won out and he forced some of it down. Next, he chewed on the tough, bland buffalo hide, doubting it contained enough nourishment to make up for all the effort of chewing it.

That night, he went to bed early while light in the western sky still showed through the crack over his door. He dreamed he walked with Smoke Man through a buffalo herd. The large animals weren't disturbed at all with the two humans, but carefully stepped aside to let them pass and even made friendly comments about them. "Good evening, gentlemen," said one especially large bull. "Are you hunting today or just visiting?"

"My God!" thought Wes. "They know we hunt and kill them and they still treat us with such respect?"

"Of course," said the bull. "You kill and eat us and we become you. We are only showing respect for ourselves."

"Is this correct, Smoke Man? Can this bull be telling the truth?"

Smoke Man smiled and stroked a tan calf. "I have never known a bull to lie. Of course, a badger is another animal and they lie all the time."

One of the cows laughed. "*Osota Wicasa*! You say such things against the badger because you are always riding your horse into one of his holes. If you keep your pony out of badger's holes, you will begin to believe him."

Wes woke to the blackness in his cabin and the sound of the wind whistling outside. Another morning and he had to get up. Or was it afternoon. It must be day because he could see a bare suggestion of light over the cabin door. His home was very cold. He must light a fire if he could just manage to get out of bed. Pieces of his dream kept coming to him. "Is this it, *Osota*? Is this the vision with the animal in it? Can I come home now?" It seemed only fair that the medicine man come for him now that he'd had his vision. Of course, he had no idea what the dream meant.

He was so tired, he would just shut his eyes for a moment more of sleep. When he opened them again he sensed that buffalo were crowded into his little dark cabin and fear grabbed at him for if they moved about, they would surely trample him. "Now, move out, fellows. This cabin is too small." He heard them stomp about but saw only their dark outlines.

"Of course we'll go," one of them said and out the door they went. The whole thing was just too tiring and Wes had to close his eyes again. He dreamed of walking in the buffalo herd.

When Wes next opened his eyes he knew it was day and that it was very cold. His blankets were stiff and the cold hurt his mouth when he breathed in. In the back of his mind he knew he was in great trouble. It had been more that just a day since he crawled under the covers and he had to get up, start a fire and catch some fish. If he lay here, he would die.

He couldn't gather enough energy to throw back the covers. Deciding to wait until his strength was up, he lay still, barely

A Vision-Quest

breathing. He thought of Crocker, sitting in Fort Laramie's canteen, drinking whiskey and eating mountains of roasted boudins and it angered him; that damned Crocker was the one who put him here! The anger combined with his fear was just enough for him to move. He pushed back the covers and wrapped a blanket about himself. He wasn't sure just how long it took him, but finally, he managed to get a fire started. The warmth from the flames began to thaw his mind and body. Realizing how close he'd just come to giving up and going to sleep forever he began shaking. "See what you've done! See, Crocker? It's all 'cause of you!"

Wes decided to get more firewood for heat and then make a fishing trip to the lake. He pulled on his boots and looked around for his coat, confused until remembering he'd eaten it. Wrapping the blanket tighter about his shoulders, he opened the door, only to have a sea of fine snow swish down and bury him above the knees. Only the top foot of the cabin door was open to the outside, the rest blocked by a snowdrift. Wes looked out and saw that another storm had doubled the depth of the snow cover. Going as far as the lake was out of the question.

For the rest of that day, Wes cleaned up the snow that had come into his cabin and then managed to make a path around the side of the cabin for firewood. Done with these two chores, he sat before the fire getting warm and recovering his strength. He would start digging a trail to the lake in the morning.

Snuggling under his covers, he swore not to let the cabin get so cold. Suddenly Wes realized he didn't feel hungry any more. He shut his eyes and found himself with Crocker and Smoke Man. Smoke Man sat on his haunches and stared into his palm.

Crocker pointed to Smoke Man. "See that, Wes? Smoke Man says he made a mistake. Says you're not to go in the mountains for the winter. You're to wait for summer and then climb a mountain and capture an eagle."

Wes couldn't believe it. "Holy Christ! What are you saying? A mistake? He made a mistake? I'm not supposed to be in the mountains? God, Crock, I'm already dead! I died in the Wind River Mountains. It's too late!"

Crocker looked at Wes with suspicion on his face. "Gone under, huh? Well, like this coon says, ya can never trust them fucking Injuns."

Wes felt himself going insane. "What? You're the one who took me to Smoke Man. He's your medicine man!"

Crock looked genuinely puzzled. "He is?"

Wes opened his eyes and tried to look about but it was too dark. He heard the wind making a terrible racket. Looking at the crack above the door, he realized it was day, but today he was supposed to go to the lake and catch a fish. It couldn't be storming today! Tears came to his eyes. He wouldn't last another night; he would go to sleep and die. He needed warmth and he needed food and neither was coming. He closed his eyes.

* * *

Inside Carl Martin's cabin Anna worked to prepare a fresh pot of soup. When she had the pot over the fire, she checked on Kathleen and found her sleeping, even though her fever was still high. Carl, in bed beside his wife, was awake and obviously in pain. Anna warmed water and, with a damp cloth, began to wash him, but his legs were so tender that he grimaced each time she touched them.

"Just do the rest of me," he pleaded. "Do the legs later."

She nodded and covered up his poor swollen limbs.

"You know," he said. "Back on the trail and in Iowa I saw lots of black-leg and pleurisy. I never thought it would happen to me and look at me now."

"Don't worry," she said as she sponged down his upper body. "Pa says they're bringing catfish back from Utah Lake. I told him to bring some for you."

He took hold of her wrist, stopping her work. "Thank you, Anna. Thank you for caring for Kathleen and me and especially thank you for watching the kids. I don't know what would have happened if you'd not been here. It's like you're part of the family already."

She gently pulled free and continued to wash him. "If it hadn't been me, someone else would have been here. Oh, I forgot to tell you: Brother Wheeler has gone quite mad. He's mad or possessed by at least a dozen devils; no one's sure which. I saw Paul this morning and he says his pa is running around screaming about the Devil and sin and all kinds of things."

Carl shook his head. "This is what comes when a wife runs off with another man. That's when poor John's troubles all started. Now look at him. I wish someone could go get Sarah Wheeler and bring her back and show her the mess she's made."

Suddenly Anna thought of something. "If Brother Wheeler is mad then they'll have to replace him as First Counselor of the Seventh Ward and that means you'll be First Counselor."

He looked at her again and his eyes flashed with a strange passion. "He went mad because of Sarah! And I'll go mad if you don't marry me! I swear, I will. I will go mad and kill myself."

That night, the air was bitter cold on their walk to the Bishop's house, and Anna had to watch her step not to fall on the ice covering the path. A visit to Bishop Lissman's home could mean serious Church business, but on this occasion it was for fun: Luke and Linda Allison were throwing a party to celebrate their expectant baby. Luke's little house was too small for a gathering, so they were holding the party at the Bishop's. The guests were young people, and Anna was eager to hear all the latest news. In the middle of the winter, the Saints were confined much of the time to their cabins by the freezing and snow and everyone was coming down with cabin fever. Anna was anxious to meet with friends and enjoy a moment of merriment. She only wished Joey and Gwen could be there, but they were snowbound in Bountiful.

Michael held Anna's arm as they walked up the icy path to the front door. Sister Lissman answered the door and showed them into the parlor. Already present were Linda and Luke Allison; Jason and his new wife, Ellen; Ernie Fontana and his sister, Mary; Billy Irvine, Paul Wheeler and Cory Tobbs. Anna and Michael quickly removed their coats and joined the others. A small table stood to the right of the fireplace and on the table rested a bowl of red punch plus a small selection of cookies. Looking at the table, Anna felt a pang of sadness, for in times past the table would have been covered with many good things to eat. But now, with the food rationing, Anna was certain the cookies had been carefully counted to insure each guest would receive one. She wondered if Bishop Lissman had acquired the flour and sugar himself from the Commissary.

Anna and Michael stepped up to Luke and Linda to congratulate them on their expected new baby. Anna looked at Linda's stomach, but the young woman wasn't showing. "Isn't it wonderful," said Linda, her face shining. "Ours isn't the first, of course. Many babies were born last winter, but ours will be one of the first born in Zion. He will never know the hurt of being chased from his home."

"Are you going to have lots more?" asked Michael.

The father-to-be put an arm around his young wife. "I will if she will. I'd like an army of children. We have to turn this land green and it'll take an army."

"We didn't turn it green enough last summer." It was Jason speaking. "This winter is worse than last. We've got to do better next summer because if this continues, we'll have to eat all our livestock."

Ellen slipped a hand under her husband's arm. "It's not so bad. More wagons will be coming in the spring. We just have to make do a little longer."

"On thistles?" said Ernie Fontana. Everyone remembered that the Fontanas had planned giving up and moving to California, only to be convinced to stay when the seagulls saved the crop.

"The trail," said Billy, "might not be open until late March or even April because of all this snow. I think the rationing is going to get worse before it gets better. I hear the flour reserve at the Commissary is so low only the Apostles are allowed in to see."

"I don't believe that!" objected Michael. "That's just some rumor."

Linda frowned. "Let's not talk about the rationing. This is a party; we're supposed to have fun." She handed her cup to her husband. "Luke, darling, pour me some more punch." Luke was quick to move, and everyone smiled to see his attentiveness toward his pretty wife.

Cory leaned close to Anna and whispered. "I wonder if he'll be that polite to her after he's married his fourth or fifth wife."

Anna turned to Cory. "You shouldn't say that!" she said, speaking softly. "It's not something we should mention in public."

Cory took Anna's arm and guided her away from the others and toward the warm fireplace. "This isn't exactly public. I'll bet most in this room know about Celestial Marriage."

Anna looked over the group of young people. "Who, besides you and me?"

Cory smiled. "I'll bet Michael and Jason know. After all, your mother and Louise are married to your pa. Don't you think they know?"

A Vision-Quest

Anna had never talked to her brothers about plural marriage, she had been warned to keep it secret, and they had never mentioned it to her. Yet, it was certainly reasonable for them to know by now. "All right, they probably know. Who else?"

"Well, that's four of us. Now, let's see, I'll bet Jason told Ellen."

"I'll give you Ellen: that's five."

"And I know that Linda knows. She was asked by Herbert Souder to be his third wife."

Anna's ears burned with the news. "No! You're kidding! He already has two. He's as old as Moses, why would he want to marry anyone as young as Linda?" Suddenly both Anna and Cory realized the simple answer to her question and both had to put hands to their mouths, trying not to laugh out loud. "Oh, Cory, does Luke know?"

"I don't know, but he might. That would make seven of us. I don't think either Ernie or his sister know, but Paul might know; his father is First Counselor in the Seventh Ward. You know John Wheeler has gone crazy. He's probably blabbed it to Paul a hundred times. That would make eight out of..." she stopped to count how many were in the room. "...eight out of eleven!"

Anna was thinking about Linda's proposal. "Linda told Brother Souder that she wouldn't marry him? How'd she do it?"

Cory looked intensely at Anna's face. "You haven't told Carl Martin that you don't want to marry him, have you?"

"No, but how did Linda tell Souder? Tell me, Cory."

Cory brushed a red lock of hair from her forehead and smiled a mischievous smile. "She just said she was secretly engaged to Luke. And she was! But it was too late, old Souder had already spilled the truth about Celestial Marriage. Anna, when are you going to tell Carl? I know you don't love him, or at least last time we talked, you didn't."

Anna sighed. "I don't know, Cory. Sometimes I feel very fond of him and think that being his wife would be just fine. But that's it–it would be fine. I always thought that marriage should be exciting, even thrilling. I don't want to settle for 'fine.' I get hints from my father and mother all the time that Carl is the right man and that marriage starts with just fondness, but I just don't know. I want to do what's right, but deep down inside I get nervous when thinking of marrying Carl."

Cory moved even closer to Anna. "I'm going to tell you something and you must act natural. Do you promise?"

Anna couldn't stand it! "Of course," she whispered.

Cory spoke so low that Anna had to lean until her ear was at Cory's lips. "I'm married to an Apostle. I can't tell you which one, but, of course, I'm not his first wife."

Anna's mouth dropped open as she stared at her friend.

"And," continued Cory, "we did it secretly last month. We're married under Celestial Marriage. I will be bound to him for all eternity."

Anna grabbed Cory's arm and spoke just a bit too loudly. "Cory! What's it like? Who is it? What happened?"

Cory looked around. "Shhh! Not so loud."

"Oh, Cory, you have to tell me everything. You have to tell me about the ceremony and the whole thing."

"I can't, I'm sworn to secrecy, but I can say this: they plan on making it public someday. He told me that. Someday it will all come out and everyone will know who is really married to who and everything. Then we can do it all openly; it will be grand."

Cory's news was just too tantalizing, and Anna moved about the party and talked to her friends with a flood of questions just under her controlled exterior. Linda had turned Souder down, yet Cory had entered into a plural marriage! Later, Anna found herself standing before the punch bowl with Luke by her side. He filled her cup with punch. "What do you think, Anna?" he asked. "Are you pleased?"

"Of course, Luke. Linda will have a strong baby. You'll see, it will be wonderful."

He looked at his wife, and Anna saw the love in his eyes. Turning back to her he smiled. "Do you remember the day we climbed the rock and drank the whiskey?"

"Do I? I was so sick. That was also the day my aunt died."

"Oh yes, I remember." For a moment they were silent and Anna felt the awkwardness. "Did you know," he continued, "that I was sweet on you then?"

Anna laughed. "Yes, and I was sweet on you, too."

He looked as if he was going to say something, but didn't know how to put it in words and, suddenly, Anna realized Luke was trying to tell her something.

"Why didn't you say something then?" she asked and gave him a smile to let him know it was a friendly question.

A Vision-Quest

"I think I would have, but Brother Martin was always around."

"But Brother Martin is married and was then," She said in a quiet voice.

Luke nodded. "I know, but Anna, we both know what's going on, it's really no secret. I was young and I admit, I was put off by Martin." He took a sip of his punch, continuing to watch her over the rim.

She felt he wanted to say more. "What do you mean, 'put off?'"

He put his cup down on the table, quickly looked about and moved closer to her. "There have been others–young men interested in you." She was surprised and wondered who they were, but she waited for him to continue. "But the word went out."

"What word?"

Now he was nervous, as if he'd said too much. "You know– it's the same with Cory. When an older man, an elder, takes an interest in a young girl, we back away."

She couldn't believe what he was saying. "You back away? You mean you won't call on a girl if you think an elder has shown signs of wanting to marry her? But why?"

"There is never anything actually said, however if a young man shows too much interest in the wrong young lady, he gets a sudden call to go on a mission in England or he gets sent to settle some far off valley."

Anna was having trouble believing all Luke was saying. "The Elders send you off if you court someone they want. That's what you're saying? And, you're saying no young men have been to call on me because of Brother Martin!" She felt the anger boil up inside. How many opportunities had she missed because of Martin? How dare he try to corner and cage her like some little bird, to keep as his own! Without thinking, she took Luke by the lapel of his old patched coat. "What about Linda? Linda was asked to be Brother Souder's wife. Why weren't you sent off?"

His face grew red and he looked about the room, as if someone should be coming to his aid. "I don't know–it was her. She told old Souder she was engaged to me."

She let go of Luke's coat and turned away, her anger so intense she didn't pay attention to the others. "Damn!" she said, just loud enough to be heard. Everyone stopped and looked. "Damn!" she said even louder.

"What's wrong?" asked Michael.

She was no longer interested in the party as she went for her coat. "Come on!" she ordered her brother. "We're going."

Michael hurried to her side as she pulled on her coat. "What is it?" he asked. "What's happened? The party's not over. Why do you want to go? Anna, talk to me."

Finally she looked at him. "You stay if you want, I'm going home." She didn't wait for him but hurried from Lissman's house and down the street.

Michael put on his coat and soon caught up to her. "At least you can tell me what's troubling you to make me miss the rest of the party!" he complained.

"God!" she swore. "I'm so mad! That damned Martin has chased off all the boys."

Once home, Anna put her coat away and went straight up to the loft where her mother had already prepared for bed. "Did you have a nice time, dear?" she said, not noticing the anger in Anna's face in the dim light.

Anna plopped down on her bed and put her face in her hands. "God! I'm tired of being a Mormon and I'm tired of eating nothing but roots and most of all I'm tired of Carl Martin!"

Mary moved close to Anna and put an arm around her daughter. "What happened, Anna?"

Anna looked at her mother and suddenly the tears came and she buried her face on her mother's shoulder. She told her mother what Luke Allison had told her. "Don't you see? That stupid Carl Martin has chased all the boys away and that's why he's the only one that ever comes around."

All the while her mother listened in silence but now she spoke quietly, but firmly. "Listen to me and quit feeling sorry for yourself. This rumor about boys being sent on missions is a lie! Sometimes when a young man is asked to do his duty, he looks about for an excuse. If he's calling on a young girl, it's only natural for him to think someone else is trying to separate him from her. To listen to Luke you would think all the girls are married to old men. Well, they're not! Look at Luke and look at Jason. And think of the older men. All of them have families and yet they go on missions and some of them are gone for two or three years. When they come back, sometimes wives are dead or run off with someone else.

A Vision-Quest

Your own Aunt Alice died while Stan was away. Sarah Wheeler ran off while John was gone. These men give up a lot for their Church and for the Lord and I won't have you talking them down."

"But is it fair?" complained Anna. "Is it fair for Carl to chase them off?"

"Carl hasn't chased anyone off! If these young men Luke talked about had any spine they would be here anyway. Carl couldn't keep a serious suitor away. What if it had been your father? Do you think someone else could keep your father, Stan, away if he were serious? Why, he'd pitch a tent at your door. I know you're taken with that mountain man, Wes Tucker. But where is he? He's off with his friend trapping with the Indians. Now, I want you to dry those tears and stop feeling sorry for yourself. You're too big to cry. Be thankful you have a real man, Brother Martin, interested in you."

Anna was even more confused now, for she hadn't completely abandoned the idea that Luke had put in her head. Yet, she couldn't dispute her mother and she now felt silly and just a little ashamed of herself. "You're right, I am making a fuss."

"That's better," said her mother. "Remember, we have a kingdom to build here in the mountains and we just don't have time to be self indulgent. I know how difficult Carl's proposal is. After all, I had to make the same decision with your father."

"But you love Uncle Stan."

Mary smiled, yet furrows showed in her forehead. "You're right, I do love Stan and I loved him when I said I'd marry him. Whether you have love for Carl is something you must answer in your own heart. If you do, don't let plural marriage stand in your way: marry Carl. If not—well, you'll have to turn Carl down and hope someone else comes along."

CHAPTER 29

Buffalo Man

Wes awoke to the sound of the storm still raging outside and, opening his eyes, saw nothing but the blackness of his cabin. Was he still alive? Was this a dream or was he really awake? He moved his hand from under the blanket, felt the freezing air and listened again to the howling wind. He must be alive—death could never be this horrible.

The wind blew even louder, moaning in its agony. Did he hear something outside in the blizzard, something more than just the wind and snow? Straining his ears, he caught only the wind, yet he felt a presence—someone outside his cabin. Had someone come to rescue him? Was this the end of his trials? He closed his eyes and listened again, feeling the presence still out in the storm. If only Wes could get up, if only he could go out, he would confront this specter. Rescuer or the Grim Reaper—it was out there, not drawing closer nor going away as it continued its silent beckoning. Whoever, whatever it was, Wes had to go. He gathered all his energy and, pulling back the blankets, twisted and sat up, dizzy from the effort. For long moments, as the wind howled and the specter called, Wes struggled to clear his mind and remember what he meant to do. Finally, collecting his strength, he found his boots and pulled them on. With a blanket over his shoulders, he stood and, one slow step at a time, made his way to the door.

Lifting the latch, he pulled the door open. The light from outside showed either early morning or late evening, he wasn't sure which, with the storm scattering much of the available light into a gray nothingness. Snow blew in freezing sheets in front of him and he could hear the pines creaking in the wind. The elements waged an awful war, and he was caught in its overpowering energy.

Wes knew the phantom stood somewhere before him. Straining to see, he spotted a black form in the midst of the storm. He couldn't make out its features, but its strength to summon him was increasing. Wes stepped out into the snow, and the wind caught his blanket and tore it away. Shivering, arms around his middle, he walked several steps toward the apparition. At first, the shape was fuzzy, but suddenly the storm lessened and Wes saw it in perfect detail—the body of a giant man with the head of a bull buffalo, standing in the eye of the storm and gesturing for Wes to come.

Nothing existed for Wes back in the cold dark cabin but death; he had to go forward. Struggling against the wind, he plowed through the snow and drew closer to the beast. Within arm's reach, he stopped and looked up into its red, burning eyes. Wes knew this couldn't be death as its true name hammered at his brain. "Who are you?" he cried.

The beast's great tongue slithered out and hung to one side as the monster held Wes' shoulder with one hand and slowly, very slowly, moved its other hand toward Wes' stomach. What could it want? Wes' stomach had been empty for days.

Wes looked down at his bare belly as the beast's hand pushed into Wes' skin and cut it apart, the fingers slipping into his insides. Wes felt the hand in him, moving about, searching for his stomach and he saw his own blood run down the beast's arm and drip into the snow. The beast found what he was after and, extracting its hand from Wes' insides, held it open for Wes to see. In the beast's palm were bits of partially digested meat.

How could that be; he'd eaten no meat! He looked again at the beast's palm and recognized the flesh–rabbit. The beast had pulled rabbit from his stomach! As Wes looked at the rabbit meat, he saw where the meat had come from, he saw the rabbit den.

The compelling was gone; Wes was released. Looking again into its large red eyes, Wes saw the buffalo head tilt to one side as he felt the beast let go of his shoulder. Wes turned and walked back toward the cabin. He would rest now, time to let the wound heal. Back in the cabin, with the door secured, he curled up on his bed and pulled one of his blankets about him.

The next morning he awoke in the cold cabin, the memory of the beast clear in every detail. He quickly felt his stomach and discovered it unhurt. Had it been real or a dream? Of course it had been only a dream. Yet, in some manner, which Wes failed to understand, the vision had told him how to survive, the message being the rabbit den.

Wes pulled on his cold boots and again wrapped a blanket around his shoulders. Opening the door, he saw a bright sunshiny day, the brilliance of the sunlight reflecting off the white landscape. The fine powdery snow was deep, but Wes lifted his legs high and pushed through it. He stopped a few feet from the cabin and cocked his head to one side. Which way had Buffalo Man told him to go? He looked down and saw a piece of cloth sticking out of the snow and, bending down, pulled up his frozen blanket! He remembered now, on the way to Buffalo Man the wind had blown his blanket away. But that couldn't be right for it was all a dream. Then Wes understood; while dreaming he'd walked from the cabin and lost his blanket.

Wes heard snow falling from a tree and walked toward the right where Buffalo Man had shown Wes the rabbit warren. Now it was up to Wes to find it. He worked his way along the lake's right shore, the snow making his passage difficult and forcing him to stop frequently to regain his strength. "Am I doing this right, *Osota*? Is there something here or have I gone insane? Am I dead already and is this the dream of a dead man?" However, he continued and, after working for over an hour and travelling several hundred yards, he spotted an opening in the trees. In the opening stood a large wind-swept granite rock, and he knew it was the location for the warren.

Drawing closer, he saw rabbits sunning themselves, trying to capture the rays of the winter sun. Wes had failed to bring a weapon, but didn't believe he had enough energy to return for one now. He continued to the rock and, to his astonishment, discovered the rabbits didn't move, but continued laying in the bright sunshine and dreaming rabbit dreams. Wes approached the first rabbit, which sat on a low shelf of the rock and simply watched as Wes reached down and picked it up by the skin of the neck.

Holding the rodent close to his chest, Wes gently stroked it. "You're all right, I've got you. You're going to make a fine meal. Don't cry, you'll be part of me very soon." The walk back to the cabin was surprisingly quick, but Wes was in no hurry. He looked out over the perfectly still landscape and marveled at the serenity of the world at this very moment. Nothing stirred and no noises reached his ears. Nothing existed except the trees, the mountains, the snow and, of course, the rabbit.

Back at the cabin, he quickly killed the animal–it would be a sin to prolong it's suffering. Roasting it over his fire, the tantalizing odor of cooking meat filled the room and made Wes sick with anticipation. This would surely be the best meal he'd ever eaten. When finished with the feast, exhaustion swept over him and he crawled to his bed and covered himself with a blanket. Tomorrow he would bring back two rabbits.

During the next week, Wes returned daily to the warren and each time he did, he found the rabbits. Without traps or weapons he approached and simply picked them up. Had they never been hunted by humans before? Was that why they were so tame? He felt his strength return, yet thinking back on the previous two weeks before the vision, he had a difficult time distinguishing between reality and his dreams. And, above all his memories, stood the remembrance of Buffalo Man, the beast's eyes reflecting in the snow and his breath whispering in the trees.

Early in the morning of the eighth day, Wes was making his fire when he thought he heard a knock at the door. Startled to think anyone could approach the lake through all the snow, he slowly opened the door and peered out. No one was there. It must have been his imagination, which wasn't surprising after the events he'd lived through. He returned to his fire-making only to hear another knock. Again, no one was at the door. He sat on his pine branch bed and listened. The knocking came again, yet it wasn't really a knocking but much more subtle, as if someone were only thinking of knocking.

Wes rushed to the door, pulled it open and hurried outside. Not far from the cabin he spotted an individual sitting in the snow, covered with a blanket. As he approached, he decided it was an Indian, but a small Indian–a child. Reaching the Indian, Wes knelt. "Hello! Do you speak Lakota?" The figure didn't move. He pulled the blanket down from the face and discovered not a child, but an old woman, her eyes closed and small particles of ice clinging to her eyelashes and graying hair. Wes touched her and found her stiff and cold. Was she frozen? Was she dead? Gently, he lifted her small body and carried her back to the cabin. Inside, he placed her on the bed. Her arms and legs weren't frozen, just stiff, so he carefully stretched her out and covered her with a blanket. He built up the fire to warm the air and reheated the remains of the previous night's soup–just in case.

After performing his chores, he turned to the bed and discovered she was breathing. He knelt down beside her and, taking her cold hands from under the blanket, rubbed them to bring back the circulation. She was so cold! He removed her moccasins and rubbed her feet. Her eyes opened and she began watching him. "Do you speak Lakota?" he asked as he continued rubbing.

Her lips opened and the sound barely came out. "Yes. Sit me up on the bed."

He tenderly pulled her to a sitting position.

"Thank you," she said and gave him a sweet smile.

"Who are you? What are you doing here?"

"I'm Laughing Woman."

"What are you doing here?"

She looked about his cabin. "Where am I?"

"You're in the Wind River Mountains. But, it's winter."

"Oh, yes, now I remember. I was looking for something up here."

"But where are your people? What tribe are you?"

"The Lakota call me *Miwatani*."

Wes thought for a moment and then it came to him. "You're *Miwatani*?–Mandan? You're of the Mandan Tribe? I've heard of your people. I thought all the Mandan had been scattered and killed."

Buffalo Man

She smiled and gently touched his arm. "Well, you can see one Mandan is left."

"Yes, your people lived on the Upper Missouri in the Five Villages and grew crops!"

"That's right. You're a very smart boy. What do they call you?"

"*Wicasa Ozu.*"

"My–I'm very impressed. You have a Lakota name but you're a Whiteman. How did you come to be here in these mountains?"

"I'm on a vision-quest."

"All winter? Who sent you?"

"*Osota Wicasa*–Smoke Man."

"Oh, yes. I know that old bag of bones. He likes to puff the pipe a lot. In fact, do you..." she looked about the cabin.

Suddenly Wes was embarrassed; he'd forgotten to offer her the pipe. He quickly secured the small corncob he kept for such occasions. "Can I offer you a smoke?"

"That's not very Lakota! You say 'let us smoke in peace.' Now tell me, have you had your vision?"

He cut tobacco and filled the pipe. "Yes, but I'm not sure you're not a vision."

She tilted back her head and giggled. "Me? I like that–me, a vision!" Her hair was gray and her face covered with a thousand wrinkles, but her eyes where alive and flashed with merriment. "I'm no vision. I'm just an old woman who would have frozen if you hadn't brought me into your cabin."

Wes lit the tobacco and, drawing in a lungful of smoke, blew it up above his head as he held up the little pipe. "Thank you Great Spirit for allowing me to live to see one of your Mandans even though she is only an old woman lost in the mountains." He handed her the pipe as she laughed at his words.

"That's very good, *Ozu.*" She puffed on the pipe and blew her smoke up into the cabin air. "I thank you Great Spirit for sending this one to save me even though he is only a child and a man at that!"

Wes chuckled at her tease and, looking into her watery eyes, couldn't remember when he'd had a more delightful time. "My Lord, you must be starving. Do you want some rabbit soup? You do eat rabbit, don't you?"

"Oh–soup, that would be wonderful, but just a cupful. I have not eaten for awhile and I must be careful."

Buffalo Man

He fetched her the soup and then sat cross-legged on the floor and watched her. "Why are you called Laughing Woman?"

"I gave that name to myself. I was so tired of everyone having names of animals. 'Little Beaver,' 'Big Horse Penis,' 'Flying Owl.' Why does everyone have to be named for an animal? Does the Whiteman tribe do that?"

Wes just shook his head, too entertained to want to interrupt her monologue.

"Well, I decided to have a different name. I entered our lodge and told my husband I was *Tanka San*—big vagina! I wish you could have seen his face. He was furious. Poor Walking Elk, he was a good hunter and brave warrior, but he...how do you say it? He couldn't understand things. He had no way to tell a laughing story."

"What happened?"

"He beat me! So I changed me name again to Laughing Woman." She passed him the cup. "More soup!" He hurried to refill the cup as she continued. "Why are you here? Why do you have such a hard quest to do? Is it a woman? Are you in love?"

Wes stopped his pouring and looked at the old Indian. How did she know?

She laughed again. "Yes, that's it! You're in love and she doesn't love you?" She searched his eyes as he handed her the cup. "No, that's not it. You love her but can't have her. Yes, that's it now."

"How did you know?"

"A woman can tell such things, especially an old woman like me. I've had many braves and I've learned to recognize the eyes of lovers."

"She is a Mormon—do you know who the Mormons are?"

"Yes, they're the Whitemen who are so disagreeable that even the other Whites won't live with them. Don't they take many squaws?"

"Yes, well that's part of it. She's a Mormon and I'm not. She has to marry another Mormon."

"So, become a Mormon."

"Oh, I can't do that—they have some rather strange beliefs."

"Then pretend, fake whatever you have to! Do you want to sleep with this woman? Do you want her to be yours?"

"But I can't believe in things just because it's convenient. I have to really believe they're so."

"Do you really love this person or are you just pretending? Love is precious! It is like the gentle mist on a spring morning that comes without warning and only stays for a minute and then is burned away by the sun. It is the murmur of a happy baby when asleep. It is loving under a buffalo robe in the black of night and laughing so hard your sides hurt."

Her words struck him like a boulder dropped on his head and he bit his lip and, wrapping his arms about his middle, moaned at the thought of holding Anna in his arms, her naked breasts pressing against his chest.

"Yes," said Laughing Woman, "you're in love, but there's more. You didn't tell Laughing Woman everything."

"Yes. She doesn't know my real name. If she did, she would know I was the one accused of killing her father, but I didn't. I'm innocent."

Her eyes grew wide as she listened and when he finished she burst out laughing. "Bull dung!" she exclaimed. "You really are in need of a big quest. Maybe you'd better stay here another winter. Just one isn't going to do it."

Later that day he went to the warren and returned with three rabbits. She cooked all three in the Indian manner–boiled with hot stones in a rawhide lined pit dug in the cabin's floor. She talked continuously, but her words were such strange twists and convolutions that she was always interesting and entertaining. Wes asked questions and she rambled on, sometimes answering and sometimes just getting lost in the attempt. Her person was so animated with energy that Wes kept forgetting she was old.

A week passed with Laughing Woman as his guest and all that time he felt he was privileged to be in her company. When she talked, it wasn't just another person talking in the same room: it was a woman talking to him. She spoke and looked directly into his eyes and held his attention, her words soft and golden. Seeing her now, Wes wondered what she must have been as a young woman and envied Walking Elk. At the end of the week, Wes could see the snow cover had diminished under the late winter sun. He had almost emptied the rabbit warren, but soon he would be able to hunt bigger game. Laughing Woman announced she would be leaving.

"Before I go," she said one night, "I want to give you something. After all, you saved my life. You don't wear a medicine pouch. Let me make you a nice pouch and you can go to old *Osota Wicasa* and have him fill it and bless it."

He put a hand at his throat and remembered Crocker's pouch. "That would be nice. Thank you."

Immediately, she scrounged about his cabin, looking for an acceptable piece of leather. "Now remember, after settling this little misunderstanding, you're to become one of those Mormons and take that girl as your squaw. Do you understand, *Ozu?*"

"But Laughing Woman, I can't do that. I don't believe in all the strange things they preach. How can I become a Mormon? What if their preachers want me to do things I don't believe?"

"*Ozu*! You have to use your head. You have to think like the fox and outwit the rabbit. Now, if the Mormon medicine man comes to you and tells you to kill a baby, what would you do?"

Wes was horrified. "I wouldn't do it!"

"Of course. That is because you know it is bad to kill babies. If he said to love babies, could you do that?"

"Of course."

"Good. You understand that loving babies is good. Now do you understand?"

"No!"

"Son of a hairy dung eater! Use your head! You are not stupid. You know good and you know bad. When your god says to do good, you know that your god is speaking to you. When your god says bad—it is man speaking. Go be a Mormon and don't do bad. This is not a difficult thing. If you decide you don't like this Anna person, throw her away, give up the Mormon god and come find me. I can still couple with a brave. I'm not dead yet!"

Wes laughed until tears ran down his cheeks. "*Tanka*," it was his pet name for her—the second half understood, "I love you already. If these Mormons will give me two wives, I will come and get you. You do want more children, don't you?"

"More children!" she screamed. "Never." Suddenly she was quiet as she tilted her head and looked into his eyes. "You will do one thing more for *Tanka*, won't you?" Her voice was low and warm. "When you couple with Anna and it is late, think of your pleasure and think of me—I will feel your pleasure. Can you do this?"

He reached out with his hand and gently touched her wrinkled old cheek. "I will do it often," he said.

Two days later she had finished his pouch and she packed to go. As he watched from the cabin door, she turned to face him. His eyes narrowed as he took in all that hung from her clothes.

"Don't look that way, *Ozu*. Yes, I took some of your things because you did not couple with Laughing Woman and she is mad. So she stole your little cooking pot and your snow shoes and one of your hunting knifes and one of your blankets and..."

"Please," interrupted Wes. "Take it all. I love you, *Tanka*."

She smiled. "Next time you will love Laughing Women as a good brave should." Without further goodbyes, she turned and started off over the snow. He stood and watched her go until she was out of sight. Would he ever see her again? Had she been real or a vision?

Soon he would prepare to leave. He must go to Smoke Man on the Clarks Fork at once. Yes, the Blackfooters would kill him if he were caught, but for some reason, he didn't think he would be. He had learned some things but he felt there was still much more he must learn. Besides, he must get his pouch blessed before returning to civilization.

When Wes finally left his cabin in the Wind River Mountains, the lake had begun to thaw and the ground snow was rapidly melting, turning the mountain streams into torrents of icy, muddy water. Wes failed to find the Shoshoni family when he reached the desert floor, north of the Green River, so he walked to Fort Bridger, a journey requiring four days. He discovered the Shoshoni had spent the winter camped near the Fort and had taken good care of Jeff. With many thanks, Wes retrieved his horse.

The few Whitemen wintering at Fort Bridger just shook their heads when they saw Wes. "God!" exclaimed a big trapper with black hair and a salt-and-pepper beard. "You look awful! You seen yerself? Go look in a mirror. Yer skin and bones."

"I been in the mountains," said Wes, scratching his dirty beard–amazed at the sound of his own voice.

"You wintered with the Injuns?"

"No, just by myself."

The trapper looked at Wes again and a smile slowly crept across his lips. "Alone! That's a thrill. But ya stink to heaven–go wash! Ya smell like a bufler that's been rolling in its own turd."

Wes washed with real soap and shaved off his beard. He had nothing to trade at the Fort, but the trapper contributed a new shirt, a used

Buffalo Man

buffalo coat and provided a little powder. With his Kentuck rifle and Jeff, he didn't need more.

From Fort Bridger, Wes returned up the Green River and continued on to Clarks Fork. He wanted to see Smoke Man even though he knew the Bug's Boys had warned him to keep out of their territory. Rising before sunup, he travelled early in the morning, picking his way with care. He wasn't sure the Blackfeet were still in their winter encampments, but he didn't want to take unnecessary chances.

Early one morning, as he traveled down the Clarks Fork, the sun came out from behind a small cloud and turned the countryside into a patchwork of spring colors while a breeze blew and stirred the new leaves on the ash and alders. Wes rode along the bluff above the river swollen with spring runoff, and kept alert for any fresh Indian sign. Approaching a gully blocking his path, he stopped and looked about before urging Jeff down the steep slope. Riding up the opposite side, he felt a strangeness in the air. The back of his neck tingled as he reined Jeff to a stop and, tilting his head, listened. Somewhere in the back of his head was a sound–like a flute or fiddle–its lonesome, high pitched notes singing out to him. The wind filled leaves added a harmony that soon divided to expose the silent spaces. These spaces were notes, too–notes from the rocks and trees, the grass and creek. Into this song intruded the thunder of horses' hoofs and the smell of a hunt–Indians and they were close!

Dismounting, he walked Jeff back to the gully's bottom and found a hiding place between a boulder and several ash. With slow deliberateness, he withdrew his rifle and checked the pan's prime. Before long he spotted the Blackfeet hunting party spread out in a line across the river's valley and moving quietly up river, trying to spook any large animal. The Indians moved past the gully's entrance into the valley and soon disappeared. Wes smiled to himself. He wasn't sure how he'd detected them, but he felt he'd had help.

Later that morning, Wes found Smoke Man's tipi just where it had been the year before. He dismounted, hobbled Jeff and scratched on the tipi flap. Soon *Osota's* head popped out. He looked at Wes and motioned for him to come in. Pulling back the flap, Wes ducked inside, noting the tipi looked much the same. *Osota* motioned Wes to the back of the lodge and urged him to sit down. "*Ozu* looks bad. Didn't you eat? You are a skinny man now. You should eat more."

Buffalo Man

Wes sat down as *Osota* prepared a pipe. "I was on a vision-quest, Smoke Man. Don't you remember? You sent me!"

Smoke Man looked at Wes with his simple face and smiled. "I told you to go on a quest? Why would I do that?"

Wes could hear the rush of the river water outside and the sound of *Osota* chopping tobacco, but his own head was spinning. Was *Osota* pulling his leg? "Don't you remember, *Osota*? You cut my palm and looked at the blood and said I was to go and starve myself during a cold winter. You sent me on a special vision-quest."

Osota tilted his head and the furrows bunched up over his eyebrows. "I did?" He carefully looked again at Wes' face. "I did! Now I remember. You're to go out during a cold winter. Do not eat for many days. Do you understand?"

"But Smoke Man, that's why I'm here. I've already done that. That's why I'm so skinny." Wes wished Crocker were here helping him make *Osota* understand.

"That's why you are skinny? You shouldn't go without food for so long. I mean, a few days, until the vision comes, but this..." and he pointed to Wes' body. "...this is like a bird that has had all the feathers removed. Did you bring whiskey? No, of course not. You Whitemen always drink it yourself." He lit the pipe, took a drag of smoke and passed the pipe to Wes. Leaning closer, *Osota's* eyes opened wide. "Did you see something? Did you see a vision?"

Wes still couldn't tell if the old Indian were teasing him. "Yes, I had a vision. That's why I'm here." He began to suspect that the man really was half-witted.

Osota pointed to the pipe. "Smoke the pipe first."

Wes drew in a deep breath, held the pipe up and blew the smoke into the air over their heads. "I saw the Buffalo Man." He watched *Osota's* face for any reaction, but the Indian just took the pipe from Wes' hand and held out his own hand.

"Give *Osota Wicasa* the pouch."

"What?"

"Give me the pouch!" This time he said it with force and his eyes flashed.

Wes reached into his shirt pocket, extracted the pouch Laughing Woman had made and handed it to *Osota*. "This?"

Osota nodded as he fingered the rawhide. "This is good. I know this one—it is Laughing Woman, I can tell."

"You know Laughing Woman?"

"Of course. She calls herself Mandan, but she lies. She says she is old, but she lies. She makes good pouches."

"I can't believe you know her!"

"Now, *Ozu*, it is time for me to prepare and for you to sleep. Lie down there and take a nap. I will wake you." He gently pushed Wes back. Wes didn't think he needed sleep, but he would humor the old man. He lay back on a robe and before he realized what had happened, he was asleep.

When Wes woke, he knew it was night, the only light coming from a little fire in the center of the floor. He looked at *Osota* and saw the Indian's cheeks and forehead painted in wide stripes of red and black paint and that he was wearing a headband of feathers and leaves. The old man gestured for Wes to sit up.

Wes slowly straightened, noticing the pungent odor of burning herbs mingling with that of cooked meat.

"Come," said the Indian, "eat. You do not eat enough. You are too skinny. Remove your shirt." He pushed a wooden bowl of cooked dog toward Wes.

Wes was hungry and quickly removed his shirt to began eating. When he had finished, *Osota* moved closer and, dipping two fingers in small bowls of paint, drew stripes on Wes' face and chest. "You must join a lodge. There are many lodges. *Ihoka* is the Badger Lodge, it is a warrior society. You are not a warrior." He continued painting and soon Wes' chest, arms and face were covered in red, yellow, black and white stripes. *Osota* put the paint away and filled a pipe. "There is the *Takala* Lodge; it is warrior also. You are not a warrior. There is a lodge for scouts and a lodge for arrow makers and a lodge for deciders and herdsmen. These are all good lodges but you, *Ozu*, are none of these things. Some lodges are secret. You will belong to a secret lodge. Tell Smoking Man the name of your Lodge."

Wes looked into Smoking Man's black eyes and was held by their depth and strength. "Buffalo Man," he answered.

Osota smiled and nodded. "That is good, *Ozu*. You are not too stupid! Now listen. Many know of the Buffalo Man Lodge, but they do not know our secret." He puffed on the pipe and passed it to Wes before continuing. "You have been visited and so it is meant for you. Tonight I will make you a member of the Buffalo Man Lodge and you will keep it a secret until the day the Great Spirit comes and takes you to the next hunting ground. Do you understand?"

Wes nodded.

"Good. You have lived with the Lakota and the Absa and so you know that many spirits exist in this world. They can hurt or they can help. It depends on the man. Touch the rock and its spirit will talk to you. Touch the earth and the earth spirit will talk to you. Touch the wind and the wind will talk to you. Now I must sing." He puffed once more on the pipe and, holding it up above his head, began a chant. At first, the chant sounded like 'hihihihi-yayayaya' repeated over and over. Wes had heard this singing many times around the fires of the Sioux and Crow.

However, as Smoke Man sang, Wes realized that the old Indian was singing words–words that were disguised by the monotone and rhyme of the chant. Wes began piecing together phrases and realized *Osota* was singing to the Buffalo Man. Suddenly Wes remembered his trial and his being near death. He remembered not just the scenes, but the feelings, too. He saw again and felt again the Buffalo Man standing before him. He saw the red eyes and the large tongue; he felt the Buffalo Man's hand on his shoulder. Watching *Osota Wicasa* and feeling Buffalo Man, Wes cried, the warm, salty tears filling his eyes, running down his cheeks and falling on his chest. They were not tears of pain, but tears of joy for he was being touched by the spirits of the world, spirit of stone, of earth, and also the Great Spirit and this touching made him whole.

Osota's singing was alive with its own spirit, coming to Wes and entering his body. Wes looked into *Osota's* eyes and saw he was being watched. The Indian stopped. "You will sing now." And he passed the pipe to Wes.

Wes drew in a deep breath, blew it out and held up the pipe. He began the chant, the words coming easily. He thanked Buffalo Man for saving his life. He thanked Buffalo Man for coming and showing Himself, for touching Wes and opening Wes' eyes to all there was in the world. He told Buffalo Man all about his friends, Crocker and Fego and Smoke Man and how he loved his friends. He told all about Anna Sinclair and how he loved her. At times *Osota Wicasa* joined in and they sang together.

Smoke Man stopped singing and looked at Wes. "There is a great boulder on your heart. What is this boulder?"

Buffalo Man

Wes was not sure what Smoke Man meant. "I love the Mormon girl."

"No," replied Smoke Man. "It is a different hurt. It is deep."

Wes tried to think. What could it be? Smoke Man leaned closer and lowered his voice. "Think of something you have done that you should not have done. Think hard."

For some moments Wes considered his life. What could it be? He thought of the killing of Jack Sinclair, but he hadn't done it. What else could it be. Suddenly, the memory rushed back to stab him in the heart. "I know," he announced. "I killed two Blackfoot boys. I didn't mean to, I didn't want to. They were only defending their home." He began to cry.

Smoke Man nodded. "This is good. You see it now. You took their spirits from their bodies and from their families. You sent them back into the Great Spirit world. They will now be your spirit warriors. They will travel with you and you will honor them as they watch over you." Wes saw the streaks made by the tears on *Osota's* cheeks as it made a trail through the body paint.

After several hours, *Osota* stood and left the tipi, and Wes knew he was to follow. Outside, Smoke Man sat on a large flat rock and faced the east, where the horizon showed that the sun was soon coming up. Wes joined him. *Osota* pointed toward the horizon with his finger. "The sun will be here soon and then you will be in the lodge. So that you remember, I have prepared this." He held out the pouch to Wes. On Laughing Woman's pouch *Osota* had painted the figure of a buffalo horn. As Wes took the pouch and the attached rawhide thong, *Osota* turned over his own pouch to show Wes the horn. Wes tied the thong about his neck so the pouch rested on his chest.

Osota smiled. "I have put herbs in the pouch for you. Some people believe their pouches are magic and will protect them. This is not so. The magic is inside of us. The pouch and the herbs are just to remind us who we are, what we have done, and what we must do. Do you understand?"

Wes nodded.

"Good. Our pouches have the horn to show we are in the same lodge."

"And Crocker is in our lodge," said Wes.

"Crocker?"

"*Mahtola*."

"Yes, *Mahtola* is in our lodge." They sat in silence and watched as the first rays of the sun spilled over the eastern mountains and struck them with loving care. Wes looked down and saw his medicine pouch

Buffalo Man

alive with the sun's rays. When the sun was up and free of the horizon, Smoking Man looked at Wes. "No whiskey? You should have brought me whiskey, *Ozu*. Whiskey would be very good right now."

They slept most of that day, having been up all the previous night. In the evening, after the sun had set and they were comfortable before *Osota's* fire, they talked. Wes told *Osota* all about his vision and his experiences, and *Osota* told Wes about his life as a medicine man. They smoked the pipe.

"Now," said Smoke Man. "I want to give you a little present, because you may need it."

"You have given me so much. There is nothing more I need."

"I will give it to you. If you don't need it, give it to another. If you use it, it will be gone, not to return. You know, of course, that some sounds have power, just as some words have power."

"I don't understand. Words are just words."

Osota shook his head. "Not so. Some words, like 'love,' have a power other words do not. Your mother's name has a power for you."

"Yes, I see."

"But other words have a greater power." Suddenly *Osota's* eyes grew large and he pointed at the ground at Wes' side as he yelled: "Snake!"

Wes jumped to the side and tried to draw his pistol, but he wasn't carrying the weapon. Looking at the ground he saw nothing there! He looked at *Osota* who just grinned back. "You see! It is not just the word, but how it is said–that is just as important. When I yelled 'snake' you jumped because the word and how I said it had power over you."

"Now I understand," said Wes, still not sure just where the old man was going.

"Good. Now I can give you my present. Some words have very much power. Long ago these words–sounds–were known and used. But it has been so long that they are forgotten. I will give you such a sound now. Get your gun."

"My rifle?"

"No, the little one."

"My pistol?"

"Yes."

Wes reached to his belongings and retrieved his handgun. "Good," said *Osota*. "Now, cock it and hold it on me."

"Are you sure? You want me to aim it at you?"

Buffalo Man

"Yes—do it!"

Wes pulled back the cock and aimed the gun at *Osota*.

The old man smiled. "Now watch and listen and do not forget!" He stretched out his arms, tilted back his head and his eyes rolled up under his eyelids. *Osota's* mouth opened and his tongue curled, and Wes saw it all distinctly even in the dim firelight. From *Osota's* stomach and then his mouth came a sound—a sound that was more terrible than any sound Wes had heard and that struck straight into Wes' brain, and from somewhere deep inside Wes the sound uncovered a fear which had no face, but was the grandfather of all fears.

Without knowing how it happened or seeing it happen, Wes sat empty handed and looked at *Osota* who held the cocked gun on him. *Osota* smiled. "Did you understand how it is done? Should I do it again?"

Wes trembled and knew he was going to be sick. He shook his head, leaned over to one side and threw up. Remembering the fear made him throw up again.

"Isn't that a good gift?" asked *Osota*.

"Yes," said Wes. "A very good gift. Thank you." He wiped the spittle from his chin and tried to stop the shaking.

The next day it was time to go. Wes certainly didn't understand everything that had happened to him at Smoke Man's tipi, but he sensed that understanding wasn't always necessary. He definitely felt different—more in control of himself and more in tune with the world. He was also feeling strong, not just strong of limb, but strong in his heart.

He thanked *Osota* and promised to protect the pouch and remember the fine gift. *Osota* nodded. "Yes, you are a Whiteman. You will go and forget Smoke Man. You will go and drink the whiskey and you will forget that Smoke Man has none. Whiskey brings good visions and *Osota* needs it for his work." The old Indian poked Wes in the chest with two fingers. "Next time—whiskey! Do you understand? And tobacco, too. Oh! And a shirt, too. Bring me a shirt like *Ozu* wears; a Whiteman shirt."

Wes mounted Jeff. "I will bring all those things. *Tecihila, Osota Wicasa.*" Smoke Man waved him away and returned to his tipi.

Wes returned by way of the Powder River and the Black Hills, finding Crocker with Red Eagle on the upper reaches of the Niobrara River, not far from Fort Laramie. As Wes rode into Crocker's camp, the mountain man jumped up and danced about. "Jesus Christ Almighty!" he yelled. "It's Farm-boy! He's alive!"

Wes slipped from Jeff's back. "I'm back, Crock."

The older man grabbed Wes by the shoulders and shook him. "I thought you was gone under. I figured you'd froze up in them mountains."

"I almost did, but I made it and I had a visitor."

Crocker looked confused. "A visitor? In the winter? In them mountains?"

Wes reached in and pulled out the pouch and let his friend see the horn painted on the outside. "*Pta Wicasa*," Wes whispered, preferring to use the Sioux words.

Crocker's eyes grew large and a broad smile came to his lips. He mouthed the words himself and unconsciously reached up and touched his chest where his pouch rested. "You've been to see Smoke Man."

Wes nodded.

Crocker slapped him on the back. "God Damn, boy! Let's have a drink of blue-ruin. Let's celebrate. This coon ain't had a real hos to talk with since I don't know when. These fucking Injuns is all the same, they just come by to steal my whiskey. Holy cow–look at you! You're all bones! God, ya must have half starved. Sit down here and tell me your story and I'll fetch the Taos."

They sat before a fire, drank whiskey, ate cooked tongue and talked. Wes told all about his adventures in the Wind River Mountains. When he reached the part about Laughing Woman, Crocker took special delight. "Hell, boy, that's just the kind of Injun I'm looking fer–one with spunk. I don't care if she's old as the moon; this hos will couple with her! Say, that little *Gnuska* has been around asking 'bout ya. I told her that her people, the Blackfooters, caught ya and ate ya! Oh, she didn't like that!"

"She has no brave yet?"

"No, she's waiting on you, I'll bet."

"Crock, there's something I got to do. I got to go back to the Salt Lake Valley and tell Anna Sinclair who I am."

"Now why," asked Crock, smiling, "didn't I think of that? Course ya got to go back. Ya still love her, don't ya? The only way to get on with things is to square with her and see what she does."

"It could get messy. Them Mormons might try arresting me, or worse, they might just string me up."

"Hogwash! Them Mormonites will have to first deal with this coon. Ain't no Mormon alive can mess with my friends."

CHAPTER 30

May, 1849

The Bargain

As Wes and Crocker rode down the broad street, Crocker marveled at Salt Lake City's growth. "Look there, Farm-boy! Look at them houses! This is a city—a real city! Look how wide these streets are."

Wes nodded and answered with little enthusiasm. "Ya, it's a city." He was preoccupied and only half listened to his friend.

Crocker waved to a man on the street. "Howdy, Brother!" Turning to Wes, he spoke in a low voice. "That's what they call each other: 'brother' and 'sister.' Like they was all in one family."

Wes only grunted.

"Howdy, Brother. Good day, Sister," called Crocker again. "These is nice people, Wes. Can't figure why they was run out of Illinois."

Wes turned toward Crocker. "What if she's married? What if she has a husband? God, she could be having a baby!"

"Well, that's a real possibility, Farm-boy. It's something ya got to consider. If she is, we'll just go find that *Gnuska* maiden. She'll make ya a fine squaw. I thought you was just interested in telling her who ya were? Let's take one thing at a time and get this telling over. Then ya can cry about whether she's married or not."

"Ya, you're right–that's what I'll do. I'll find her and I'll tell her and not worry about the other."

Crocker looked at Wes with suspicious eyes. "You ain't gonna take one look at her and vamose, are ya? Ya ain't gonna get cold feet?"

"Of course not. I've come to see her and talk and that's just what I'm gonna do."

Crocker reined in and looked about. "Now, which way is that Sinclair cabin? Everything is so built up, I don't recognize anything. Is that it?" And Crocker pointed to a log cabin a block and a half down the street.

Wes shook his head. "No, can't be, it's too big."

"It's the one! A room's been added. Come on." They rode toward the house and finally Wes conceded they had arrived. Hitching their horses to a rail in the street, they walked up the path to the house. The woman they knew as Louise stepped out on the porch, her stomach swollen with child. "Hello. I didn't expect to see you two again."

"Hello, Ma'am," said Crocker as he took off his hat and pointed toward her stomach. "Looks like ya got yerself a little Mormon coming soon."

She smiled. "Yes, next month, I think." She patted her belly. "It's a wonderful feeling."

Crock laughed and slapped his black felt hat against his rawhide pants. "Lord Almighty, that's what my second wife used to say. She just loved being with child. Made her all shiny and happy, just like it does you, Ma'am."

"Please, call me Louise." She backed away and gestured toward the front door. "But come in. I'm afraid they're all out in the fields. This is a busy time of year for us."

The two men entered the Sinclair home, followed by Louise. Wes removed his hat. "Yes," he said, "I know. I grew up on a farm, and spring is a busy season."

She pulled two chairs up to the table. "Please sit down. I'll put some coffee on. I wish I could offer you some whiskey, but we don't drink spirits anymore so there's none in the house."

The Bargain

Wes and Crocker quickly sat and Wes placed his hat on the table. "That's all right, coffee is just fine," he said.

"Hi," came a little voice from behind Wes. He spun around and discovered a little girl. "Where did you come from?" Wes asked.

She pointed toward a door leading to another part of the house.

"How old are you?"

"Three," she responded, looking at Wes with coy eyes.

"Who are you?"

"I'm Lou Ann."

Wes looked at her again, hardly believing his eyes. "You're Lou Ann? I remember you as a baby. Just last year you were no higher than a frog. Look at you now."

Louise placed coffee cups before the two men. "Now, Lou Ann, don't you bother these gentlemen. Go find Billy, I need him."

Crocker smiled as he watched Louise move about the kitchen. "If I remember right," he began. "Your first husband drowned."

"Yes, that was in '46."

"Well, congratulations on your new marriage. I hope we'll get a chance to meet your husband."

She turned and smiled at Crock. "Oh, I expect you will."

Within a half hour all the Sinclairs still living in Stan's house had assembled. The men drank coffee around the table, and Stan sent Michael for something stronger as the women prepared an early supper in honor of their guests.

As he listened to the conversation, Wes tried catching Anna's eye, but she fluttered about the kitchen, too busy to pay attention to him.

"Yes," said Crocker. "There is a great hoard of people aiming to come through your valley for California. They's already on the Oregon Trail and some as far as the Platte. None had reached Fort Laramie when we went through, but it won't be long."

"When will they get here?" asked Stan.

"Oh, let's see. Six weeks for the first, maybe two months. They call themselves the Forty-Niners and they're all heading for them gold fields in California. That means they'll be coming through this-here Valley, sure as shooting."

Stan looked worried. "We heard that some pioneers might be passing through on the way to the gold, but we didn't expect so many."

"From what we heard," said Crocker, "there's thousands on the Trail. They're coming from everywhere. The boys at Laramie say they ain't half equipped fer the trek and most will probably die on the trail, just like them Donners did."

"Or worse, they'll want to settle here."

"Not much chance of that," offered Wes. "They have the gold fever and nothing is keeping them from the gold fields."

Michael was intrigued with the stories of gold. "Is there really that much gold there, Mr. Sloan? Can ya really just pick it up out of the streams?"

Crocker shook his head. "Can't say fer sure, cause I ain't been there, but I hear ya can pick nuggets up that are the size of yer fist. The biggest danger is filling yer pockets so full that ya step in quicksand and 'plop'– yer gone! No one can find ya cause the gold holds ya down."

When the women served the food, Wes painfully noticed that the meal consisted of wild plants and little else. He looked about and saw the familiar hollow cheeks and dark-rimmed eyes indicating the Valley had been through another starving winter. Anna sat at the other end of the table, distracted and withdrawn. Wes still didn't know if she was married, but no husband was about so he guessed she wasn't.

After supper, the men talked as they sipped whiskey, and Crocker smoked his pipe. The women hurried to wash the dishes and then joined the men at the table. During a pause in the conversation, Mary stood up. "Come, Mr. Sloan, I want to show you and Wes how the town has grown."

Wes, out of politeness, stood and took hold of his hat, but he didn't really want to go. He needed to be alone with Anna. Just before the three of them left, Mary turned to her daughter. "Anna, you come, too, dear. You need the fresh air." Wes' heart jumped and he could hardly wait to get outside. Because of the early supper, the sun still shone from the southwestern sky. As the four of them walked down the path that ran beside the street, Mary commented about the different homes they passed and related news about her other children. Gwen and Jason had married and built their own homes and Jack Jr. was on a mission in England. Finally, she stopped. "Anna, you take Wes and show him where the temple is to be built. I'll show Mr. Sloan where Brigham Young lives." She didn't wait for an answer, but took Crocker by the arm and led him off.

The Bargain

Wes turned and saw Anna staring at him with large dark eyes. "That," he said as he gestured toward her mother, "was planned by your ma."

She took his arm as they began walking again. "Yes, it was obvious, wasn't it, but it's hard for a young woman here to be alone with a man. It's just the way we are. Especially, when the young woman is engaged to be married."

Her last words sank into him like a great hot shaft of iron. "You're engaged?" he asked, trying not to show any emotion in his voice.

"Yes, to Carl Martin, he's a bishop. The wedding is set for July. I'm almost eighteen and it's time I married and started a family of my own."

He couldn't think, let alone speak, his mind a whirlwind of contradictory thoughts and feelings. She led him to a large, level field that showed signs of construction work, but the purpose wasn't obvious to Wes. "This is our temple square," she said. We're building a magnificent temple, even bigger than the one in Nauvoo." She found a log on which to sit and they stopped to rest.

He wanted to scream in his disappointment, but tried to control his frustration. "Yer ma gave us this time for you to tell me that you're engaged."

She nodded and slipped a hand under his arm. "I never believed you would return. In fact, I'm not sure why you're here now. You know I cared for you and I thought you cared for me. What I can't understand is why you came here before and then just disappeared. I suppose it's our religious difference. I can't be anything but a Mormon, and you aren't going to become one. That really puts us in different worlds."

As she talked, she faced forward, toward the south and the young City that was spread out before them. Wes turned and studied her face, taking note of her mouth, eyes and hair. She was no longer a girl, she was a young woman and the sight of her swelled his heart with a love he thought would kill him. He was only half listening now, as he leaned closer to her and kissed her thick black curls above her ear. He hadn't planned doing it, it just happened.

She turned and, with her hands, pushed him away. Holding her, he saw her pink lips and her pale, ivory skin. Bending down, he kissed her full on the lips. She pushed away harder with her hands, but her mouth responded and they continued the kiss for a long blissful moment. Finally, she broke free. "No," she pleaded "please, no! I can't! Not here–not now!"

Buffalo Man

He wanted to kiss her again, but she continued pushing with her hands as she turned her face away. Then, in a compromise, she relaxed and rested her head and shoulders against his chest. "Why?" she whispered, "Why didn't you come? I waited–I waited as long as I could."

Everything he felt for her was balled up in a burning mass in his chest. That one kiss ignited his passion and he couldn't stand the idea of not possessing her completely. "I love you, Anna. I didn't want to, but I do."

From her trembling, he knew she was crying. Her words came out in a half-whisper, half sob. "Why didn't you come?"

He knew it was time. If he was ever going to explain to her, he had to do it now. "There is something I have to tell you. You have to promise me that you'll listen to the whole thing and not run away. Do you promise?"

"Wes, I know you're a wanted man. I know you're accused of killing someone and the law is after you. Did you really think that would matter to me?"

He held her tighter in his arms and prayed no one would come and interrupt. "You have to listen, please. Let me tell it now."

"All right."

"Think back to the day your father was killed on the bank of the Mississippi River." She said nothing and just barely nodded her head, showing she'd heard. "On that day, I was going to the Newtown Mill to see Sam Davidson about a mule." He told the story slowly, carefully, not leaving out or changing a single detail. Once he started, it was easier than he had thought. All the time he talked, Anna rested her head against his chest and listened. When he reached the part about her father in the River, he felt her cry again.

By the time he finished, he was wiping the tears away, too. For long minutes they just sat on the log, her letting him hold her as the sun set and the sky grew darker. Finally, she pulled free and looked at him. The sight of her face, with her hair messed and great red rims about her tear-filled eyes, made his heart open and bleed.

"You're Wes Hamlin!"

"Yes."

"Oh, God! Wes!" She reached up and put her wet face against his neck and kissed him. "Oh, sweetheart, I believe you. I know you wouldn't murder anyone. I know you're innocent. Why didn't you tell me?"

The Bargain

"I was afraid you'd hate me. I couldn't stand that!"

"I thought you'd forgotten about me. That you'd married an Indian."

"I love you, Anna." He bent down and tenderly, gently kissed her lips. "I'll always love you." He continued holding her as she pressed her face against his neck. They were still, neither wanting to move, neither wanting to break the special moment they now shared. The sky was growing darker and Wes wondered if someone would be sent to find them.

She kissed him again on the neck. "I'll always love you," she said.

"I didn't know what you'd do when I told you who I was. I was afraid you'd run off and never see me again. I'm sure you've hated Wes Hamlin for years."

"Yes," she said. "It's true. I wanted him–you–caught and punished for my father, but I somehow got over my father's death. It was my sister, Lisa–when she was lost. I blamed myself. I'm still not over it, I still have bad dreams. I dream she is alive and with a man who is hurting her."

"Sheriff Hawes didn't ever find any trace of her?"

"Yes, he did, but it went nowhere. He learned that a family running a tavern on a river boat had a little girl fitting Lisa's description, but when Hawes went there, the boat was gone and he couldn't find it. We don't even know for sure if it was my sister."

"Is that all?"

"Yes. The boat had been docked on the River below Nauvoo. I think the family's name was McNaughton."

At the sound of the name, Wes sat straight and turned her to face him. "What did you say? What was the name?"

"McNaughton–why?"

"I know that place. It was a rumhole where my half-brother used to go. I was there once, myself. You say that when Hawes went there, it was gone? Did he try to find it?"

"Yes, he said he tried, but didn't know where they went."

Wes was quiet for a moment, staring off beyond the temple grounds as she continued to watch his face. Finally he looked at her again. "Listen to me, Anna: I love you! We can overcome this religious difference. You have to break off with this other man. You don't love him, do you? You can't marry him!"

In the half-dark, she reached out and stroked his cheek. "I'll break the engagement."

"There's something else; I have to do something before we marry. I must try to find your sister."

She was silent for several moments before touching his face with the tips of her fingers. "Why? Why is it important now? How can you hope to find her after all this time?"

"First, I know that place on the Mississippi and I know some of the people who used to go there to drink. Maybe, if I'm lucky, I can find one of them and find out what happened to the McNaughtons." He was quiet, not sure he should say more.

"Is there something else?" she asked in a whisper.

He took a deep breath before starting. "During the Mormon War, some of our people made what we called 'wolf hunts,' sneaking out at night to attack one of your farms."

"Yes, I remember. We were always terrified of wolf hunts."

"Well, I never went on one, but I was young and carried away like the others—I wanted to. I was only sixteen and thought the war was a grand and glorious thing. That day, as I rode down toward your farm, I wanted to join my brother, Gunner, for a wolf hunt. When I saw Gunner, I tried to get to him—to join him in the raid on your place. I didn't shoot your pa, but I could have. I could have done it just as easy as my brother or his friends. I'm guilty inside, even if I'm innocent in fact. Maybe if I can find your sister, maybe I can make up some of the hurt my family has caused you and your family."

She held him very close and whispered in his ear. "God, I do love you, Wes! I'll wait. When you come back, with or without her, I'll be yours."

He held her tight, not wanting their time alone together to end. She was so soft, so small—like a beautiful bird he was meant to protect. Her black curls brushed against his cheek and her fragrance filled his head. When it was late, she pulled away and faced him. "We have to go back. It's dark and they'll wonder where we've been."

"We have to tell your folks tonight that we plan to marry. They have to know."

She looked down toward the ground. "It'll be difficult, but I'm sure they'll understand."

"You're not going to tell them who I really am, are you?"

"Not tonight. I'll wait until the right moment. I know they'll believe me and accept you—don't worry."

The Bargain

They stood and walked back to the Sinclair home, moving slowly, prolonging their time together. Arriving at the cabin, they saw lanterns lit and the Sinclairs and Crocker sitting at the dinner table, still sipping coffee. Everyone turned when the two young people entered, but no one said a word.

Anna pulled Wes before the table, a nervous grin on her face. "We have something to tell you all." Wes noticed Stan frown at Mary. Anna put an arm around Wes' waist. "Wes and I are going to marry. As soon as he returns, we'll marry. We love each other."

Wes looked down at her and saw the glint in her eyes and knew she was speaking from her heart, filling him so full of joy he thought he would burst. But then he looked back at the table and saw the stone faces of the Sinclairs. Only Crocker smiled and nodded his head.

Abruptly, Stan stood. "You don't know what you're saying, Anna. You can't marry this man."

Anna squirmed beside Wes. "But Pa, we love each other!"

Wes felt he had to say something. "Mr. Sinclair, I know I'm not a Mormon and I'm not a rich man, but I love Anna and I'd do anything for her!"

Mary shook her head. "You two don't know what you're saying. You can't marry! Anna is a Latter-Day-Saint and Wes, you're not. It is not permitted for Anna to marry you. Now, you can argue all you want, but that's our law."

Louise sat with Lou Ann on her lap. "Anna," she said, "you're already engaged. You're engaged to Carl Martin. You're to have a Celestial Marriage."

Wes held open his hands and pleaded. "I don't know what this 'celestial marriage' is, but if that's what you want for Anna, I'll go through it."

Mary gave a little laugh. "You don't know anything about it! You have no idea what our faith demands. You can't have a Celestial Marriage; only those men holding our Priesthood can enter into such a marriage. This whole idea of yours is simply absurd."

Anna wrung her hands. "Wes is going to search for Lisa! When he finds her he's returning and we're getting married."

Mary stared at Anna and then Wes. "Lisa? You know where she is? She's still alive?"

Wes shook his head. "I'm not sure, but I knew the McNaughton river boat and I'll search for her."

Michael spoke up for the first time. "But Sheriff Hawes searched and we searched. We sent Saints out all up and down the River. We found nothing–nothing! How can you think you can do better?"

Stan stood at the head of the table, grinding his teeth and staring at Wes. "I want a word with Mr. Tucker–alone. You'll all please excuse us." He walked to the door and opened it, waiting for Wes to join him.

Wes pulled away from Anna. "I'll be right back," he whispered. She looked back with anxious eyes, but said nothing.

They left the cabin and walked down the street toward the fields. In the dark, Wes couldn't see the expression on Stan's face but he heard the determined tone in the Mormon's voice. "I thought it best if just two of us talked, away from the others."

"I understand."

"I don't think you really do. Anna is a Latter-Day-Saint, a Mormon. She believes in our religion with a great faith, a faith born of years coming here to build Zion. I know this because she is my step-daughter and I have lived with her, I have seen her faith grow. She saw her natural father killed, her sister lost, an aunt and cousin die on the trail. Yet, she has seen the miracles God can perform. She is a Mormon through and through and nothing you nor I do will ever change that. You can't marry her and expect her to abandon her faith, and she can't marry you and remain in her Church."

"Then I'll become a Mormon!"

Stan tilted back his head and laughed. "You–a Mormon! Sure, you might join the Church to have her, but you don't believe as we do. It would be a sham and you'd soon drop away. You and my daughter would be headed for disaster as sure as we're standing here."

Wes felt desperate–Stan Sinclair wasn't wavering. "Why can't I become a Mormon? What better reason to find God then for the love of a woman? It's just as reasonable as a child being a Mormon because his or her parents are Mormons."

"You don't understand our religion or what is required to be a good Mormon. How can the elders accept you if they know you are insincere and are joining just because of Anna?"

"What's to keep me from running off with her?" Wes said it but once the words were out, regretted it How would any father react to such a brash statement?

The Bargain

"You forget where you are, Mr. Tucker. You're in Salt Lake City! There is no Federal marshal here. All our men belong to the Mormon militia. We can field hundreds of troops in minutes. I could have you brought back before you were half way to Fort Bridger."

"Why didn't your people go after Sarah Wheeler when she ran off with Taylor Hawes?"

"Because it was Sarah Wheeler and not my daughter. John Wheeler never asked the Church to go after them. He thought she was controlled by demons–maybe she was."

"Are you saying that there's nothing I can do to receive your blessing and if I run off with her, you'll chase me down?"

"That's about it."

Wes saw the outline of Stan Sinclair next to him. Stan was a big man in his late forties and the years had made him strong, a kind of strength that rippled just under the skin. Wes could sense Stan's strength, like he could sense Crocker's strength, born of living hard, each day filled with labor and trials. Wes knew Stan Sinclair wasn't a man to be easily tricked or swayed if he believed he was in the right. "I'll make you a bargain," said Wes. "If I fulfill my part, you will give your blessing to Anna and me. If not, I'll go and never return."

"What is this bargain?"

"I'll go and search for Lisa. If I find her, or find out what happened to her, you'll consent to my marriage to Anna."

Stan stood in the dark, and Wes knew the older man was watching him, thinking. "You seriously believe you can do this when half the Saints in Nauvoo failed?"

"It's the chance I'll take."

"I don't accept, but I'll make a counter offer. You go and find Lisa and bring her back here–alive! You do that and I'll personally see that you and my daughter are married."

"But, My God, what if she's already dead? I won't be able to do it!"

"Take it or leave it."

"How long do I have?"

"Until the end of August. That's over three months."

Wes was trapped. He could try stealing Anna and might even succeed, but he could also try to find her little sister. What should he do? The two men stood in the dark street while Wes struggled with his decision.

Finally, he held out his hand. "You have a bargain. By the end of August or I won't be back. Agreed?" He felt Stan's hand slip into his.

"Agreed."

The next morning, as Wes and Crocker saddled their mounts and prepared to leave, Anna approached Wes, taking him by the arm, her eyes flashing with fear. "Why did you agree? It's impossible!"

He quickly bent down and kissed her fully, but quickly on the lips. "You have to have faith in me! I know you have faith in your god and, if I'm to be your husband, you must trust me."

She laid her head against his arm. "Oh Wes, will I ever see you again? I love you so much it hurts!"

"You'll see me, don't worry."

Her hands held on to his arm with such force that her fingernails dug into his skin. "If you can't find her, come back. I'll run away with you."

He put his foot in the stirrup and swung up on Jeff. Looking at her he shook his head. "I gave your pa my word." Her eyes threatened to fill with tears. "Anna!" he scolded. "I don't want to remember you like this. I want a smile." She tried smiling as she wiped her eyes. He reached down with his left arm, encircled her body and lifted her off the ground to give her a kiss. "I'll be back."

As Wes and Crocker headed up the road in Emigration Canyon on the way to Fort Bridger, Crocker reviewed the situation for his young friend. "Now, let this old dog get things straight. You have to go after this here little girl that was swept away in a boat on the Mississippi River back in '46, who might already be dead, and find her and bring her back alive in just three months. That's it?"

"Yep."

"And ya got to do this in just three months?"

"Yep."

"Don't sound too hard, but you'll need yer old friend, here, to help out."

CHAPTER 31

The Search for Gunner

Wes and Crocker hurried to Fort Bridger, through South Pass and down the Platte Valley. Before even reaching Iowa Territory Wes realized how futile his search really was. Three and a half months had sounded like a long time when he made his bargain with Stan Sinclair. Yet, Wes now realized most of his time would be spent just traveling from the Salt Lake Valley to the Mississippi and back, which would leave precious little time to actually conduct the search. Had Sinclair known this when they shook hands? Had it been part of his strategy to defeat Wes and Anna's plans?

Crossing Iowa, the two travelers returned to Hancock County, Illinois and the ruins of Nauvoo. With the abandoned city as their starting point they searched up and down the Mississippi River, seeking out anyone who could tell them the whereabouts of the McNaughtons and their rumhole river boat. However, they received few clues other than a description of the members of the McNaughton family. A careful search of the boat's abandoned mooring revealed nothing. Already the middle of June, and they had no real leads.

They moved down the bank of the Mississippi River, checking all the despicable saloons and whorehouses as they went. Reaching St. Louis, they were still empty handed. With the dust of the trail in their mouths, they decided to visit the Rocky Mountain House and study the alternatives still open to them. Inside the Rocky Mountain they ran into an old friend. "Professor Sterling Harkless!" yelled Crocker. "You old alligator! Where you been all this time?"

The Professor lifted his head from the table and showed his red, watery eyes and blue veined nose to the two men standing over him. Wes was shocked at how the man had aged although only three years had passed since meeting him. Harkless rubbed his eyes. "Is that you, Crock? God, I though you were dead." He sat up straight and tried brushing crumbs from his dirty suit. "Sit down, men, sit down. Barkeep whiskey! These gentlemen have acquired a thirst in their travels."

"Professor, you look awful!" cried Crocker. "You been drinking yerself into ruin. Now confess: it's so, ain't it?"

Pulling a stained handkerchief from his pant pocket, Sterling wiped his face and eyes. "No, I'm just taken with a touch of pleurisy. A lot of it has been going around St. Louie. Then there's the consumption." He turned toward Wes. "Who's this young fellow? He appears to be attired in the mountain man dress. Are you a trapper?"

"Professor," answered Crocker "this here is Wes Tucker, we call him Farm boy. You met him back in '46. Don't ya remember?"

Sterling leaned closer and stared into Wes' face as the bartender placed glasses of whiskey on the table. "You're very right, Crocker, this is young Wes. Now I remember. Didn't we talk one night of killing Indians? Well, young man, did you kill your red brothers?"

Wes shook his head. "I was stupid, I was just a kid."

"Professor!" interrupted Crocker. "We need some information. Maybe you could ask around for us."

Sterling's eyes threatened to close but the drunkard fought to keep them open as his long, slender fingers found and encircled his glass of spirits. "Certainly, I will put all my resources at your disposal."

The Search for Gunner

"We're looking," continued Crocker, "for a river boat that's used as a tavern and run by the McNaughton family. There's three: a mother named Mary, and two sons, Toby and Jake. We think an eight year old girl is with them. Can ya put out the word? We ain't got much time."

Harkless rubbed his head as if he could force the thoughts out. "I think I remember them."

Wes leaned forward and took Sterling's arm. "You do? They was here?"

The Professor's face screwed up as he concentrated. "Yes. Is one son a big fat man with a diminished capacity of the mind?"

"Yes, that's him," answered Wes.

"And he's the one called Toby," continued Harkless. "He was in here several times, getting drunk and being thrown out. He bragged about the establishment he owned down at the wharf. Being in a mind to test their credit arrangements, I went there once myself. Well, I must say, I was very disappointed. It was small and dirty and the whiskey was watered. They tried to cheat me, too. I'm sure they spent more time robbing people than serving them liquor."

"But are they gone?" asked Wes.

"Oh, yes. I returned once, just to validate my earlier impressions and discovered the barge, or boat, or whatever, had disappeared. I don't know where they've gone. This Toby fellow has not returned to the Rocky Mountain."

Crocker leaned back in his chair. "We know one thing: they was here. That means we're on the trail."

"Professor?" asked Wes. "Do you remember seeing a little girl when you visited the tavern? She has dark hair and would have been about six or seven. Do you remember?"

A pained expression crossed the Professor's face as he considered the question. Looking at Wes, he tilted his head to one side and bit his lip. Suddenly his face brightened up. "Yes, I do remember. She was sweeping the floor with a broom, which was much too large for her. I remember now, I remarked at the time that it was cruel work for a child, only to receive a rebuke from the management. I decided to still my tongue, not wanting to interfere in a family matter."

"Do you remember what they called her?" asked Crocker.

Sterling thought a moment and then shook his head. "No, I heard no name."

The next day the three men fanned out in the City to search for any information on the whereabouts of the McNaughton river boat. Returning that evening to the Rocky Mountain House, they were sad to report that no one seemed to know anything about the vagabond family. "I can't believe one of us didn't turn up something," said a tired Professor.

Crocker shook his head. "We got a difficult decision now. Do we go down river to New Orleans or up the Missouri to Independence? I think they're the two logical choices."

"What if the boat's been destroyed? What if it sunk?" asked Wes. "The family could be anywhere."

"But we don't know that, Wes," replied Crock. "We got to believe they just moved on to a new location. But we don't have time to be wrong on this. If we go one way and the McNaughtons went the other, we probably won't have time to backtrack and pick up their trail. We got to leave for Salt Lake no later than the first week in August."

Wes felt dejected. "There won't be no use in leaving for Salt Lake if we don't find her."

The three men remained silent for several minutes until Harkless took a deep drink, shook his head and addressed his friends. "There is only one solution, of course. One of you must go down the Mississippi to New Orleans and the other must go up the Missouri to Independence. I will stay here and act as messenger. If either of you discovers that the McNaughtons went in your direction, send word to me. If I hear anything from either of you, I will dispatch a letter to the other addressed to the Sheriff's office in Independence or New Orleans, whichever is appropriate."

"That's a ripsnorter plan, Professor," cried Crocker. "You stay here and this coon will go down river. I've been to New Orleans and know my way about. If I get there and find no trace of them I'll head back up here. Wes, you go west to Independence. If you find nothing, return here and we'll meet. Hopefully, we'll find them one way or the other."

"All right," said Wes. "We'll leave tomorrow."

Crocker reached into his belt and withdrew his single action, Navy Colt six-shooter and placed it on the table next to Wes.

Wes looked at the gun and then his partner. "What's that for?"

"I want you taking it. If I tell ya to buy a six shooter, you'll just ignore me, you're so in love with that pea shooter of yours. I'll buy another before I leave town."

"But Crock!" objected Wes. "I can't take your gun! I don't need it anyway."

"Listen to me, Wes. These here McNaughtons is just a bunch of Jim Crows, living off the misery of others and doing anything fer money. If you run into them without warning ya best have a gun that will put 'em all under if need be. Now yer to take this gun and that's all there is."

"Then you take my single shot," insisted Wes.

"Haw!" yelled the mountain man. "That low down good fer nothing toy? It can't shoot but once and this tired dog never gets in a fight that one shot will get me out of. I'll buy a real gun tomorrow, if you please."

Early the next morning Wes left for Independence while Crocker went shopping. Moving west and checking the River would take time and slow him down, for Independence was over two hundred miles away and the road didn't always follow the River. Wes was forced to detour frequently, checking small settlements on the River's bank.

As each day slipped by and Wes drew closer to Independence, his hopes of finding anything gradually diminished. So many possibilities existed for what could have happened, and he wasn't even sure the little girl with the McNaughtons was Lisa Sinclair.

Late in the afternoon of the sixth day out of St. Louis, Wes spotted an old tavern sign laying in a clump of bushes next to the road. Looking about he discovered an overgrown path leading toward the Missouri River. Realizing the path hadn't been used for some time, he decided to check it out anyway. He urged Jeff down the path and soon came to the river bank. From the charred timber at the shore, he could tell that a large boat had burned. He tied Jeff up and walked about, looking for some piece of evidence that would tell him the owners of the destroyed boat, but found nothing. Could it have been the McNaughtons' boat? He hoped not, because if it were, they were long gone.

Back on the road to Independence he decided to stop at the next farm and, in less than three miles, came to an old farmhouse set several hundred paces back from the road. Knocking on the rough cut door, he tried to peek in, the house appearing deserted. Suddenly he heard the cocking of a rifle. Slowly turning, Wes found himself looking down the barrel of a large flintlock fowling piece held by a skinny, mean looking old man. "What the hell ya want?" the man asked.

Wes held up his hands, not daring to even look at the six shooter and the single shot pistols in his belt. "I'm just looking fer information. That's all, just information."

The old man continued holding the gun as he cocked his head to one side. "You a river rat?"

"No sir!"

"You a mountain man?"

"Yes."

"Ya know Jim Bridger?"

"I met him. I've been to Fort Bridger."

"Ha!" he yelled as he put his gun down. "I knowed it! I could tell you was a mountain man. Come in, boy, and we'll sit a spell. I got red-eye." The old man led Wes into the cluttered house and found him a seat. He then pulled an old crock from a cupboard. "Now, try this. It's real stuff!"

Wes lifted the crock to his shoulder and took a drink of the bitter liquor. "Good, good Taos."

The old man smiled. "Knew you'd like it. Now, what ya need?"

"You know that big bend in the River? Well, a river boat burned back there. Did you know the names of the owners?"

"You a relative?" he asked.

"No."

"Good. 'Cause they was the down lowest, meanest, cheatingest critters on the river bottoms. Couldn't go there without being robbed or cheated or just made sick with bad whiskey. They came here to buy vegetables and meat and tried to cheat me every time!"

"But do you remember their names?"

"Yes, of course. It was McNaughton!"

Wes sat up straight. "McNaughton? You sure?"

"Yes, but that was the old woman and she died. There were others. Her boy, Jake, came over mostly fer supplies. He weren't too bad, best of the lot. The real skunk was that Gunner. He weren't a McNaughton, but he run their whores."

"Gunner?" repeated Wes as the hair on the back of his neck stood up. "Gunner who? Do you remember?"

The Search for Gunner

"No. He were a tall, skinny man in his late twenties, but he was a mean one. Had a friend just as bad called Roland, I think?"

"Roland Palmer!" cried Wes.

"Yeah, I think that was him Roland Palmer."

The breath was sucked out of Wes' lungs and he began shaking. "And this Gunner, was it Gunner Hamlin?"

"Hamlin? Yeah, could have been, sounds right. Say, what's wrong with you? You look like ya saw a ghost! You all right?"

"Please, try to remember. Was there a little girl? About seven, with black hair, a pretty girl."

"Not that I ever seen. I only went there a couple of times. That was enough. I don't recall seeing a little girl. Say, what's these people to you?"

"I'm looking for a little girl, named Lisa, that was living with them. At least I think her name was Lisa. When did the boat burn?"

He took another drink of whiskey before answering. "I'm not too sure. Maybe a year ago."

"You say Mary McNaughton died?"

"Yea, was sick fer a time and just died. Probably drank her own whiskey!" He laughed at his joke.

"Was anyone killed in the fire?"

"I don't think so. Some of us went over to the River the next day to see what all the smoke was about. That's when we found the boat had burned. We never found no bodies in the ashes but they could of floated away. We just never saw any of them folks again. And, it's good riddance, too."

"Which way do you think they would have gone?"

"Independence, probably. It's 'bout fifty miles west."

"You say this Gunner ran the whores. What else did he do?"

"Anything that needed a gun. He liked using that gun of his. His friend, Roland, bragged how this Gunner could shoot the eye out of a crow at a hundred yards."

Back on the road, Wes hurried Jeff along, his mind spinning with the discovery that his own half brother was mixed up with the McNaughtons. That day on the Mississippi River back in 1846 had come full circle. He wanted to marry Anna, and Lisa might be living with Gunner. But if Gunner was caring for Lisa then it would be a simple matter to get her back. Gunner was his brother! Yet, it occurred to Wes that he had been learning things about his brother, things that meant Gunner might not be too anxious to see Wes again.

He had to get to Independence and send word to Professor Harkless that he'd found the river boat. The McNaughtons and Gunner could be in Independence at this very moment and Lisa could be with them. He urged Jeff on even faster. It was the first week in July, his time was slipping away.

As he drew closer to the frontier town, the road became crowded with the Forty-niners headed for the gold fields in California. Every make and description of wagon and coach had been pressed into service to carry a conglomeration of Missourians, Easterners, and immigrants forward. They were the rich and the poor, the strong and the weak, but they all had one thing in common: they were greedy for gold. As Wes rode past them, dressed in his mountain outfit, they stared at him and whispered "mountain man!"

Reaching Independence, Wes was even more amazed at the impact the California bound travelers were having. The town had grown considerably since he last passed through in the spring of 1846, and now it was crowded to overflowing with the new pioneers. They were mostly men, but some were families, and the families were the most pitiful men and women who had already lost one dream in life and were frantic not to miss out on this one.

Wes rode straight to the sheriff's office where he found Sheriff Hillman sitting with several deputies in a small, rundown jail house. The Sheriff, in his fifties with a stocky frame and dark, greasy hair, wore a dark wool suit and carried two six shooters in black holsters on his hips. After a quick introduction, Hillman pointed Wes to a chair and poured him a cup of coffee. "Just what can I do for you, Mr. Tucker?" Wes was still using his adopted name.

"I'm looking for an eight year old girl named Lisa who was separated from her Mormon family three years ago."

"You've been hired by this Mormon family?"

Wes cussed himself for mentioning the Sinclairs were Mormon for he knew the Missourians had no love for the Mormons. "Not exactly, but I am trying to reunite the girl with her folks."

Hillman, at first warm and cordial, now looked at Wes through suspicious eyes. "Why do you think she's here?"

The Search for Gunner

"I think she's in the company of a family by the name of McNaughton, Jake or Toby McNaughton. Or, she could be with a man named Gunner Hamlin."

Hillman looked at his deputies and then back at Wes. "Why do you think she might be with these McNaughtons or this Hamlin?"

Wes grew impatient. "It's a long story. I'm just wondering if you know of these people and their whereabouts."

The Sheriff held up a hand. "Now, just a minute. You came in here with some far fetched story about some Mormonite girl and you won't answer a few simple questions."

"All right! The girl, Lisa Sinclair, was separated from her folks when a boat she was in drifted away on the Mississippi River. The McNaughtons owned a saloon boat on the River bottoms and were reported to have a little girl with them fitting Lisa's description. Later, they joined up with Gunner Hamlin. I'm just trying to find them."

Sheriff Hillman withdrew a bottle of whiskey from a shelf next to his desk and poured several ounces into his coffee cup. "Now, just why are you interested in all this, three years after it happened?"

Wes looked at the ceiling and let out a sigh. "I'm engaged to Lisa's older sister."

Hillman leaned forward in his chair. "You're a Mormonite!" he yelled.

Wes threw his arms out to his side. "Look at me! Do I look like a Mormon? I've been living with the Injuns for years. I'm just engaged to the sister." Wes was now feeling very uncomfortable under the hard gaze of the Sheriff.

"You ever met Old Gabe?"

"Yes, I've met Jim Bridger. Last time I saw him was at Fort Bridger on the Oregon Trail."

This seemed to satisfy the Sheriff because he gave Wes a warm smile and picked up the bottle of liquor. "Here, have some good drinking whiskey. So, yer marrying one of them Mormonite girls, huh? How'd ya get her away from her bishop?" The Sheriff and his deputies gave hearty laughs, and Wes forced himself to join in.

Wes patted Crock's six shooter and winked. "I just persuaded him with my persuader."

The Sheriff lunged forward, slapped his knee and gave out a roar. "That's good oh, that's good! That's what they all need."

"Sheriff Hillman," interrupted Wes. "Do you have any information on the people I'm after?"

Hillman poured whiskey into Wes' cup. "It's interesting you came by, cause ya just walked into a hornet's nest of trouble. If I knew where Hamlin was, I'd bring him in here fer a little chat."

"He's wanted?" asked Wes.

"In a manner of speaking. The McNaughton boy, Jake, was shot to death right in the street here in Independence. I can't say fer sure, but I think that Gunner Hamlin did it. I think it was over some whore, some girl."

"What about Toby McNaughton?"

"Don't know him, just this Jake and Hamlin. If you learn where this Hamlin is, I'd appreciate ya letting me know. As fer Jake McNaughton, he's up the hill, under six feet of earth."

Wes sensed the track fading on him. "Where would Gunner Hamlin be? Could he still be in town?"

The Sheriff laughed and his men joined in. "God Almighty, boy, look outside! The town's overrun with these Forty-niners. It's all we can do to keep them from shooting each other before they get out of town and become someone else's problem. He could be anywhere. I've kept an eye out for him, but we've had dozens of murders and I'm catching 'em and hanging 'em as fast as I can."

"Sheriff," asked Wes, "if you were wanted, where would you go?"

Hillman stroked the stubble on his chin. "Well, I'd slip over the border into Kansas Territory. Not much law there, just the army and they don't get around much. Ain't enough Federal marshals to clean things up. Lots of Jim Crows have put up shacks on the Kansas River just inside the Territory. It's out of our jurisdiction and they do just about what they please. Unless ya have to, I wouldn't go along the river bottoms between here and the Papin Ferry where the Oregon Trail crosses the Kansas; it's nothing but mean rumholes. But, if I were this Gunner, that's where I'd go. He was running whores on a boat to the east of Independence before it burned. I'd assume he's still running whores."

"What about Westport?"

"He might go there. I've told the Sheriff to keep watch and he hasn't been seen yet, but Westport might be worth a check."

"Can I ask a favor of you Sheriff?"

The Search for Gunner

Hillman nodded.

"I have a partner coming here from St. Louie, Crocker Sloan. If he comes here, would you tell him we've talked? I'll check back with you every few days."

"When do you expect him?"

"Not for awhile, I'm afraid."

"What are you going to do now, Tucker?"

Wes looked out the jail's window at the mobs in the street.

"I'm not sure. I suppose I'll check around Independence and see if anyone has seen Gunner. Maybe I'll mosey over into Kansas."

Hillman pointed a finger at Wes. "If you find where Gunner Hamlin is, you have an obligation to report it to me. Do you understand?"

"Of course, Sheriff, of course."

By the time Wes left the jail, the day had already turned to early evening, but Wes didn't have time to waste. Immediately, he found a street crowded with taverns and began asking in each one if anyone knew Gunner Hamlin or Toby McNaughton. After five saloons and as many whiskeys, the only new information he'd acquired came from a little whore named Riva. She told Wes that over a year ago, her friend Sally had been kidnapped by a man calling himself Gunner, but she had no idea where Sally had been taken.

On a dark street in Independence, Missouri, leaning against Jeff and listening to scores of drunks yelling and fighting, Wes felt very alone.

* * *

As Roland stood guard, Gunner felt in the darkness for the stranger's money purse. Finding a large leather pouch, he opened it and felt the paper money and coins inside. "I got it," he announced in a low voice. "Let's get rid of him before he stinks up the place."

"How much?" asked Roland.

"Now how the hell do I know? It's dark, ya damn fool. Come on, let's push him into the River. He'll be past Westport before he comes up." They picked up the limp body, and swinging it between them, released it on the count of three. In the dark, they didn't see it go in, but the splash was loud, making Gunner wince. "Come on, Ro, let's get out of here." They found their horses and hurried back to the saloon. Inside, they stepped up to the bar and ordered drinks.

"Ain't ya gonna check?" whispered Roland.

"Shut up! I want a drink first. We'll count it later." They began drinking in earnest, the stranger's purse bulging under Gunner's shirt.

After their third whiskey, just as the fourth was being poured, Friendship Brown entered the saloon. Spotting Gunner he hurried to stand beside his friend. "Sam! I just got back from Independence."

"I can see that!" said an irritated Gunner.

"I got to talk to ya. Someone's looking fer ya."

Now Friendship had Gunner's full attention. "Who? Who's looking fer me?"

"I don't know. Somebody by the name of Wes Tucker is asking all over Independence about you." Friendship leaned closer and whispered. "He's asking fer Gunner Hamlin."

Gunner stared at Friendship as he spoke the name. "Wes Tucker? I don't know any Wes Tucker. What's he want?"

"I don't know!" replied Friendship.

A tall Mexican, in his sixties and wearing the rawhide of a mountain man, stood on the opposite side of Friendship. He turned and faced Friendship and Gunner. "Excuse, 'Senor.' You know Wes Tucker?"

Roland leaned over the bar, looking past Gunner and Friendship at the Mexican. "Shit! When we start serving Bean Eaters?" He turned and yelled at the fat bartender. "Toby, I told ya no Spaniards in here!"

Gunner suddenly slapped Roland with his open hand. "Shut yer fucking mouth, Winston. This here Mexican is my friend, can't ya see that?" Gunner turned back to the stranger and held out his hand. "My name is Sam Gruber. What might yours be?"

The Mexican looked suspiciously at the three men standing with him at the bar. "I am Elfego Rodriguez Baccala."

"Well, Senor Baccala," said Gunner. "You're welcome in my saloon any time ya want. Now, I understand this here Wes Tucker is looking for me and I don't even know the man. Who is he?"

Fego hesitated for just a moment before answering. "He is the one we call 'Farm boy.'"

The Search for Gunner

Friendship and Roland laughed. "What kind of stupid name is that?" exclaimed Friendship.

"Quiet!" warned Gunner. "Now, just who is this Farm boy?"

Fego's eyes narrowed. "He is a mountain man. He rides with Crocker Sloan. You have heard of Sloan?"

Gunner tried to remember but couldn't. "Yeah, sure, Sloan. But why is this Farm boy looking fer me?"

"I do not know, Senor, but if Farm boy wants you, he will find you. Good night!" Without warming, the tall Mexican turned from the bar and walked through the door, disappearing into the night.

Gunner turned back to the bar and his drink. "Why the hell would this mountain man be looking fer me? I don't know him."

Roland shook his head. "I don't like them mountain men. They got that mad look in their eyes, like they had the demon inside. And they'll fight anything Shit, I once saw..."

"Would you shut up!" yelled Gunner. "Just shut the fuck up, and let me think."

CHAPTER 32

Battle on the Kansas River

Wes ran up the brick steps of the Independence jail two at a time for everything he did now was filled with haste. He had already checked every tavern and whorehouse in both Independence and Westport and, although he kept running into people who knew Gunner, none of them could tell Wes where his half brother was. August first was less than a week away, and if he didn't leave for Salt Lake City by that date, he might not return by the deadline. The distance from Independence to the Great Salt Lake Valley was over eleven hundred miles, and he would need thirty days to make it with any margin to spare.

Hurrying into the office, he discovered Sheriff Hillman was away. "Any word for me from Crocker Sloan?" he asked a deputy sitting behind a desk. The deputy shook his head, and Wes turned to leave when the deputy called him back. "You got a letter here!"

Buffalo Man

Wes stepped to the desk and accepted the envelope offered by the lawman. Breaking the seal, he pulled out a sheet of paper and unfolded it. It was addressed to him, but the text was in Spanish, yet at the bottom of the page he recognized the name of Elfego Baccala. He turned to he deputy. "Can you read Spanish?"

The officer shook his head. Wes realized he'd have to find someone to translate it. He remembered one of the saloons he'd been in just the night before and a Mexican woman behind the bar. Leaving the jail, he hurried back to the saloon. The woman was still behind the bar, trying not to look too bored with the few customers in the establishment at this early hour. Wes ordered a whiskey and then produced the letter. "Can you read this for me? I don't read Spanish."

She took the letter and smiled back at him. "You want me to read it to you?"

"Yes, please."

She stared back at the letter. "It is addressed to a Senor Tucker from Senor Elfego Baccala. He says he is looking for you. He says if you look for a Senor Sam Gruber, the man owns a cantina just north of the Shawnee Mission on the south bank of the Kansas River. He then says he will look for you in Westport. He says if you get this letter, leave one for him in the *carcel,* jail." She glanced at Wes and pointed to the last line of the letter. "Here he says Senor Gruber is *malo cabron.*"

Wes shook his head. "What's a *malo cabron?*"

"Oh, Senor! It is an outlaw, a bad man."

Wes asked her to read the letter again in case he'd missed something. He didn't know any Sam Gruber! Why would he want to find this Gruber? Then an idea struck him; it might be Gunner using another name, just like Wes used the name Tucker. But how did Fego know he was looking for Gunner? There were just too many questions to be answered. He paid the woman for her trouble and left the saloon to fetch Jeff. He'd just have to check out this Sam Gruber.

Leaving Independence, Wes passed through Westport and a mile farther entered the Indian Territory of Kansas. A few miles farther brought him to the Old Shawnee Mission, a large two story brick building housing a Methodist school for Indian boys. Here the Oregon Trail turned southwest before bending back to the Papin Ferry. A narrow dirt road led north from the Mission to the River. Wes followed the road until he came to a gentle hill that ran down to the River's bank. There he saw the tent building with the false wooden front. In large black letters over the door he read "Samual Gruber's Road House." Beneath, in smaller letters, was "Girls! Whiskey! Gambling!"

Wes hitched Jeff to the post where several other horses patiently waited and walked up onto the porch. Almost noon, a hot sun beat down on his head so he removed his hat, wiped the sweat from his forehead and entered the tavern. Inside, a bar ran along the right wall and six large round tables stood beside a small dance floor. Two customers sat at a table, engrossed in some private conversation. Behind the bar, Wes saw a tall fat man with an ugly face and narrow eyes, and knew at once it was Toby McNaughton.

Wes started for the bar when Roland Palmer entered the saloon from a back room. Roland and Wes stopped and, standing fifteen feet apart, stared at each other. "Roland?" said Wes, not believing he was seeing the man.

Roland leaned forward and narrowed his eyes. "Wes? Is that you, Wes? Wes Hamlin!"

"Yes, it's me!"

"Jesus Christ, I don't believe it Wes Hamlin! I ain't seen you fer years, boy. You're all growed up!" He turned and called back into the room he had just left. "Sam, get out here! See who's come!"

The tent flap flew to one side, and Gunner stepped into the room, wearing pants, long underwear and no shirt. He held a towel to his face, caught in the act of removing soap from his chin. He looked at Wes and the recognition flashed in his eyes. "My God, I don't believe it! My little brother, Wes!"

Wes suddenly remembered the love he'd had for Gunner and the warmth swelled inside him. "Gunner, I've been looking fer ya." Both men walked, closing the distance between them. Gunner threw his arms around Wes and gave him a big bear hug, and Wes hugged back. "God, Gunner, it's been ages."

"Sure has, boy. You're all growed. Let me look at ya." He pulled away and appraised Wes. "Jesus, yer a mountain man."

"That's right, Gunner!"

Gunner leaned closer and lowered his voice. "Wes, I don't use that name anymore, a little disagreement with the authorities. I'm Sam Gruber now. All right?"

"Sure...Sam. And I'm Wes Tucker. I don't use Hamlin no more."

Gunner stared at Wes again and affectionately slapped him on the shoulder. "Tucker? You're Tucker? My God, I heard a mountain man was looking fer me and I had no idea it was you! Jesus, Wes, it's good to see someone from home. Come on, let's have a drink." He moved to a table and pulled out a chair. "Toby bring a bottle of the best. This here is my brother! Come on, Wes, pull up a seat."

Wes sat down next to Gunner. "I've been looking for ya all over Missouri. You're a hard person to find."

Gunner smiled at Wes. "When you're in this business ya got to keep moving." Gunner yelled at Roland. "Win, come and pull up a chair; this is a celebration. Hell, a man don't run into a brother every day out here." He leaned close to Wes. "We call Roland 'Winston Smith' now. He got in a bit of trouble, too." Toby McNaughton placed a large green bottle on the table along with three glasses. Gunner yelled in the direction of the tents behind the barroom. "Friendship! Get out here." Turning back to Wes, he slapped him on the back. "That's another friend I want ya to meet."

A fat woman in a fancy gray dress entered the room, and Gunner waved her over to the table. "Get over here, Nancy. I want ya to meet my half brother, Wes. He's the one been looking fer me."

Nancy walked up behind Wes and messed his hair with her hands. "My, you're a handsome one. Ya look better than your brother." She nudged Gunner. "I'll bet he's good in bed, huh, Sammy? All you Hamlin boys is good in bed. Pour me a fucking drink, Win, I'm parched."

"Sit down," ordered Gunner. "We got to celebrate." A short, stocky man in his forties entered the room. "Friendship, get over here. Meet my brother, Wes."

Friendship Brown walked to the table and took Wes' extended hand. "Glad to meet ya."

"Sit!" ordered Gunner. "We're going to have a drink." He turned once again to Wes. "Jesus! It's so ball busting good to see ya! I ain't seen no one from home for years. When were ya there last?" He picked up the bottle. "Here, everyone have a drink. This is a party."

"Gunner...I mean Sam," The name sounded strange in Wes' mouth. "I got to ask ya something."

"Ya, what is it? Ask me anything."

Battle on the Kansas River

"Why did ya say I was the one who shot that Mormon that day back on the Mississippi?" Everyone sitting around the table was silent as they looked at Gunner.

"Wes, that's a lie! I never said that. That fucking Hawes said I did, but I didn't. It was Cyrus who shot that man. Weren't it, Ro?" Gunner had forgotten to use Roland's assumed name.

Roland quickly nodded his head. "That's right, Wes. Me and Sammy told Cyrus not to shoot, but he was mad in the head and he started shooting, anyway. It was him that killed that Mormon. Sammy told that to Hawes and so did I, but he wouldn't believe us. No one would. Everyone just assumed you did it cause the Sheriff said so."

Wes felt much better. He had hoped it was something as simple as that. "God, ya don't know how much better that makes me feel."

Gunner scowled at him. "Wes, ya didn't think bad thoughts about yer own blood brother, did ya? Hell, we got to stick together. You go back to Hancock County and tell them folks old Gunner said ya didn't do it. Tell 'em it were Cyrus Maggio. He's dead now, did ya know that, Wes?"

"Yes, and Sheriff Hawes ain't sheriff no more," reported Wes. "He left Illinois and run off to Oregon with a Mormon woman. And guess what? My brother Bert is married! Her name's Lacy, a pretty little thing."

Gunner looked at Wes and a grin covered his face. "God, Wes, it's good looking at someone familiar. Holy shit, we're having a party tonight! We're all getting drunk. I got some sweet little whores here, Wes, who'll screw yer balls right off! If ya like 'em dark skinned, Tamla is a real beauty, but the best lay in this place is sitting right at this table. Nancy is the best whore this side of St. Louie."

Wes suddenly remembered why he was here and leaned closer to his half brother. "Gunner, I got to ask ya about a little girl."

Gunner's brows came together. "What girl?"

"Her name's Lisa, Lisa Sinclair. I been looking for her and I thought she was here."

The men looked at Gunner, but Nancy pointed a finger at Wes. "Now, you're welcome to sleep with any of my girls, young man, but Lisa is being saved. We got plans fer her."

Wes felt the excitement tingle through his body. "You have her here? God Almighty, you don't know how hard I've been looking fer her. Where is she?" Wes looked about the room.

Gunner put a hand on Wes' shoulder. "Now, don't go getting all fired up. Yes, she lives here with us, but we got plans fer her. What ya want with a little shit like that, anyway?"

"But Gunner, she's the little sister of the woman I want to marry. I got to take her back or I can't marry Anna."

"Bullshit! The McNaughtons found her and adopted her. When Mary McNaughton died, I adopted her. How do you know who her family is?"

"Because she was lost in a boat on the Mississippi River back in '46. Her family's been looking for her for years. She belongs with them, Gunner."

Nancy pointed her finger at Wes again. "Now you listen to me, young man. That little shit eats us out of mountains of food and don't do her work around here. We got a lot invested in her and we plan to get it back."

Gunner held up a hand. "She's right, Wes. We've raised that child for years. We got rights, too. What about all we've done for her? We stand to make a pile of money on that child soon."

"I don't understand! You're going to make money on Lisa? How?" Wes looked from Gunner to the fat whore.

Nancy smiled and nudged Gunner. "He ain't so smart, is he? Don't you know nothing, boy? This here is a whorehouse. We fuck fer money, and that little shit is going to start making her share of it."

Wes couldn't believe his ears. Lisa was only eight years old! "You can't! She's a child! Ya can't do that!" He was half yelling.

Gunner scowled and shook his head. "Don't be stupid, Wes. You're not a kid no more. This is the West and we survive any way we can. We could 'a throwed the little turd out in the snow years ago and no one would 'a known a thing, but we didn't. We fed her and cared for her and protected her. Now she's got to pay us back. God, she's worth hundreds! Do you understand? She's worth hundreds of dollars if we work her right."

The others at the table were nodding in agreement with Gunner as Wes stood up. "I'm not letting it happen. Ya can't do this. It's wrong! I won't allow it!"

Everyone else stood and, as Gunner and Roland grabbed Wes' arms, Wes tried reaching for Crock's six shooter, but Friendship forced his head down hard on the table, painfully smashing his nose into the wood. Wes struggled to turn his head to one side, but all he could see was Roland drawing out a long knife, and then Wes felt the cold metal against his throat. The voice he heard was Gunner's as his half brother put his lips next to Wes' ear and spat out the words. "Ya fucking little shit head! What the Christ do ya mean coming into my place and telling me what to do with my whores? I treat ya like my own brother and ya give me trouble."

Another voice broke in and Wes recognized it as the one called Friendship Brown. "We got to kill him, Sammy. Brother or not, he'll tell Hillman. We got to kill him."

"Shut the fuck up!" yelled Gunner. Again, Wes felt Gunner's lips close to his ear. "You're either with us or you're against us. Ya can't be in between. Hell, Wes, I wanted to make ya part of my gang, part of this operation, but now I see ya ain't with us. I can't let ya go, ya know that, don't ya? Ya know too much. You'll bring the army down on us. I'll make it quick, you'll see..." Suddenly an explosion filled the room and the center of the table, just inches from Wes' face, disintegrated into wood chips. Wes felt the pressure diminish on his arms and heard the distinctive voice behind him.

"*Saludos a todos, campanyeros. Dejar de!*"

"Fego! Is that you?" yelled Wes.

"*Si, companyero.* We must vamose now. *Si?*"

Wes pulled against the arms that held him and felt them give way. He stood and turned to see the Mexican standing in the door of the whorehouse, rifle in one hand and a six shooter pointed at Gunner's head.

"Who is this fucking Mexican?" cried Gunner. "Tell him, Wes, that this is family business!"

Wes slowly backed away toward the door, trying to keep an eye on Toby McNaughton behind the bar and the group at the table.

"Come, Farm boy. *Pronto!*"

"Toby!" called Gunner. "Shoot that son of a bitch! Shoot that fucking Bean eater!"

Toby whined. "I can't, Gunner. He's got a gun!"

Wes now stood beside his friend. Nancy was holding her hand down by the side of her dress when, suddenly, she raised it, pointed a small silver pistol at Fego and fired. The Mexican pointed his revolver at her, pulled back the hammer and pulled the trigger. The force of the bullet striking her chest forced her back several feet. Everyone stood frozen in place as the fat whore looked down at the hole between her breasts and watched the blood spill out and stain her dress. Her eyes glazed over and she slumped to the floor.

"Holy shit!" escaped from Roland's lips.

Gunner, white with rage, turned back toward Wes and Fego. "Ya fuckers!" he yelled. "Ya killed my best whore! God damn it, I'll get you, you'll see, I'll get you, both of you. I'll get you, Wes and I'll get that fucking Spaniard."

"Let's go," said Wes in a low voice and he backed out the door.

Fego nodded his sombrero toward those at the table. "*Hasta la vista!*" He backed out and joined Wes on the saloon's porch. "*Pronto*, Farm boy. We go!" They hurried to their horses, keeping an eye on the door and windows of the whorehouse. Once up the road and over the hill, Fego reined to a stop. "Farm boy! Wait!"

Wes wheeled Jeff around and rode back to his friend. "Don't ya think we should get down the road a piece before we call a halt?" Fego shook his head, and Wes noticed the Mexican holding his right shoulder as blood oozed between his fingers. "Fego, she hit ya! Come on, we got to get ya to a doctor! The Mission is just down the road. We can get there and then I'll go to Westport for a doctor."

"Wait! Is the *Senorita* back there? Do they know you look for the little *Senorita* Lisa?" Fego pointed back toward the tavern.

Wes nodded. "Yes, she's there and they know I'm after her."

"Then we cannot go, my *companero*. Hillman told me you look for *Senorita* Lisa. If we go now, she will be gone! You will not find her. Senor Gruber will take her."

"No, Fego, I've got to take care of you. We'll bring back men from Westport for her."

"No. You know she will be gone by then. We will go back. Together we will take her." Fego reached down and attempted to withdraw his rifle, but the pain was too much and he swayed in the saddle, unable to shoulder the weapon. "We go back, take her now! I am good."

Wes shook his head. "Look at ya. Ya can hardly stay yer mount."

Fego scowled and shoved his rifle back into the scabbard. "You're right. Fego is no good. You go for the *Senorita* and I will go on to the Mission. You know it must be this way."

Battle on the Kansas River

Wes looked at the wound in Fego's shoulder and winced. It was bleeding and the blood soaked Fego's shirt. Wes slid off of Jeff and ordered Fego to dismount. "I'll just tie you up first." He cut away the Mexican's shirt and closely examined the wound. It was high on the shoulder and a small hole, obviously from a small caliber gun. He pulled off Fego's bandana and balled it up. Placing it on the wound he used his own bandana to tie Fego's in place. "There, that should do it fer now. How ya feel?"

Fego nodded. "Much better. I'll be fine. You go."

"All right! I'll get Lisa. You go down the road to the Mission, and if anything happens to you, I'll find ya along the way." He helped his friend back onto his mount and then got back on Jeff.

Fego reached out with his hand and took Wes' arm *"Takpe, Wicasa Ozu."* he said, using the Lakota for 'attack.'

Wes checked both the six shooter and the single shot pistol and then drew out his rifle. *"Takpe!"* He yelled, holding the rifle high and jamming his heels into Jeff's sides. The horse responded by jumping forward and galloping back down the hill toward the saloon.

Wes hoped his quick return would take everyone by surprise. No one was outside the whorehouse as he reined to a stop and slipped from Jeff's back. Carrying his rifle he ran into the tavern, coming to a stop just inside the door. Toby still stood behind the bar, but a large bore scatter gun rested on the bar in front of him. Gunner, Roland and Friendship were gathered around the body of Nancy. Roland looked up and, spotting Wes, let out a little cry. "Oh, shit!"

Gunner looked first at Wes and then at Toby. "Toby!" he yelled. The fat half wit reached for the scatter gun. Wes raised his Kentuck, cocked it and shot from the hip just as Toby's hand gripped the gun. The resulting explosion filled the room with blue smoke, and the force from the rifle's ball smashed Toby against the wall. He held the scatter gun up and squeezed the trigger, blowing a hole in the top of the tent.

Wes dropped his Kentuck rifle and drew Crock's revolver as he turned back toward the others. Both Friendship and Roland were drawing their revolvers and Gunner, who wasn't wearing a weapon, moved backward toward the rear exit.

Roland aimed his gun at Wes, having beaten him to the draw. Wes dropped to one knee and aimed his own weapon as Roland fired. Not waiting to discover if he were hit, Wes pulled the trigger on Crock's gun. The pistol jumped in his hand as smoke spit from the muzzle, but Wes had no time to see the results. He aimed at Friendship Brown and pulled the trigger again. After his own gun bucked in his hand, he heard someone else's gun go off as the tent filled with smoke. Roland was still standing, so Wes aimed and fired again at the man. Marching forward, Wes saw Friendship sitting on the floor, holding his revolver with both hands and pointing at Wes. Wes shot at Friendship a second time, putting the ball right between the man's eyes and blowing the back of his head against the tent wall.

Roland lay on his back, his eyes glassed over, but still moving the hand holding his gun, so Wes pointed at Roland's breastbone and pulled the trigger, blowing a hole in his chest. Just then Wes heard a scraping noise behind him and turned to see Toby laying on the floor behind the bar holding a single shot pistol. Smoke spit out of the pistol and the ball slammed into Wes' left arm, twisting him around. He turned on Toby and shot him through the top of the head.

As Wes looked around the room, checking the bodies on the floor, stabbing pain spread throughout his arm. Nothing in the room moved, but Gunner was gone! Wes walked to the tent flap that exited the back of the room and, moving it aside with the barrel of the revolver, stepped into a large second tent that served as a kitchen. At the opposite end of the room stood Gunner, trying to place percussion caps on the nipples of his own revolver. "Don't make me shoot," said Wes as he aimed Crocker's six shooter.

Gunner's face distorted into that of a trapped wild animal that would rather kill than give up. "Fuck you, Wes," came out of Gunner's mouth as he closed the gun's cylinder and began aiming.

Wes had to do it, even though it was his own blood; he squeezed the trigger. The hammer fell on the percussion cap but nothing happened and, with a suddenness that made him cold all over, he realized he'd already fired all six charges, the gun was empty.

Gunner realized it too as he aimed his gun at his half brother. "Looks like ya went and fired all your shots. Too bad! Now, it's old Gunner's turn to do the killing." Gunner's eyes flashed with excitement and his mouth turned up in a smile.

Wes reached out both arms, tilted his head back and saw in his mind just how the sound had to start deep in his chest and how it had to come out. He shut his eyes, curled his tongue just as he'd seen Smoke Man do it and, with every fiber of his body, made the sound come out in a perfect replication. For a long moment, the ancient sound filled the tent and then Wes was done. He opened his eyes and saw Gunner standing still, his eyes wide in wonderment and the gun still aimed at Wes.

With one fluid motion, Wes drew his single shot from his belt and shot Gunner in the center of his forehead. For just the fraction of a second, Gunner's eyes cleared and a look of terrible understanding came to his face before he crumpled into a heap on the floor.

Now the pain returned to Wes' arm with double strength. He bit his lip and stepped over Gunner's body. He still had to find Lisa. Moving into the next tent, he discovered a storeroom filled with boxes and barrels. Wes saw no one and was about to leave when he felt a presence, he wasn't alone! Both guns were empty, so he withdrew his knife and searched behind all the supplies, but he couldn't find what he knew must be here. Looking down, he saw a sliver of light pass between the floor boards to the crawl space below. He carefully searched the planking and, behind a whiskey barrel, found what he was after. Reaching down, he pulled the loose board up and saw part of a girl's arm.

"Lisa?" he gently called. There was no answer. "Lisa? Come out." Still nothing moved. He reached down and took hold of the arm and carefully pulled. Slowly, the girl came out of the crawl space and sat on the storeroom floor. Wes couldn't believe the poor creature before him; she was dirty and skinny and covered with scratches and bruises, her eyes filled with fear and her cheeks sunken and pale.

"What's your name?" he asked.

"Lisa."

"Lisa what?"

"Lisa Sinclair."

"My name is Wes. Do you remember your sister, Anna, or your mother, Mary."

Her eyes grew large. "You know Anna?"

He nodded. "I've come to take you home, Lisa. I've come to take you home to Anna."

CHAPTER 33

August 27, 1849

A Tragic Killing

As Wes rode down the streets of Salt Lake City he felt such a wonderful excitement that he barely noticed the changes in the city. Thousands of Forty niners had reached the Valley and passed through to California, but many were still in the Mormon capitol. Their wagons, filled with personal belongings and mining equipment, lined the streets while they milled about, watering stock or trading goods with the Saints. The City's normal industriousness and ordered activity were replaced with a group frenzy; a frenzy of the Forty niners hurrying on to the gold fields, and a frenzy of the Saints to send them on their way.

But none of this commotion bothered Wes as he rode Jeff down the busy street. He reached back a comforting hand and patted Lisa's leg. "This is your new home, Lisa. This is Salt Lake City. What do you think?"

He felt her weight shift before she answered. "It looks like Nauvoo, but different. It's so dry. Where are the trees?"

"There were no trees when your folks came so they had to cut logs in the canyons and bring them down in wagons to build houses." He reined to a stop. "Look, Lisa." He pointed to a large log cabin one block away. "That's where your family lives."

She didn't answer but tightened her arms about his waist.

"Come on," he said, "let's say hello to your folks."

As they approached the Sinclair home, Louise, hanging wash on a line by the side of the house, stopped her work and used her hand to shade her eyes while seeing who was coming. Suddenly, she dropped her hand, turned and ran into the house. Wes reined to a stop at the hitching post just as Louise and Anna rushed from the cabin.

Wes felt Lisa shift her weight to catch a glimpse of who was coming down the path and then a slight cry left her lips. Wes reached back and, holding Lisa's arm, helped her slide from Jeff's back.

Anna Sinclair's eyes were riveted on her sister. Holding out her arms, she gave a scream as she scooped her sister up in her arms and began covering her face with kisses. "Oh, God!" she yelled. "Oh, God! Jesus!" she cried. Lisa threw her arms around her older sister and buried her face on Anna's neck. Louise put her apron to her face. "Oh, my! Oh, my!" was all she could say as she cried and watched the two sisters.

Wes turned to see Mary and Stan Sinclair running down the street, Mary in front. When Lisa's mother reached them, she just stopped and stood as if in a trance. Lisa and Anna pulled apart, their faces covered with tears, and looked at Mary. Mary fell on her knees, held out her arms and gave out a cry. Lisa dashed into her arms.

Suddenly, Wes was aware that Stan Sinclair was standing beside Jeff. "Oh, Christ!" he said. "It's a miracle! It's God's miracle!" Other Saints now gathered about the Sinclairs. "Get down!" said Stan, directing the command toward Wes.

Wes dismounted and tied Jeff's reins to the hitching post. "I brought her back, Mr. Sinclair."

Stan grasped Wes by the arm. "You did! You really did," he said, staring at Wes' face. All of a sudden, tears came to the Mormon's eyes and he pulled Wes into his arms and gave him a long, powerful hug. "God bless you, boy. God bless you, Wes."

A Tragic Killing

Wes pulled away and wiped a tear from his own eye. "Did Anna tell you who I am?" he asked.

As Stan turned to watch Mary hug her youngest daughter he nodded. "Yes, you're Wes Hamlin. We know."

All at once Anna threw her arms around Wes' neck and pulled his head down. She forcefully kissed him on the lips and then kissed him a second and third time. "Oh, God, Wes, you did it, you found her."

As he held her in his arms and listened to her soft voice he felt his joy would explode his heart. She was his, she would be his wife. He watched as the Sinclairs become reacquainted with their lost Lisa. He cared for these people and knew in time he would come to love them. He felt it would be an easy thing to become a Latter Day Saint.

"Wes Hamlin!" someone shouted from the assembling crowd. Wes looked up and saw a powerfully built Mormon in his mid forties and wearing a black beard. He was holding a pistol. "Wes Hamlin," shouted the man again. Now everyone stopped to look at the newcomer.

Anna, still in Wes' arms, turned to face him. "Carl!"

Carl Martin took several steps forward and pointed the pistol at Wes. "Wes Hamlin, I'm arresting you for the murder of Jack Sinclair."

Stan shook his head. "You don't understand, Carl," he said as he took a step forward.

Carl suddenly pointed the gun at Stan. "Don't move!" He swung around, pointing the gun at those gathered around him, and the crowd backed away. Carl again aimed at Wes. "Don't anyone interfere. I have been ordained to arrest and hang this man. He is a murderer, he is the one who killed our Brother Jack Sinclair on the River."

Those Mormons gathered around began to nod their heads and point toward Wes. Someone in the crowd yelled, "Get a rope, the Bishop's caught a murderer."

Stan's voice boomed out. "Listen to me! This is Wes Hamlin but he didn't kill Jack. He's innocent. He just returned my daughter, Lisa, and he's to marry Anna."

Suddenly, Carl took several steps forward, still holding the gun on Wes. "Anna," he pleaded, "you're to marry me. We're to have a Celestial Marriage. God has ordained that WE be husband and wife."

Anna hugged Wes about the waist. "I love Wes. I don't love you, Carl, I never did."

With pain written on Carl's face, a craziness came to his eyes as tears streamed down his cheeks. "God, Anna, I love you. I've always loved just you! I can't live without you."

A terrible frustration gripped Wes, for he suddenly realized that this Carl Martin was going to shoot. His love had made him insane. Wes looked behind Carl at the crowd, hoping someone would step forward, but everyone was just standing and watching.

"I've given my word," said Stan, "and I'll not go back on it now, Carl. You're my Bishop, but this man..." and Stan pointed toward Wes.

Carl shook the pistol at Stan's face. "Shut up! Just shut up! She belongs to ME! Do you hear?" He aimed the gun again at Wes' face. "She's MINE!"

Wes noticed that the gun was a percussion pistol, and that a percussion cap was in place on the nipple, but it was still uncocked. He itched to reach for Crocker's revolver in his belt. Yet, he didn't want to hurt this Mormon; the man was obviously out of his mind with jealously. "Please," he said, "just put the gun down. We'll talk."

"NO! She's mine." Carl put his left hand on his forehead and, grinding his teeth together, moaned, "Oh, God, oh, God Lord cast thy might in my arm to slay the wicked."

"Please," pleaded Anna, "put the gun down, Carl."

Suddenly, the muscles in Carl's face relaxed as he stared at Anna. "Jesus, Jesus, if I can't have you, no one can." He cocked the gun as he aimed it at Anna's head.

Without thinking, and in one quick, fluid motion, Wes cocked his revolver as he drew it, aimed, and fired at Carl's chest. In a moment the smoke cleared, and Wes saw Carl laying on the ground, his eyes open, but seeing nothing.

A woman in the crowd screamed, and a man yelled out, "He shot the Bishop, the mountain man killed Bishop Martin."

Stan grabbed Wes' arm. "Quick, get on your horse." He pushed Wes toward Jeff and untied the reins as Wes slipped his foot in the stirrup. "Get out of here, now," said Stan. "I'll try to give you a head start. Stay off the road, go through the mountains."

"But he was insane!" objected Wes. "What was I to do?"

Stan shook his head. "He was a bishop. Go before it's too late!"

A Tragic Killing

Wes swung into the saddle and turned to look for Anna, but she was gone! How could this happen? One moment he was holding her in his arms and now he was running for his life! He saw several people bending over Carl Martin and others running down the street. Then he saw three men approaching with rifles. There was no time to argue. He touched his heels to Jeff's ribs, and the big horse jumped forward.

Bending forward, Wes urged Jeff on and, at full gallop, rode out of Salt Lake City. He followed Stan's advice and quickly abandoned the road to Emigration Canyon and headed north up into the mountains. Reaching a dominant hill overlooking the valley he stopped and looked at the road from Salt Lake. More than a dozen horsemen were riding toward Emigration Canyon at full gallop. A Mormon posse was coming and Wes knew they'd be difficult to escape–this was their territory, not his.

34
CHAPTER

Despair at Fort Hall

Wes was exhausted as he walked the road toward Fort Hall, leading Jeff by the reins. A slow rain fell, turning the road into sloppy mud. Both he and Jeff were wet, dirty, and worn out, and he was so tired that he could hardly put one foot in front of the other. Yet after twelve days of hiding and running, he'd eluded the Mormon posse in the mountains north of the Great Basin. He would be safe at Fort Hall. However, with safety, came the torment of his loss. He knew he could not return to Salt Lake City to claim Anna, for the only authority in the Salt Lake Valley was the Mormon Church.

Fort Hall was a smaller version of Fort Laramie with adobe walls surrounding blockhouses. Wes saw pioneer wagons outside the Fort's wall and dark columns of smoke pouring from two of the Fort's three chimneys. Once inside the Fort's gate, Wes led Jeff to the stable and found the stable hand, a redheaded boy with a limp. Handing the boy a silver dollar he give instructions for Jeff to be unsaddled, rubbed down and given oats.

"It's too much," said the boy as he stared at the dollar in his hand.

Wes was too tired to consider change. "It's an advance on several days." Without further comment he headed for the canteen. He needed a meal and a drink–especially a drink.

Inside, a small fire burned in a huge fireplace, fighting off the chill of the summer storm. A dozen occupants sat at several rectangular tables. Wes walked to a small round table at the back of the barroom and sank into a chair. A tall skinny bartender in his thirties, wearing a dirty top-hat, came forward. "Whiskey?" he asked. Wes nodded and laid his head upon his arms folded on the table. "You don't look so good," continued the barkeep. "You want some food?" Wes nodded his head without looking up. "You want a steak?" Again Wes only nodded and then heard the bartender walk away.

Escaping from the Mormons had, to a degree, kept his mind busy, but now he was overcome with the full sense of his loss. How could this happen? After his impossible agreement with Stan Sinclair and his rescue of Lisa, and then successfully returning her to Salt Lake City, all had been lost! Why had he fired at the Mormon bishop? Why didn't he use some other tactic to disarm him? Yet, reviewing it over and over he couldn't see any other sound alternative. He now understood that the Mormon bishop, Carl Martin, was the man that Anna had been betrothed to. Yet Martin was much older than Anna, at least in his forties. Suddenly, it came to Wes that Martin, as a middle-aged Mormon bishop, must have already been married. That meant that Anna had been facing a polygamist marriage! He just couldn't understand it all: polygamy, the Mormons, their new Zion–it was too much.

He was tired, wet and hungry yet nothing compared to the great hurt in his heart. The thought of Anna in his arms, her lips on his made him groan in unfulfilled desire. What could he possibly do now? Returning to Salt Lake City was out of the question. What about finding Crocker? His friend must be traveling up the Platte River by now. Maybe he could join up with his partner and they could sneak back into the Mormon city and steal Anna away. Yet that strategy seemed doomed for the Mormons controlled the entire territory around the Great Salt Lake Valley. What about finding Smoke Man? But what could his holy man do? It was so unfair, he had fulfilled his part of the bargain and was now deprived of his life mate. He heard the sound of a plate being placed on the table in front of him, yet he didn't bother moving, ignoring both the food and the whiskey. Life was just too empty for him to care.

Wes woke fully dressed, laying on a mound of hay in the stable. His mouth was dry with that peculiar stale whiskey taste and his head hurt. Sitting up, he remembered that he'd been drinking a good portion of the previous night. He did not remember coming to the stable. Wes struggled to think out what he should do next. He tried to sum up what his life had meant to date. He had partnered with Crocker and lived with the Indians. He had killed those two Blackfoot boys, the memory jolting him. Then he killed fat Toby, Friendship Brown, Roland Palmer and his own half-brother, Gunner. Finally, he'd killed the Mormon bishop. At nineteen, it seemed his life was about killing, he was a good killer. But he didn't want to be a killer, he hadn't started out to kill, only to find his way in life. Crocker had been right: some men aren't meant to live in society, some are meant to live by themselves in the wilderness. He must be such a man.

Standing up, he brushed the hay from his rawhide pants. Walking toward the door he spotted the redheaded boy in the shadows. "You staying?" asked the boy.

Wes hesitated. "No, I'll be leaving soon." He walked from the stable and headed for the tavern. Approaching the steps leading up to the front door, he stopped. He was frozen. Should he go in and drink some more? Should he drink himself into a stupor? Should he return to the stable and get Jeff? But where would he go?

"Wes Hamlin!" yelled a male voice behind him.

Someone was calling his name, someone who knew him. With heart racing, Wes spun around to see Stan Sinclair standing in front of him, holding the reins to a horse. Had the Mormon come to arrest Wes and return him to Salt Lake City?

"You forgot something back in Salt Lake," said Stan and he moved aside to let Wes see that Anna was on the horse. She slipped off the mount as he rushed to her. Opening his arms, he scooped her up. His ears rang with the sound of her voice. "Oh, Wes, I'm here–I'm yours." She reached up with her hand and pulled his head down, pressing her lips against his.

Suddenly, Stan was standing beside them. "You kept your bargain and I'm keeping mine."

Still holding Anna close to his chest, Wes nodded. "I'll take good care of her, Mr. Sinclair."

"Lordy, Wes, I know ya will."

"This religion thing still isn't settled."

Stan smiled. "I know. But you found Lisa and brought her back. That was a miracle. It was God telling me that you were meant for each other. I guess you'll just have to work it out between you." He extended his hand and Wes took it. "When you get settled, write me a letter. I'll want to visit my grandkids some day."

Epilogue
Crocker and Friends

On the South Fork of the Powder River three men sat around a small fire and roasted buffalo boudins. Crocker Sloan, Elfego Baccala and Smoke Man watched the guts cook and passed a jug of whiskey. "Ya know," said Crocker, addressing his remark to the Indian. "Ya got to be careful with this blue-ruin. You Injuns always get so blind-drunk."

Smoke Man retrieved a burning twig from the fire and lit his pipe before answering. "Smoke Man understands. Absa and Lakota, we have no head for whiskey, but it makes good visions." They were silent for a moment. "Did you know," said Smoke Man, "that the Whiteman has no head for the pipe?"

"Tobacco?" asked Crocker.

"No, the medicine pipe–the medicine smoke. Whitemen act like crazy horses when they smoke."

"Well," responded Crocker. "This coon hadn't thought of that."

Fego finally spoke up. "Men are finding much gold in California. They are getting rich, no?"

"You want to go to California?" asked Crocker.

"No," said Fego, "I only want to be rich." The three men were silent for several minutes before Fego spoke again. "There is a valley, Senors. It is high in the Bitterroot Mountains. There is gold there."

Crocker nodded his head. "The Bitterroot Mountains, ya say? Well, ain't that something! That's where them Blackfooters is guarding a secret valley what has giant beav! These beav is big–big as a horse!"

Smoke Man puffed on his pipe and nodded. "I have never seen the beaver so big. I would like to see that."

"Well, hell, men–let's do 'er. Let's go up into them Bitterroots and get that gold and trap them beav. We aren't getting younger, ya know."

"And when we are rich," said Fego, "We will visit my friend, Wes and his Mormon wife."

"Your friend!" yelled Crocker. "I taught that young stallion everything he knows. He's my friend."

Smoke Man smiled, gave a little cough, rocked back and forth and patted his medicine pouch. "*Wicasa Ozu* is my friend."

"Jesus Christ!" yelled Crocker. "How'd I get mixed up with a dumb Injun and a Bean-Eater?" He was silent for a moment before another thought came to him. "Now, this is how I got 'er figured. You, Fego, will tell them Blackfooters you're a half-breed, half Blackfooter and half Bean-Eater."

THE END

Made in the USA
Las Vegas, NV
16 December 2021